THE SORCERESS QUEEN
AND THE
PIRATE ROGUE

HEIRS OF MAGIC
BOOK TWO

BY

JEFFE KENNEDY

Book Two in the adult fantasy romance adventure series from award-winning, bestselling author Jeffe Kennedy. Follows the prequel novella, *The Long Night of the Crystalline Moon*, in the Under a Winter Sky romantic fantasy holiday anthology and Book One of Heirs of Magic, *The Golden Gryphon and the Bear Prince*.

A Lonely Road

Stella has always been one to count her blessings. Empath, sorceress, shapeshifter, and healer, she's grateful for the gifts the goddess of shadows has bestowed upon her. Yes, she's sensitive to emotions and can't bear to be in large crowds for long. And yes, that means she'll never be able to take a lover, as she's unable to withstand physical contact with anyone but her twin brother. Certainly now that he's found his true love, she feels more alone than ever. None of it haunts her, however, more than the vision of the lonely tower where her life path ends.

An Unrequited Love

Jakral Konyngrr is a man of simple tastes: good whiskey, some coin in his pocket, and a fine blade in his hand. Though he's no prince, not a shapeshifter, and not blessed with any magic, he's happy in his skin. And yet he seems doomed to live the life of a hero from a tragic ballad, because the only woman he's ever wanted barely knows he's alive. As much as Jak longs for Stella, he's resigned himself to being forever in the background. At least he can guard her back.

A Quest to Stop a Monster

But now Jak and Stella have been thrown together—along with a mismatched group of shifters, warriors, and sorceress friends—chasing and attempting to avert magic rifts that release monsters into their world. Worse, the strange intelligence behind the bizarre and deadly attacks seems to have developed a fascination for Stella. Battling for their lives and the good of the realm, they must fight—and perhaps love—together to alter the course of the future before it's too late.

ACKNOWLEDGMENTS

Many thanks to beta readers Emily Mah Tippetts and Darynda Jones, at the last minute, as usual.

As always, love to Grace (Darling) Draven for all the things. Thanks and love to Carien Ubink for all the assisting.

Special thanks to Ravven, for helping this cover come to life—and to all the readers who sent suggestions for how Jak should look, in particular.

As ever, love and immense gratitude to David, who is there every day, and who makes everything possible.

Credits
Proofreading: Pikko's House (www.pikkoshouse.com)
Cover: Ravven (www.ravven.com)

THE SORCERESS QUEEN
AND THE
PIRATE ROGUE

BY
JEFFE KENNEDY

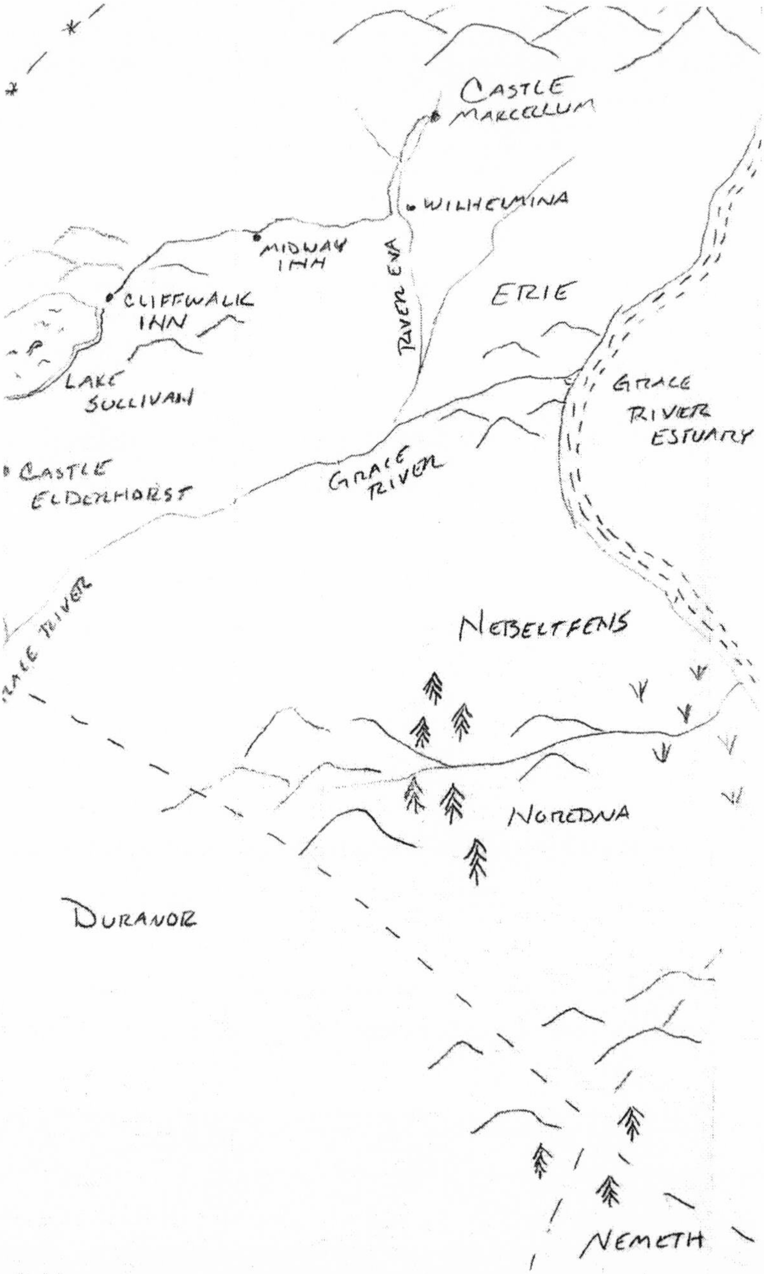
CASTLE MARCELLUM
WILHELMINA
MIDWAY INN
CLIFFWALK INN
RIVER EVA
ERIE
LAKE SULLIVAN
GRACE RIVER ESTUARY
CASTLE ELDERHORST
GRACE RIVER
GRACE RIVER
NEBELTFENS
NOREDNA
DURANOR
NEMETH

~ PROLOGUE ~

"NILLY! DEAR NILLY! Heya, wait up."

At Jak's call, Stella obligingly halted, stepping out of the busy foot traffic of the marketplace that crowded the road. Jak jogged up the incline, dodging a cartload of fruit, then ducked a vee of colorful staymach birds when they zoomed at his head. Reaching her, he dramatically clutched his side, panting as if out of breath. "I swear this cliff path gets steeper every year," Jak complained, a boyish grin lighting his face, cheeks dimpling.

Stella shook her head at his antics, not at all taken in by his jesting. Of all of them, Jak devoted himself the most to physical conditioning. His wine-red shirt hung loose over his narrow hips—the full pleated sleeves that buttoned at his wrists giving him a piratical air—and the collar hung open, the laces untied. Beneath, he wore tight black trousers, and his lean and agile gymnast's body showed the results of his diligent efforts.

Not that Stella looked. At least, not when anyone, particularly Jak, would notice.

"Seeing as how the road is centuries old and carved into the cliff face, I suspect it has remained exactly the same as the last time you were here," she replied gravely. "Perhaps you've gotten soft from lolling on the beach in Nahanau." He definitely looked as if he'd been much in the sun, his skin darker than usual with a healthy tanned glow, glints of gold highlights in his tousled dark hair.

His grin broadening, he swept her a gallant bow. "Ah, my lady sees through me. I'm afraid the surfing and beach-frolicking have indeed taken their toll." Straightening, and clearly not out of breath at all, he patted his stomach, then lifted his shirt while hooking a thumb in the waist of his trousers to tug them a hand's width down his flat belly. "Tell me true, dear Nilly—have I got a pot belly now?"

She looked—of course she looked, she wasn't that oblivious, no matter what people said about her—and immediately noted that his tan went all the way down. And that, far from being flabby, his abdominal muscles looked like they could cut glass. Her fingers itched with the temptation to touch, a rarity for her, when touching others brought such unpleasant consequences. *Jak is not for you,* she reminded herself. *And he's barely more than a boy, regardless.*

Except Jak didn't look like a boy anymore. In the last year away, he'd filled out, gotten more masculine. She tried to summon her usual image of him as a bratty younger brother. That had always been her best defense against his flirtatious charm. He'd suddenly become a man, she realized uneasily, and she needed to stop looking at him.

"You appear to be safe from the effects of indulgence so far," she told him, turning to resume her errand. "Though it's probably a good thing you've returned to Annfwn to walk the cliff path and get back into shape."

"Did you just make a joke?" he asked, his expression delighted as he paced alongside her.

She slid him a bemused glance. "You know I have no sense of humor."

"I know you always *say* that"—he tipped his head jauntily—"but I don't think it's true."

Sadly, it *was* true. Maybe being an empath had affected her emotions, as it seemed that strong feelings, in all their variety, tended toward grief and anger, even among the outwardly joyful Tala. Maybe even particularly among the Tala, a people still emerging from centuries of generational struggle and isolation. Still, she sensed the effervescence of humor in others, so she knew she didn't share that native gaiety.

Her lighthearted mother positively despaired of her, forever saying that such a solemn girl would never attract a lover. That wasn't news to Stella. She had seen her own future, and it was a lonely one. Even without her visions of isolation, the practicality was that the intensity of physical touch was simply too much to bear for long. She'd reconciled herself to the fact that she could never take a lover. The prospect saddened her, but she couldn't change who she was.

"I didn't mean to make you sad," Jak said earnestly, his own eyes shadowed now, his mood losing its sparkle.

"You didn't." She added a serene smile, sorry that she'd dampened his enthusiasm. "Did you just arrive? I didn't see the *Hákyrling*."

"I came adragonback," he informed her, his natural ebullience restored. "Kiraka and Dafne gave me a ride."

"Lucky you," she replied in all sincerity. "You must be in good favor, then."

3

He grimaced cheerfully. "It wasn't all surfing and beach-frolicking in Nahanau. Dafne had me in the library most of the time. But she did say I'm not entirely hopeless. You should have come to join us."

She shook her head automatically. "Everyone agrees that the best thing I can be doing is studying with Auntie Andi."

"You can't work on your sorcery *all* the time," Jak protested. "I know! Let me teach you to surf. It's the best fun."

No. That would not happen. Jak would no doubt strip down to nearly nothing for swimming, and Stella didn't care to test herself that far. If someone caught her looking—particularly Jak—then she'd perish of mortification. She slanted him a repressive, older-sister look. "I've surfed many times, young Jak."

"As a porpoise isn't the same," he countered, a hint of irritation wafting off him that she'd called him young. Good. That should quell his flirtatiousness.

"Of course it's the same," she replied loftily. "Surf is surf."

"Don't do that," he gritted out, definitely annoyed.

Pasting on a surprised look—one advantage of being an empath was one learned to recreate the appearance of emotions—she lifted her brows in surprise. "Do what?"

Hopping in front of her with nimble speed, he planted himself in her path, forcing her to stop. "Don't pull that older-sister, more-mature-than-thou routine," he said.

"I *am* older than you," she pointed out.

"Not *that* much older, and you are definitely not my sister, or even my cousin," he shot back, stepping closer. Even aggrieved with her, he took care not to touch her. But his proximity still infiltrated her senses, along with the clean smell of salt and sweat. He was taller than her now, she realized with a jolt of surprise. When had that happened? "We're not related at all, in fact," he murmured suggestively.

"I babysat for you," she reminded him tartly.

He rolled his eyes. "This again? The pack of us ran around together."

"I was still responsible." She narrowed her eyes at him. "And *you* were a naughty kid."

Instead of being daunted, he smiled, a sensual curve to his generous mouth that had warmth fluttering deep inside. "Guess what, dearest Nilly?" he murmured, leaning even closer. "I'm no longer a kid, but I'm even naughtier."

She caught her breath, blushing at the frankly sexual heat coming off of him. "Jak!"

"Don't sound so shocked." Very carefully, he picked up a long lock of her hair without brushing her skin, winding it through his fingers. "You know how much I like you. Stella. My guiding star."

Her mouth gone dry, her heart hammering, her body— Moranu help her—filled with longing, she didn't know what to say.

"Come swimming with me," he coaxed her in a throaty voice, his dark eyes dancing with wicked mischief.

Searching for anywhere to look but those alluring eyes, she focused on the small gold hoop in his left ear. "You got your ear pierced."

His smile widened, dimples deepening. "Do you like it? I think it makes me look like a pirate."

She did like it, but she gave him a reproving shake of her head. "Not an appropriate image to aspire to, young Jak."

"Oh, I know you're not that stuffy," he replied, undaunted. "Come swimming with me. Give me a chance to show you I'm not the kid you try to pretend I am."

"I know you're not a kid." Her voice came out breathy.

Jak smiled, tugging her even closer, his heated gaze on her mouth. "I missed you. I've been thinking about you. I think about you all the time. And I have ideas, things we could do that won't hurt you."

Though they weren't touching, her mental barriers had gone wobbly, images insinuating themselves into her mind, of her and Jak, naked together, and coils of rope…

With a gasp of shock and dismay—surely not desire—she jerked backward, the lock of hair he still held yanking painfully on her scalp. "No!" she burst out, loudly enough that several people turned to look. When had she forgotten they were surrounded by a crowd? And not just anyone, but her own people, who she'd serve someday as their sorceress, possibly their queen.

Jak, who'd immediately released his grip on her hair, held up his hands. "I'm sorry. I apologize. What can I do to help?" His sharp, dark gaze fastened on her left hand, and she realized she'd stuck her two littlest fingers in her mouth, the nails snapping as she bit down.

Stella yanked her fingers from her mouth, tucking her hand guiltily behind her back. Moranu take her, she'd broken that habit, one she'd had since she was a little girl. Another failing her mother had despaired of. *Just look at your poor, wrinkled*

6

fingers! How will you ever have pretty nails if you're forever chewing them down to nothing?

"Stella, my star, please." Jak's forehead creased in worry. "I didn't mean to upset you. I—"

"You didn't," she lied, drawing herself up and letting the magic settle around her like a protective cloak. There. That was better. She should know better than to let her mental shields weaken like that. "It takes more than the offensive flirtations of a silly boy too young to know better to upset me."

Jak's mouth fell open, and he closed it hastily, dark eyes glittering. "You can keep saying that, but I won't always be too young for you."

At times like these, Stella felt positively ancient. "Oh, Jak," she said. She wanted to sound pitying, but she didn't have it in her to be cruel. "You are now and you always will be."

He curled his hands into fists, frustration radiating off of him. "You're wrong. I'll prove myself to you. Just wait and see."

Jak stormed off, leaving a cloud of roiling emotions in his wake, and Stella watched him go. Once again alone, she continued up the road, telling herself she hadn't been shaken by the encounter. Jak would grow out of this phase, this youthful infatuation, and he'd find lovers to absorb his considerable energies.

Her future didn't hold him in it. It didn't hold anyone at all. Just an isolated tower in an endless field of lilies. And herself, forever alone.

~ I ~

Seven Years Later

T HE *HÁKYRLING'S* BELLS rang the advent of dawn in his
head, popping Jak awake.

Hot and restless, he groaned as he moved, his body aching
where it wasn't stiff and numb. They'd all been up most of the
night, dealing with Lena and Zeph's dramatic return to the
land of the living—not that he'd been able to contribute
much—so you'd think that for once he'd sleep in. But no.
Dawn it was. Though, to be fair, sunrise in these northern,
wintry climes was admittedly significantly later than his father
would've rousted him out of his berth on the *Hákyrling*.

Since his bed was a cold and lonely one, he might as well
get up. The beds at King Groningen's manse on the shores of
Lake Sullivan were well-appointed and comfortable, but
without company, there wasn't much reason to stay there if he
couldn't sleep. Plus, he felt like crap. Previously undetected
deep bruises made themselves felt as he levered himself to his
feet. Padding naked to bathing chamber—all his, as these were
indeed nice digs—he surveyed himself in the mirror, wincing
as he noted the sickly greens and purples, particularly over his
ribs. Fucking Rhy sure packed a punch when he wanted to.

The fall from the wrecked carriage likely hadn't helped either.

Jak tentatively fingered the bite marks from Rhy's wolf teeth and lacerations from his claws. Just flesh wounds, as his father would say, in that dismissive Dasnarian tone—but they stung like a copper viper's bite, all swollen and crusty, too. Good thing Rhy was such a close friend, or Jak would be seriously pissed at taking this beating from him.

Rhy had also been out of his head over a woman at the time—a kind of insanity Jak understood all too well.

With a sigh for that, which became an unmanly moan as his ribs creaked, Jak dunked his head in cold water to try to clear it, missing the hot, running water at Castle Elderhorst. Still, as lovely as a hot bath sounded, running some dagger forms would be the best thing to work the aches out of his body. His ribs bit again as he towel-dried his hair. Cracked, most likely. Two or three of them, he decided, after some judicious prodding. Still, he was better off than Zeph, who'd nearly died after falling through a portal in the sky escaping from wherever she'd gone to rescue Lena.

Lena had been bad off, too, having nearly bled to death from the lacerations covering her body. If they didn't have Stella with her magical healing abilities, they'd have lost Zeph and Lena, no doubt. Stella would be exhausted from that effort, so Jak could handle a few flesh wounds on his own. Not to mention that he tried very hard not to ask Stella to do anything for him.

Not wanting to bother any of the servants either, given the night they'd had dealing with their newly arrived guests' emergency, he found the shirt he'd worn the day before—a new one that Rhy had also ripped all to hell and gone—and completed its untimely demise, reducing it to strips of cloth.

Binding his ribs, he tied off the ends, then tried some dips and twists. It wasn't an ideal solution, but they'd at least hold his ribs in place. Glancing outside, he verified the beach was empty in the gray dawn light. Plenty of room to run some forms. And, as it was oddly balmy down here at lake level—as opposed to the arctic winter up on the heights—he decided to forgo a shirt. He only had one intact spare with him and no reason to stink it up with sweat if he didn't need to.

He got winded just pulling on his pants, ribs grinding unmercifully. Fucking Rhy.

Normally it would be tempting to make the short jump from the room of his balcony to the pebbled beach as a light warm-up, but he didn't trust those ribs. All he needed was for one to separate into a full break and puncture his lung. Then he'd have no choice but to ask Stella to heal him. Hopefully, she was sound asleep, as she deserved to be.

The manse was dark and quiet as he made his way through the deserted halls. Lena and Zeph would no doubt be sleeping off their ordeal and the massive healing for some time, too, The last Jak had seen Astar, he was holding anxious vigil over Zeph. Rhy had been watching over Lena, too, though more surreptitiously. Gen had gone to bed around the same time Jak had, worn out from nerves and patrolling the skies, looking for Zeph and Lena to return. But she'd never been an early riser, even under the best of circumstances.

Jak would be lucky if he saw any of them all day.

Reaching the beach, he studied the deep black mirror-still

water of Lake Sullivan and shivered. Balmy by comparison, yes, but hardly warm. Odd, he'd been hot up until that moment, but now he felt chilled. Well, exercise would take care of that.

Pulling his twin daggers—using the real thing would sharpen his attention—he started the opening movements of Danu's Dance. His ribs burned, the bites and lacerations on his neck and arms pulled with hornet stings of pain, then broke open enough that blood streaked down his chest. But the familiar stances and twists of the martial dance pulled his head into a different space.

Ignoring the minor distractions, he worked his body, letting his thoughts dissolve into the bright clarity of Danu's presence. The spring of sinew and muscle warmed him so that sweat poured down his body, the rising sun burning off the lake mist and flashing off his daggers as he spun, ducked, and wove.

Coming to the finish, he leapt into the air, somersaulting into the final spin out of habit—his forgotten ribs seizing with a lance of agony so he landed with an ungainly one-footed thud that put him on his ass. One rib audibly broke. "Fuck!" He doubled over his knees, mastering the nausea from the agonizing prod of the bone shards, his healthy sweat turning into a cold and greasy one.

"Maybe working out and exacerbating untreated injuries wasn't the smartest decision," said a cool voice.

Stella. Just wonderful. Turning his head, he eyed her. She looked as fresh and lovely as the winter morning. Swathed in her white fur cloak, she studied him, her eyes fulgent as mercury as she looked *through* him. "Unless it was your plan to puncture a lung?" she asked, raising a dark brow.

Somehow Stella had a knack for making him feel eternally fifteen, so he produced a cocky grin, gritting his back teeth against his rising gorge and the bone-shivering pain. "You know me—anything to attract the attention of a beautiful woman."

She huffed out an exasperated sigh. "Do *not* get up," she instructed when he made to rise. "You'll only make more work for me to do."

"You don't have to heal me," he said, though his voice came out weak, and he couldn't seem to catch a good breath.

She knelt on the pebbled beach next to him, her scent enveloping him, like night-blooming flowers carried on a warm tropical breeze. Her dark hair spilled in gleaming loose waves over the white fur cloak, rosy highlights catching the morning sun. Her skin flawless, her face pale as the moon, Stella possessed a calm and shining loveliness that staggered him every time. Daughter of the most beautiful woman in the Thirteen Kingdoms, if not the entire world, she still wasn't flashy or glamorous. Instead, and in keeping with her withdrawn nature, her beauty lay like banked coals, smoldering quietly with subtle hints of crimson and gold, like the sun catching the glints in her shadowed hair. Jak liked to think he was the only one who saw and appreciated what others failed to notice.

"Not only do I have to heal you," Stella said with tart exasperation, breaking into his romantic reverie, "I should've healed you long before this. *When* did you get these wounds?

Not last night, I think. Lie back."

"Here?" He shivered in anticipation of lying back on the cold pebbles. He was cooling down fast in the chilly air, his sweat chill now that he'd stopped moving.

"Yes, here," she replied firmly. "It would be dangerous for you to stand, let alone walk, you cocky idiot. If you'd been less stupid, we could've done this in a nice, warm bed."

Savoring the image of Stella with him in a warm bed got him through the surprisingly difficult journey to lying down. Stella supported him, a good thing, as a black haze nearly took him under. For a moment he worried about her touching his bare skin, then realized she wore fine leather gloves. Hmm. That gave him an idea. Not that he'd ever get to do anything about it. At least turning over that fantasy in his head helped distract him from the pain that had increased by leaps at the change in position.

"This looks like a bite mark," she remarked, prodding the shoulder wound with a gentle touch that nevertheless made him wince. "Wolf teeth, if I don't miss my guess. Rhyian?"

"Yeah," he gritted out through clenched teeth. He really hoped he wouldn't puke. That wouldn't be any way to convince Stella to see him as a man. Plus, the pain that heaving would bring... He shuddered. *Get tough*, he ordered himself. "Rhy and I had a bit of a scuffle yesterday afternoon." He swallowed convulsively, which also hurt. Everything hurt all of a sudden.

"Are you nauseated?" She studied his face as she ghosted her gloved hands over his cracked ribs.

"A little," he admitted.

"That would explain why you've turned green," she commented dryly, stripping off her gloves. "Not surprising with the broken bones dumping marrow into your bloodstream. Plus, several of the bites are festering. You have a fever. Clearly you realized the ribs were cracked because you had the sense to bind them, if badly." She worked quickly, deftly unknotting his makeshift bandages, then murmuring in dismay at the bruising. "Moranu take it, Jak! Explain to me why you didn't tell me about these injuries yesterday?"

"I didn't want to bother you." Focusing on her face helped him deal with the shudders wracking his body now.

"So you decided that waiting for infection to set in, then working out so you'd completely fracture a cracked rib wouldn't be bothering me?"

"I didn't think about that," he admitted.

"You never do, Jak."

"I didn't think it was that bad," he added, though it was a weak defense. "Plus we had more important concerns worrying about Zeph and Lena. Then I knew you'd need to sleep off healing them. Why aren't you sleeping now?"

"I was about to. I finally knocked Rhy and Astar out, over their objections, since the stubborn fools seemed to think they needed to keep holding vigil. On my way to bed, I spotted you out here, your ribs bandaged, working out like a crazy man who was apparently trying to kill himself."

"Sorry," he muttered, truly chagrined. The last thing he wanted to be was an additional burden for her.

"Yes, you will be, because this is going to hurt."

More than her disdain? He opened his mouth to make a joke

along those lines, but gasped out a mewling shriek when she laid hands on him and popped the rib back. Actual tears sprang to his eyes as she aligned the broken ends—he could swear the grinding fragments made an audible noise—before a burst of healing magic flooded the area, bringing blessed relief.

Flinging his head back, he slammed his eyes shut, hoping she wouldn't see the moisture there, and he panted, biting back any more unmanly whimpers.

"You're doing well," Stella murmured, her voice throaty and soothing, a sensual purr she never used with him. Her warm hands stroked over his bare skin, and it just figured that the only time he'd get these crumbs of attention from her were under these circumstances.

It was enough to make a grown man weep. Oh wait, he already was, Danu take him for a sniveling fool.

"Still with me?" Stella asked, sounding truly concerned for him.

He stared up at the gray sky. The parting in the clouds hadn't lasted long, and now a swirl of light snowflakes showered down on him. He shivered violently. "Right here where you left me," he replied through chattering teeth.

"I'm sorry about the cold." Her green healing magic intensified, a small sun over his chest, the delightful heat, so quintessentially her, flooding outward to suffuse him with well-being. "I am warming you, but some of what you're feeling is the fever breaking. I'm almost done with the cracked ribs," she murmured, "and now I'm purging the infection."

Feeling slightly more human, he focused his gaze on her intent face again. Her eyes were half closed, fulminous silver through the lace of her dark lashes. She had a widow's peak, he realized with considerable surprise. And here he'd thought he'd studied everything about her, but this was new to him, the fine dark hairs forming a point on her brow, elegantly gracing her high forehead. She usually pulled her hair down around her face, so that was why it didn't normally show. But while she healed him, she'd tucked her hair back behind her ears to keep it out of her way, instead of hiding her face in the tenebrous depths of it like usual.

In wonder, he stretched out an unsteady finger to touch the fine point, careful to make contact only with the hair, even though she had her hands on his skin. He knew she'd be guarding against his thoughts and emotions, using the flow of healing magic to ward him out. Flicking her gaze to his face, she raised a brow.

"You have a widow's peak," he said, as if that explained anything, dropping his hand quickly.

She wrinkled her nose and shook her head so her hair fell heavily over her forehead again. "I know. I hate it."

"It's beautiful." Like a natural diadem, crowning her queen without interference by mortal instruments.

She snorted in a decidedly unlovely way, making him laugh—which hurt, but not nearly so much as before. Unfortunately, with the recession of the pain and nausea, he began to experience the other notable effects of Tala healing, the spring-green vitality bubbling through his bloodstream and heating his loins. *Not now,* he told his cock sternly as it engorged, pressing hard against his pants, not listening in the least.

"My mother used to pluck it," Stella confided, and for a wild moment of disconnect, Jak thought she meant his unruly cock.

"The widow's peak," he exclaimed in relief, drawing a puzzled half smile from her. "Queen Amelia would... pluck out your hair?"

"She thought it marred the line of my forehead when my hair was styled up for fancy balls and such. You know how Mother is about grooming." Stella rolled her eyes a little. "Strong opinions."

"I'm sorry," he said impulsively. It galled that she'd had any reason to think she wasn't perfect in every way.

Stella shrugged it off. "I hated the plucking—she'd have to sit on me to hold me still—so I put a stop to it when I got old enough."

"But you hide it."

"To be fair, now that she can't make me, I simply don't ever put up my hair." She slanted him a mischievous smile. "An advantage of being an odd and awkward sorceress is people aren't surprised when I don't adhere to court fashion. I'm going to heal the bites and lacerations while I'm at it, unless you'd rather go in and get in bed for that part? You can walk without harming yourself now, and you'll be wanting to sleep when I'm done with you."

The way desire for her pumped through him, he had no intention of compounding the problem by going near a bed with her. "Leave them," he said, feeling as desperate to escape her touch now as he'd ever been to have it. The warrior goddess Danu teaching him a lesson in being careful what he wished for. His cock, trapped in a bent position, ached furiously as it swelled, and he sincerely prayed that Stella wouldn't sense *that* particular pain.

"I'm healing all of it, either way. Call it professional pride. Stay still, or *I* will sit on you."

If only... "Do it here," he grated out, wrenching his gaze to the sky and thinking hard—no, not that word—concentrating on chilling images. Snow, and ice, and freezing water. Stella lifted her hands from his burning flesh and began tracing the various lacerations with a light brush of her fingers. He suppressed a groan, forcing himself to stay still, banishing the fantasies of her bending to follow the caresses with her soft lips, perhaps nipping him with her kitten teeth and—With an involuntary twitch, he clapped a hand over his eyes, willing the sting to penetrate his lust-fogged brain.

"Am I hurting you?" she asked.

"Not at all," he gritted, then considered he should've said yes, so she'd stop.

"Want to tell me why Rhy attacked you?"

Not particularly, but it gave him something else to think about, especially since, as she worked her way up his body, a lock of silken hair fell over her shoulder to trail over his bare chest. He wasn't going to survive this torture. "Astar and I were getting the horses ready to take the carriage down to the lake—you and Gen were already on the wing, scouting—when Rhy plummeted from the sky in raven form. The horses spooked, which is how the carriage got wrecked. We all took a spill, and I must've landed wrong. None of that is really on Rhy. He was out of his head with worry about Lena, not in his right mind. He'd sensed that Lena was no longer in our same reality, and—"

"He did?" Stella asked, pausing in her considerable surprise. "How?"

Jak shrugged, taking the opportunity to wriggle a little, hoping to adjust his erection. Not enough. *Gah.* "I don't think he knows." Rhy had been gone for days, possibly never to rejoin their mission, so his sudden reappearance had come as a surprise to all of them. He'd also arrived when they were already in an uproar, since Lena had fallen through one of the rifts in reality the high queen had sent them to investigate— and repair—and Zeph had gone to rescue her.

"Hmm. So why attack you?"

"He thought we were holding out on him, not telling him where Lena went. It took a while to convince him *we* didn't know either—and to subdue him. Then he talked trash about Lena and me, and I had to correct his stupid assumption."

"Lena and you?" Stella paused infinitesimally.

"He found out I've been teaching Lena how to defend herself with a dagger."

"Ah." Stella relaxed, and he wondered if he should have fanned that little flame of jealousy, if that was what it had been. Knowing Stella, she'd been thinking about something else entirely. "I've been meaning to ask about that," she said. "Astar thinks you should teach me to use the Silversteel daggers Ash gave me, so I don't do something foolish and cut myself with them or something."

"You are never foolish," he replied fervently.

She grimaced. "I tend to be absentminded, I know. I don't

19

need to learn self-defense, just enough so I'm not a danger to myself."

"I'd be delighted." If he'd been standing, he would've swept her a bow. Teaching Stella bladework would give him all sorts of opportunities to charm her, to work his way inside her emotional guards—and perhaps the physical ones, too. Besides, she did need to learn self-defense. He'd hesitated to nag her about it, but this request gave him the opening he needed.

"And that was enough to set Rhyian off?" she asked.

"Well, and I foolishly mentioned that she and I discussed how the shapeshifters have been more animal lately—not you—and Rhy leapt to unsavory conclusions, which only proved my point. In the meanwhile, I took some hits."

"Hmm." The noncommittal sound seemed unjustly accusing.

"I gave as good as I got," he said, hearing the defensiveness in his own voice. "I just can't shapeshift all healed up again like he can. If he were a mossback like me, he'd be in worse shape than I am."

"Don't call yourself that. You know I don't like that word. Not being a shapeshifter doesn't make you lesser." She'd reached the bite at the juncture of his shoulder and neck, having to bend over him to see it, her face close enough that her breath wafted warm over his chilled skin, those night-blooming flowers filling his head with thoughts he shouldn't have. If he put his arms around her, she'd fall against him, her slender curves nestling against him. His cock twitched painfully at the image, and he moved his hands well away from her, lest they get notions of their own.

"How about Astar turning into a dragon, huh?" he said, going for a different topic of conversation. Though Astar had several forms, he'd never taken dragon form before. The shapeshifting Tala tended to be closed-mouthed about their arcane mysteries, but so far as Jak understood, only one person in living memory had attained dragon form. Until Astar spontaneously became one to catch Zeph and Lena before they smashed into the lake. "That was a surprise."

"Not to me," Stella said, so matter-of-factly that he realized she must have seen that future for her twin brother. A few times, he'd nearly asked her what she saw in his—until he regained his better sense and kept his big mouth shut. "You're lucky Rhy didn't snap your collarbone," she observed in an absent tone, absorbed in what she sensed. An intense burst of magic surged through that area, relieving a nagging ache he hadn't been totally aware of until it was gone. "As it is, he barely missed nicking a major artery. You could've bled to death, Jak."

"I would've called for your help if that had been the case."

She lifted her head, staring intently into his eyes. "Would you?"

"You know me." He tried for a cocky grin, but something about her somber gaze checked him.

"Yes, I do know you. Just like I know you didn't ask me to help you yesterday. You had to realize you were injured by last night. Or you could've asked me this morning, after everyone else was handled. Why, Jak? I had to force myself on you."

I only wish you'd force yourself on me, an irreverent voice piped up, but he managed to keep the words from reaching his lips. Unfortunately, that meant he also failed to give her a reply.

"I wish you would *talk* to me," she said in the face of his silence, a hint of pain in her voice. "Don't you trust me at all? I know that things have been... awkward between us, but—"

"No," he burst out. "They're not—"

"But I thought that," she forged on, talking over him, "if nothing else, we are friends. Closer than that, even. You're like a brother to me and—"

He clapped his hands to his head, yanking on his hair, unable to bear it. Speaking of being out of his head. Between the sexual side effects of the healing and her proximity, he couldn't pretend to his usual insouciance. "I don't *want* to be like a brother to you!" he nearly shouted, startling her enough that she reared back, her face blank, eyes wide and dark gray with shock.

"Jak," she whispered, actually scooting away from him. "What are you—"

"*Look* at me, Stella." He pushed up to a sitting position. His body responded with elastic vigor, full of the renewed vitality she'd given him, so he jumped to his feet, appreciating the ease with which his body responded, and swept a hand at himself. The turgid erection throbbed against his trousers, a blessed relief as it finally extended from its cramped position.

Stella blushed, averting her gaze. "That is a natural side effect of the healing," she said, almost primly. "It happens to everyone, so you don't need to—"

"Put on your gloves," he told her, nearly snarling the

command, and her eyes flew to his face like startled birds. He bent and picked up her discarded gloves. "Put them on."

Watching him warily, she drew the pretty leather over her slender hands. "Jak, I don't know what—"

As soon as she had the second glove safely covered her skin, he seized her hands and drew her to her feet, holding her as close as he dared. This was his chance. With Astar and Zeph finally consummating their long chase, this could finally be his opportunity with Stella.

If he didn't fuck it up like he had so long ago, too much the impetuous boy. *Danu, let this be the right time.*

"It's not just the healing," he told her, tightening his grip when she made to pull away. "It's you. I'm like this whenever I'm around you. Sometimes even when you're nowhere near." He choked out a laugh, searching her face for any glimmer of shared feeling, seeing only embarrassed shock. "If I even *think* about you. Which is Danu-cursed inconvenient, since all I ever do is think about you. Stella, my star, I—"

"Jak, let me go," she said firmly, her expression cool and remote.

Not the right time, clearly. *Thanks for nothing, Danu.* Never ask the goddess of the bright sword and swift justice to help with matters of the heart. With chagrin, annoyed at himself for the grievous misstep, he released his hold on her, raking his hands through his hair instead. "I'm sorry. I shouldn't have done that, said anything. Let's forget this."

"No, we should talk about it." She looked troubled, drawing the cloak around herself. "I've never wanted to lead you on. I know the others make their jokes about us being a couple—and you know I don't understand humor very well, so I let them slide rather than saying anything—but I think maybe I've been careless in letting you flirt with me. In not putting a stop to it."

Well, that burned. "I know I'm not good enough for you."

"It's not that," she replied firmly, the words even more crushing because that meant she had another reason to refuse him.

"Then what is it?" The question had been a firm demand in his head, not the puppyish plea that came out.

"Jak…" She sounded so sad, turning away to look out over the glassy lake. "You're such a good person. A fearless fighter. A loyal friend, handsome, fun. You make everyone laugh."

Each word flayed him open more surely than Rhy's wolf teeth had. "Please don't say any more," he whispered soundlessly, mostly a prayer to his merciless goddess, but Stella's keen shapeshifter ears heard him anyway.

She glanced over her shoulder at him, pity in her gaze. "I mean it, Jak. You really are the finest of men."

"This isn't helping," he told her, grateful for the rising anger. Far better than feeling so pitiful in the face of her uncaring rejection. At least she hadn't called him a boy. This time.

"I'm sorry. I don't know what words will help. All I have is the truth, and that is that I just… don't feel that way about you." Her serene face, the clear gray eyes, just a shade darker than the lowering clouds, showed no hint of emotion. "I don't feel that way about *anyone*," she continued remorselessly, holding up her gloved hands in demonstration. "I'm not a person meant to have lovers. I'm meant to live my life alone. That's the price I pay for my magic, and I pay it gladly."

"Gladly," he spat. "I don't believe you."

"Maybe not gladly," she allowed, "but I am at peace with it. I have to be, because that's who I am. I'm asking you to understand that—and to be my friend anyway."

"You're asking an awful lot, Stella," he shot back, full of unreasoning anger. How she could be so cool, so remote and unfeeling, he simply didn't understand.

"I know." Her poise faltered slightly, and he glimpsed some of the turmoil beneath the smooth surface. "And I understand if this is too much to ask. I can sense how you feel about me, the strength of your attachment and—"

"Please stop." He wiped a hand over his face, unable to bear it a moment longer. Stupid idiot. Of course the empathic object of his unrequited love had sensed it from him. She'd known all along and afforded him the courtesy of pretending not to, until he'd forced the situation. "Can we agree to move on, and never reference this very painful conversation?"

"Of course," she replied with gentle compassion that was so her—and made everything so much worse.

"Thank you," he replied with forced dignity. "I'm going inside."

"You should sleep," she said to his back as he turned to go. "To complete the healing."

"I know how it works," he bit out ungraciously. In fact, he wouldn't be able to help it, the exhaustion of rapid and deep healing crashing over him. That must be why he felt so much like shit—because Stella crushing his heart was nothing new.

"Jak," she called after him. "Will you promise me something?"

He paused, not looking back at her. Not wanting to hear it. "What?"

"That when you need help, you'll ask me for it."

"Sure," he said, turning to look at her. "If you'll promise me the same."

After a bare moment's hesitation, she dipped her chin. "I promise."

"Then I do, too," he lied. No way was he letting Stella get close to him again. His heart couldn't take it.

~ 2 ~

STELLA HELD ON to her composure with everything in her as she watched Jak go back up the walk to the manse. Tasting leather, she jerked her left little fingers out of her mouth, digging her gloved nails into her palms instead. This was no time to be sucking on her fingers like a child, even if she desperately craved a bit of self-soothing. She was a grown woman, with responsibilities—and one of those was taking care of the situation with Jak. That painful conversation had been a long time coming. No matter how excruciating, at least it was done.

But she still couldn't take her eyes off of him.

He moved with his usual fluidity again, and she told herself that she was doing her job as a healer by watching. She could even kid herself that she studied his leanly muscled back to be certain his ribs floated properly, their clean lines tapering to his narrow hips, his taut ass in those tight pants flexing as he—She forced herself to turn away and face the lake, blowing out a shuddering breath.

Then, feeling her thighs go to water, she folded into a sitting position, drawing up her knees to wrap her arms around them, struggling to contain the fierce need to weep. The chill of utter loneliness settled over her heart in a gentle snowfall. If only Astar were awake... But her twin would be asleep for a long time. She should know, as she'd put him under.

Besides, Astar was no longer solely hers. He was focused on Zeph now. That was how Astar lived: fully, ardently, and with unconditional commitment to whatever course of action he settled upon. Astar's attraction to Zeph had always been there, the love he'd refused to consciously acknowledge and tried to imprison with duty and propriety clear to Stella from way back. Now that he'd shed those chains, he'd given himself utterly into Zeph's keeping, the withdrawal of his deep attachment to his twin a palpable severing. Which was as it should be. Stella wanted that for him. If anyone deserved that kind of love, Astar did.

Stella hadn't realized how cold and lonely it would leave her, however.

She would learn to live with it. And she'd been meticulous in ensuring that Astar had no inkling she felt so bereft. She'd die before she did anything at all to impinge on Astar's happiness. And he *was* so happy, fulfilled and at rest—even when he fought his fear that Zeph would be lost forever—in a way he'd never been before. Stella savored that happiness vicariously, like warming her hands at a fire.

And she would let him go. If she did her job well, he'd never guess at how profoundly her world had changed.

It was just terrible timing that she'd had to separate herself so firmly from Jak at the same time. That was also her own fault, that she'd let the flirtations go too far between them. Much as she envied Astar's newfound joy—and, oh, how bitter that was, to feel the green monster gnawing at her heart, and about the most important person in the world to her—she had to be realistic and let Jak go. It had been unkind of her not to cut him off before this.

Love and companionship were not in her destiny. She'd seen her fate, and her life path ended always at the same place: a lonely tower in an endless field of lilies.

Much as she longed to take what Jak offered, she couldn't do that to either of them. Any time she was tempted, she need only look at her own future to see that she never would. That was also as it should be. No need to shed useless tears over it. She'd done the right thing, and now Jak would move his affections to someone who could return them. And when that happened, she'd be happy for him. Just as she was for Astar. Neither of them would ever know how she died a little inside from losing them.

No doubt she felt so morose from the drain of healing, so she withdrew the Star of Annfwn from a pocket of her cloak to rejuvenate herself. The perfectly smooth and round topaz glowed with its own light, as if embedded with a star of its own, even in the gloom of the increasingly thick snowfall. It sang to her native magic, restorative and comforting.

Her relationship with the Star had been evolving since Aunt Andi gave it to her. She'd worked with the magic-focusing jewel before—though always under the sure guiding hand of Andi's experience and powerful sorcery—but having it in her sole possession had changed things.

Pulling off her glove, firmly banishing the visceral memory of how it had affected her for Jak to take control like that—

ordering her to put on the gloves, holding her hands with such fierce passion in his eyes—she wrapped her palm around the Star's heat. The eroding weariness that came from healing began to fade, leaving her refreshed, her magic fully restored. An extraordinary benefit of having the Star. She'd done more healing in the last day than in her entire life leading up to this, and now felt none of the usual aftereffects. She no longer needed to crash into the restorative sleep to recover.

Too bad, as she'd actually welcome a bit of oblivion at the moment.

Had Andi ever felt this alone in her sorcery? No, because she'd married Rayfe before she knew much of anything about her magic. And while Andi and Stella shared many of the same talents, Andi wasn't an empath like Stella, with all the attendant, devastating side effects of being so porous to the world. Debilitating impacts the Star did nothing to alleviate, alas.

At least it was peaceful out on the beach of this empty, wintry lake. Being alone always helped. With most everyone still asleep—but for a few servants she sensed quietly going about their chores—Stella was blessedly free of the chaotic emotions that battered her on a daily basis. Even with her shielding as good as she could make it, just being around other people in normal circumstances left her drained. Her friends understood, to an extent, but she didn't like to make a problem of herself, so she rarely mentioned it. Even Astar didn't realize how much simply living at Castle Ordnung had been an ordeal for her.

But she had only herself to blame there, as she'd made sure

he didn't know how bad it had been at times. She'd had no intention of leaving him to the elegant wolves there, dressed in their silks and satins and slavering to take a bite of the next high king. Stella would never abandon Astar in his time of need, no matter the cost to her peace of mind.

But now Astar would have Zeph as his companion. She'd be a good partner for him, giving him the unconditional support and occasional wake-up kick he needed. Astar would no longer need—or want—his sister hanging around. Stella would be free of Ordnung now. The insight came as a shock— and explained why her future held a lonely tower and nothing else.

She shouldn't mind that, knowing that she'd be alone all her life. Being alone was a good thing for her. She needed that time to herself to rebuild her shields, to refill the well within that drained away just being around other people. Being around anyone but Astar, that was.

Jak had always been considerate of her, protective even, and more careful than most about her sensitivities. But, like Astar, even he didn't realize how being around him could be painful. His scorching desire and his excruciating longing for her just now had left her feeling flayed from the inside out. He made her want what she couldn't have, his wanting and her own tangling together to make an internal blade, the bitter edge of it leaving her gutted. Feeling Jak's crushing disap- pointment at her rejection, experiencing his grief at the slicing knowledge of what could never be, along with hers, had been almost more than she could bear.

Bad enough that she broke her own heart, but she'd had to

feel every drop of blood she'd drawn from his. At least it was done.

But far from being cleansed by the catharsis of the break, only gritty misery filled her.

"Wallowing in self-pity will get you nowhere," she said aloud, her voice echoing softly over the mirror-smooth black water of the lake. It seemed a whisper of *something* replied. More than an echo. Hmm.

Gazing over the water, she focused her vision—physical and internal—on the far distance. She wasn't nearly so good as Aunt Andi at projecting her consciousness beyond her body, but she could selectively shapeshift, increasing the focal length of her eyes to farsight, and adding a dollop of magic to extend it even farther. *What is out there?*

Lena and Zeph had gone through that rift into another realm. Both of them had sensed it as a sort of fold or doorway in the walls between different realities. Logically, those must be smaller versions of the vast metaphysical rift that had yet to occur in their future, the disaster to come that Andi had seen and that the high queen had sent their crew to stop.

Stella had caught glimpses of that future in confusing fragments. When they'd battled the stone giant at Gieneke, Stella had sensed something of that same overlap in different realities—something she'd also caught a sense of from Lena and Zeph's minds as she'd healed them from their ordeal in that world. She'd like to discern more for herself, and she might as well do something productive while everyone else recovered.

The *something* moved through the opaque water, and her

heart quickened with excitement. Could it be Lake Sullivan's famous, seldom-glimpsed lake creature? She'd love to see it. It would be useful, too, to get a feel for the creature, to determine if it indeed belonged to the world Zeph and Lena had unwillingly visited. It could be that the lake creature moved back and forth between worlds through one of those rifts. If so, it—or its ancestors—had been doing so regularly for centuries, since the stories about it stretched back that long. Sifting her mind through the dark waters, she *looked* for the lake creature.

The waters parted, and a dark head rose.

Gaping in astonishment, Stella tried to make sense of what she saw. Gleaming black as the water it rose from, as if formed of the water itself, the triangular head of the creature continued to rise on an impossibly long, sinuous neck. It rose high enough to look into the second story of the manse if it wished, then tilted to gaze at her with an obsidian eye. A thin line across the snout delineated its reptilian mouth, but besides that—and the eyes that blended into its skin seamlessly—the head was featureless. No nares in evidence, no pinna or sign of openings for ear canals. The skin wasn't scaled, but seemed to be a soft mucus membrane, like an amphibian. Behind it, coils of its long body emerged from the water, leaving no ripples, no sign of limbs moving beneath.

With an unsteady blend of trepidation and delight, Stella realized she'd never seen any creature in the world like it before, not living nor in any text or illustration. Something she would've said was impossible before this. Living among the shapeshifting Tala, she'd thought she'd seen every possible creature in existence—and a few supposedly mythical ones, too.

The lake creature continued to gaze at her, no hint of threat in its posture. Instead it seemed more... curious? With a start, Stella realized she sensed nothing from it whatsoever. No glimmer of emotion, no thoughts, murky or otherwise. Its presence blended seamlessly with the water that birthed it. If she closed her eyes, she wouldn't know it was there at all. All living things had some kind of presence to her internal sight, even the simplest of plants or the tiny organisms that lived in the soil at their roots. This creature had no more sense of life than the pure waters of the lake it dwelled in.

Either it was something undetectable to anything but her eyes—or its shields were so impenetrable even their existence couldn't be felt. Unprecedented.

"Hello," she tendered, extending a mental wave of greeting as well.

Nothing. It simply looked at her, motionless in the water.

Then, as silently as it had arrived, it withdrew, sinking back into the water as if dissolving into it, leaving not even a ripple behind.

"Good morning," Gen said behind her.

Stella shrieked, clapping a hand to her thudding heart so it wouldn't burst out of her chest.

"Sorry," Gen said, plopping down beside her, her soft indigo eyes full of puzzlement. "What's up with you? You're usually impossible to sneak up on."

"Did you see it?" Stella asked breathlessly.

"No! See what?" With eager excitement, Gen scanned the silent, undisturbed water. "Did you get a glimpse of the lake creature?"

"More than a glimpse." Or... had she? Gen had walked up behind her within moments of the creature disappearing. It wasn't that short of a walk from the manse, so Gen should have seen it. There was no way she could've missed it. Unless the encounter hadn't been real. "Maybe I imagined it," Stella said on a considering breath.

"Most people only see bits of it." Gen shook back her long chestnut hair, studying the water. "A head or tail poking up, a loop of body. There and gone again."

"I saw more than that. Or I think I did." With Gen beside her, reality had regained a firmer feel—and the incident with the lake creature began to seem even more dreamlike.

"Tell me." Gen now studied her with gentle concern.

So Stella described the incident, Gen listening thoughtfully. "How could I have not seen it?" she asked when Stella finished.

"Maybe because I dreamed it?" Stella ventured. More and more, that seemed like the most reasonable explanation. She'd been upset, needing something to take her mind off the confrontation with Jak, off the mourning for her twin, the icy prospect of a life lived without love. Off that abrupt ending to her life path, in an isolated tower in a sea of lilies.

"I doubt it," Gen replied in a practical tone. "More likely it's a sorceress thing. Like the creature can't be seen with mortal eyes or something."

"There are stories of sightings by non-sorcerous types," Stella pointed out. "And I'm mortal, too."

"Not like the rest of us," Gen commented without rancor, and without noticing how Stella flinched internally at the assessment. "Besides, the stories surrounding sightings of the lake creature always include some aspect that only the chosen, or the pure of heart or something, can see it. If any of us is pure of heart, it would be you."

"I'm definitely not that," Stella replied, an unexpectedly bitter edge to her voice. One that took Gen by surprise.

"Is something wrong?" she asked with a concerned frown. "I mean, besides seeing a mythical lake monster and then me scaring you out of your skin."

"Not at all," Stella said as serenely as possible. "Just a little rattled, as you say. But I also don't believe in the purity-of-heart or chosen-one explanations."

"Yes, well, the stories conflict," Gen agreed. "And there's a lot of superstition tied in around it, with the good luck and conferring of blessings. It would take serious study to sort the grains of truth from all the chaff."

"How do you know so much about it now?" Stella didn't think Gen had known more than the rest of them when they'd first discussed the creature.

"Henk," Gen replied bleakly. A world of misery in the one word.

Stella winced. That was a good reminder that other people had problems far worse than her own. "I'm very sorry it didn't work out with Henk."

"I'm very sorry Henk turned out to be such a heel," Gen said on a sigh. "I only saw what I wanted to see in him."

"That's easy to do."

Gen snorted. "All of you immediately disliked him. None of you were surprised that he lost his mind at the sight of Zeph becoming a gríobhth, or that he abandoned us after…" She trailed off, flushing.

"After you shapeshifted into a white saber cat and put the fear of Moranu into him," Stella finished with a smile. "That was one of the most satisfying moments I've been privileged to witness." Zeph's gríobhth form—or gryphon in Common Tongue—tended to shock people with her golden beauty and the sheer improbability of her existence, but saber cats hadn't been seen in centuries, and Gen had been a particularly large and astonishing example of the breed.

Still flushed with chagrin, Gen made a face. "Not a solid method for finding true love, however."

"I don't know. Seems like a good test to me. If he loves you as a saber cat, then he's more likely to embrace all the aspects that make you special."

Gen gave her a grateful smile. "Thank you. You're always so kind."

Not always. Jak's furious disappointment still strummed along her nerves, and she let out a heavy sigh.

"Maybe we should go swimming," Gen suggested, eyes brightening. "I was planning to do a bit of aerial reconnaissance, since the other shapeshifter scouts of the group are abed, probably for the day, but it would be fun to go look for the lake creature, too."

Stella considered that dubiously, mentally measuring the size of the creature's mouth. It didn't look to have had much in the way of teeth or claws, but that didn't mean it wasn't dangerous. "We'd have to take the form of something that's a decent size," she decided out loud. Astar wasn't awake to weigh the risks and make a decision as the group leader, so she'd do her best by him in his absence. "Preferably something fierce—just in case—and cold-water tolerant. There may not be ice on that water, but it's close to freezing."

"I have an orca form."

"You have an *every* form," Stella retorted with a laugh. Gen had more forms than anyone, even Zeph. "I can't do that, but I can do a sea lion."

"Yes, let's explore," Gen urged. "Zeph and Lena will probably sleep all day after what they've been through."

"Absolutely. So will Rhy and Astar, because I saw to that."

"Did you?" Gen's eyes widened in interest. "I didn't know you could do that."

"It's a new skill I've been honing."

"Useful. So that just leaves Jak." She deflated. "It wouldn't be fair to abandon him to the sleepers, but he can't shapeshift."

"He's sleeping, too. I just healed him, and he'll be out a while. Did you know Rhy attacked him yesterday?"

"No." Gen shook her head, sighing. "What came over him?"

"I don't know, but—" Stella paused, the words echoing oddly in her head. "You said those exact words yesterday, when you became the saber cat and stalked Henk, that you didn't know what came over you."

"I was so angry," Gen admitted. "Like seeing-red mad."

"Astar has been growly, too, the bear close to the surface in his emotions," Stella mused. "I thought it was Zeph's effect on him, but…"

"Zeph has definitely been acting wilder. More so than

usual. I thought she was going to shift into a gríobhth and disembowel Princess Berendina on the ballroom floor."

"A sentiment I could sympathize with," Stella said wryly. There'd never been much chance that the social-climbing princess from Jorrit would win Astar's hand in marriage, but Berendina been determined. And her thoughts and emotions had been unpleasantly mercenary and acquisitive. There weren't many people that Stella couldn't find something to like about—having intimate insight into people's heads tended to make her sympathetic, even with those personalities unpleasant on the surface—but she hadn't cared for Princess Berendina. If the woman wanted a throne so badly, let her turn her ambitions to winning one on her own merits, not marrying into the privilege. "Jak mentioned it, too," Stella noted. "He said he and Lena had also observed that the shapeshifters were acting a bit more animal than usual."

"Except for you," Gen said, her gaze keen on Stella. "You are as serene and poised as ever."

Maybe not. Maybe she hadn't been as reasoning as she thought, repudiating Jak like that. If so, she owed him an apology. Except... things were better this way, even if he hated her now.

"I bet it's the sorcery side of you," Gen added, wiggling her fingers in the air, making Stella smile. "Come on, let's go exploring. I want to see this lake creature! If I can. The outing will do you good. You seem down today. Are you worried about Zeph and Lena?"

"No. Everyone healed fine." Stella stood and walked the short distance to the water. "I'm dying to hear their story, however."

"Me too. And I want to hear how Astar suddenly just grabbed dragon form. I didn't know he'd been working on it."

"He hadn't," Stella replied. "But it was always in him, waiting to be released."

"Figures," Gen muttered.

"Do *you* mind?" Stella asked. She knew the answer, felt Gen's frustration over it, her disappointment with her life in general. Gen's mother Zynda was the only other shapeshifter to attain dragon form, and Gen had long been trying to follow in her mother's footsteps. Stella privately thought Gen didn't need to follow anyone else's path, but she was willing to listen if Gen wanted to talk about it.

Gen made a face at her. "I'm sure you can sense that I mind. I'm envious, but I'm also happy for Astar. A good swim will work out the green meanies." She waded into the water. "Moranu this water *is* cold! I should've become a bird and then shifted over deeper water. This wading in for a deep-water form is miserable."

"You still could," Stella pointed out, waiting politely. Sea-lion form would let her shift on the beach, then wade in. Cold water wouldn't bother her then.

"My boots are already wet," Gen said philosophically, "but I'm going for a fish first, or I'll never make it. Guard my back?"

"Always," Stella said with a smile, and became the sea lion, taking her clothes and the Star with her. Keeping an eye on fish-Gen, she plunged into the water. A good swim would work out her own sad mood.

Who knew what they would find?

~ 3 ~

"NOTHING," GEN DECLARED, shaking back her glossy chestnut hair, waving her fork in the air emphatically. "Not a Moranu-blessed thing in that lake. How is that even possible?"

Jak regarded her with amusement, grateful for Gen's presence at their cozy dinner. Stella wasn't exactly avoiding his gaze, but she also wasn't acknowledging his existence in any significant way. She had that remote, faraway look to her, like she did when she'd had enough of being around people and was heavily protecting herself from their emotions. He doubted that was the case, however, since only the three of them sat around the small table by the fire in the smaller dining room. Zeph and Lena had apparently both awakened, as had Astar. Everyone had heard him roaring at finding her gone.

Good thing Jak had crashed into his own bed with his pants still on, because he'd been in the hall, blades in hand, before he fully awakened. By the time he figured out there wasn't an actual attack, Astar had carried Zeph back to bed—and not to sleep that time.

Lucky guy. But Astar deserved it, if anyone did. Zeph was

certainly pleased with herself.

Fully awake after that false emergency, and feeling considerably restored, Jak had washed up, dressed fully—and found himself still kicking his heels alone. Lena had eaten and gone back to sleep, in a new room, leaving hers to the still-sleeping Rhyian. Or the apparently still-sleeping Rhy. Jak had his doubts there. Astar had gotten the same knockout treatment from Stella, and he'd woken up after a few hours, but if that was how Rhy wanted to handle things, then so be it. Better for him to sulk quietly than subject everyone else to his undoubtedly foul mood.

There'd been no sign of Gen or Stella until the pair of them returned from exploring the forbidding lake. Good thing dusk fell early this far north in winter. Jak might've lost his mind pacing around and worrying about them if he'd had to wait much longer. Not that he'd let on to Stella, who'd greeted him with her usual polite distance, her only sign of concern a formal question about his ribs.

Normally he didn't mind not being a shapeshifter. He fell in with those who were perfectly happy having one skin and keeping it in place. But it was Danu-cursed frustrating to be left behind. Also something he wouldn't let on to Stella. If she was going to be eavesdropping on his emotions, then he'd give her ones *he* chose. Carefree and happy Jak was the order of the evening.

"You saw *nothing* in the lake?" he teased Gen. "No rocks? Not even a bunch of water?"

She glared at him, mouth set mulishly. "You are not funny, Jak. I meant no fish, of any size. And certainly no lake creature," she added with glum disappointment.

"Maybe the lake creature ate all the fish," he suggested, gaze wandering to Stella—who seemed entirely focused on her meal. She always ate slowly, as if not entirely convinced she'd like the taste by the time she put it in her mouth. Not like him, who'd been raised by two warriors with the ethic that time spent eating was an opportunity for an enemy to put a blade in your back.

"Maybe," Gen said, the kind of *maybe* that meant *I think you're an idiot but I'm too polite to say so.*

Jak kicked his chair back onto two legs and toasted her with his whiskey glass. At least he could get drunk on Groningen's excellent liquor supply. "Are you sure there are no fish at all? Surely you two didn't canvass the entire lake." Though he addressed the question to Stella, too, she didn't look up, dark hair falling in a curtain, obscuring most of the pale oval of her face.

"True enough." Gen swirled her wine thoughtfully. "It's an enormous lake, and deep. So deep that not much light penetrates beyond a certain level, and even my orca vision failed. Much as I wanted to see Stella's creature, I was also wary of falling through one of those rifts. What if they're in the water around here, too? Nilly might sense it, but I don't know that I would."

"Oh, it's Stella's creature now?" It would be nice to get *some* reaction from the silent Stella.

"Well, she was the first to see it," Gen explained. "This morning."

His chair came down with a thud. "You saw it? When this

morning?"

Stella—finally—lifted her gaze to his, gray eyes calm as winter morning. "After you went inside. It rose up from the water, right in front of me."

He fought a myriad of emotions, worry wrestling with aggravation. She'd been in danger, and she hadn't called him back. "You promised," he said softly, the lethal anger giving the mild words a keen edge. "Not moments before that, you promised to call me if you needed help."

"I didn't need help," she replied smoothly, but he caught a shadow of defensiveness in it. "Besides, I knew you would be already asleep, which you needed to complete the healing."

"Aha!" He kicked his chair back onto two legs again, balancing there. "I get your reasoning: the promise is conditional. Thus, if I decide it's better for you, then I don't have to keep my promise either."

Stella gave him a long look, silvery sparks belying her calm expression. "It's not the same thing."

"Isn't it?" He snatched up his whiskey glass without unbalancing the chair. "Do you think you're the only one who cares about other people? That you're the only one who's here to see that we all make it through this quest alive?"

Her gaze grew thunderous, storm clouds gathering on the horizon. "I never said that, Jak."

"No, you keep your own counsel," he bit out, more viciously than he meant to.

"Did I miss something?" Gen asked, looking back and forth between them, a line between her brows.

"No," Stella replied firmly, pushing back her chair to stand.

"I'm tired and going to bed."

"You barely ate," Jak pointed out, feeling both guilty that he'd disrupted her desultory eating and irritated that she'd run away like that. "Sit down again and finish your supper."

"I'm not hungry," she shot back defiantly. "And you don't order me."

"Jak's right," Gen put in with concern. "We burned a lot of energy today. You need to eat more than that. Jak will behave himself."

"I wasn't behaving badly," he complained.

"You're being an ass," Gen hissed at him under her breath, as if there were any way in the world Stella wouldn't hear that. "You're as bad as Rhyian."

"Did someone blacken my name?" Rhy slouched against the doorway, one eyebrow arched to demonstrate how much he didn't care.

"Oh, wonderful," Gen muttered. "Now there's two of them."

"Hey!" Jak protested. Quite the comedown indeed if Gen really thought he was being like Rhy. Gen smirked, and Rhy paused beside the still-standing Stella, glancing from her face to her plate.

"You probably should eat, cousin," he said with surprising gentleness. "Don't deprive yourself just because Jak's being an ass."

"You weren't even here," Jak countered.

"I didn't have to be." Rhy held Stella's chair until she sighed and sat, then snagged a chair of his own and wedged it between the girls. He grinned at Jak. "I could hear you all arguing from upstairs."

Finding his whiskey glass empty, Jak got up for more.

"Get me one, too," Rhy called after him, and Jak made a rude gesture but snagged a second glass. And because he *wasn't* an ass, he poked his head through the doorway to ask someone to bring Rhy a plate.

"I had to heal four cracked ribs on Jak this morning," Stella was telling Rhy as he returned. "And clear him of infection from the wounds you put on him."

Rhy raked a hand through his unruly black hair. "Shit, man—I'm sorry. I forgot."

"It was nothing," Jak said, handing him the whiskey and clinking his own glass against Rhy's. Sliding a glare at Stella, he went back to his own chair. "Not even worth mentioning."

She met his gaze coolly. "A mere flesh wound?"

Now she was talking to him, and it wasn't any better than the silent treatment. "It's between me and Rhy and it's handled."

"A guy thing. Really?" Gen rolled her eyes.

"If you like," Jak said.

"I don't like," Gen retorted, "because it's the women who have to patch you up from your manly manly bro stunts."

"I seem to recall Zeph nearly killing herself fighting the stone giant," he countered. "And then she and Lena both needed extensive healing after *their* latest, all-female stunt."

"That was in the course of duty for the quest!" Gen banged down her now-empty wineglass. "Not whatever dick-swinging you two were up to." She leveled a furious glare on Rhy, who held up his hands in surrender.

"I swear, I never touched Jak's dick," he said solemnly, making Jak choke on his whiskey.

"Let me get you more wine," Jak said to Gen, using his smoothest courtly manners. She made a face at him but handed over her glass. A group of servants bustled in just then, setting a full plate in front of Rhy, clearing away Jak's and Gen's cleaned ones. One man hesitated at Stella's side.

"I'm done," Stella told him with a soft smile.

"Do you have soup?" Jak asked as he brought Gen's glass back and took his own seat.

"Soup, milord?" The man looked startled.

"Broth, chowder, stew. Something like that. She prefers that kind of thing." He tipped his chin at Stella. "And sweets. Anything sweet you've got would be welcome."

"Of course, milord. Right away." The man bustled out, and Jak didn't bother to correct his error in giving him a title. No lord he, and all the happier for it.

Stella was eyeing him. "Thank you, Jak. That was thought-fully done."

"One day you'll learn to just ask for what you want," he told her. She raised one dark brow, and he nearly bit his tongue wanting to take that back, since she'd very clearly told him what she wanted—and didn't want—that very morning.

"Here we go again," Gen muttered darkly.

"No, we don't," Stella said with unusual firmness, turning to Rhy. "Jak mentioned that you found us because you sensed Lena was no longer in this world. Can you tell me what exactly you felt?"

Rhy considered her as he chewed. "Want to just look in

my head? That might be easier than me trying to explain."

"It wouldn't be easier on Stella." That was just like Rhy, to take the easy route at the cost of someone else. "That kind of thing is hard on her."

Rhy gave him a bemused look. "Don't forget who my mother is," he replied. "The omnipotent Sorceress Andromeda has been rummaging around in my head all my life. I know how to let them see what they're looking for without soiling their magic with my foul emotions. Sweet Nilly has been trained by the best and knows what she's doing. Besides, I assume it's important or you wouldn't be asking?"

He directed that last at Stella, who nodded cautiously. "It might be. And I do know what I'm doing," she said to Jak. "So stop acting like a mother hen."

"Am I an ass or am I a hen?" he asked philosophically.

"It's entirely possible to be both," Gen shot at him, but only half-heartedly, because her attention was on Stella and Rhy.

It shouldn't annoy him, watching Stella lay light fingertips on Rhy's bare forearm, making skin-to-skin contact, but it did. Rhy closed his eyes, holding still for her as the magic gathered around her like mist condensing over the ocean as the air cooled and the sun set. With their dark heads bent together, the family resemblance was apparent. Their mothers were sisters, and the three of them—including Astar—had always been a tight-knit group. Especially when the twins were little and learning to control their shapeshifting, they'd spent a lot of time in Annfwn. They were close cousins, practically like siblings.

I don't want to be like a brother to you! his own voice shouted in his head, words hurled like weapons at her. And she'd reared back as if wounded, pale, frightened by his vehemence. He'd well and truly fucked up. Worse, he didn't see any way to fix it.

His whiskey glass was empty again, and he still wasn't drunk enough, but even as he moved to get a refill, he caught Gen's sidelong glance, the subtle shake of her head. Fine, then.

Resigned and in the doldrums, stuck like a sailing ship without oars on a windless day, he excused himself and went to his room to lie awake and brood. Stella didn't even notice that he'd left.

IN THE MORNING, Astar sent around a request that they all convene to hear Zeph and Lena's tale of their adventures—and to plan next steps accordingly.

Jak was the first one to arrive, that Dasnarian sailor timeliness thing prodding him as always, not to mention that he'd been up since dawn, running forms and testing his body. It had been a relief to perform Danu's Dance to the best of his ability. At least that was one arena where he wasn't a disaster.

The small salon they were to meet in overlooked the lake, providing spectacular views, so he stood at the big window studying the unruffled surface of the black water for signs of Stella's lake creature. The snow-capped mountains all around plunged dramatically to lake level, a considerable drop in altitude from the peaks. On the heights, winds whipped snow across pristine ridges, looking like the ghosts of deer racing from unseen predators. Below, not a breeze disturbed the lake's glassy surface. The difference between the two bothered him in a way he couldn't quite identify. They were like two worlds, juxtaposed together.

A sound at the door alerted him, and he glanced over his shoulder, expecting a servant with the promised hot beverages and breakfast pastries. Instead he caught Stella on the verge of sneaking out again.

"Afraid to be alone with me?" he asked, and she started guiltily, a rose blush gracing her fair cheekbones.

With a heartfelt sigh, she entered the salon. "I'm surprised you heard me. Most people don't."

Most mossbacks, she meant. He had to give her credit that she hadn't lied about trying to avoid him, much as it pained him that she felt she needed to. "You know Mom," he said lightly. "She'd skin me and use me for shark bait if I let someone sneak up on me."

Stella smiled a little and nodded, relief releasing the lines around her solemn mouth. Relaxing, perhaps, that he'd let her off the hook. "Jepp is impossible to sneak up on, too. I've tried."

"I'm surprised you didn't sense me in here before you walked in the door," he said, trying very hard to sound friendly and not at all bitter, even if he did feel like actual shark bait. *Don't be like Rhy.*

"I try not to listen like that," she replied, coming to his side. "I thought you knew that. I observe privacy whenever I can."

Except when someone hurls his emotions at her like rocks.

She came to his side, gazing out the window also. "I'm

very sorry, Jak," she said quietly, just loud enough for him to hear and probably hoping none of their keen-eared friends would. "I never wanted to hurt you."

"You didn't," he replied, willing it to be true. When she slanted him a dubious glance, he grinned. "A mere flesh wound, right? Yes, it hurt in the moment, but it had to be done. I appreciate your honesty, and I won't be like Rhy, mooning after what I can't have. You can rest easy on that account."

Stella smiled at that, some genuine warmth in it. "Speaking of flesh wounds, how are you feeling?"

"Good. Excellent, really. I had a decent workout this morning, and I'm happy to report all is shipshape."

"Yes, I saw you. On the beach, from my window." She was blushing. How fascinating. "You looked good—healthy, I mean." She pressed her lips firmly together.

Tempted to tease her, he instead took a deliberately different tack. "I'm sorry, too," he said. "For how I behaved at supper last night. I—" He broke off, realizing she wasn't listening to him.

With an arrested expression, she looked past him to the doorway, so he turned to see what had distracted her. Zeph and Astar entered, his arm around her shoulders, her arm around his waist, both of them positively glowing with love, and reeking of sex. Not literally on the latter—not to his human nose anyway—but it was obvious in the languid lines of their bodies, the way they *fit* against each other, that they'd been tangled around each other in every way possible.

He had to look away, taken off guard by the stab of envy.

Not that he'd ever desired Zeph, though she'd offered, and not because she wasn't beautiful. Zeph had just never interested him that way. He wasn't drawn to her bright, flirtatious nature. Not like he was fascinated by Stella's shadows, her silent storminess, the black-water depths where she hid herself away.

Stella glanced at him, expression wry, and he realized he'd been staring at her as he wondered about those depths. He also caught the sadness in her eyes, the yearning she quickly erased with a serene countenance. But he'd seen the truth: Stella was broken-hearted over losing Astar. Of course she was. Jak was an only child, and had been the only kid on a sailing ship full of adults for a lot of that childhood. He had no idea what it was like to have a playmate or a sibling, let alone a twin. Running his finger along a lock of Stella's hair, he extended a sympathetic thought. Her eyes widened, a plea in them, and he nodded.

No, she would never want Astar to have any idea how bereft she felt.

"Color me astonished," he called out jauntily, giving Stella cover to regain her poise. "You two appear to be in one piece. Judging from the noises coming from your room, I expected to be cleaning up the bloody shreds this morning."

"Ha-ha," Zeph tossed at him, making a face, while Astar blushed. "Nilly, can I talk to you a moment before we get started?"

"You can talk to me anytime," Stella replied, going with Zeph to the far corner.

The servants came in, one young woman practically staggering under a heavy silver tray, so Jak stepped over to relieve her of it. "Oh, milord!" she gasped, face turning redder. "You needn't—"

"Already done, milady." He gave her a wink and set the tray on a low table. "You have brought sunshine to a gray morning because I dearly wanted..." He surveyed the offerings with some disappointment. "Hot tea," he finished gamely.

"If it please you, milord," she offered shyly, picking up a silver pitcher, "I have coffee imported from Annfwn, too. I could fix you a cup."

"You are my own true love," he exclaimed, bowing elaborately. "Lots of cream, and make it as sweet as you are."

"Stop flirting with the woman responsible for our breakfast," Astar said with an easy smile, not meaning it.

Wonder of wonders, amazing what getting laid did to pull the stick out of a man's ass. Jak nearly asked if Zeph had taught him any of the more stimulating things that could go up there, but decided Prince Charming wasn't ready for that level of ribaldry yet. The dimpling servant handed Jak a cup, along with tea for Astar, who accepted it with a thank-you.

Stella's voice rose in a squeal of happiness, and Jak looked over to see the two in a rare embrace. "What's going on there?"

Astar cleared his throat. "I asked Zephyr to marry me. I gave her Grandmother Salena's ring."

Jak didn't exactly choke on the hot coffee—delicious, if overly sweet, probably Stella would like it—but he did raise a brow. "What about Her Majesty's infamous list of suitable princess brides? I know Zeph wasn't on it."

"Yes, well." Astar firmed his jaw, looking more noble than

ever. "Auntie Essla doesn't have any room to criticize, seeing as how she married for love, not politics."

"Which is arguably why she hoped you'd take up that torch."

"She'll have to live with the disappointment, then—or find another heir. I'm sending a missive to Ordnung to inform her of my decision."

"Who are you and what have you done with the spotlessly honorable Crown Prince Astar?" Jak inquired, not bothering to contain his amazement.

"He grew up," Astar retorted, "and learned something about what truly matters in life." His gaze lingered on Zeph, who was telling Stella a story regularly interrupted with sighs and squeals. "I nearly lost her, Jak. Twice over. I'm not going to face a third time without giving her everything that's in me to give."

"Good man," Jak said, clapping him on the shoulder. "I wish you both well. I think our Zeph will actually make an amazing queen."

"I think so, too," Astar murmured.

"An amazing *what*?" Gen demanded as she came in the room with Lena. She spotted Zeph and Stella in the corner and beelined for them without waiting for an answer. Lena followed right behind. A new chorus of squeals went up, and Jak stuck a finger in his ear, making a show of digging at it.

Astar laughed. "They'll work off the excitement quickly."

"I hope so," Rhy said sardonically, slouching into the room with his hands deep in his black trouser pockets. "They're hurting my ears," he added in a carrying voice.

"Poor sensitive baby," Zeph sang out.

"Do I dare ask?" Rhy asked, surveying the offerings and popping a glazed roll in his mouth.

"That pitcher has Annfwn coffee," Jak said, pointing.

"Bless Moranu." Rhy sighed happily, pouring a cup.

"They're excited because Zephyr and I will be getting married," Astar told Rhy, who sloshed his cup in surprise, burning his hand, which he shook absently.

"So much for Willy's Moratorium," he snarled at Astar.

"Are we still doing that?" Jak asked. In truth, he'd forgotten the rule Astar had imposed on the group at the beginning of their quest, that there would be no romantic entanglements among themselves. Of course, it was a moot point for him now. "In point of fact, Zeph ducked agreeing to it from the very beginning—and tricked Astar into doing the same." When Rhy frowned, he added, "Think back to our first meeting."

Rhy's expression cleared in dawning comprehension—and irritation at the duplicity—while Astar looked chagrined. Jak lifted his coffee in a toast toward Zeph. "You have to admire her planning."

"Why is it admirable planning on Zeph's part to persist in chasing Willy and win his hand in marriage," Rhy ground out, "and when it's me wanting to win Lena back, I'm the villain?"

Astar growled deep in his chest, opening his mouth, but Jak pointed a finger to stop him. "If you don't know the answer to that excellent question, my friend, then *that* is what makes you the villain."

Rhy drank down his coffee, hissing at the burn. "Since when are you the philosopher?"

"Danu's lines are clear ones," Jak replied cheerfully, adding a silent reminder to himself to abide by them.

"Apparently Willy's Moratorium wasn't in lines nearly as fixed as Danu would make them," Rhy bit out, glaring at Astar.

"It's true," Astar replied evenly. "As I am only a man, and I lack the goddess's clear-eyed wisdom. Therefore, I'm rescinding the rule. I bear responsibility for failing to seal my own vow to the agreement, and then later making another vow in violation of my implied promise. You are free to do as you please, cousin."

When Rhyian's eyes lit with fierce glee, settling immediately on Lena, Astar put a hand on his shoulder. "But I'm warning you, Rhyian: this is a make-or-break opportunity."

"To do what?" Rhy asked, shrugging off the hand irritably.

"The right thing," Astar replied with firm resolve.

"According to you?" Rhy sneered.

Astar just shook his head sadly. "You still don't get it. According to Lena."

"And how am I supposed to know what *she* thinks is the right thing?" Rhy snarled.

"Here's a startling suggestion," Jak replied with raised brows. "You could ask her."

"And how am I supposed to do that when she won't talk to me?" Rhy waved his empty cup in the air.

Jak shook his head and snagged the cup, going to refill for them both. This would be a long morning. "Maybe figuring *that* out would a good place to start, if you're smart enough," he called over his shoulder, laughing when Rhy made a rude gesture.

~ 4 ~

"ALL RIGHT, PEOPLE," Astar called out from where the three guys were clustered around the food, interrupting Zeph's swooningly detailed—and third—description of the actual proposal. As happy as Stella was for her and Astar, she didn't need to hear the story yet again. "Time for Lena and Zeph to give us the report. We've waited long enough."

"I know I can't stand the suspense any longer," Stella agreed.

"Me neither," Astar said. "So, grab some food and drink, and find a seat so we can hear where Zephyr and Lena went, and what happened there. Then we need to plan next steps."

"You don't know already?" Jak, holding an incongruously delicate cup, elbowed Astar. "You two have been closeted nonstop since the girls returned. I figured Zeph had told you everything."

"We weren't *talking*," Zeph replied to Jak sassily, giving Stella, Gen, and Lena a wink and a pleased smile. Then Zeph's mood darkened as she held out a hand to Lena, and they shared a long look. "And I only wanted to have to tell it once."

"Agree completely with that," Lena replied fervently. "Let's get this over with."

They all took their seats, the festive mood sobering, and Stella sifted through the emotional currents. Worry. Fear. Curiosity. While she'd told Jak the truth—that she tried not to overhear thoughts and feelings people wanted to keep private—sometimes she had no choice. And sometimes, like this, it was useful to keep her mental finger on the pulse of the group. Astar and Zeph's good news had been a welcome happy distraction from the uncertain future they all faced.

And she greatly appreciated that Zeph had wanted to tell Stella first, in private, though the engagement hadn't come as a surprise. Zeph had been earnest, even vulnerable in a way Zeph never was, concerned about Stella's approval. Fortunately, her blessing was something Stella could give with a full heart. Zeph had always been like a sister to her, so having her as an official heart-sister only formalized the relationship.

I don't want to be like a brother to you! Jak's pained and furious words echoed in her mind, and she flinched internally.

"I made it sweet," Jak said, appearing in front of her as if conjured by her thoughts, and pushing a pretty cup of black coffee into her hands. "No cream, right?"

"Right," she replied faintly, rather astonished.

He put a plate on the table in front of her, piled high with pastries. A lemon tart glowed like sunshine, another spilling with glistening blueberries. Buttery, flaky popovers oozed with cream that glinted with strawberries. Her stomach growled at the sight. "Thank you, though I can't eat all that."

"It won't go to waste," he replied. "And unless you ate a great deal after I left last night, you need it."

"Why are you feeding me?" she asked, aware of Gen nearby, listening with interest.

"Don't sound so suspicious. I'm feeding Gen, too." He pointed at the plate Gen was holding. "Unless we're sailing or fighting, I don't have many responsibilities. Might as well play waiter." He grinned and snagged a chair with one foot, picking up his own coffee cup and raising it to her as he lolled back in the fussy chair, a lock of unruly brown hair falling over one eye. The gold hoop in one ear glinted, and he looked decidedly piratical. If pirates drank from elegant, hand-painted ceramic.

"I'll start," Lena declared, "since it began with me." She pushed back her waving caramel hair, a line between her brows. "I should lead off by offering an apology to you all, but especially to Zeph, who risked her life to come after me. I didn't mean to step through that fold into another realm, but I'm aware I jeopardized all of you with my carelessness."

"It *was* extremely careless of you," Rhy said, pushing up from his chair he'd barely sat in and pacing toward the window. "You could have died."

"I very nearly did, several times," Lena agreed soberly, watching him with mingled sorrow and longing. Something she immediately hid when he turned. "And I already stated that I regret my carelessness. It was an accident, however. I was simply trying to track the oddness I sensed in the atmosphere, using my weather magic to get a bead on it, just to gather more data. I was circling what felt like a weather front between high- and low-pressure systems when suddenly I was falling."

"Falling?" Gen echoed. "But you'd been on solid ground."

Lena nodded. "I know. Still, it felt exactly like that—as if I'd put my foot down wrong and fallen off a cliff. Except it was a forest. I fell through branches, then into this deep leaf litter. Deepest I've ever encountered."

"Easily as deep as Astar is tall," Zeph put in. "Maybe more. It was compressed at the bottom, looser at the top. I never did determine where the soil was, if there was any."

"If there was a forest, there had to be soil," Gen offered.

"Not necessarily." Lena shook her head, gaze haunted. "This world worked by different rules. I had some magic, but not all of it, and what I had was—twisted from the usual."

"And I couldn't shift back from gríobhth form," Zeph said. "I never thought I'd dislike my First Form, but the prospect of being trapped in it forever, no words or thumbs..." She trailed off with a shudder, and Astar put his arm around her on the settee they shared. She sagged against him, closing her eyes.

Jak had discarded his cup and pulled out a silver dagger, spinning it through his fingers thoughtfully. "Given the wounds you returned with, I'm guessing something nasty lived in that leaf detritus."

"Zeph dubbed them tentacle things," Lena said. "If there was more to them than that, I never saw." She raised a brow at Zeph.

"Whatever the tentacles were attached to, it was buried deep," Zeph said. "I could hear it—or them—moving down there, but was never sure if it was one creature or thousands. Thousands of tentacles, though. I thought there was no way Lena could've survived those things—they had a sting to them and could strip your flesh away with a touch."

So that was the source of the many lacerations and what

had looked like burns on both Zeph and Lena. In some places, they looked like they'd been flayed. If Stella hadn't had magical healing skills, and the assistance of the Star to renew her magic, neither of them would've lived.

"I was lucky to land near that rock outcropping," Lena replied. "Once I figured out I couldn't climb any of the trees— smooth surface, no limbs below several man-heights—I managed to get on those rocks." She threw a grateful smile at Jak, nodding at the blade walking through his nimble fingers. "I fended them off with the dagger you gave me. I meant to thank you right away. Without your lessons in bladework, I'd have been dragged off that rock in no time."

Jak grinned in sincere pleasure. "You're a good student. It makes me happier than I can say that the lessons stood you in good stead. I'm happy to work with all of you. Best to be prepared," he added, a hint of challenge in the dark eyes that lingered a moment longer on Stella, a reminder that she'd asked him for help. Something she now regretted, given the tension between them.

"I have claws, thank you," Rhy replied, glaring at Jak, his jealousy ripe in the air. "I can protect Lena, too."

"Not if you're not there," Lena countered, "which you weren't. I'm not blaming you for that," she added, holding up a hand when he opened his mouth to argue. "My point is that any of us could be isolated as I was. We have to be able to fend for ourselves."

"And you can't count on claws, Rhy," Zeph pointed out. "Whatever that place is, I could *not* shift. If I'd been in human form, we'd both have died there."

"Everyone is taking lessons in hand-to-hand," Astar decided. "In human form only, no shapeshifting tricks or enhancements. Jak, thank you for the offer."

Jak stopped the spinning blade by tapping the flat to his temple in a jaunty salute, while Rhy groaned, muttering about being forced into mossback ways. Everyone ignored him.

Zeph and Lena went on to describe their escape from the forest floor, the attacks by the canopy denizens, the endless circling to locate another rift to return to their own world. Stella comprehended even more, hearing all that they didn't say. She bent her own rules a bit more to probe deeper into the black emotions clouding around Lena, who sat by herself in a high-backed chair, fingers digging into the padded arms. Though she reported the details of their harrowing adventure in a precise, even tone, the remembered despair plagued her inside. Stella experienced with Lena the moment of decision to let herself fall, to save Zeph by killing herself, crystal clear and bleeding shards of residual grief.

Though it was an invasion of Lena's mind, Stella was glad to have probed. Sometimes healing the body from trauma was the easiest part. To have decided on suicide, to the point of taking that action and throwing herself into the arms of death, and then awake to a life she'd thought she'd relinquished... That changed a person.

Lena would need help, perhaps more than Stella could give. Lena also needed to be not so alone. Speculatively, Stella observed Rhy, with his restless pacing and helpless rage. Was he the answer? That very much depended on Rhy, she supposed. But when she took a look at the future between them, it didn't look likely. Not unless something changed. *Hmm.*

Zeph, having also grown too restive to sit still while she told the last bit, now perched on the edge of the settee. She described her frantic dive through the fold, which stripped her of her gríobhth form—the last thing she remembered—before it dumped her naked and near death to plummet through the night sky over Lake Sullivan.

"So," Astar said, breaking the thoughtful silence that had fallen, fingers laced between his spread knees. "Let's connect pieces of the puzzle. Was the intelligence you encountered at Gieneke from this world you visited?"

"'Intelligence' sounds so bland," Jak complained. "Let's give it a nickname. And I think we need a name for the place, like the Evil Realm."

"We don't know that it's necessarily evil," Lena countered, frowning at him. "That's an unfair value judgment."

"The alter-realm, then," he suggested with a lift of his brows.

"Fine," Astar said. "Was the Gieneke intelligence from the alter-realm?" Jak opened his mouth, and Astar pointed a quelling finger at him. "Don't."

Lena and Astar both looked at Stella. "How should I know if it was the same intelligence?" Stella asked. "Lena would know better than I would, as she had contact with it in both places."

Lena shook her head. "I only assisted you at Gieneke. You're the one who connected to the intelligence, who understood it well enough to take in its emotions and use them

63

as a weapon against it. Can't you see in my mind whether it was there in this alternate world or not?"

"I haven't looked," Stella replied, which was true. She'd been observing Lena's mental and emotional wounds, not rummaging through her head for everything.

Lena heaved an impatient sigh. "Then look."

"It's not always that simple," Stella cautioned.

Jak cocked his head, watching her thoughtfully.

"You looked in *my* head last night," Rhy said, ceasing his pacing to stop by Lena's chair, hand hovering as if he longed to touch her, before he shoved it in his pocket.

"You're different," Stella replied automatically. Aware that Astar was looking at her with considerable surprise, she added, "I looked in Rhy's mind to determine how he knew Lena had gone to another world."

Astar raised a brow. "What did you find?"

Lena regarded her with wariness, too, but also a considerable edge of morbid curiosity. Stella debated how much to tell them. Really, she should've planned this out, should've realized the question would come up.

"Just tell us," Lena said, though her internal tumult didn't match her outward calm. "We're all in this together. I'd rather know, and for everyone to know."

Stella sighed to herself. She disliked causing pain, for whatever reason—and it seemed she'd been doing a great deal of it lately. "Lena and Rhy have a connection. Perhaps formed when you were in love in your youth. It's not something under your conscious control, but it is there."

Rhy stood still, thoughts racing behind his blue eyes, a

triumphant—and possessive—smile twitching his lips. Lena, also frozen in place, revealed nothing. Despair still clouded around her, but Stella couldn't be sure if that was due to this information or a residual emotion from her traumatic experience.

"When you left our world, Lena," Stella continued, as gently as she knew how, "it severed the connection between you and Rhy. He felt the break, like a wound."

"Then it's gone now," Lena said with enough relief that Rhy frowned at her.

Stella shook her head regretfully. "It snapped back into place as soon as you reentered our world. I saw that in Rhy's mind also."

Lena took that in, then came to a decision. "Well, that's neither here nor there and not relevant to solving the puzzle of the rifts, or to deciding our next steps." She held out a hand again, looking like a queen in her high-backed chair, her hair a cloak of bronze around her. "Look in my mind. If what Zeph and I went through helps to solve this puzzle, then it will have been somewhat worth it."

"Better than nothing," Zeph agreed.

With no reason to refuse, Stella rose and went to Lena. She sat on the stuffed footstool Jak supplied with alacrity and a gallant bow. Bracing herself for the onslaught of Lena's emotional din, she cleared her mind and reinforced her barriers to all else. Opening the door to another person's mind was different every time, even with the same person. What she'd tried to explain to Jak the night before was true: for all of Rhy's lack of discipline in other areas, he'd learned a great deal from his mother. He possessed a mental organization that allowed him to offer a clear pathway to what she sought, closing off the clutter and chaos of other parts of his mind.

Lena's mind was easier to sort than many. She had her librarian mother's clean catalogue of thoughts and memories, and her disciplined search for knowledge, her scientific approach to life, gave her an orderliness other people lacked. However, the strain of recent weeks had also left her mind like a library after a devastating flood. The mud of despair, rage, love, grief, and furious frustration coated everything, thoughts still floating unfocused in the debris.

Stella's heart went out to her, and she did something she'd never tried before, channeling healing into the place, like a cleansing light. Not changing what was there, but lightening the load of it, making the mud less dense, sweeping it together so that Lena could begin dealing with it on her own. Behind a door, however, the looming wave of death remained.

She didn't dare approach it.

Lena relaxed gradually, her mind sinking into sleep while Stella continued her housekeeping. When a hand touched her shoulder—Astar's familiar, comforting essence in it—she gradually withdrew.

Then blinked at the bright midday light coming in the windows of the salon empty but for the three of them. She'd been in Lena's mind for hours—and Lena herself slumbered peacefully.

"I wasn't sure if I should interrupt or not," Astar said, crouching beside her and searching her face.

Stella nodded, setting Lena's hand gently in her lap, then

standing to stretch her stiff body. "She was hurting, mentally and emotionally," she explained.

"I figured as much," Astar said, studying Lena's sleeping face. "Should I send Rhy away again?"

"It wouldn't do any good. I don't think he could stay away. The next time something happened to her, he'd simply be drawn back again."

Astar nodded thoughtfully, a new understanding in his eyes. "I hate to say I sympathize with the bloody idiot, but I do."

Stella knew he did, and smiled at him, so truly happy for the love he'd found with Zeph. *I refuse to be bitter or envious.* "And it's not only him that's causing her distress. What happened to her has left her wounded on many levels."

Astar searched her face. *"Can you tell me?"* he asked subvocally, using their longtime method of private communication. It did her heart good to feel that connection to him. She'd been so deliberately walling him out, to give him privacy with Zeph, that she hadn't realized how much of him hadn't been in her head.

"I'd want her permission first. Zeph knows about it, however, if you want to ask for her version. Ask her if she'll tell you what happened right before they went through the fold to come home."

A line between his brows, he nodded. *"And Zephyr—should I be worried about her, too?"*

"I'd give her plenty of opportunity to talk about it, but our Zeph has an admirably resilient spirit. And she has you. That makes a difference." She slipped her hand in Astar's, like folding her own hands together, the one person she could touch without

struggle. The memory of Jak's smooth skin haunted her senses, how she'd wanted to touch more, taste... She shook herself from the foolish longing.

"*Meanwhile, Lena is locked in this battle with Rhy.*" Astar sighed aloud, gaze going to Lena again, who was stirring now. "*I wish I could do more for her.*"

"*She has us,*" Stella replied firmly. "*That's more than you realize.*"

Lena opened her eyes, bemused at the time that had passed, just as Stella had been.

"Welcome back, fair Lena," Astar said, giving her a warm smile. "If you're up for it, I'll gather up the strays and we can reconvene."

"Yes, of course," Lena replied, sitting up and running hands through her hair. Her gaze settled on Stella. "I don't know what you did, but thank you."

"You are welcome," Stella replied gravely, then gave her a smile. "Call it a bit of housekeeping."

"THE SAME INTELLIGENCE was indeed in the alter-realm," Stella confirmed for the group, once everyone had assembled again. "From what I was able to glean from Lena's memories, the 'tentacle things' were appendages of the same intelligence, or one of the same breed."

"There could be more than one?" Jak asked, fingering a dagger with a glittering look in his dark eyes.

"There could be an entire world of them, for all I know,"

Stella replied calmly. Would he try to stab all the creatures to death? Probably. "To recognize a given individual, I'd have to have direct mental contact with them again."

"It doesn't matter if there's an entire world of these entities," Astar said. "The problem occurs when the intelligence comes here, or we go there."

"Or when its ugly pet monsters do," Jak inserted, then pretended to cringe at Zeph's glare. "Not you, charming Zeph. You're the most beautiful monster I know."

She threw a glazed bun at him, which he speared neatly on his dagger, using it as a skewer to munch happily.

"I'm willing to concede that the m-word is appropriate for the tentacle things," Zeph said. "I think we can avoid going to the alter-realm from now on, as I'm better at sensing the rifts now. Lena is the expert, though."

Lena grimaced. "*Not* something I wanted to be an expert in."

"Aunt Andi said as much," Stella pointed out, "back at Ordnung, that understanding and repairing the rifts would likely fall to you."

Sagging back in her chair, Lena sighed, nodding in acknowledgment.

"I think we all agree that the crux of the problem is twofold," Astar continued. "The rifts allowing creatures to come here, and the rift itself, given the visions of the future. The question I'm posing now is—is there any reason for us to linger here at Lake Sullivan?"

"Not unless we want to try for another look at Stella's lake creature," Gen said.

They all looked at her with varying expressions, Jak's tight with remembered displeasure.

"*Another* look?" Lena said, sitting up, eyes alight with curiosity.

"*Stella's* lake creature," Astar repeated, a hint of betrayal in his face.

"Moranu forgive me," Stella said, rubbing a hand over her face. "I forgot to mention—though this is the first time we've all compared notes—I saw the famous lake creature yesterday morning." She described the visitation, emphasizing that she'd never felt threatened, while Jak spun his dagger with a too-bland expression.

"I don't love that you two went exploring the lake alone, looking for that creature," Astar said at last.

"*You* were otherwise occupied," Gen retorted pertly. "And nothing messes with an orca."

"That you know of," Rhy inserted with a mischievous smile.

"Why do you think you were the only one to see it, Nilly?" Lena was studying her. "By the sound of it, either Gen or Jak were close enough that they should have heard the splashing at least.

"It made no sound," Stella remembered. "I've wondered if I'd dreamed it up."

"We certainly saw no sign of it when we searched the lake," Gen added glumly. "Or anything else, really."

"If the lake creature is moving between realms, as we're theorizing," Lena mused, "then there could be rifts underwater."

"It was just blind good luck Stella and Gen didn't inadvertently swim through one of those," Astar said. "I don't want to take the risk again."

Stella didn't think it was chance that they hadn't, but she didn't say so. The lake creature had deliberately shown itself to her and only her, thus it was up to her to determine why. "I don't have any reason to linger here," she told them, a bone-deep certainty informing the decision.

"I'm happy to leave this place," Lena agreed fervently.

"Back to Castle Elderhorst, then?" Gen posed the question with a bit of trepidation. No, she wouldn't want to confront vile Henk again. The others all thought Gen had moved past that. Only Stella knew how much Gen still smarted over the brief affair. Something more had happened than Gen had told them, given the way her pain lingered.

"I'd rather simply continue directly on to Erie and Castle Marcellum, so we can make the voyage to the Isles of Remus as Her Majesty directed." Astar tapped his fingers together as he thought. "It would be a more direct route than looping back down to Elderhorst, but we should retrieve our things. Jak will need his sailing charts." He gave Zeph an intimate smile. "Those of us who can't shapeshift into fancy outfits could benefit from a change of clothes."

"I would take exception to that remark," Jak said, "if it weren't particularly true for me. Jak might need his sailing charts soon, but he needs a new shirt sooner." He flicked a black look at Rhy, who returned the look blandly. "The good news there is, I sent to Castle Elderhorst for our stuff. Yesterday, while everyone was sleeping, chasing lake creatures, or otherwise occupied."

"Waiter *and* stevedore?" Gen teased.

"Exactly so." He lifted a shoulder and let it fall, a fatalistic Dasnarian gesture. "Figured I could make myself useful."

"But how did you send to Castle Elderhorst?" Gen asked.

He gave her a mock-sympathetic look. "Sweet Gen, you have to get used to our newly elevated circumstances. This place is oozing with servants wanting to do stuff for us. After the fifth time someone asked me if I needed anything, I thought of that."

"But what if we'd decided to go back to Elderhorst?" Gen persisted.

"Then we'd just take our stuff back with us. I figured whatever we decided from here, we'd be set." He looked to Astar. "Carriages and trunks should be here by evening."

"It was good thinking." Astar nodded at Jak. "Thank you."

Jak slipped his dagger into a hidden sheath, stood, and clapped his fist over his heart in the salute used by the high queen's personal guard. "I live to serve, Your Highness. Just don't forget that sinecure we discussed."

"Pays well, an unreasonable amount of power, no effort on your part." Astar ticked off the criteria on his fingers. "I have something perfect in mind." Though he didn't look at Stella, a tingle through their twin connection made her wonder...

"All right everyone, we leave in the morning," Astar declared. "Until then, you may do as you please. I suggest rest if that's what you need, or commencing with those hand-to-hand lessons."

"I know some hand-to-hand I could teach you," Zeph

purred to Astar. "We could—"

Gen clapped her hands over her ears. "I don't want to hear this!"

Zeph snickered, pleased to have annoyed Gen so easily. "In all truth, I was kicking myself that during our… adventure"— she slid a rueful smile to Lena—"I hadn't practiced taking off from the ground in gríobhth form more than I had. I think I'll find a quiet place away from prying eyes to do just that."

"I'll keep you company," Rhy offered, surprising everyone. "I need to practice shapeshifting too."

"That would be terrific, Rhy," Zeph replied with a dazzling smile. "I need to build up to being able to lift off from the ground with a person on my back. Maybe you could take various forms and gradually increase weight?"

"Sounds like a plan."

Zeph gave Astar a lavish kiss, fluttered her fingers at the rest of them—Lena studiously avoided Rhy's searching look— and they left.

"What do you say, Jak?" Astar said. "Shall we teach these lovely ladies some weapons work?"

"Indeed we shall," Jak replied, his grin sharp.

Gen groaned. "I hate you both."

~ 5 ~

I T HAD BEEN an especially keen torture, Jak reflected, to instruct Stella in the skill of using the twin Silversteel daggers. He'd somehow made it to the next morning without imploding, but the need she stirred in him showed no signs of abating. Having "volunteered" to drive the carriage—let's face it, he was the only one who knew how to handle regular horses and mossback conveyances—he perched on the coachman's seat, guiding the team of horses along the winding road that bordered Lake Sullivan. The views were spectacular, the silence welcome, and the crisp air bracing enough that it should've cooled his heated thoughts.

Turned out nothing in this world was cold enough to diminish his ardor. Worse, it only seemed to be increasing. The afternoon before should've been a distraction. He liked bladework, and normally it allowed him to focus on nothing but that.

Then Stella had shapeshifted into a set of fighting leathers. He couldn't get the image out of his head. Her delicate body in the form-fitting black that delineated every perfect curve, her hair coiled into a tight braid that set off her hauntingly lovely face, the way she'd set herself to the task with a solemn determination that only made him love her all the more…

Don't think about wanting her! The horses threw up their heads, protesting his death grip on the reins, and Lena poked her head out the carriage window. "Everything all right up there?"

"Thought I saw Stella's lake creature!" he called back. It was a plausible excuse, the lake serene and smooth to the left, falling away as the road climbed higher, a steep and rocky hillside to their right. "I got all excited, but it was just a log."

Lena studied the lake surface anyway. "Too bad. I'd like to see that thing for myself." She glanced up at him again, narrowing her eyes. "Sure you're not lonely up there? I could come up, help you keep lake-creature vigil."

He grinned at her. "You'll get cold, Princess of Nahanau."

Sticking her tongue out at him, she added a narrow glare. "I'm not *that* much of a weenie."

Pretending to think about it, he finally shook his head, looking sorrowful. "I'm sorry to have to say it, but you *are* that much of a weenie."

"Just for that, I should make it rain on you," she grumbled, then withdrew to rejoin Stella and Astar inside the carriage. Gen, Zeph, and Rhy were on the wing, scouting ahead. Like him, they were happy to be outside. The arrangement allowed the group to consolidate to a single carriage, and put them in a position of greater freedom, no longer reliant on drivers prone to abandoning them in the middle of nowhere. It was just a side benefit that driving gave him a respite from Stella's intoxicating presence.

He didn't know how much longer he'd be able to pretend

that he didn't want her with every fiber of his being. What would be best would be to figure out how to not want her at all. Stella didn't want him—he kept repeating that painful truth to himself, like poking at an unhealed wound—and he needed to get a grip on that bald fact. Unlike Rhy, Jak did understand the difference between Zeph's diligent pursuit of Astar and Rhy's apparent inability to understand why he needed to leave Lena well enough alone.

Unfortunately, knowing the right thing to do didn't change his feelings. Oh, he could make himself stand back, treat her like the sister she wanted to be to him—love her from afar as he'd *been* doing for the last seven bloody years—but that didn't kill the craving for her, the sheer longing she stirred in him, the endless need.

Oh yeah, on a viscerally wrenching level, Jak fully understood why Rhy couldn't let go of Lena.

And wasn't that a shameful realization? The difference was, Rhy had *had* Lena and threw it all away. Jak had never even come close. Stella forever treated him like a bratty little brother, while her gaze stayed on some future only she could see.

The easiest solution would be to stay away from Stella entirely. His sailor's soul could be at peace with that. It would even be romantic, in a tragic-Dasnarian-ballad way. The broken-hearted sailor, traveling the world, never forgetting his lost love.

The problem with that, however, was that living a tragic love story lasted your whole damn life, not just for the space of a beautifully rendered ballad, drunkenly sung with good friends, the tears shed all vicarious and quickly forgotten. Jak was a gregarious kind of guy, and he didn't want to live his whole fucking life pining after Stella. And it was all his own Danu-cursed fault. He couldn't even blame it on some inner bestial, mate-for-life deal.

His mother would tell him to find someone else, preferably any number of someone elses, and his father would likely agree. Neither of them would understand him fixating on one person. Well, maybe his father would, having fallen so hard for Jepp that he gave up a chance at being emperor for her. Maybe that was where Jak had gotten this self-destructive urge.

Whatever caused it, he'd never found anyone who compelled his interest like Stella did. Who made him want to wrap her up in safety and also kiss her so thoroughly that she'd lose that dreamy distance and *see* him. Danu knew, he'd tried to stay away from her. He'd been doing exactly that, all these years, when circumstances allowed. Now, not only did he have to be flung into her company daily, but he had to work with her in close physical proximity.

Like they had the day before.

In another stroke of truly terrible luck—just an extra dollop of torture for him, because Danu was clearly enjoying Herself in giving him what he'd asked for—most of teaching the use of the daggers had fallen to Jak. Though Astar helped with the lessons, he knew mainly sword work and, on top of that, he'd been training with a broadsword in the last year. None of the gals were going to be swinging a broadsword. Astar had been useful as a sparring partner, but it had been largely up to Jak to show Lena, Gen, and Stella how to use the smaller blades that fit their hands, strength, and lower center of gravity best.

Lena practiced with a fevered determination that made him worry for her. He kept picturing her on that rock outcropping, surrounded by flailing tentacles, fighting gamely on, though she had no reason to think anyone would be coming for her. She had the skills down and just needed to work them, so he got out of her way.

Gen had showed a surprising talent for using a dagger, picking up the movements quickly, wielding it with a shapeshifter's elastic muscle. Of course, that was Gen all over. She practiced everything she wanted to learn with diligence and keen mental focus.

That left Stella needing the most intensive tutoring. Not that Stella lacked the same abilities as Gen—though everyone knew Gen was the best shapeshifter among them, probably better than anyone alive except her own mother, Zynda—but Stella had a tendency to hold back. She was so afraid of causing harm that she ended up poking tentatively with the blade and withdrawing it with an immediate apology if she came anywhere near another person with it. Her trepidation also led her to hold the dagger like a bird with folded wings, as if she feared it might burst from her hand at any moment. He'd had no choice but to repeatedly fold his hand around her gloved one, reinforcing the grip, guiding her strike, her fragrant form tucked up against his groin, and...

Don't think about wanting her!

At least this time he managed to spare the poor horses as he reined himself in. They trotted along in good spirits—much better than his own—heads high and ears lively.

The sudden pinning of those ears was the only warning he got.

The horses reared, screaming as only huge animals that see themselves as mouse-sized prey can, thrashing in the traces as they scrambled to escape what landed in the narrow road ahead. Jak couldn't quite believe his eyes, though he didn't have much time to look, what with trying to keep the horses from dragging the entire carriage over the cliff's edge and into the lake. It had *looked* like the sky had opened in a narrow slit and rained scaly bright-green monkeys.

But that couldn't be right, could it? Swearing in Dasnarian, he sawed at the reins, sparing a second glance. Scaly bright-green monkeys bounding toward them, baring viciously sharp teeth they sank into the panicking horses. The carriage wheels lurched onto the rocky verge. The horse on that side tossed its head in panic, three monkey things clinging to its back as its hooves scrabbled in the scree.

Jak pulled hard on the horse on solid ground, trying to get her to pull them away from the edge. She put her head down and leapt forward, fortunately away from the cliff's edge, unfortunately straight toward the waterfall of monkeys. He braced his feet, pulling back hard to stop their careening flight, unable to even get a hand free to draw a throwing knife.

Astar climbed out the window of the jouncing carriage, hanging on to the side. "What in Moranu?" he shouted.

"Monkey-lizards," Lena yelled back, hanging out the other window.

Astar drew his sword, gauged the distance, and leapt to the ground, swinging the broadsword in great, lethal arcs. At least he had the sense not to take grizzly form, though little could frighten the horses more at this point. Jak had his full body weight braced and straining to slow the horses. The terrified steeds shied from the onslaught of monkey-lizards, careening toward the only open path—the cliff's edge. Lena and Stella would be dead if the carriage went over.

A black jaguar leapt from the carriage, bounding up the road and diving into the swarm of monkey-lizards. Stella in her First Form. Glorious, powerful, and out of her fucking mind. She laid about with lethal claws, but the monkey-lizards outnumbered her—and continued to rain from the rent in the sky. He needed to get to her. He didn't dare let loose of the reins.

"I'm going to cut the traces!" Lena shouted in his ear.

She crouched on the carriage seat next to him, a dagger in her hand. He hadn't seen her climb up to the top of the bucking carriage, but he shook his head wildly. "If you fall, you'll be crushed!" he yelled back.

But she was already hanging over the footboard, feet tucked under the lip as she stretched down, sawing at the leather traces. With a mighty jerk, the horses, still in tandem, burst away, the carriage skidding to such a grinding halt that Jak—who'd been braced backward with all his strength—flew forward over the footboard. Fortunately, his training kicked in, and he changed the fall into a flip midair, pulling his twin daggers and landing on his feet between the grounded shafts, Lena in a heap beside him.

A monkey-lizard flew at his head, and he spun in Danu's Dance, making a whirlwind of his twin blades, the vicious little monsters falling away from him as he made a shield around him and Lena.

He might tease Lena about being a weenie princess, but she was tough. Even tougher now after her trial in the alter-realm. She got to her feet, her own dagger in hand. "Go help Nilly! I'll get to the horses."

He didn't bother to argue—she was already running after the horses, who at least hadn't leapt over the cliff's edge, but were rearing and bucking to try to dislodge their monkey-lizard attackers. Jak followed her example and ran full tilt, dodging the creatures that bounced up at him, cleaving a path through them, aiming for where Astar and Stella fought together.

Still in jaguar form, Stella fought with tooth and claw, batting the hapless monkey-lizards in Astar's direction. His broadsword cut through the creatures like they were made of butter—creepy bright-green butter—but the massive blade wasn't meant to be wielded at speed. Several of the creatures clung to his thighs and back, gnawing with single-minded fury.

Jak threw a dagger, piercing a monkey-lizard through the neck and knocking it off Astar's back. Keeping one dagger, he drew his own sword. It was a lovely double-edged blade with a shining curve, a gift—if a grudging one—from his father, who finally acknowledged that Jak would never grow into the Dasnarian bulk that wielded those heavier swords well.

It was perfect for this kind of dance.

Sword in one hand, dagger in the other, he lit into this fight with glee. *This* was how you burned off unrequited yearning. Jak put his stupid heart to work, pumping blood to his singing muscles, a far better use for the aching thing. Working in tandem with Astar and Stella, he methodically cut apart the monkey-lizards, littering the narrow road with them. But they kept coming, pouring from the unseen rent in the air.

"Stella!" Astar roared, fighting his way to her. "We have to close the rift. Get to Lena. Do what you have to."

Did they even know how to do it? Apparently Stella planned to try, because she went leaping in Lena's direction, bounding over the piles of dead and still-twitching monkey-lizards. Jak was already turning to follow when Astar yelled at him to guard the girls as they worked. Where in Danu were the shapeshifter scouts?

Lena had the horses against a nook in the cliff, back around a bend in the road. She'd weighed down their dangling traces with rocks. Right now, the exhausted creatures weren't going anywhere, but that would change if they were sufficiently spooked. The rocks wouldn't hold them against any serious pulling.

Stella morphed from jaguar into running human in her fighting leathers. That meant he was able to catch up to her. "Where are your daggers?" he shouted, jogging beside her.

She cast him a startled look. "Go help Astar!"

Jak shook his head grimly. "His orders. I'm on you two while you close that rift."

"Then I don't need my daggers, do I?" she shot back, a mulish tilt to her mouth. "I have you."

He could wish she didn't sound so annoyed about it.

"Besides," she added as Lena jogged toward them, "I have to hold the Star." She showed him the glowing topaz orb in her palm.

"Hold it in one hand," he told her. "Dagger in the other. Look, Lena has hers."

"Lena can actually *use* her dagger," Stella snapped. "I'll stick to magic."

Lena looked back and forth between them. "What's the plan?"

"We're closing the rift," Stella replied, turning her back on him.

His fingers twitched to throttle her, but instinct had him spinning, slicing a monkey-lizard in half as it flew toward them. "Get busy," he advised, ignoring what sounded like a very feline snarl. It almost made him smile. He'd take her being pissed at him over that cool indifference.

BY THE TIME Rhy arrived to help—Gen and Zeph following right after—Stella and Lena had managed to slow, then halt the inrush of monkey-lizards. The shapeshifters helped with cleanup, which consisted of dispatching the remaining creatures and pitching them, or their remains, in the lake below.

"I really don't think adding exotic animals to the lake eco-system is a good idea," Lena commented, frowning at the black water.

"What ecosystem?" Rhy snorted. "I thought Nilly and Gen said there's nothing in it."

"We don't even know if they're composed of the same

materials as creatures from our world," Lena continued as if Rhy hadn't spoken. "They might not decompose properly."

Astar grimaced as Stella tended to his wounds. She'd healed Lena first, then went to her twin, as Astar wasn't able to heal himself via shapeshifting. Jak had assured Stella he was fine, and he needed to cobble the harness together or they'd be spending the night in the middle of the road. Though she'd given him the hairy eyeball, she hadn't argued. "I agree," Astar said, "but I also don't want to leave these things littering the road."

"Why don't you take dragon form and incinerate them for us?" Gen asked.

"A better question is," Rhy put it, "why didn't you take dragon form and blast these monkey-lizards to nothing?" He kicked one limp body into the lake.

"I, ah, tried," Astar admitted, looking pained. "I don't know how I did it the first time, but it doesn't seem to be a form I can just pull like my others."

Zeph stroked his hair in comfort, and Stella gave him a thoughtful look.

"So," Astar continued, "unless Lena and Nilly can figure out how to reopen the rift and send them back through…"

"First of all," Stella said absently as she worked, "the rift isn't closed, it's just too narrow for the monkey-lizards to fit through."

"It's also entirely possible they ran out of the poor things on the other side," Lena added.

"Poor things?" Rhy repeated, incredulous. "Those vicious beasties nearly killed you all."

"They were tools, Rhyian," Lena ground out with exaggerated patience. "Innocent creatures used as a weapon against us."

He opened his mouth—and Jak readied himself to step between them—but Rhy clamped his lips shut. "Good point," Rhy conceded.

Wonder of wonders. A small silence fell as they all processed that, and Stella flashed Jak a warning glance, as if she suspected him of being on the verge of making a smart remark. Hey, even he knew when to leave well enough alone.

"The harness is as good as it's going to get without replacement parts," he said instead. "It should hold us to get to the Cliffwalk Inn, the one the manse staff told us about. Or to get us back to the manse. One or the other. Staying near this rift is probably a bad idea."

"The manse would be warm," Lena observed wistfully, "but I hate to backtrack."

"This is one of the only roads we can take," Astar said, "unless we want to circle back to Castle Elderhorst, and that would add days to the journey. And complications." He smiled ruefully into Zeph's heated glare. Yeah, putting Zeph in the same castle—even one as big as Elderhorst—with Astar's erstwhile potential fiancée, Princess Berendina, was just asking for trouble.

"We've already come this far," Gen put in. "Let's keep going. I have no desire to revisit old friends at Elderhorst either."

Jak felt bad for Gen. That Henk had been a genuine ass, and Gen was simply too trusting, too earnest to see through that asshole's façade. "Better to have seen his true colors early on, sweet Gen," he told her, and she smiled gratefully. Why couldn't he have fallen for Gen? She wasn't enigmatic or moody. And she was an open book, much like himself. Generous, kind-hearted, familiar with mossback ways from so much time spent with her father's family. Of course, they were farmers, so about as different from his footloose family as one could get and still be approximately the same species. She was lovely, too, in an understated way, with her soft blue eyes and rich chestnut hair. And *she* felt like a sister to him.

Why did it have to be Stella who fascinated him so? With her hair pulled back still, the widow's peak showed clearly, her black hair forming a point on her pale forehead, marking her a queen, even without a kingdom. He wanted to kiss her there, then between those stormy eyes, on the tip of her sweet nose—and then plunder her full lips until she gasped his name. As if she sensed his gaze resting on her as he brooded, she glanced up just then, eyes thundercloud dark with magic from healing. Her solemn mouth twitched in wry acknowledgment. Danu take him—when would he learn to mind his thoughts?

"Jak is right," Astar said.

"My favorite phrase," Jak said, once again paying attention to the ongoing conversation. "What am I right about this time?"

"We shouldn't stay here any longer," Astar replied, unperturbed. "At any moment, whoever is on the other side of the rift might have restocked their monkey-lizards."

Jak regarded him with some amusement, picturing a stockpile of quiescent monkey-lizards ready to be fired through the rift. "Do you think that's what happened here?"

Lena glanced at Zeph, who nodded with uncharacteristic solemnity. "Probably," Lena said. "When Zeph and I saw the creatures in their natural habitat, they were territorial, but not aggressive otherwise."

"These were frightened," Stella said, dusting off her hands, finished with healing Astar. She became aware of them all looking at her. "What? I can feel their emotions, just like with people. They were out of their minds with unreasoning fear. I think they thought they were defending themselves from us."

"Interesting," Jak commented. He pulled a dagger and spun it through his fingers. He always thought better with a blade in hand. Sharper. Old habits died hard. "Do you think the alter-realm intelligence could have instilled those emotions in the monkey-lizards, prodding them to want to attack us?"

Stella returned his gaze thoughtfully. "It's an idea."

"Let's discuss on the road," Astar declared. "I want to get moving."

"Good idea," Lena agreed fervently.

"Jak still needs healing," Stella countered.

"I'm fine," he assured them all. "Just a—"

Stella cut him off, rounding on him with quiet fury. "Don't you dare say they're only flesh wounds, Jakral Konyngrr!" She lowered her voice. "You *promised*."

He blinked at her unexpected wrath and sheathed the dagger. "Not even my mother calls me that."

"I'm not your mother," she retorted, then blushed at his slow grin.

"Not even close," he purred, just to see her blush deepen.

"No doubt Jepp calls you more colorful names than that when she's pissed at you," Astar observed wryly. "Nilly can ride with Jak up top and heal him there."

"Not while he's driving," Stella said. "And several of his wounds are on his legs. I can't get to those with him upright."

"The horses are too tired to pull the carriage, anyway," Lena said. "I hate to suggest it, but it would be better if some of the shapeshifters don't mind playing draft horse and letting the real horses walk behind."

"Zeph and I can be draft horses," Gen volunteered, looping her arm around Zeph's waist and smiling sweetly.

Zeph shuddered, making a face. "Ugh. *Harnesses.*"

"You don't have to—" Astar began, but Zeph waved a hand in the air, a shining black and well-muscled horse standing where she'd been.

"Hmm." Gen became an even larger breed, prancing in place and flicking her tail. Zeph's black horse became a white one, a truly massive breed with hooves the size of Jak's head.

"Smaller," he advised them, laughing at their competitive spirit as he helped Lena unharness the natural horses. "Or you won't fit in the traces."

"That's settled, then," Astar said. "I'll sit up top, since the ladies don't need any direction, and hold the reins out of their way. Stella can heal Jak inside the carriage. Rhy, will you take scout duty? Stick close, though."

"Gladly." He became a raven and launched into the air, circling above.

Jak finished strapping the restive Zeph and patient Gen into the traces and showing Astar the components. Astar was a quick study, largely from chagrin that he'd always had servants to handle this sort of thing for him. Now that the excitement of the fight was wearing off, Jak was feeling the half dozen or so injuries he'd taken. Flesh wounds, for sure, but still painful.

Stella had healed the worst of the real horses' wounds while Lena rubbed them down, soothing them as she attached their leads to the back of the carriage. To Jak's surprise, when Lena finished, she climbed up to sit beside Astar.

"Come ride inside, Lena," Stella said, frowning in puzzlement. "You'll get cold."

Lena shook her head. "I want to keep my feelers out for more rifts." She pulled up the fur-lined hood of her cloak. "I'll be fine up here."

Jak narrowed his eyes at Lena in suspicion, but she only smiled cheerfully and gave him a little wave. "Get healed up, Jak. We need you. We'd be in pieces in the lake with the monkey-lizards without you."

Not believing her innocent act for a moment, he nevertheless swept her a bow, stifling a squeak as a wound he hadn't felt until that moment stabbed with unexpected pain. This was getting old. "At my lady's service," he managed to say more or less smoothly, then held the carriage door open for Stella.

She slid him a side-eyed glance, but stepped onto the stoop and ducked in—giving him a gut-wrenching view of her perfect, black-leather-clad, heart-shaped ass. He groaned for real, wondering what further torments Danu had planned to test his willpower.

"I knew you were hurt worse than you were admitting," Stella said as he settled into the seat across from her. The carriage lurched into motion, jerking a bit from side to side as Zeph and Gen tried to outpace one another. This might be a long and uncomfortable ride. "Take off your pants."

The suggestion from her enticing mouth did obscene things to him, and he covered his reaction by grinning at her. "You just wanted to get me alone in here to get into my pants?"

She gave him a steady look. "Believe me, darling Jak, with you covered in blood and gobbets of monkey-lizard, I'm not swooning with desire here."

"No, you never are," he muttered. Unsheathing a pair of daggers, he set them on the seat beside him so they'd be within easy reach, then unbuckled his sword belt, toed off his boots, and unlaced his pants. He paused in the process, glancing at her. "I'm not wearing anything underneath."

"Of course you aren't." She sighed with exasperation. "I'm a healer. You don't have anything I haven't seen before."

He waggled his eyebrows at her. "Oh, I think I might surprise you there."

She arched one eyebrow of her own, regarding him coolly. "Really? You're going with that gambit? I'm not some girl hanging out at the tavern looking for a nice tumble from a randy sailor."

"If only," he retorted, the words coming out more wistful than he liked. The salacious banter had been a bad idea, as his cock—which was well-endowed, thank you very much—had only gotten harder. Oh well, she'd asked for it. And by the feel of it, most of his injuries were on his legs—what he got for battling knee-high beasties. With resolve, he tugged his shirt down to cover himself, then pushed down his pants, gritting his teeth as several sluggishly bleeding bite marks opened again, the rents in his pants sticking to the drying blood. They'd been a fresh pair, too. At this rate, he'd be entirely out of clothes and have to run around naked.

Stella hissed a breath through her teeth—and sadly, he didn't think it was out of impressed admiration for his endowments. Released from the confines of his pants, his erection pressed against his loose shirt, struggling to get free like it needed to breathe or something, so he kept his grip on the hem, holding the fabric down—and feeling not unlike a shy virgin from a comical ballad, fighting to keep her skirts in place.

"I cannot believe you," Stella muttered. "How were you even standing?"

"I'm just that tough?" he ventured. She slid onto the jouncing floor of the carriage, kneeling at his feet. *Not* a helpful image for quelling his unruly cock. "Ah, Stella, my only love—what are you doing?"

"Getting a better look so I can see the wounds through this bloodbath," she replied tartly, shooting him a wry glance through her lashes. "It's not what it looks like, so don't be brewing up any prurient fantasies."

She traced her fingers over a wound on his thigh, the shock of healing energy combined with her touch and her unfortunately very sexy proximity to his groin just about making him come right then and there. "How would you even know what it looks like to me?" he asked, somewhat desperately. "You're a virgin still."

"Maybe I'm not," she countered, prodding another wound, then extracting a cloth and water flask to clean the edges of it. It hurt like a bitch, but focusing on the pain helped.

"You're not?" he asked with surprise—and whoa, a considerable amount of jealousy. "Who have you been with?" he demanded.

"None of your business, Jak," she replied coolly. "You've been at sea a lot."

True. Still, it was hard to swallow, thinking of her taking lovers and still walling him out. If she was going to be able to touch anyone, it should be him.

"Besides," she continued, sealing another wound while he fought not to squirm under her galvanizing caresses, "inexperience doesn't equal ignorance. Girls talk."

"Zeph," he said with relief. "I should've realized."

"And Lena," Stella replied with a secretive smile. "Gen wanted to know, so they gave us pointers." Was it his imagination that her gaze lingered on the outline of his thrusting erection? Yeah, he was kidding himself, because she was only bending her head over a particularly ragged place on his upper thigh where a monkey-lizard had apparently tried to make a meal of him.

"Were you all scantily clad for this conversation?" he asked. Not like he could get any *more* aroused than he already was. "Maybe lounging around on pillows wearing scraps of silk and lace, practicing your techniques on sausages—ouch!"

"Serves you right." She flashed him a rare, bright smile, pleased with herself, dazzling his senses. "I'm going to wash off the rest of this blood, make sure I didn't miss anything in the mess."

"Maybe I should do that," he suggested, then groaned and dropped his head back as she drew the wet cloth down his thigh. "You're tormenting me on purpose," he realized.

She made a sound that might be a muffled giggle. "That's what you get for picturing your friends naked."

"I was only picturing *you* naked." The words popped out of his mouth before he realized his stupid brain had formed them. Biting his tongue, he considered if he wouldn't be better off simply cutting it out. Danu knew it got him into trouble often enough.

~ 6 ~

S TELLA ABSORBED THAT startling declaration. It shouldn't be
such a shock. She'd known Jak liked to flirt with her, for
whatever reason, but she also knew perfectly well that she
dulled in comparison to Zeph's stunning beauty, Lena's lush
sensuality, and Gen's gentle loveliness. When you grew up as
the daughter of the most beautiful woman in the Thirteen
Kingdoms, possibly the whole world, you didn't harbor many
illusions about your own looks.

She'd learned early on to spare herself the futility of com-
paring herself to her mother. If anything, Stella had gone in the
other direction, steadfastly refusing Ami's earnest attempts to
teach her cosmetic tricks and how to style her hair in a more
flattering way. There were sayings about putting makeup on a
duck, and Stella had an uncomfortable image of herself
similarly bedecked. So she tried not to think about it at all.
She'd gotten pretty good at it. Just living day to day gave her
enough to deal with.

Mostly, she didn't think of herself as a sexual person.

But Jak had pictured her naked. And he imagined her learning Zeph's tricks for giving pleasure, lessons Gen and Lena had
absorbed with fascinated interest. As usual, Stella had sat a

little apart, glad to be with her friends, but not really fully in the conversation. She'd figured—as the rest of them had, too—that she'd never have opportunity to employ such techniques. Everyone knew that Stella was destined to life a life alone and apart.

Everyone but Jak, apparently.

And there he was, laid out before her like a feast, tension in those lean thighs, so deliciously corded with muscle. His skin was hot beneath her hands as she washed him, tempting her to touch him even more—something she normally knew better than to want. With his head thrown back, his throat was exposed, the skin smooth where he'd shaved that morning, his short beard outlining his jaw with silky dark hair. He was valiantly trying to cover his arousal with that thin white shirt—and she guessed that he was as well-endowed as rumor suggested. Everyone had heard Jepp's lustful boasting about Kral, how he was hung like a stallion and had the staying power of a man half his age. Whenever Jak visited Annfwn, or Nahanau, or Ordnung, he'd always set off titillated speculation about whether he took after his father.

Apparently he did. To her utter shock, a heated desire filled her, and she itched to touch him, to wrap her fingers around that impressive shaft. Impossible for her to do, and yet...

"Stella?" Jak had lifted his head, gazing down at her with his keen dark eyes, his voice hoarse in the swelling tension between them. "Is something wrong?"

"I'd better check the rest of you," she said throatily, though she'd been aiming for clinical. "Take off your shirt."

He lifted one eyebrow, glancing ruefully at his straining

erection, the gold hoop earring winking at his ear. "I think, under the circumstances, taking off my shirt is a really bad idea. Let me put my pants back on first."

"I think they're ruined." She cast a dubious eye at the bloody pile of ripped leather.

"Likely, but I'm not hopping out of the carriage bare-assed to dig out a new pair from the trunks strapped on the back."

"I can see blood seeping through your shirt. Just take it off so I can heal you, then you can put it back on again. I'll get Willy to grab some pants for you when we stop next."

He eyed her. "I'll wait," he decided. "I'm not going to bleed to death in the next few hours."

"Jak," she said, exasperated now. She waved a hand at his erection, hoping she wasn't blushing—and hoping the lie wasn't apparent to him. She'd caught an enticing glimpse of the mysterious dark hair between his thighs, the masculine flesh taut there. Whatever was possessing her, it was driving her to want more. "I don't care about... that."

Unexpectedly, he grinned. "You can't even say the *word*. I'm not showing my erect cock to a blushing virgin who has told me in no uncertain terms that she wants nothing to do with me." He paused, searching her face as he sat up a little. "Unless you've changed your mind?"

Her mouth had gone totally dry, and she became abruptly aware that she still knelt on the floor of the carriage. Zeph had been extremely detailed about various positions for pleasing a lover with mouth, lips, and tongue, and... Hastily, Stella scooted up onto the seat across from Jak.

He watched her with an amused smirk, a hint of bitterness

in it. "Thought that would do it," he murmured.

"Stop calling me a virgin," she snapped, stung and embarrassed. "I might not be."

"Yes, you are," he replied with confidence. Reaching to the floor, he deftly snagged his pants and draped them over his lap.

"Almost no one my age is sexually inexperienced," she pointed out. "It's not a reasonable expectation."

"I don't expect it. I just know you."

"You do not know me that well."

"I'd like to," he replied simply, but with an underlying intensity. "Aren't we friends, if nothing else?"

She shrugged, averting her gaze to the window, but the curtains were closed to keep out the chill, so she ended up staring at brocaded burgundy velvet like an idiot. Giving up, she made herself face him. "Of course we're friends. Only friends," she emphasized, but even she didn't believe herself.

Jak smiled slightly, not acknowledging that. "Sexual inexperience *is* a reasonable expectation in some cases. For example, as we both know, Astar was a virgin until just recently, until Zeph finally managed to knock some sense into him."

She sighed mentally for the truth of that. Her twin was obstinate in clinging to his ideals, forever trying to live up to the heroic image of their long-dead father. Though their stepfather, Ash, had always been good to her and she loved him like a father, sometimes Stella wondered if she would've turned out differently if Hugh had lived. Maybe she wouldn't be so... odd. "Astar is different," she said, knowing she meant it about herself, too.

"Astar is your twin."

"I'm aware of that."

He chuckled. "Don't get prickly, little star. It's just an observation. The pair of you are cut from the same cloth."

"My reasons for remaining a virgin have nothing to do with Astar's," she replied with heat, then stuttered to a stop, realizing what she'd admitted. Really, she didn't know why she'd tried to claim otherwise. Something about his snide comment that she was never swooning with desire. It had rankled, probably because it was true. *Poor Stella, such an odd and awkward duck.*

Jak didn't call her on the admission, though. He cocked his head, considering her. "Then what are your reasons?"

"I'm not discussing this."

"You're the one who accused me of not knowing you. How can I know you if you won't talk to me?"

"Not about this, Jak."

"Why not?" He gestured to his groin. "You've witnessed me in my extremity."

"I didn't see that much."

"But you looked," he teased.

Her face went hot. "It was in my face."

"Oh, no, my star," he purred. "You'd have known if it was."

"Fine. I am obviously a virgin—and always will be," she flung the words at him, pushed past reasonable discretion. "Because I. Can't. Touch. Anyone." She spaced out the words clearly for him.

He only cocked his head, giving her a polite smile.

"I might be innocent of experience, but even I understand that sex requires touching," she added.

He didn't move, listening with alert interest. Thoughtfully picking up one of the daggers lying on the seat beside him, he spun it between his fingers. "I know this about you, and I feel compelled to point out that I've always been careful about protecting you from being touched."

That was true. For all of Jak's carefree ways, he looked out for her, always careful not to touch her skin, guarding her in the press of crowds so the unwitting didn't distress her.

"But you were also touching me just now," he pointed out in a low voice.

"That's different."

"How?"

"That was healing."

His lips quirked with amusement. "How is healing-touching different than *other* touching?" He floated the word "other" with a mental image of very specific touching.

She nearly buried her face in her hands—would have, if it wouldn't give away just how much he affected her. "It just is. I can't explain it."

"Can't?" he asked softly. "Or won't?"

"You don't understand," she ground out, clenching her fists in frustration.

"No, Stella," he replied in the same tone, "I don't. That's why I'm asking the question. This is how people who can't read minds discover stuff about each other. I can't understand you unless you explain."

"I never asked you to understand me," she fired back.

"No. You've never asked me for a Danu-blessed thing, have you? Stop treating me like a child who can't possibly comprehend grown-up things. I'm a man now."

"I know you are!" She was more excruciatingly aware of that truth than ever in her life.

"Then throw me a bone here. What's the deal with you?"

She wished she knew. Feeling cold now that the heat of anger and embarrassment had fled, she drew up her knees and curled in the corner of the seat. Taking up her thick cloak that she'd left behind in the carriage when she shifted, she pulled it around her and extracted her fur-lined gloves from the interior pockets, drawing them over her chilled fingers. Jak wore his padded leather jacket over the thin shirt, but surely he couldn't be comfortable bare-legged like that. "Aren't you cold?"

He tipped his chin at his lap. "The cold helps. And don't try to dodge the question."

"I don't actually know what my 'deal' is," she told him steadily. "I've learned so much about sorcery from Aunt Andi—for which I'm so grateful—but she's not an empath like me. There *aren't* any empaths like me, anywhere, maybe ever."

He arched a brow. "Never, in all of history?"

She shrugged, irritated with it all. "Believe me, Dafne has looked."

"Well, if Dafne can't find the information, it's not out there to be found."

"True." She smiled back, enjoying the shared amusement, before she sobered again. "I'm better than I used to be, not always so impacted by it. Shielding helps."

"To wall people out."

He made it sound so punishing, like she already lived inside that stone tower, shunning human company. Though, she had to admit, there were certainly times—especially when she felt overwhelmed with people—that retreating to an isolated tower sounded like an exquisite relief.

"I have to wall people out, Jak," she said, realizing that she sounded like she was pleading with him. She didn't want to be this person, didn't relish the future she saw for herself. "You have no idea what it's like if I don't."

"Tell me," he urged, dark eyes quiet, his expression composed. He was restraining himself, holding back from impinging on her senses, she realized. It wasn't easy for him, such a naturally exuberant person, to hold back, but he was trying. For her.

"It's like… being invaded by noise. Like people shouting in my ears, but also my other senses. So I see things, too, intense and larger than life. I smell things, everything at once, so much that it chokes me. And touching someone…"

"Makes everything even more intense," he finished for her, and she nodded, feeling perilously close to tears.

"Yes. The touch itself is overwhelming, and then it's like it opens a door for all the other stuff to be even louder, brighter, more, more, more." She stopped herself, aware of the hysterical edge to her voice. There was a reason she didn't discuss this with anyone, not even Andi, though her aunt had a better idea than most. So did Astar, though he had more important things to think about than his strange twin. Their mother mainly worried to death about it, so Stella had gotten in the habit of concealing the worst ravages from all of them. She hated that everyone thought she was so fragile—almost as much as she hated *feeling* so fragile.

"I'm sorry this is so hard for you," Jak said softly, and the compassion in his gaze nearly broke her. She'd rather have him relentlessly teasing her.

Impatiently wiping at the tears that had fallen despite her best efforts, she shook her head. "It's not so hard, really. There are many people in the world who have much worse problems than I do—and without the gifts I'm blessed with."

He nodded, then cocked his head thoughtfully. "You touch Astar all the time—why is he different?"

She shrugged helplessly. "I'm not sure. Maybe because we shared a womb? Touching his hand is like holding my own."

"So, a matter of familiarity and trust, perhaps."

Sighing in exasperation, she shook her head. "I don't know. Nobody knows. I just... I have to accept there are certain realities about who I am." Firming her resolve, she met his gaze. "*You* have to accept that, too, Jak. No matter how much I want you, that's something that can never happen."

His smile lit his face, dimples winking like stars. "You *do* want me!"

"There were two parts to that sentence," she said, bitterly regretting that slip, "and you pounced on entirely the wrong half."

Undaunted, he continued to grin at her. "Not from where I'm sitting." He glanced ruefully at his lap. "Though, admittedly, that welcome news did not help with my current problem."

Her face heated at the reminder. "It's just the residual

effects of the healing."

He sobered, giving her a long and serious look. "It's you, my star. It's always you."

Shifting uncomfortably, she wondered if she should offer to help him. His discomfort was a palpable tension. Other people's pain always distressed her, and only the reality that she'd kill herself helping everyone kept her from trying. She cleared her throat. "You could, ah, take care of it. I'll look away, cover my ears."

He regarded her with smoldering intensity. "Would that make a difference? I mean, you sense everything even with your eyes closed and ears covered."

It was true. "I can make an effort to… not pay attention." For some reason, she couldn't look away from his intent dark gaze.

"What if I want you to watch?" he purred. "This is something we can do that isn't touching." He tossed the dagger aside and put his hand under the draping concealment of his shirt and the ruined pants, clearly grasping himself. Holding her gaze, he stroked upward, his face going tight with need.

The heat in her face poured down her throat, scalding over her breast. "Jak…"

"Am I embarrassing you?" he asked, never taking his gaze from her face. "Or is this arousing?"

Definitely arousing. And here she hadn't thought of herself as a sexual person. She was practically melting into the seat, her cloak suddenly much too warm. But she pulled it tighter around herself.

"Stella, my star." Jak stroked himself again. She couldn't look away, utterly riveted. "Do you want to see?"

Mutely, she nodded. A distant part of herself stood back, shocked and appalled—certain she was opening the door to a world of problems—but in the moment, she did want this. She wanted to see him, more than she'd ever wanted anything.

Moving slowly, Jak pushed aside the draping pants, leaving only the thin shirt barely concealing his upright cock, firmly gripped in one hand. The head of it pressed against the white fabric, dark with blood and need. He spread his legs, giving her a teasing glimpse of his scrotum, then toyed with the hem of his shirt with his other hand. His arousal filled the carriage like woodsmoke, thick and richly scented. Rapt, she watched as he slowly drew up the shirt, revealing bit by bit his thickly veined cock, the head of it a deep rose, glistening and enticing, his scrotum drawn up tight beneath.

It was surprisingly beautiful. And, yes, quite large. Disconcertingly so.

Her gaze flew up to find his still intent on her. He breathed a laugh, a half smile on his lips. "I have to know what you're thinking. It's only fair, since I'm an open book to you."

Licking her dry lips, she didn't really have any coherent thoughts. She wanted to be on her knees again, to take him in her mouth, to trace those veins with the tip of her tongue. She chewed on her lip to stop those reckless thoughts.

"Danu," Jak swore lightly, his voice rough. "The way you're looking at me. I'm not going to last."

"Don't last." She dropped her gaze. "Show me everything."

With a groan, he stroked upward, his hips following the movement, his shirt riding high in his grip, showing off those gorgeous abs. His movements grew faster, jerking harder, much harder than she imagined would be comfortable, his grip tight, expression fierce.

In another moment, it was over. Jak threw back his head, teeth clenched, throat working to swallow the growls of incoherent desire. His whole body convulsed, his hips lifting as his seed shot in a stream that he caught in his bunched-up shirt. While he was preoccupied, Stella squirmed, the liquid need slick between her own thighs. She wished he would touch her there.

If only.

Jak breathed a hoarse laugh, staring up at the ceiling of the carriage, still holding his softening cock and using his shirt to wipe up the mess. His body had gone languid, as tempting in the aftermath as in the peak of his need. "I'm going to have to just change clothes entirely," he observed. Then he sat up, finishing the cleanup, eyeing her as he did. "How are you doing over there?"

"Fine," she answered, after taking a moment to find her voice.

"Fine," he echoed musingly. "Have I frightened you off forever?"

"You are very large," she replied bluntly.

He paused, clearly taken aback, then laughed, shaking his head. "Only you could make that sound like a bad thing."

"It's not," she hastened to assure him. She hadn't meant to hurt his feelings. She was simply not processing what had happened very well yet. "It's beautiful. I mean, you are, all of you. I liked... all of it."

He tugged his shirt back down, far more relaxed now, considering her, a half smile on his lips. "Did you? Total honesty."

"Yes." She searched for more to say. "I felt your ecstasy with you. Like nothing I've ever experienced."

"Huh." He mulled that over, his smile tipping into a wicked slant. "I confess that's one of the hottest things I've ever done. Especially without touching anyone."

"I'm glad," she said softly. Now that the moment was over, reality was setting in—and she was finding it difficult to believe she'd just done this. "I do wish you happy, Jak. I want you to know that."

He frowned. "Why does that sound like a goodbye?"

"Because we can't be together," she replied with considerable exasperation. The man did not listen.

"We just were," he pointed out stubbornly. "We are. We can be, just like this."

"What, me watching you?"

"I'd be delighted to watch you." His smile had gone entirely wicked. "I'll watch you now. Slip your hand into those unfairly tight pants and touch yourself."

She nearly choked on the thought. "Jak!"

"Tell me, star," he murmured, "are you wet? I bet you are."

How did he know? Probably her face revealed everything.

"You don't have to show me anything," he coaxed. "Watching your face would be enough."

"I am not doing that," she informed him, not crisply, but at least with some backbone to it.

"Have you ever?" he asked, his voice a sensual sound that went straight to the part he was talking about.

"What?" she nearly stammered in her shock.

"Touched yourself. Made yourself come. Parted the slick

folds of your—"

She clapped her hands over her ears and squinched her eyes shut, feeling childish but also pushed past bearing. The worst part was, she couldn't stay that way. After a few minutes of pretending to have her head in the sand—and a few more of wildly considering shifting into a bird and flying out the carriage window—she finally peeked at him. Maybe he'd be asleep. Didn't men fall asleep after? If not from that, then the healing should have done it.

But no. He watched her, wicked mischief glinting in his eyes. "Still here."

She dropped her hands. "I'm not discussing these things with you."

He cocked his head, as if listening for something more than her words. "It's nothing to be ashamed of."

"I'm not." She sounded entirely too defensive.

"You watched me come all over myself," he pointed out, that wicked smile playing on his lips.

She pinned him with a furious glare. "You are enjoying teasing me."

He grinned, putting his hands behind his head and kicking his long legs out. She tried very hard not to look between them. "Yes," Jak said with satisfaction. "I am."

She groaned and raked back her hair, then remembered she had it braided back for fighting. It was matted and wet with unmentionable substances. Wonderful. Her mother would have a fit to see her. "Why?" she demanded.

Jak quit playing around, sitting up and leaning his forearms on his knees, that sexual intensity in his expression again. "I want to be with you, Stella. If I can't touch you, then I can at least talk to you."

"I don't understand." Though maybe she did. She rubbed her thighs together, and he noted her movement, steepling his index fingers against his lips.

"If I could touch you, my star, I would tease you past endurance," he said, his voice as caressing as if he'd touched her indeed. "I'd start seducing you with occasional touches. Nothing too intimate. All publicly polite. My hand on the small of your back. A brush of my fingers against yours as I handed you something. And you'd wonder if they were accidents, but they wouldn't be. I'd go slow, so I wouldn't frighten you. Just little caresses, until you began to look forward to the next one, began to yearn for the feel of my hand against yours. And when I kissed you for the first time..." His voice lured her in, painting pictures that seemed to hang in the air between them. Not pushing into her mind, but offered for her viewing, if she cared to look. In that image, Jak drew her into his arms, bending to brush her lips with his, sweet and tender. She found herself pressing her fingers to her lips, imagining they were his. Jak's intense eyes focused entirely on her.

"When I took you to bed," he continued, "I'd undress you as slowly as possible, kissing every fingertip of your beautiful skin. You think I'm teasing you now. This is nothing to how I'd torment you, caressing, touching, tasting until you couldn't hold still. Until you were begging me to let you come. But I wouldn't. Do you know why?"

"No." Her whisper barely had any sound, but he knew.

"Ask me."

"Why wouldn't you?" she asked, feeling like she was dying to know.

He smiled slightly. "Ask it with all the words."

Her face flamed, but she had to know. "Why wouldn't you let me come?"

"Even if you begged me."

"Even if I begged you."

"Because, my shining star," he said in a lower voice, "I'd make you wait, make us both wait, until I was inside you, fully immersed in you, touching you inside and out, so we could come together."

A ragged groan sounded in her ears, and she realized it came from her own throat.

"But you can come now," he crooned, a demon tempting her beyond rational thought. "Put your hand between your legs and climax for me. You know you want to. You need it. I can see it in your face."

She did need it, because she also couldn't do this. "I can't."

"You can. It won't take much."

"No." To prove it, she uncoiled her legs, sitting up and smoothing the leather over her thighs, even that caress tingling. Her sex felt swollen to bursting, and she crossed her ankles firmly, pressing her thighs together. "I'm not going to touch myself while you're watching, Jak."

His gaze caressed her, as if he could see through her clothing. "All right. Then when you make yourself come tonight, you can imagine me watching you. Better, imagine that it's my hands, my mouth on you."

"I am *not* going to do that." She couldn't look at him, feeling scalded inside and out.

"Stella." He waited for her to meet his gaze. When she did, he didn't smile, his eyes sharp as a hawk's. "Yes, you will."

~ 7 ~

S HE DIDN'T DO it. Though not because the thought wasn't plaguing her.

By the time they reached the Cliffwalk Inn, it was well into the evening, and despite the desolate landscape and icy weather, the place was nearly full. Fortunately there were two rooms available—the expensive ones, which they could afford and which fit their cover story of being wealthy young nobles on a travel lark—so the girls shared one and the boys the other.

"I'm sorry you and Astar have to be apart tonight," Stella told Zeph as they all settled in.

Zeph rolled her gorgeous eyes. "I can live without him for one night."

Making a snorting sound of disbelief, Gen remarked, "That remains to be seen."

"Ha-ha." Zeph shifted, briefly becoming a small cat, then came back in cozy lounge pants and a draping shirt. "It wouldn't have been fair to cram five of you into one room, even if I were thoughtless enough to make Lena endure Rhy's company for that long."

"I could handle it," Lena replied, a bit terse. "You all shouldn't have to walk on eggshells because of us."

"Being considerate of you doesn't mean we feel tense," Stella reassured her, following Zeph's example and shifting into sleeping clothes. She was frankly just as glad not to share a room with Jak, even with the others present. Though he would've been perfectly circumspect, she wouldn't have been able to shake the excruciating awareness of him. She simply had no practice at this. Now that Jak had opened that door between them, his presence was like being near a lighthouse, the bright light of his attention flashing with distracting regularity, coloring everything with his personality.

"Besides," Zeph said, "a girls' night lets us catch up." Her bright sapphire gaze lit on Stella with disconcerting intensity. "Stella can tell us about having sex with Jak."

Stella choked on the mulled wine she'd just sipped as Lena shot up straight from the trunk she'd been rummaging through. "What?" Lena demanded. "You had sex with Jak? When did this happen?"

Ambushed, and very much unused to being the center of attention, Stella found herself backing up and had to make herself stop. "I didn't," she protested, but it came out weak and far from convincing.

"She did," Gen told Lena. "In the carriage."

"The sweet, sweet scent of sex was all over both of you," Zeph confirmed cheerfully. She sat cross-legged on one of the two beds and patted the spot next to her. "Now tell us *all* about it."

"No," Stella replied. They all continued to look expectant. "We didn't have sex, and I'm not talking about it."

"Yes, you are," Zeph informed her.

"You're blushing," Lena pointed out with a delighted smile. "*Something* happened."

"And we want to know every little detail," Zeph said.

"Maybe not *every* detail," Gen countered. "But we definitely want to know what happened between you. Was it romantic?"

Was it? Probably not by any reasonable definition. It had been surprising, and hot, and so very sexy.

"The look on your face, Nilly," Lena murmured. "You *have* to tell us."

"At least tell us if the rumors are true," Zeph pleaded. "Is he as well-endowed as the stories suggest?"

"Don't you know?" Gen asked with surprise.

"Why would I?" Zeph seemed genuinely perplexed.

"I figured you and Jak had been lovers at some point," Gen replied.

"No way." Lena shook her head, finally extracting her own sleepwear from the trunk. "Not Jak."

"I haven't had sex with *everyone*," Zeph complained.

"Almost everyone," Gen corrected. "And I know you flirted with Jak."

"So did you," Zeph retorted, but without heat, her gaze lingering on Stella thoughtfully. "And maybe I suggested a romp to him a time or two, but he wasn't interested. We all know that Jak has only ever had eyes for Nilly."

"True," Gen agreed on a sigh. They all looked at Stella again. "So…" Gen drawled. "Are you still a virgin or not?"

Clearly, she wasn't escaping this room without telling them something. "I *am* still a virgin," she replied, sounding prim to her own ears. "And going to stay that way, as you are all perfectly aware that it's difficult for me to have physical contact with anyone."

"Difficult is not impossible," Lena said, meticulously folding the clothes she'd shed and wriggling into a set of bronze velvet pajamas that complimented her brown skin and gorgeous caramel hair. She settled onto the bed next to Gen, fluffing the pillows behind her. That left Stella facing her inquisitors—or taking the spot next to Zeph.

"Nevertheless," she said, "we did not touch. Aside from what I needed to do to heal him, we did not have any physical contact."

"That's not saying much." Zeph sipped her wine, eyes knowing over the goblet's rim. "There's a lot of sexy stuff you can do without touching. Aha! She's blushing harder. Was that it? Did Jak put on a little show for you?"

How does she know? Stella's blush had gotten so fierce it felt like her cheeks might burst. Clutching her own goblet, she put her head down and sat on the bed next to Zeph. At least that way she wouldn't have to face them. "Maybe," she admitted in a small voice.

Zeph clapped her hands, crowing with delight, an echo of her gríobhth First Form in it. "Go, Jak! Ha. I love it."

"Wait, what do you mean?" Gen asked. "What kind of show?"

"He jerked off for her," Zeph explained patiently.

Gen's soft indigo eyes grew round, and she leaned forward to stare at Stella. "Really?"

With a huff of impatience, Lena crawled around Gen and

sat on the edge of the bed, bare feet dangling. "I'm with Zeph now," she said. "I want to know *everything.*"

"That's all there is to know," Stella tried, to a chorus of protests.

"Is this something that guys do?" Gen demanded.

"Not for me." Lena sounded disgruntled about that.

"Some of them," Zeph said, stretching out toward the foot of the bed to lean on her elbow. She slid a grin at Stella. "The confident ones. Our Jak is comfortable in his skin. And I bet he was happy to show off for Nilly. Wasn't he?"

Still mortified, Stella simply nodded. Then drained her wine. At a nod from Zeph, Gen plucked up the carafe from the warmer on the table between the beds and refilled Stella's goblet. Stella didn't normally drink much, as the alcohol tended to make her shielding more permeable, but tonight she needed the release. Besides, she'd grown up with these three and was used to their psychic presences. That could be true about Jak, too, she supposed...

Zeph nudged Stella's hip with her toes. "How big?"

"I don't have any basis for comparison," Stella informed her.

Lena held up her palms about a hand's length apart. "This big?"

"Bigger," Stella admitted, and all three girls hooted with glee. "Shh. Someone will hear."

"Pfft," Zeph scoffed. "Only Rhy and Astar have the ears for it, and all three guys were planning to hit the tavern and do some drinking."

"All right, Nilly. Enough dancing around this." Lena pointed at her. "Put down that goblet and show us. Length and girth."

Knowing her friends would never give up—and that they'd forgotten their troubles in the merriment of the conversation, which they all needed—Stella complied. Putting down her wine, she held her hands apart.

"No!" Gen gasped. Lena fell onto her back as if struck dead, and Zeph whistled, then poked her toe into Stella's hip again.

"And the girth," she reminded her.

Lena popped back up again, mouth falling open as Stella approximated Jak's girth with rounded fingers.

"Moranu take me," Zeph murmured reverently. "I should've tried harder with Jak."

"You were too busy chasing Astar," Gen retorted, more out of habit than anything, as she sounded a bit in shock.

"And very pleased to have caught him," Zeph agreed happily. "Though Astar is more like—" She levered up to demonstrate with her hands, and Stella shut her eyes and clapped her hands over her ears.

"Lalalalalala," she sang. "I do not want to know about my brother's member!"

All three girls broke out giggling, so Stella figured it was safe to look again.

"His *member*." Zeph rolled her eyes. "Nilly, sweetheart, if you're going to be doing nasty sex games with Jak, we need to teach you the proper filthy terms."

"I am not going to be doing any such thing," Stella informed her.

"Was it a one-off?" Lena asked very seriously, then lost it

when Gen collapsed into more giggles.

Stella regarded the pair of them with an expression of disappointment. "I had no idea you two were so immature."

"We had no idea that you are such a sexual adventuress," Gen said, wheezing with laughter.

"It's always the quiet ones," Zeph said solemnly, then gave Stella a smile. "I'm proud of you. If you'd asked me, I'd have predicted you'd turn into a bird and flee the carriage."

"I nearly did." Stella put her hands to her cheeks. Still burning hot. She might blush for the rest of her life over this.

"But you didn't." Gen clapped her hands together. "Because you two are in love."

"No, we are not," Stella replied definitively. "This was... an exception."

"I'll say Jak is *exceptional*," Lena quipped, snorting.

Stella ignored her. "We all know that the magical healing can be... stimulating, particularly in that way. He was uncomfortable, and I suggested he... relieve himself. As his healer, I didn't want him to suffer."

Lena and Gen stared at her, incredulous, and Zeph nodded, her face a picture of innocent agreement. "You were only thinking of his comfort."

"Exactly."

"Which is why you watched," Zeph added, raising her brows.

"Closely enough to memorize his dimensions," Lena pointed out.

"It was memorable," Stella replied. Then buried her face in her hands and groaned. "Oh, Moranu! I have no idea why that happened. *Why* did I watch?"

"Hey, Nilly. Drink your wine." Gen pushed the goblet against her hands, and Stella took it and sipped, the rich flavor reminding her of Jak's heated desire filling the carriage space. "Of course you watched," Gen continued earnestly.

"How could you *not* look?" Lena asked wistfully. "That had to be so hot."

"You may be a scary sorceress and bearer of the Star of Annfwn and all that," Zeph said, "but you're also a woman. You've held yourself aloof from relationships all this time. It's good and normal for you to have some kinky fun."

"And Jak is an excellent choice," Gen said, getting up to refill the wine for everyone. "There's no finer man."

"Except for Astar," Zeph amended for her.

"Except for Astar," Gen agreed, lifting her goblet in a toast.

They were quiet a moment, all aware of which man's name remained unspoken. Lena blew out a sigh. "Rhyian is a good man, too," she said. "But you can trust Jak. He'd die before he hurt you."

"None of that matters," Stella replied, "because Jak and I will not be having a relationship."

The others exchanged knowing glances. "Does Jak know that?" Zeph asked meaningfully.

"I told him so." Stella lifted her chin. "Several times."

"Uh-huh." Lena tapped her finger on her chin thoughtfully. "For the record, did you tell him this before or after he, shall we say, demonstrated what you'd be missing?"

At some point, she'd stop blushing. This was what came of being a sensitive person. "I'm not answering that."

"Definitely before," Zeph decided.

"This will be interesting to watch," Lena agreed.

"We should start a betting pool," Gen declared, clapping her hands together.

"That won't work," Lena said. "We'd all be betting on Jak to succeed. Who'd bet against us?"

"I would—" Stella sputtered, but they all talked over her.

"We could bet on timing." Zeph gave Stella a mischievous smile. "I say Jak will have divested Stella of her virginity within a week."

"What?" Stella nearly choked on her wine again and set the goblet firmly aside. "That will *not* happen."

"Define virginity," Lena demanded, then snickered. "Because her eyes sure have lost their innocence."

"Penis in vagina," Gen said, almost primly. "That's the usual standard."

"What about between two women or two men?" Zeph argued. "You can't say they're virgins, but a penis goes nowhere near a vagina."

"Zeph has a point," Lena agreed. "Penetration, full stop."

"Even digital?" Gen frowned. "That falls more under foreplay than sealing the deal."

"Let's not attempt to define this for everyone." Zeph waved that away. "We're talking about a single case, Jak and Stella, so I say penis in vagina, standard intercourse between male and female, any position."

"This is never going to happen," Stella told them, but they ignored her.

"Done," Gen said. "But I think eight to ten days."

Lena was studying Stella intently. "Four days. Or fewer."

"Salena Nakoa KauPo!" Stella burst out. "I am not having intercourse with Jak *ever*, much less in four days."

"That's why I say a week," Zeph said. "But I'll take five to eight days, to keep the spread even."

"The guys might want in on this, too," Gen mused. "Maybe we should give them the option to bet before we set it in stone."

"You *cannot* tell the guys about this," Stella yelped. "Especially not Jak!" She groaned, putting her hands over her heart. "No, especially not my *brother*."

"I don't know," Zeph said doubtfully. "Jak loves to gamble."

"But he could skew the results," Lena countered. "Advance his seduction schedule to ensure his win."

"Jak would not be above that," Gen agreed.

"His seduction schedule?" Stella echoed on a squeak. "He does not have any kind of plan like that."

They all regarded her with sympathy. "Think about who Jak's parents are," Lena said. "Both Jepp and Kral are masters of strategy."

"And highly sexed individuals," Gen said, nodding.

"I'm afraid you don't stand a chance, Nilly," Zeph said with mock pity. "You're going down like a felled tree. You just don't know it yet."

"Four days." Lena nodded sagely. "No more."

"You are all forgetting that I can't touch anyone," Stella nearly screeched, beyond exasperated with all of them.

"I bet Jak is figuring out a way around that," Zeph said. "I can think of a few techniques offhand. He's a clever guy."

"And powerfully motivated," Gen added cheerfully.

"You're all wrong," Stella objected. "It's not going to happen."

"Willing to bet on that?" Zeph asked cagily.

"She can't be in the betting pool," Lena argued. "For the same reasons Jak can't. She'll try to skew the outcome."

"I have a right to bet on my own mind," Stella replied with dignity. "And, as this bet is a sure thing, then yes. I'll stand against all three of your bets that I will not lose my virginity to Jak in any way, shape, or form."

"No cock in pussy?" Zeph asked doubtfully, squealing when Stella threw a pillow at her.

"It sounds too big to fit in there anyway," Gen said. She looked to Zeph and Lena. "Doesn't it?"

Zeph shook her head, and Lena smiled with a hint of smug satisfaction. "It will fit," Zeph replied, "and it will feel fantastic, I promise." She patted Stella's velvet-covered knee. "It's all about the arousal. And I feel confident that Jak is the kind of lover who is patient, slow, and absolutely devoted to making sure his partner is more than ready."

This is nothing to how I'd torment you, caressing, touching, tasting until you couldn't hold still. Until you were begging me to let you come. Jak's words echoed in Stella's memory, and she didn't doubt Zeph was correct about that. "Again, it doesn't matter," she said firmly, "because it's never going to happen."

"Nilly, darling," Gen said softly, chewing on her lower lip, concern wafting off of her. "I hope you won't let wanting to win this bet get in the way. Zeph is right about that—you deserve to enjoy a flesh-and-blood love affair. If anyone would do right by you, it's Jak. He understands how you are."

"He's always looking after you," Lena agreed.

"And he has nimble fingers," Zeph pointed out with salaciously raised brows. "Good with his hands."

"Not to mention his other endowments," Gen said on yet another giggle.

Stella sighed. "Have your fun, but don't be disappointed when you lose this bet."

"Oh, don't be that way, Nilly." Gen pouted. "I want this for you. More than I want to win the bet."

"Think of it this way, Gen," Zeph said, eyeing Stella. "If you lose, at least you won't be only virgin among us."

"Oh. Hrm." Gen lost all sparkle, a cloud of regret condensing around her.

Stella swung her legs off the bed. "What happened?" she asked, abruptly worried. This must be what had been bothering Gen.

"Happened?" Zeph sat up, too, and Lena took Gen's hand.

"You slept with Henk," Lena said, watching Gen's face, trying to contain how appalled she felt. The strong emotion from her—and Zeph—however, became palpable to Stella.

Gen nodded, looking miserable, tears leaking down her face. "At Elderhorst, that last night."

"Oh, honey." Stella moved over to wedge in on Gen's other side. "Did he hurt you?"

"No." Gen released a wobbly breath. "It wasn't like that. I was willing and all."

"Why didn't you tell us?" Zeph asked gently, no teasing in her now.

Gen gave her a watery glare. "Tell you what? That I took your advice and kicked off the shackles of sexual innocence with the first guy who would have me and it was awful?"

Stella stroked Gen's chestnut hair, sending calming love into her. "I'm so sorry it was awful," she murmured.

"It just… wasn't what I thought it would be," Gen said in a small, wretched voice.

"And Zeph told you to do this?" Lena asked, casting a doubtful eye at Zeph.

"No," Zeph replied firmly. "I decidedly did not."

"It's not Zeph's fault," Gen said, giving her cousin a rueful smile. "She just advised me to stop evaluating everyone I met for true-love potential. I thought I could go about it like shapeshifting, trying out various forms to see what I like." She huffed out a harsh laugh. "Well, I guess I know what I *don't* like."

"Henk is an ass," Zeph said, grimacing.

"We thought so before," Lena agreed, "but now we know beyond a doubt."

"He was definitely not a considerate lover," Gen said. She leaned against Stella. "That's why I want you to be aware of how lucky you are. If Jak is your first, you'll be so much better off."

Stella absorbed that with considerable chagrin, feeling that she'd been terribly selfish. "I wish your first had been better."

"Me, too," Gen said with some force. Then she laughed a little. "At least it didn't last very long."

"Was it…" Lena asked on a grin, "…very long?"

Gen held up her pinky finger, and they all collapsed into laughter.

~ 8 ~

"DO YOU THINK they talk about us?" Rhy asked suddenly. When both Jak and Astar frowned, he added, "The girls. Do you think they discuss us, talk about what we're like in bed, who has the biggest dick?"

"That's easy," Astar said. "Jak does."

"It's true," Jak replied equitably, drinking the very excellent ale. "But I try not to brag."

Rhy snorted. "Since when?"

"Also true," Jak said, conceding the point.

"Besides," Rhy continued, "shapeshifters have an advantage that way. Selective shapeshifting can be a beautiful thing."

"Selective shapeshifting is beyond my skills," Astar said, not sounding at all bothered. "But Zephyr is happy with me as is." He smiled the smile of a man well sated, and Jak drowned the stab of envy with a draught of ale. The interlude with Stella that morning had been intensely erotic. So much so that the release had been sadly all too temporary. She'd also been avoiding him ever since.

"I come by mine naturally," he informed Rhy. "No cheating necessary."

"Shapeshifting isn't cheating," Rhy countered. "Mine is as natural as yours."

"Are we seriously swinging dicks here?" Jak asked.

"Yeah, why are you wondering, Rhy?" Astar signaled for another pitcher of ale.

"About Jak's dick?" Rhy deadpanned. "I'm not."

Jack grinned easily. "You, my friend, *are* the biggest dick."

Rhy gave him a narrow glare, the wolf glinting out of his eyes. "Care to go another round with me? You won't get the drop on me again."

"Nobody is fighting anyone," Astar said, his tone making it clear he was very serious. "We have enough problems without fighting among ourselves. Stella is taxed already keeping everyone healthy without us creating unnecessary work for her."

"That's the problem with having mossbacks along who can't heal themselves," Rhy replied with a shrug and a snide curl of his lip for Jak.

"Did I do something to offend you?" Jak asked. He'd like to pull a blade to toy with, but that sort of thing in a crowded tavern was asking for trouble.

"Stella is my cousin," Rhy replied.

Jak's fingers itched for that dagger—nothing like being a regular human guy keeping company with shapeshifters who could attack with tooth and claw in a blink—but he settled for setting down his ale and tapping his fingers on his thigh conveniently near an easily pulled blade.

Astar looked between them. "What's this about Stella?"

"They did the nasty in the carriage," Rhy said with a smirk.

Oh, fuck him.

Astar swung his head, a heaviness to him like the grizzly bear within. Slow to rouse to anger, terrifying when he made it there. What Jak got for keeping company with predators.

"They *what*?" Astar demanded.

"Sex," Rhy answered. "Didn't you smell them?"

"I try not to smell my sister," Astar growled, glaring at Jak.

"I did not have sex with your sister." Jak met Astar's gaze steadily. This moment had been inevitable. Jak loved Astar, as a friend and as his liege. Astar would be high king someday, and he'd be a good one. For all that Jak teased him about it, he fully intended to serve Astar's rule in whatever capacity he could. "But I *am* in love with her," he added. Funny to say it out loud for the first time. And to the entirely wrong people.

He didn't hold his breath because that was death for a bladesman. It only added tension. But he waited, fully aware that Stella would *not* be happy about this.

Astar stared back at him, struggling to assimilate this shift in his world view.

Rhy, clearly out to make trouble, made a scoffing sound. "Love," he sneered. "Is that what you call it?"

Jak leaned back so he could keep both men equally in his sights. "Yes."

"What happened with Nilly in the carriage?" Astar demanded.

"Are you asking as the crown prince, as my friend, or as Stella's brother?" Jak countered.

That gave Astar pause. "I'm all of those things."

"Yes and no." Jak gave in and pulled the dagger, spinning it through his fingers down by the side of his chair. It made him feel much better. Claws for everyone. "My prince has the right to demand an answer, if he feels the question is important to our mission or the good of the realm. My friend might ask because he loves me and wants me happy. Stella's brother, however, should recognize that his sister is a woman grown and what she chooses to do is none of his Danu-cursed business."

Rhy snickered, and color flooded Astar's face. Usually the most easygoing of men, Astar was no pushover. "My twin sister is my responsibility, Jakral Konyngrr. It has always been my job to protect her." He stabbed a blunt finger at Jak. "*You* will keep away from her."

"She's not fragile," Jak retorted. "She doesn't need your protection from me. And the only way I'll keep away from her is if she asks me to."

"She *is* fragile!" Astar snarled. "Sensitive. You don't know Nilly like I do, she—"

"I've known Stella my entire life." Jak deliberately slowed the spinning of his blade, willing himself to keep his temper. "And I feel I should point out that Stella would not appreciate you calling her fragile, nor would she be happy about you making decisions for her."

"Stella isn't here," Astar fired back.

Rhy smiled, very pleased with the trouble he'd caused. The payback for this would sting, Jak would make sure of it.

"No, Stella isn't here, is she?" Jak replied. "And she wouldn't be pleased that the three of us were discussing her *private* business." He slid his gaze to Rhy while still keeping

Astar in his peripheral vision. "That's what this is, isn't it, Rhy? You resent all of us for interfering with your pursuit of Lena, so you're going to sabotage this for Stella and me."

Rhy narrowed his gaze to lethal slits. "There is no you and Stella. There's just you taking advantage of her trusting nature. I'm with Astar. Stella does need protecting—from you, pirate."

"You're perilously close to insulting my honor," Jak said softly.

"Then let me make it loud and clear for your mossback ears," Rhy hissed. "You're not good enough for Stella. She'll be queen of Annfwn, and you're nothing but a mixed-breed Dasnarian, mossback bastard—" Rhy broke off, stunned by the dagger that pinned the loose sleeve of his shirt to the back of the wooden chair. Glancing down, he looked at the rent in the fabric, and the bright trickle of blood where the blade had grazed his arm.

"Payment for the insult to my mother," Jak told him, "you sanctimonious prick."

Rhy *moved*, his shapeshifter speed making him a blur as he lunged across the table. Jak threw himself back barely in time, somersaulting and rising to his feet in a crouch, a dagger in each hand.

"No." Astar's booming order startled them both. He pointed at Rhy. "Sit. Do not shift, on pain of my royal displeasure."

Rhy held up his hands, blue eyes glittering. The tavern had gone silent except for chairs scraping as people craned to see the excitement.

"You." Astar pointed at Jak. "Sheathe your blades. We are friends. We do not draw on each other. We do not fight each other."

Jak sheathed his blades and gave Astar the Hawks' salute. His mother, Jepp, had been in Ursula's elite guard from when Ursula was a young princess to after she ascended to being high queen. Though Jak hadn't served the high throne similarly, he expected he might someday. Jepp had prepared him for that honor, should it come his way. Holding his fist over his heart, he bowed deeply. "Apologies, Your Highness," he said with all the respect he could muster. "I hear and obey."

Astar stared at him a moment longer, then raked a big hand through his hair. "Just... sit down, Jak."

Jak did so with alacrity, ignoring Rhy's smoldering glare.

Astar finally sat, too, then righted their cups and filled them all with ale. Eyeing Jak, he drank. "And if I order you to stay away from Stella, will you hear and obey that, too?"

"You are an honorable man," Jak replied, instead of directly answering the question. "A noble and decent leader. It would be a rare exception for you to use the power you hold in such a dishonorable way."

"He didn't answer the question," Rhy remarked.

"Shut up, Rhy," Jak and Astar said together, but they didn't smile, their gazes locked.

"I could order you to do it," Astar finally said.

"Yes," Jak acknowledged. "And I would obey a royal command. I would also make sure Stella knew about it."

"You don't play fair," Astar grumbled.

"Would you?" Jak asked baldly. "You told me you wouldn't risk losing Zeph without giving her everything that's in you to give. Would you ask me to do less for Stella?"

Astar wrapped his hands around his mug and stared into the ale as if it held all the answers. If only it did, Jak would be the wisest man in all the realms. Rhy started to say something, and Astar flicked up his gaze briefly. "Not a word, cousin, if you know what's good for you."

Rhy subsided, sighing as if terribly bored and folding his hands behind his head, kicking out his long legs and pretending to watch the dancing that had resumed when their fight came to nothing.

"She means that much to you?" Astar asked, pinning Jak with a stern gaze.

"She does."

"You're in love with her."

"I am."

"Does she know that?"

"Not in so many words." Jak had to keep from squirming. He'd never quite imagined himself being grilled by a prospective bride's father, but this came close. Much sooner than he'd planned, thanks to fucking Rhyian. Still, sometimes *hlyti* had ideas of its own. The smart man seized the moment. "I've made my interest clear. We talked about it, in the carriage—and don't snicker, Rhy, as I will be unhappy with you disrespecting the woman I love—and I'm going slowly with her." Now he did look at Rhy. "I don't want to pressure her in any way."

"What is that supposed to mean?" Rhy snapped, breaking off when Astar's meaty fist pounded once on the table, rattling their mugs.

"Not. One. More. Word. Or I will order you confined to

the borders of Annfwn and you will very likely never see Lena again so long as you live. If you think Her Majesty won't back me on that, or that your own parents won't, you are gravely mistaken." Astar stared hard at Rhy, who finally slouched in his chair, miming sealing his mouth. *If only.*

"May I respond to that?" Jak asked Astar, tipping his head at Rhy. At Astar's nod, he answered calmly. "It means that telling Stella of my strong feelings might create a sense of responsibility on her part," he explained. "Especially for Stella, who feels everyone else's pain so keenly. If she decides to be with me, it will be on her terms, because that's what *she* wants, not because she feels the burden of making me happy."

Rhy glared mutely, then looked at Astar expectantly, finally raising his hand like a child in class.

"No," Astar replied. "Jak has reminded me that—though I regard you two as my closest friends—I am also the crown prince, whether I like it or not." His grimace made it look more like not at the moment, and Jak regretted his role in that. Still, his own happiness, and Stella's, were too important. Astar inclined his head at Jak. "You may court my sister."

A smart remark sprang to Jak's tongue, which he fortunately managed to squelch before it escaped.

"But I will speak to Stella about it," Astar continued, "and satisfy myself that she is receiving your suit willingly."

Hmm. Would he be able get to Stella first, explain his intentions? She might not take Astar's interrogation well. The simplest route for her would be to simply wash her hands of Jak. Stella was a tough nut to crack, and it required persistence to penetrate her walls and discover whatever idea had her believing she'd be alone all her life. And then to talk her out of it.

Astar watched him closely, as if following Jak's thoughts. He'd learned well under Ursula's relentless mentoring, and understood how to discern what people didn't say. "I want your word, Jak," Astar continued, confirming the insight, "that you will not attempt to speak to Stella about this before I do. You, too, Rhy. That should go without saying, as you don't have my permission to speak at all."

Rhy opened his eyes wide, lips pressed firmly shut, expression indignant.

"Yes, I mean it. Until I rescind the order. Maybe in the future you'll think twice before using your wit to cause trouble," Astar replied, as if Rhy had spoken. Then he looked back to Jak. "Your word, please."

"You have it, Your Highness," Jak answered, giving him the Hawks' salute again. So be it. Either Stella would cut him off at the knees or she wouldn't. He'd made his best case—and the second opportunity had been more than he'd hoped for even that morning, so he'd put himself in Danu's stern hands. In Moranu's, too, as Stella looked to the goddess of shadows. For that matter, he'd say a prayer to Glorianna, also. Astar and Stella were Queen Amelia's children, after all, Glorianna's avatar. Maybe the fierce goddess of love would stand up to her crueler sisters and sling Jak a much-needed favor.

"All right, then. I will talk to Stella in the morning." Astar shook his head, bearlike, then drank down his ale and re-poured. "Can we get back to being drinking companions? I'd like to shed the crown for a while."

"We can, Willy, my boy," Jak replied cheerfully, clinking his mug against his friend's.

Rhy pointed to his mouth, raising his eyebrows.

"Oh, fine," Astar sighed. "Since you asked politely. But one wrong word and I'm slapping you mute again."

"Thank you, cousin," Rhy replied with a half bow, almost managing to keep the snide tone out of his words. "May I make a request?"

"Is it going to piss me off?" Astar returned.

Rhy considered. "Possibly. But it's important to me."

Astar waved a hand in resignation.

"I don't want to lose Lena without giving her everything that's in *me* to give," Rhy said, giving emphasis their words that he echoed. "I'd like Your Highness's permission to court her, just as you've given Jak."

Astar considered his cousin with a weary expression. "Sure, Rhy. Why not?"

Rhy sat up, excitement sparking in his eyes.

"And I'll hold you to the same terms," Astar continued. "I will put the question to Lena."

"She'll say no." Rhy deflated again.

"Then there's your answer. Unless she changes her mind, you have to live with it."

"But she won't listen to me," Rhy protested.

Astar grinned, not at all nicely. "What was it Jak advised you? Maybe figuring *that* out is a good place to start, if you're smart enough."

Jak toasted to that, feeling grim. He couldn't enjoy Rhy's setback in this case, as he figured the odds very high that Stella would take the safe and easy route and tell Astar she'd rather be left alone. *Glorianna, Moranu, and Danu,* he sent mentally, deciding to up his own odds by applying to all three goddesses equally, all of them the various faces of woman. *Smile on my efforts, and I will...* What? It was beyond reckless to offer open promises to the deities. *I will give my blades and life to Your daughter, Stella, who You love so well, and upon whom You've showered Your gifts.* There. He could live with that. He'd do it anyway.

"So, boy." An older man, skin toughened from wind and weather, loomed over Jak. He jerked his chin at the blade still buried in the back of Rhy's chair. "Can you aim those gnat-stickers from any distance?"

Jak deftly snagged the dagger and spun it through his fingers, blood tingling at the prospect of a wager. "I can put a blade through your gnat's eye at twenty paces. Have a contest in mind?"

"Me and the boys have some throwing targets out back, if you've got coin to match your boasts."

He had a nice stash from the unwise pockets at Elderhorst. Sliding a glance at Astar, he cocked an eyebrow, implicitly asking permission.

Astar pulled out a sack of coin, pouring a few onto the table, Ursula's likeness stamped in the fresh and shining gold. "This enough to make it worth your while?" he asked.

Jak rubbed his hands together with glee. This would be fun.

~ 9 ~

"NILLY! PSST," ZEPH hissed, grabbing Stella's sleeve and pulling her into an alcove.

Stella, who'd been just about to descend the inn steps to breakfast, briefly teetered from surprise before she found her footing again. "Is something wrong?"

"Not exactly *wrong*," Zeph whispered cryptically, gaze sweeping the otherwise empty corridor. "But it is vital that I talk to you. Immediately."

Despite her urgency, happiness radiated off Zeph, so Stella believed her that nothing dire had happened. Zeph's sapphire eyes were bright, her glossy black hair in untidy waves—no doubt from Astar's hands. She hadn't been there when Stella awakened, Zeph's side of their shared bed decidedly cool.

"Did you sneak off for a morning interlude with my brother?" Stella demanded, trying to sound indignant but too amused to carry it off.

Zeph rolled her eyes at herself. "It turns out I *couldn't* live without him for one night after all. Don't tell anyone or you'll ruin my reputation as a scandalous flirt."

"That's really lovely," Stella said, meaning it with all her heart. "I'm truly so happy for you both."

"I know you are," Zeph replied, very serious now. "And I appreciate your blessing more than you could possibly know."

Stella did know, because Zeph's mind and heart were more open to her than most. Zeph's free-spirited nature meant she had nothing to hide. Though others didn't see past Zeph's lighthearted demeanor, her devotion to Astar and his happiness had never been in question for Stella.

"That's part of why I'm returning the favor," Zeph said, quickly checking the hallway once more. "Come with me." Zeph led Stella back down the hall and into an empty room.

Favor? "What is the mystery?" Stella asked, intrigued.

"All right, I didn't tell you this, but: Jak told Astar that he's in love with you, and Astar tentatively agreed to let Jak court you on the condition that you tell him that you welcome Jak's suit. Astar is going to talk to you about it sometime this morning, and Jak gave his word of honor not to talk to you about it first."

"He... they... they *what?*" Stella groped for some place to start.

Zeph nodded in sympathy. "It's a lot. Which part do you want me to repeat?"

"Let's start with the part where you're not supposed to tell me this. I assume Astar confided in you and you promised not to say anything."

"I did *not* promise," Zeph corrected, holding up a finger. "He just told me not to tell anyone and proceeded to tell me the story and asked for my opinion."

"Zeph..."

"You're my friend, too," Zeph retorted. "My opinion is

that you should know they were discussing you. And at the risk of being accused of trying to bias the betting pool, I wanted you to be forewarned, so you'll know to tell Astar *yes*, you do want Jak to have the opportunity to court you."

Stella opened her mouth, and Zeph wagged her finger in Stella's face. "I know you, Nilly. Your first instinct will be to tell Astar no. That way you can weasel out of dealing with Jak, and you'll have your bearish twin to enforce the edict."

Slowly closing her mouth, Stella had to admit that option had appeal. Her friends meant well, but she and Jak could never have a relationship. It would be better for them both if Jak faced that reality now. She shouldn't have encouraged him in the carriage, shouldn't have succumbed to the temptation of... The memory gave her heated shivers, and she firmly banished it. "It would be easier that way," she told Zeph gravely.

Zeph fisted her hands on her hips. "I *knew* it! Easier isn't necessarily better, Nilly. I know dealing with our emotions is a trial to you, but unless you plan to hide away and be a hermit in some secluded tower, then—" She broke off with an incredulous lift of her brows. "You *are* considering that?"

"I've seen my own future," Stella replied simply. "Besides which, it's a logical solution for me."

Zeph waved that off. "We both know the future is fluid, subject to change according to our will, our choices. Maybe this is a crossroads for you. This could be your opportunity to open up the possibility for a different future."

That had never occurred to Stella. She'd lived so long with the image of that tower in the field of lilies, her life path ending there, that it seemed impossible anything else could be real. "But I've seen—"

"You've seen the future that results from your current decisions," Zeph interrupted, gríobhth sharpness in her eyes. With a deep breath, she softened. "Stella, back at Elderhorst, you said some things to me. When I'd been so convinced that I should let Astar go because I would make a terrible high queen, you said otherwise, remember?"

"I remember." Maybe she was reacting to Zeph's intense emotions, but her eyes filled with tears. Zeph had been so determined to be noble and unselfish that she couldn't see the truth.

"You opened my eyes to the possibility of a different life for myself, so I owe it to you to do the same. Don't seal yourself off in a tower. Let's find ways for you to live among the people who love you. That includes Jak."

Stella wiped away the tears. "Jak isn't really in love with me. It's lust, a passing fancy born out of youthful obsession."

"Sounds like me until not long ago," Zeph observed wryly, then she sobered. "If that's all it is, what's the harm? That's what courtship is: testing the waters."

"This sounds very like the advice that got Gen in bed with odious Henk," Stella felt compelled to point out.

To her credit, Zeph winced. "A fair point, and I know I need to make amends for that. It kills me that she picked *that* guy. In my defense, when I suggested she play the field instead of looking for true love, I didn't imagine she'd go to bed with the first asshole to smile at her."

"Gen can be impulsive in unpredictable ways," Stella conceded. "And I don't think you bear any responsibility for it. She made the choice."

"Even though I goaded her into it?" Remorse oozed off of her.

"Like you're goading me now?" Stella asked with arched brows.

Zeph looked aghast, then chagrined. "You're right. I've learned nothing."

"You just want your friends to be happy," Stella replied kindly. "I can see your heart, Zeph, and there's no malice in it. We are just not all quite as... fierce as you are."

"I don't necessarily feel fierce," Zeph muttered, dark emotions passing through her as swiftly as the chilling shadows cast by clouds on an otherwise warm spring day. Lena wasn't the only one suffering the trauma of their harrowing adventure. It helped that Zeph enjoyed the bloom of falling in love with Astar, but her sunny nature could be deceptive.

"Anytime you want to talk about it, about anything," Stella said as gently as she could, "I'm here for you."

"I know." Zeph smiled at her a bit mistily. "You're always here for all of us. Perhaps to your detriment, as you spread yourself very thin sometimes. You deserve to have something for you. Which is why I want you to be open to what Jak is offering."

Stella had to laugh. "You, my friend, are relentless!"

Zeph smiled, an afterimage of her gríobhth beak, shining and lethally curved, in it. "It is in my nature, I suppose."

"Very much so. Which is one of the many reasons you'll make an excellent high queen. Tenacity and ferocity will serve you well. Shall we go down to breakfast?" Stella turned to go, making Zeph catch up with her.

"What are you going to tell Astar?" Zeph hissed.

"I wonder if they have those flaky pastries like we had at the lake manse?" Stella asked. "Those were delicious."

"Come on, Nilly. Just tell me."

"It was lovely that Groningen's manse had Annfwn coffee, but I don't suppose we can hope for it here."

Zeph growled low in her throat. "You know the curiosity will drive me crazy."

"A just punishment, then." Stella smiled serenely at Zeph. "I'll have to consider whether to reveal to Astar that you talked to me about this."

Zeph's gorgeous sapphire eyes flew wide in horror. "You wouldn't!"

No, she wouldn't—she had no intention of interfering in Astar's love life, any more than she already had, that was—but it also wouldn't hurt for Zeph to worry about it a little bit. "What do you suppose his reaction would be?" she mused as they reached the bottom of the steps.

With a groan, Zeph pressed her fingers to her temples. "Moranu, I hate it when he's mad at me."

"Something to bear in mind for the future, hmm?"

Zeph lifted her head and glared. "You're trying to teach me a lesson. You bitch. You're supposed to be the nice one."

Stella couldn't help smiling. "I have my claws, too."

"Yes, you do," Zeph agreed ruefully. "Please don't tell him. I'll owe you a favor."

Unable to torture her friend any longer, Stella gave her a

fond look. "You already did me one."

THEY WERE THE last to reach the breakfast table, where the other five already sat, platters of food in the middle of the round table, their plates heaping. Astar narrowed his eyes at Zeph in suspicion as she slid into the chair beside him that he'd saved for her. "I was about to come looking for you two."

"I asked Zeph to help me," Stella replied calmly, taking the chair on his other side, though she skidded to a mental halt. What in the world would she ask Zeph to help her with?

"And I did," Zeph jumped gleefully into the breach. "I put her hair up, and it looked beautiful, but she took it down again."

Jak cocked his head, dark eyes sparkling as they would on any other morning, his emotions calm and unruffled. If he was anxious about Astar getting the verdict from her, he didn't give the least sign. Something to remember about him, how well he dissembled. "What are you talking about, naughty Zeph? Stella looks absolutely beautiful this morning. But then, she looks beautiful all the time."

Astar slid him a dark look, which slid right off Jak's jaunty mood. Was it a cover? Tempted to probe deeper, she decided that would be too unfair.

"You're awfully happy this morning," Gen noted, studying Jak. "I expected you to at least be hungover."

"Are you kidding?" Rhy grumbled. "That mossback can drink all of us shapeshifters under the table."

"It's a gift," Jak acknowledged. "To answer your point, sweet Gen, I won a tidy sum last night in a spontaneous knife-throwing competition. Additional coin always puts a man in a good mood."

"If the man is a pirate," Rhy added.

"Fairly won," Jak countered, "as you witnessed. I seem to recall some of my new coin came from your pocket."

"You bet *against* Jak?" Zeph demanded.

"Isn't that against the man code?" Gen asked, also surprised.

"We *both* bet against him," Astar put in, shaking his head. "It should've been a sure thing. He wagered he could hit a bull's-eye the size of a fingertip if he was blindfolded, knives sheathed, from a handstand, with his back to the target."

"You did that?" Lena asked, clearly impressed—and earning a sour look from Rhy.

Jak lifted a shoulder and let it fall. "It sounds harder than it is. A simple flip, pull my blades as I drop, remember where the target is."

"Did we mention he had to drink five shots of whiskey first?" Astar demanded.

"Ah." Jak waggled his fork at Astar. "That's where they made a mistake. The whiskey didn't have time to kick in. You all should've made me wait a bit."

"Noted for next time," Rhy said.

"Or you could bet that he'd succeed," Stella suggested. Because Jak was giving her empty plate a warning look, she took a roll and carefully spread blackberry jam on it. "I've become interested in wagers myself lately," she added, ignoring Gen's stifled giggle and Zeph's outright laugh.

"You?" Astar asked, bumping his arm against hers. "Since when are you interested in such worldly games?"

Was she really so dreamy and off in her own thoughts all the time? They all seemed to think so. At any rate, Astar didn't wait for an answer, listening while Gen gave her thoughts on an amended scout schedule that would keep them in closer contact with the carriage group, to avoid a repetition of yesterday's lapse in reinforcements arriving. Jak, across the table from her, lifted his brows in question, and she shrugged, making it elaborate in the Tala style. He laughed silently and toasted her with his mug.

"Can I have a word with you?" Astar asked subvocally, startling her.

"Of course," she replied the same way. *"You don't have to ask. I'm always here for you."* As she said it, she remembered Zeph saying how she was always there for all of them, perhaps to her detriment. Her gaze went to Jak, arguing cheerfully with Rhy about daggers versus claws. He winked at her without missing a beat.

"This is different," Astar replied, a growl in his mental voice as he caught Jak's wink and glared at him.

Stella nearly rolled her eyes. Really, even without Zeph's warning, she'd have guessed Astar's sudden desire for a private conversation had to do with Jak. *"So, talk,"* she prompted, just to yank his tail a little bit. She knew he wouldn't want to talk here, even if no one else could hear them.

"After breakfast. We can take a walk on the cliff path."

"Sounds bracing." She eyed the thick snowfall swirling out-

side the inn, much of it going sideways.

"*Good views, they say,*" Astar agreed, missing her sarcasm entirely.

Oh, he was wound up all right.

"THIS IS NOT a comfortable conversation for a brother to have with his sister," Astar began. Stella nodded seriously, though it took a heroic effort not to laugh. The more awkward Astar felt, the more pompous he got. Another reason Zeph was good for him—she had a knack for puncturing that and getting him to focus on the moment instead of constantly trying to live up to the expectations of their long-dead, noble father. "I expected our mother to talk to you about this kind of thing, honestly," Astar added, sounding almost paternal.

Dear Moranu, he wasn't thinking he needed to explain sex to her, was he? "Mother already explained about hairstyles," she assured him earnestly, not above keeping her teeth in his tail a bit longer. "I just find them binding."

Astar cleared his throat uncomfortably, turning his face into the biting wind. The views were spectacular, indeed. They'd climbed in altitude considerably on the journey the day before, rounding the eastern edge of Lake Sullivan. The Cliffwalk Inn was a popular destination for sightseers—though typically in warmer weather—and the full expanse of the lake stretched out below. Like a black jewel set in platinum, the deep water shone glassy and mysterious amid the snow-covered landscape.

"There's no easy way to say this," Astar said, his voice strained. "I don't want to upset you, but you are a grown woman and should make your own choices. So, even though I know what your answer will be, I have to ask. Jak has requested permission to court you. Shall I tell him to leave you alone?"

Stella did her best to reveal no reaction. She might've chided Zeph for breaking a confidence, but she was truly grateful for the forewarning. As it was, her amused irritation with her twin's foibles was ripening into annoyance, if not anger. "Why did Jak ask for *your* permission?"

He glanced at her in surprise, his cheeks ruddy from the sharp wind, blue eyes troubled. "Because, as I explained, Mother isn't here and—"

Stella shook her head sharply. "Jak doesn't need anyone's permission. Not from our mother, and certainly not from my brother. I'm capable of saying no on my own."

"I know you are." Astar regarded her more intently, as if seeing someone he didn't quite recognize. "I'm just trying to protect you from—"

"I don't need a keeper, Willy."

"I never said you do," he protested.

"No, but you're treating me that way. Like someone too *fragile* to leave unprotected." Feeling the surge of unaccustomed defiance, she threw back the hood of her cloak, letting the chill wind seize the banner of her hair and whip it with snow. Using her sorcery, she warmed the air around her skin. She so rarely used her magic for herself. Mostly she used it only when someone else asked her to, and why was that?

"I don't think you're fragile," Astar said through gritted teeth. "I know Mother has treated you that way—and I know how much it bothers you—and I've always stood up for you."

That was true, but in her current fractious mood, she wasn't ready to soothe his ruffled feelings yet. She'd never felt the influence of her First Form in the way other shapeshifters did. At least, the jaguar didn't seem to infuse her personality and outlook as much as, for example, the grizzly bear influenced Astar or the gríobhth did Zeph. She'd always put that down to being a sorceress and empath, first and foremost. Today, however, the big cat prowled through her heart, hungry for more than she'd given it. Fierce, even.

"It's just that I know something happened between you and Jak in the carriage yesterday," Astar finally said when she still hadn't replied to him.

"*Something?*" she echoed, raising a cool brow.

"Something sexual," he ground out.

"How could you possibly know that?" she persisted.

"Rhyian told me he smelled it on you two."

"Ah." She nodded sagely. "How surprising that Rhy might want to make trouble for Jak in that arena. Sounds like you played right into his hands."

"That's not important right now," Astar said after a slight pause, and she could tell she'd given him cause to consider. "What matters is you admit that something *did* happen."

"I don't have to admit or deny anything. It's my personal business."

"You are my sister," Astar growled, the bear close to the surface. "If Jak foisted himself on you, then—"

145

She raised a hand, stopping him. "Jak is your friend," she said softly. "He's arguably your closest companion who isn't family. Are you really wanting to accuse someone who's been a loyal friend all our lives of something terrible like that?"

"I don't know what to think," he bit out.

"Then don't, because this doesn't have anything to do with you."

Astar flushed, face even redder against the golden hair lashing his cheeks. "I don't understand why you're being so difficult."

"Because *you* are being invasive about my private life. Did I interrogate you about Zeph's seduction attempts?"

"That's different."

"How?" She asked it sharply, cold as the winter winds.

"Because I knew how to handle Zephyr," he shot back.

She laughed in his face. "Oh, sweet Willy. That is so not true."

He started to retort, then grimaced instead and raked his hand through his snarling hair. "Yeah. I'll concede that point. The real difference is that... it's just that I know you're not interested in... sex, and stuff like that."

"Why do you think that?" She was rather enjoying herself, though she did feel compassion for Astar in his earnest discomfort. Not enough not to let him twist in the wind a bit longer, though.

Astar was gaping at her. "Because..." He waved a hand in the air. "You're above all that."

"Sex? Romance? Human interaction?" Abruptly, she was furious with him. "Tell me, brother of mine, what do you envision for my life, now that you'll be marrying Zeph? She'll be your wife, your hostess, eventually your queen. Where does that leave me?"

He looked like she'd hit him over the head with a bucket of ice water. "I... I hadn't thought that far."

"No, I know you hadn't." Just as suddenly as it had erupted, her anger faded, and she was sorry to have said anything. She'd promised herself she wouldn't, having some tragically romantic idea of gracefully erasing herself from their lives. "And you shouldn't have to. It's not your responsibility to plan my life."

"You can live with us at Ordnung," he said, taking her hands. "You always have a place there."

"I hate Ordnung," she said gently. "I only ever stayed there for you. And now you won't need me anymore."

"I'll always need you, Nilly."

He sounded so upset that she patted his cheek. "But not in the same way, and that's as it should be. We're not kids any longer. It's natural for us to grow up and go our separate ways."

"So you're going to hand yourself over to *Jak*?" He sounded bewildered enough that she leashed her temper. Who knew she'd had one that needed leashing?

"Why do you say it that way?" she snapped, stepping away from him and feeling her claws pricking in defense of their friend.

"Because Jak is..." Astar didn't finish that sentence, which was probably wise. "He's Jak."

She laughed, rolling her eyes, a burst of affection in her

heart for the rogue. "Yes. He certainly is. The point is, however, that you're not being asked to sign over my ownership papers like I'm some sort of Dasnarian bride. I don't know if Jak and I have much in common when it comes down to it, but I'd... I would like to see what happens." The sense of freedom, of fierce adventure, was as exhilarating as the snowflakes whipping her cheeks. "You may tell Jak that his courtship is welcome."

"So gracious of you," Astar muttered, then slid her a wry grin. "And if that was payback for the permission thing, it was well played."

"You were the one to put yourself in the middle of this, Your Highness," she replied sweetly. "It's only fair that you have to tell Jak how wrong you were."

"He'll never let me forget it." Astar rubbed his ruddy cheeks, contemplating that with resignation.

"It's good for a ruler to have companions who know his human side, and who can call him on his mistakes. That's what keeps you from becoming a tyrant." She relented and sent some warmth his way, too, sliding her arm in the crook of his elbow and turning them back to reverse their path on the cliff walk, back toward the inn. "You *are* only human, Willy. That's all right, too."

"I'm sorry, Nilly," he said, patting her hand on his arm, "that I've been so selfish. I've been so caught up in Zephyr that I didn't give any thought to how you must feel."

She sighed mentally, annoyed with herself for putting a taint on his perfect happiness, something he'd waited so long to have. "I didn't want you to be thinking about me, to be worrying about me. This bloom of first love—you only get it once. I *want* you to savor that. You and Zeph both. Moranu knows the circumstances are difficult enough as it is."

He was quiet a moment. "Do you think you... with Jak?"

"I don't know," she answered honestly. "I gave you a hard time back there, but it honestly never occurred to me that I might want something like this."

Astar made a hmming sound, and she caught the words he nearly spoke, but he swallowed the thought nearly as loud as if he had spoken—that Jak had said he was in love with her. Good on her brother for deciding not to reveal that, even if the much-less-tactful Zeph already had.

"I think it would be all right just to enjoy some flirtation," she continued. "Test the waters, as it were," she added, amused to be quoting Zeph. To try to be someone who wasn't always on the fringes, cringing from strong emotions, always on the defensive. The thought niggled at her. Before she could draw it out, though, a ripple on the water far below caught her eye. The lake creature's head rose from the water, stately, terrible, and as glossy black as the water itself.

Clutching Astar's arm, she gasped. "Look!"

He tensed, hand going to his broadsword. "What? What is it?"

She pointed. "The lake creature! Do you see it?"

He squinted along the line of her arm. "No?"

Jumping up and down in her excitement, she jabbed her finger at the spot. The creature's head had to be several man-heights above the water, loops of its body bumping out of the still surface for easily ten times that in length. "Right there. It's the only thing out there."

Astar shook his head slowly. "I only see the water. Not even a ripple."

Stella could swear the lake creature was looking straight at her, that it inclined its chin in a grave salutation before it sank below the surface of the water again. Gone as suddenly as it had appeared. "How can it be that I'm the only one who can see it?"

"Didn't Jak say something about that back at Elderhorst, how only the pure of heart can see it?" Astar had a teasing smile on his face, and he hugged her arm to him. "That's you."

"I'm hardly pure of heart—if there even is such a state of being."

"Maybe it's a metaphor," Astar mused. "That magical lingo is usually vague that way."

"Well, if it's a metaphor for sexual innocence, then I might have a good before-and-after test soon," she commented. Just a last nip on her brother's busybody tail.

He winced. "Please don't put that image in my head. I'll try to stay out of it, but…"

"My growly, protective brother." She squeezed his arm. "I can respect that boundary."

"Besides," he said after a moment, "Gen didn't see the lake creature when she was right there with you, and she's complained about her virginity enough that I know about it. So it can't be that."

Stella nodded, keeping Gen's changed circumstances to herself. Knowing Astar, he'd probably want to go back and call Henk out for being a cad. Moranu knew, *she* wanted to. "Oh well," she said instead. "We'll be leaving the lake behind today anyway." Part of her felt sad about that, and she sent a mental farewell to her lake creature.

"On to Castle Marcellum," Astar agreed.

"In the heart of the Northern Wastes," she said with a shiver, even though she wasn't actually cold anymore.

"Only the eastern edge of them," he corrected with a smile.

"Practically tropical, then."

"I do love you, Nilly."

"I love you, Willy. Nothing will ever change that." Other things would change—and soon—but not that. Never that.

~ 10 ~

JAK OCCUPIED HIMSELF with checking the harness on their two valiant steeds. The inn staff had repaired the equipment perfectly, and a night of rest and excellent feed had done the horses good, the pair prancing in the traces in good spirits, their breath puffing warm and fragrant of hay in the swirling snowfall. Stella had healed their wounds so nothing showed of the battle from the previous day, and they both seemed sound. She must've calmed them too, because neither acted skittish or afraid of the carriage as he'd anticipated.

If only she could do the same for him. Well, if only she were inclined to. Stella might be just as happy to see him stewing with anxiety. Ha! Some suave and cocky guy he was now. At least working with the horses was a good exercise in maintaining his cool, as horses tended to be sensitive to nerves. Running forms for a couple of hours at dawn had helped, too. He wasn't in anything close to a meditative state, but he also wasn't quite crawling out of his skin either.

Still, how long would this conversation take? Astar had steered her out to the cliff walk—despite the blustery weather—foiling Jak's half-serious resolve to attempt to eavesdrop. Probably Astar had suspected Jak might try such a thing. His mother had been a decent spy after all, and he'd learned a few tricks. Not that he'd have gone against Stella's decision, but he'd have liked to hear how Astar framed the question. And the exact wording of her reply.

Then he considered that maybe he *didn't* want to know what they said about him. There were all sorts of cautionary tales along those lines, warnings that knowing people's innermost opinions about you could sting more than you'd expect. Though Stella had no insulation from that. She'd always know what everyone around her thought about her, what they felt.

She was going to say no to being courted. Of course she was, and he was braced for that. Hadn't she told him as much to his face? Yes, there had been that intensely intimate interlude between them in the carriage—and she'd been tempted, he'd felt it in his bones—but she was also determined to wall him out. To wall out all the world, come to that, to live her life alone, the inscrutable sorceress in her remote tower.

"Fuck that shit," he muttered viciously under his breath.

"Jak," Astar said from behind him. "A word, please."

Sometimes he really hated Astar's honorable and polite gentleman mien. He'd call it a noble façade, but Jak knew as well as anyone that Astar strove to be exactly that. Sometimes it would be easier if Astar could be a genuine asshole, now and again. More like the rest of them.

"Sure," he said, throttling his smart-ass urge to bow and throw Astar's royal titles in his face. "It's just me and the horsies here—ready for the verdict."

Astar nodded, running a hand down the flank of the nearest gelding. "They look good. Solid and ready to go."

"Willy." Jak shoved his hands in his coat pockets to remind himself not to draw his blades. "If you love me at all, you'll just tell me flat out."

With a rueful smile, Astar gripped his shoulder, squeezing it lightly. "She said yes."

He'd been so braced for the negative that he felt the same disorienting spin as the day before, when the abrupt skidding halt of the carriage had sent him flipping through the air. "Stella," he clarified, "said... yes?"

"To you *courting* her," Astar specified, his voice and expression stern, but there was a flicker of amusement in his eyes. "Nothing more than testing the waters, but I won't get in the way. I'm to stay out of her business, apparently."

"Wow." His brain still hadn't caught up, and Jak couldn't think of anything savvy to say. The moment called for a commemorative remark, and he had nothing.

"It's up to you now, my friend." Astar shook him a bit—maybe to wake him from his stunned state—then let go. "I'm staying out of it, as sternly instructed." He grimaced, then glanced around to be sure they were still alone. "I'd get in trouble for saying this, but let me issue the standard warnings and caveats."

Jak inclined his head gravely. "She's precious to me, too."

Astar frowned, opened his mouth, then firmly shut it again. "So." He cleared his throat. "Which route are we taking—along the Grace River or overland?"

And that was apparently that. Astar well and truly staying out of it. Maybe Glorianna *had* intervened with her golden son on Jak's behalf. "Diagonal overland is two days faster, at least," Jak pointed out, not for the first time.

"And harsher. A slower journey along the River Eva would be more fitting for our cover of a pleasure jaunt."

"Yeah…" Jak pulled out a map, unrolling it over the nearest horse's flank, tracing the river route with his finger. "But it's going to be like this place the whole way. Local people and tradesfolk. We don't need to be spreading reassurances around here. None of these people even heard about the bizarre eclipse, much less are worrying about it. And I hate to jinx us by suggesting it, but if that alter-realm intelligence is somehow tracking us and laying booby traps for us like yesterday, the longer it takes us to get to the Remus Isles, the more opportunities it has to cause us serious damage."

"You think that was a planned attack?"

No longer concerned that he might be tempted to hurl a blade at Astar, Jak drew a slim dagger and spun it between his fingers as he considered. "Narrow point in the road, well-placed rift, a considerable supply of those monkey-lizards in a mouth-frothing frenzy, three of our people at the farthest points of their scouting circles… Yeah, I'd say it was planned, and quite neatly, too. It very nearly had us, whatever *it* is."

"An unsettling thought." Astar looked torn.

"There's also the aspect that several of us have noticed: that you shapeshifters seem to be more vulnerable to your animal impulses than usual," Jak tendered, bracing himself for Astar to growl at him.

To his surprise, Astar nodded thoughtfully. "You think it has to do with the intelligence? Or the rifts?"

"Both?" Jak suggested, then lifted a shoulder and let it fall. "I'm not sure there's any way to know, but I do think that the longer this journey takes, the more we're vulnerable to these attacks and influences. Maybe it knows we're coming for it." He pointed to the map. "We can get to the Midway Inn by tonight if we hustle, then to the town of Wilhelmina the following night. There're apparently several inns there, and more regular lodging after that. Smart money says we get to Castle Marcellum, get the pass to sail to the Isles, and take care of the problem at its source."

"Since you won my coin, we know who's the smarter," Astar replied. "Going the overland route is going to be the hardest on you three—you, Stella, and Lena—since you can't shift into winter-hardy forms."

"We're not so fragile," Jak replied, firmly sheathing the dagger again.

"No." Astar looked wryly amused about something. "You're not. All right, you've convinced me. Overland it is."

"Maybe Lena could help us with the weather," Jak suggested. "Bring spring early or something."

Astar huffed out a laugh. "Don't think I didn't ask her. There was an involved explanation about vast weather patterns and upsetting the balance of nature on a whim, cascading effects, all disastrous. Short answer was no."

The rest of the group burst out of the inn just then, laughing and talking gaily, a couple of staff following them with repacked trunks. Stella wore her white-furred cloak, the hood drawn up around the perfect pale oval of her face, her dark hair spilling in a frame between, her eyes wide and crystal gray.

Blushing faintly as she caught him looking, she visibly steeled herself to walk up to him. "Astar spoke with you?" she asked quietly.

"Yes." A grin threatened to stretch his lips, the exhilaration he hadn't quite allowed himself to feel yet bubbling up inside. He wanted to kiss her. He also knew he had to go slowly and carefully, now more than ever. He didn't know what to do. If he'd been thinking ahead at all, he would've gotten her some kind of gift for this moment. Flowers, maybe. "Thank you," he blurted.

Her fine brows rose. "You're thanking me?"

She'd pulled her hair back from her forehead, he realized, revealing that seductive widow's peak. For him, perhaps. "Um, that was a stupid thing to say. I don't know why I said it. I'm not quite sure how to proceed now."

Blowing out a breath, she smiled. "Oh, thank Moranu—me too. I have no idea how to do this."

"I guess we figure it out together?" He held out a hand, and she placed her gloved one in his. Lifting her hand and holding her gaze, he pressed a kiss to the soft leather over the delicate spine of her knuckles. "We'll take it slow."

"That would be good," she said, watching him gravely, a world of thoughts behind her eyes. "Guess what?" She leaned closer, closing her fingers around his and lowering her voice. "I saw the lake creature again. Just now, from the cliffs."

He whistled long and low. "You have Moranu's own luck. I wish I'd been there."

"Well..." She cocked her head thoughtfully. "Astar was right beside me and saw nothing, even when I pointed him to the exact spot."

"Isn't that interesting?" Jak considered the implications. "So, you're thinking you're the only one who can see it."

A line formed between her brows. "Clearly that's not the case, as other people have seen it over time, or there wouldn't be the legends."

"Only the pure of heart," he teased, squeezing her hand.

"You, of all people, should know that's not true." But she blushed a faint rose, like her sweet lips. Oh yeah—he was head over heels for her.

"You have the purest heart of anyone I know," he told her, meaning every word. And he planned to safeguard that heart like it was made of spun glass.

"Some people might like standing out in a blizzard," Lena said archly, and she moved past them, "but the smart one is getting in the carriage." She smiled broadly at Stella and held up four fingers, then folded one down.

"What was that about?" Jak asked as Stella narrowed her eyes at their friend.

"You don't want to know." Stella returned her gaze to his with such sweet innocence that he knew something was well and truly up.

"I think I do want to know."

"Learn to live with the *prick* of curiosity," Zeph suggested, sailing past. "Rhy is taking first shift as scout, so Gen and I are riding in the carriage with you."

Good idea, that, to keep the majority of the shapeshifters with the main group for defense.

Gen paused to eye their clasped hands. "Joining us in the

carriage, Jak?"

"Someone has to drive the horses," he replied, finally releasing Stella's hand—much as it pained him—and sweeping the ladies a gallant bow. "I live to serve."

THEY SOON LEFT all sign of the lake behind, the little-used northern road ascending to a harsh and windswept plain. The advantage of the unceasing northwesterly wind was that it scoured the road clear. It also blew snow across in a knee-high blizzard that boiled thick as fog and obscured the ground, regardless of what fell from the sky at any given time. Even Jak's excellent vision struggled to make out details and keep them off the verge, and after a few hours, his eyes ached from the strain. He had his fur-lined collar pulled up around his ears, a black-knit sailor's cap pulled down over them, along with his warmest clothes and leather coat—and still the wind sliced him to the bone. He even capitulated and pulled on his fur-lined gloves, though they made him clumsier with his blades, finally deciding that losing his fingers to frostbite would impact his bladework more.

Taking the overland route might not have been his brightest idea.

Astar paced them in grizzly form, carefully staying downwind of the horses—though they were head down and miserable enough that they might not care that much even if they did scent him. A raven tumbled through the winds overhead, mantling its wings to stabilize against a gust, then dove for the seat beside Jak—becoming Rhy as it did.

"Why do people live here?" Rhy demanded, seizing the thick black cloak he'd stowed at the footboard and dragging it on, pulling the hood up around his head, then chafing his hands.

"In point of fact, they don't," Jak replied, sweeping a hand at the barren wasteland. "See anything?"

"Snow and wind."

"Besides that."

"I've forgotten if there's anything besides that in the entire world."

"How about the Midway Inn—did you spot it yet?"

"No. I suspect a mossback trick," Rhy replied grimly. "There is no inn. They're just luring us out there to die, alone, in a frozen wasteland."

"You're not alone," Jak noted. "You have us."

Rhy slanted him a dark-blue glare. "When we're trapped in our snow cave, slowly starving to death, I'm eating you first."

"You can try," Jak answered cheerfully. "But it would be smarter to get one of the shapeshifters to become something like a bison. The meat would last a lot longer. Taste better, too."

"True," Rhy mused. "You're a stringy fucker."

Jak patted his flat abs. "Clean living."

Rhy barked a laugh at that, and Jak reined up. Not like they'd find a better place to stop. "I'll check the horses while you pry the next shift out of the carriage."

Nodding, Rhy hopped down, and Jak went around to the horses' heads. Ice had collected on their muzzles, so he stripped off his gloves and warmed the tender muzzle of one with his palms. Stella appeared through the swirling snow, the white cloak making her look like a manifestation of the landscape, her clear gray eyes standing out against her pale skin.

"Can I help?" she asked, observing his actions. "We don't want your magic blade-throwing hands getting frostbite."

"If the ice collects over their nostrils, they can't breathe," he explained. "The cold already wears them out faster; not be able to breathe well makes it worse."

"I have an idea." She pulled off her own gloves and mimicked his actions, melting the accumulated ice off the other horse's muzzle. The mare lifted her head, nuzzling Stella and bumping her chest, a delighted smile lighting Stella's face. She so rarely looked that way, always so solemn, with a shadow behind her eyes. Lifting her hands, she spread a glow of green-threaded rosy light over the mare. Then she nudged him aside and did the same with Jak's gelding. The pair of horses stamped in place, their lustrous eyes brighter.

"What did you do?" he asked, taking the opportunity to put his arms around Stella from behind, putting his face beside hers. With her thick cloak, he could hardly feel her, but it was worth it to be close enough to inhale the fragrance of night-blooming flowers from her heated skin.

She stayed still, not withdrawing, still focused on the gelding. "A bit of healing to restore their energy. A bit of sorcery to make a bubble of warmth around them."

"Can you sustain that?" he asked, concerned.

"With the Star, yes," she replied after checking that Rhy

was out of earshot. "For the rest of the day anyway."

She turned in the loose circle of his arms, her mouth temptingly close. Lifting her hands, she framed his face, sliding her fingers over his beard, tingling warmth following. She stroked his earlobes, tugging lightly on his earring in a most stimulating way, and he closed his eyes, humming in pleasure at her touch. "I think you're the one with the magic hands," he murmured.

"I should've thought to do this before," she replied in a worried tone. "You're very cold."

"Feeling warmer now." He opened his eyes and grinned at her. "Besides, this is like a midsummer day in Dasnaria."

She breathed a laugh, still massaging his earlobes in that most interesting manner. "Even I know it's not always winter in Dasnaria."

"You're toasty warm," he observed, pressing her against him just a bit more.

"Zeph took tiger form, and we all piled together against her under the blankets." A wistful smile curved her pretty pink lips. "Like being kids again."

"Sounds fun."

"Maybe you should take a break, let Rhy or Astar drive and come warm up."

"I'm feeling refreshed now. I'll let Rhy ride inside. I think his raven form didn't handle this weather well."

"You're a thoughtful guy, Jak." She said it sincerely, but the faintest hint of surprise had him cocking his head at her.

"I'm heading out," Gen said as she passed them. "Finish exchanging your sweet nothings because everyone is ready to roll again. Once I get out of scent range of the horses, I'm going for polar bear form. I'll run ahead to find this Midway Inn Rhy is bitching about being a trap."

"I thought he was sure it doesn't exist," Jak called back.

"I think he'll be vindicated by either dire outcome," Gen said with a saucy wink. She became a snowy owl, flying out into the blizzard, quickly disappearing.

THEY REACHED THE inn before full dark, but just barely. Even though Gen had spotted it and assured him it was there, and though Zeph had spent her shift winging back and forth with regular updates on their progress, Jak had never been so glad to see the lights of civilization in the snow-whipped twilight.

"And so our hero lives another day without being eaten by vicious shapeshifters!" he told the horses, who nodded happily in agreement. The people in the group might've been able to survive a night on the frozen plain by all piling into the carriage and sharing body heat, but the horses couldn't have. "Yeah, us prey animals have to watch out for each other."

He guided the rig into the circle of light in front of the inn. Torches blazed in a crescent of welcome, but no sound came from within. Odd, because inns had a characteristic din, even ones in the middle of nowhere. The hairs on the back of his neck went up, and he scanned the area for signs of life. "I have a bad feeling about this, horsies."

The carriage door banged open, Lena's laugh ringing out. "Thank the three!" she exclaimed as she stepped out. "I can't wait to—"

Jak cut off her words with a hand over her mouth, having jumped down behind her. "Shh," he hissed in her ear, then glanced into the shadows of the carriage. Rhy pushed to the front.

"Trouble?"

"I don't know," Jak replied quietly, letting Lena go with an apologetic pat. She rounded her eyes in question.

"I'll check it out," Rhy said, becoming a wolf and disappearing into the shadows before Jak could stop him.

"What is it?" Stella asked quietly, moving into the spot in the carriage doorway Rhy had occupied.

"I don't know." Jak grimaced. "Maybe nothing. It's just—"

A wolf's strangled yelp rang through the cold air, cut off just as quickly.

"Rhyian," Lena breathed, face waxy under the play of torchlight.

Jak bit out a curse. What to do? Astar would be hanging back, out of sight—hard to explain a grizzly bear way out here—waiting to shift and dart inside when the coast was clear. "Can you talk to Astar from here?" he asked Stella.

She looked surprised. "No. Why would you think so?"

"You're a sorceress."

"Yes, but I need a receptive mind to speak to."

He nodded. "It just seems like you and Astar have some kind of telepathic twinspeak sometimes."

"They do," Zeph said.

"We don't," Stella retorted, then looked faintly embarrassed. "Not telepathic anyway. We have to be close together."

Jak grimaced. So much for getting Astar to make the call.

"I'm going after Rhy," Zeph declared, pushing past Stella. "The gríobhth can take on whatever it is."

"No." Jak seized her by the arm. She jerked it away with a hiss, already on her way to becoming the gríobhth. "Zeph," he said as calmly as he could. "This isn't natural. Where's the wind? You go out there, it could get you too."

"Jak's right," Lena said, her expression changing the way it did when she used her weather magic. "There's something strange here."

Stella stepped down from the carriage, Gen right behind her. "Then it is a trap?" Gen asked quietly.

Jak pulled off his watch cap and raked a hand through his hair, willing his exhausted brain to think. Fuck Rhy for being right in his pessimistic paranoia—and then getting caught. He weighed the odds. "We should leave."

"We can't abandon Rhyian," Lena said, steel in her voice.

No. No, they couldn't. But for the moment, Astar was clear of the trap, and they needed to keep the heir to the high throne safe.

Stella put a gloved hand on his arm. "Let me try something."

"And me." Lena moved to Stella's side.

Throttling back the protective urge to toss Stella into the carriage and drive her away from this place, he nodded. But he also stuffed his gloves and watch cap in his pocket, drew his sword, and readied a dagger in the other hand. Taking a few steps ahead of Stella, he studied the quiet scene.

"Jak," Zeph whispered. "What about me and Gen?"

"Take your best defensive forms," he answered quietly, "but stay close. Nothing gets to the sorceresses."

He didn't watch what forms they chose, nor did he care who spotted them now. There was no one out here to see them, and keeping everyone safe took precedence over not alarming the locals. Jak trained his gaze on the shadows. The torches that had been so welcome as he emerged from the storm now worked against him, creating bright flares of light that kept his eyes from adjusting to the deepening night. His mother had taught him all the scout's tricks for seeing well with fully human eyes—and how to recognize a situation set up to blind them.

A golden glow rose behind him as Stella invoked the focusing power of the Star of Annfwn. No chanting this time as she and Lena kept as quiet as possible. Though what good would that do? They were spotlighted out here, in a clearing of blazing light. They might as well be the bull's-eye of a target for...

The thought had him jerking his head up. Barely in time.

"Scatter!" he shouted, throwing himself backward and knocking Stella and Lena to the ground. They yelped in surprise, the orb of the Star rolling across the packed snow. He had no time to help them, leaping to a crouch as the great *thing* landed with a crash and a cloud of flying snow, ice, and dirt.

Practically on top of him.

It took his brain far too long to grapple with trying to identify whatever the thing might be, but fortunately reflex took over as he launched himself at it. It might not have a head, but it had tentacles, and Jak wasn't letting those things get near

Stella and Lena. Making a whirlwind of his sword and dagger, he sliced at the tentacles as they reached for him, vaguely aware of the horses rearing in panic and taking off at top speed, the carriage rattling over the icy ruts of the drive. Good thing he hadn't told the sorceresses to take shelter under it.

Black flesh flew, dark liquid spattering cold against his skin, and the tentacles kept coming. Several wrapped around his sword, yanking it from his grip even as they shredded themselves against the lethal edge. Without losing a beat, he pulled a second dagger. That was a better balance for this kind of infighting anyway. The thing seemed to have thousands of tentacles, from as thick as his waist to hair thin—and no matter how many he sliced away, there always seemed to be more.

On the other sides of the creature's mass, the gríobhth and white saber cat—Zeph and Gen—waged their own battle of beak, fang, and claw. Zeph's whiplike tail whistled through the air, sending tentacle bits flying, and Gen bit them off by the mouthful. The saber cat launched herself at the main mass of the creature, sinking in her formidable fangs and front claws, bringing up her powerful haunches to dig into the shapeless core, sending huge chunks flying.

Zeph followed her lead, spreading her great golden wings and pushing off with her leonine back legs, propelling herself into the air to land on top of her side of the creature. Laying about with beak, four sets of claws, and that whipping tail, she shredded the thing.

With the creature's tentacles all going to defending its core from Zeph and Gen, Jak had a breath of a moment to consider his own strategy on how to best assist them and get them all out of this.

"*Jak!*" Stella's voice shouted in his mind, and he spun to look for her.

Lena had her daggers out, defending herself against the tentacles of another monster that had arrived behind them. But Stella… she couldn't be seen for the mass of tentacles mummifying her. Terror striking his heart, he ran at the creature at full speed. Wading into the mass of tentacles, ignoring the ones that latched onto his legs, waist, and chest, he hacked away at the tentacles swathing Stella, feeling like he chased the tide, as more tentacles replaced the ones he sliced away. The creature began to move away, dragging its prize with it. Jak raced after it as it sped relentlessly into the night with surprising speed. Desperation and exhaustion sobbing through his chest, he searched frantically for something he could do.

"Stella!" he shouted. "Help me help you!"

"*Jak!*"

"Stella!" Stella's voice in his head. He didn't question it.

"*Listen! The Star. I need the Star.*"

But where in Danu was the Star? An image popped into his mind—his own memory or something Stella inserted there—of the Star rolling away across the dirty snow-rutted drive. To find it, though, he'd have to abandon Stella to the creature, leaving her to be dragged off while he essentially ran away. "*I'm not leaving you!*"

"*I'm lost if you don't. Please, Jak. I'm asking you to help me. This is how you can.*"

"Fuck!" he shouted in pure frustrated rage, sheathing his daggers to run in the other direction.

~ II ~

HEAD DOWN, FREEZING air burning his lungs, Jak did his best to maintain focus, to remember the direction so when he ran back into the now inky, snow-splattered night covering the featureless plain, he might have a fighting chance of finding her again. If the thing hadn't already dragged Stella through a rift into the alter-realm.

He made it back to the torchlit circle of hell where the gríobhth and saber cat still battled the first tentacle monster. Unable to tell if they were winning or losing—at least they were still alive—he scrabbled around on hands and knees, searching for the blasted jewel. *Glow, you fucker,* he thought at it furiously.

"There." Stella's mental finger pointed him to a deep rut shrouded in darkness. Digging with his bare hands, he hissed at the bite of ice-sharp shards piercing under his nails. "I don't see it," he said aloud.

"Let me in."

If Rhy could do it, he could. He pictured Stella, opening his arms to her. She stepped into his mind like a breeze on a tropical night. Of its own accord—seemingly—his hand reached forward, pushing into a clod of dirty snow... and closed around the Star. Without a pause to look at it, he was on his feet and running, almost blindly, into the whirling white and black infinity of the wintry plain.

Stella stayed with him—and drew him toward her at the same time. It wasn't exactly the direction he'd have gone in on his own, but he threw his trust—and the last of his strength—into following her pull.

The tentacle monster had picked up speed, and had also jagged sideways. Jak was nearly on it before he skidded to a sliding stop on the icy snow. He pulled one dagger but had to use his other hand to hold the Star. "What now?" he shouted at the creature's tentacle-wrapped lump as it moved along like an octopus on dry land, using some of its many tentacles for propulsion.

"I need to use the Star through you."

"Do it."

"You have to let me in Jak, all the way."

"I am!" he snarled.

"You're fighting me. Be still. Be calm."

"Easy for you to say," he muttered, but he tried.

"Clear your mind, Jak. Relax."

"I'm a little stressed right now," he ground out.

"Do Danu's Dance."

It seemed beyond absurd, an exercise in futility. A tentacle monster was dragging Stella away into the frozen tundra, and she wanted him to run forms?

"Do it, Jak."

"I live to obey," he snarled, and moved into the familiar steps of Danu's Dance. The one blade fit snug into his grip, if sticky with fluids he didn't want to contemplate, and in the other he balanced the Star on his palm. He wasn't as practiced at that, as he rarely performed Danu's Dance that way, though that was how it was sometimes done. The martial form was also an actual dance, performed with lit candles floating in saucers of water—or burning oil for the brave—cupped in the palms and balanced there with exquisite care. Keeping the Star perfectly balanced on his palm so it wouldn't roll off into the snow again as he swept through the increasingly rigorous and acrobatic movements of the dance required utmost concentration.

And as the ritual of the form took over his body, his mind focused on the Star, Stella's presence within him intensifying. Her magic, dark as fog on a moonless sea, swept into and around him, pouring into the Star.

It blazed into light, becoming like a small sun in his hand, and he nearly faltered in surprise.

"Keep going," Stella murmured in his head. "You're doing well. Yes, just like that."

Her praise stroked him like an intimate caress, and he strove to continue through the form, beginning Danu's Dance for the third time, distantly aware of his exhaustion and growing weakness. More than a few flesh wounds this time.

The Star grew brighter until it illuminated the landscape bright as full day, the snowscape nearly blinding in its stark whiteness. And the creature stood out, black and phenomenally bizarre. Its bulging, pulsating core burbled with shifting pustules, tentacles bristling in all directions. A grizzly roared from not far away. Astar on his way, thank Danu.

The screech of a gríobhth from above and the roar of a saber cat followed. The Star grew impossibly brighter, pulsing with such fire that Jak expected it to burn.

With a massive flare, sound boomed out, almost knocking him over—though he managed to land on his feet. The creature dissolved so abruptly that Stella went rolling over the snow like a discarded toy.

Jak ran to Stella. Her occupation of his mind was quickly fading, and her white fur cloak was tarred with black fluids. When he fell to his knees by her side, his head swam with dizziness so extreme he nearly keeled over. He rolled her limp body into his arms, but when he went to stand, his legs failed him, leaving him kneeling in the bitter snow, Stella a boneless weight.

"Let me have her, Jak." Astar had a hand on his shoulder, clamping hard and shaking him a little.

Jak blinked at Astar, in his shirtsleeves in the raging blizzard, and held Stella tighter. "She's hurt."

"I know. So are you. Let me help you both."

A draft horse pranced up behind Astar. Gen?

Astar let go of Jak's shoulder and slid his hands under Stella, tugging when Jak held on. "Jak." Astar met and held his gaze. "It's all right. We're putting you both up on Gen's back to take you to the inn. We'll freeze out here."

"It's not safe at the inn."

"It is now. Trust me."

Jak nodded mutely and let Astar wedge his twin out of Jak's arms. They felt frozen in place. "Lena and Zeph."

"They're all right." Astar stood, holding Stella. "Can you

stand?"

"I... don't know." He didn't want to move. The snow that
been so bitterly hard now felt soft and cozy as a bed. "I think
I'll lie down a moment." There, that was better. Icy crystals
cradled his cheek like a pillow, comforting as drowsy sleep
overcame him. When Astar pulled at him, he resisted, though
without much strength.

"Jakral Konyngrr, you are shirking your duty," Astar
barked in Dasnarian. "Now get up before I toss you over-
board."

"Dad?" Jak stopped resisting, wondering how Kral had
gotten there. He found himself tossed over broad shoulders,
hoisted there sideways, his arm and leg on one side firmly
gripped, the other side dangling.

"Can you balance Nilly without help?" Astar asked, breath
puffing.

"Stella," Jak gasped, struggling.

"She's fine. She's right there. If you'll behave, you can sit
with her and keep her on Gen's back."

"Please." Unmanly tears wet his lashes and froze there.
"Don't keep me from her."

"I won't." Astar sounded grim, then levered him onto the
draft horse's back. Stella lay face down, a shapeless, limp form
in stained white fur. "Stay on. That's an order."

"Yes, sir." Jak realized they'd been talking in Dasnarian the
whole time and he'd barely noticed. How odd. "Don't tell
Mom and Dad I fucked up."

"I'll tell them you're a bloody hero." Astar slapped his
thigh. "I'm right here. Your only job is to hold on."

"Hold on," Jak repeated, gripping with sluggish muscles, securing Stella against his knees as he dug numb fingers into her filthy cloak. Why did his head feel so thick and slow?

"Hold on," Astar agreed firmly. "If you do that, I'll buy you all the whiskey you can hold."

"Whiskey," Jak sighed wistfully.

"Knew that would get you. Go, Gen."

Gen began walking, slowly at first, gathering speed as Jak found his seat. Astar, back in grizzly-bear form, strode beside them, a hulking shadow gliding in the dizzying whirl of snow.

Drowsiness swept over him in waves, and he swayed, tempted to close his eyes. Just a short nap. But he had a job. "Get tough. Hold on," he muttered to himself, and the horse he rode whickered encouragingly.

The torches still blazed in the horrific semicircle in front of the inn, and Jak flinched at the sight. "Astar, no!" he shouted. "You don't—"

Astar was at his knee, human face calm. "I understand, but it's all right now. Trust me."

A winged shadow dropped from the sky, and Jak went for the dagger in his boot, his uncooperative fingers bumbling the move, the blade dropping to the snow. Astar clamped his wrist. "It's Zephyr. Stand down, man."

Jak looked again, recognizing the gríobhth's golden shine. She became Zeph, who dashed up to them. "All clear," she said. "No luck on the scent trail. You got them both?"

"Yes, but Nilly's unconscious, and Jak is half dead from blood loss and frostbite. We have to warm him up."

"I'll open the doors and Gen can just go right in. Lena's in by the fireplace. Take them there."

Gen bobbed her head and clomped up the wooden steps, ducking a bit to get through the double doors. The inn felt like an oven, the air too thick to breathe. Gen took them into a big common room, tables pushed back from a blazing fire.

"Down you go, buddy," Astar said, holding up his hands. "Or do you need me to lift you down?"

"Not a lil kid." His sharp retort came out slurred.

"Danu save me from stubborn Dasnarians," Astar said, tugging on Jak's arm and catching him as he tumbled.

"Half," Jak corrected.

"The stubborn half." Astar pulled Jak's arm over his shoulder and pretty much dragged him to the pile of blankets and pillows before the fire.

"Not too close," Gen said. Back in human form, she and Zeph carried Stella between them to the blankets. "Both of these two have to warm up slowly, but especially Jak."

Astar grabbed a blanket and hauled Jak backward, depositing him on it. "Lie down now, buddy. You're off duty."

"Take his wet clothes off," Gen said over her shoulder, working with Zeph to unwrap Stella. "Tell me what you see."

"Why does everyone want to see me naked all of a sudden?" Jak wondered.

"I'm going to pretend I didn't hear that," Astar grunted. "He's cut up all over. Lots of dried and frozen blood, but no active bleeding."

"He will when he warms up."

"He's really white, all over. Cold and clammy," Astar reported.

"Gee, thanks."

"Not surprising," Gen called. "Dry him off. Wrap him in one blanket, loosely, then see if you can get some hot water into him."

"Whiskey," Jak said.

"No," Gen replied before Astar could.

"Warm whiskey," Jak corrected.

"No alcohol!" Gen was firm on the subject.

"Sorry, buddy." Astar grimaced, having finally wrestled off Jak's boots, the pants falling away in shreds like his shirt and coat had. He was fucked for clothes now. All he had left was the scarlet suit he'd worn to the ball at Ordnung a lifetime ago. Astar began rubbing him briskly with the blanket.

"Patting, not rubbing," Gen instructed.

Obediently, Astar changed his technique.

"How do you know so much about this?" Zeph asked.

"Dad's family," Gen replied. "When your mossback family lives in the foothills of Mohraya and there's no magical healing to be had, you learn a lot about frostbite and what to do with half-frozen people. All right. Maybe turn her head to the fire to get her hair dry, but otherwise keep doing what you're doing. She needs to warm up slowly, but she should be all right. Listen to her heartbeat and tell me if it changes."

Gen appeared on Jak's other side, her brown hair incongruously smooth and shining. But then, she'd have shapeshifted to heal and clean up. Must be nice. "Lift him up, and lean him against you. Your body heat will help."

Astar slid an arm under his shoulders, levering Jak into a half-sitting position, sitting behind him. Gen pressed a mug to

Jak's lips. "Drink, slowly."

It was hot water all right. Plain hot water, with a faint tinge of bitterness, like old coffee. He swallowed that sip, then turned his head. "How is Stella?"

Gen gave him a level stare. Her eyes, usually a soft indigo, looked like the deep ocean before a storm. "Stella will be fine. You are the one we're worried about, Jak, so do as I tell you— or I'll have to explain to Stella why I let you die."

Die? A joke sprang to his lips, but Gen narrowed her eyes in warning, so he obediently drank down the flat, nasty water. "Rhy and Lena?" he asked once he swallowed. He shivered, once and hard, and his bones began to ache.

Gen and Astar exchanged looks over his head. "Lena will pull through," Gen said. "And the tentacle monsters are gone. Stella vanished them both with that last blast of magic."

"The Star," Jak said, suddenly panicked, trying to sit up. His muscles cramped painfully.

Astar restrained him without effort. "Stella has it."

"She doesn't." Did she? He couldn't quite remember what had happened. Everything was fuzzy. He was still forgetting something. "Rhyian."

A low rumble sounded through Astar's chest where he still braced Jak. Gen put the cup to Jak's lips again. "No more answers until you drink more."

He drank, feeling the warm liquid hit his stomach, then pressed his lips closed when she offered more. Her gaze went to Astar over Jak's head.

"We haven't found him," Astar admitted. "We've looked, and we'll keep looking. I found his scent trail, and it just...

stops."

"The rift." Jak forced the words past his lips, feeling out of breath, as if he'd been running. Everything hurt. Not the lacerations he couldn't see, but in his joints, his very bones.

"That's what it looks like."

"Have to... get out... of here..." *Shit.* He tried to struggle up again. "Horses?"

"Give it a rest," Astar ordered, forcibly holding him down. "We found the horses. They're safe in the stable. We're not going anywhere tonight. Let us handle things. You've done enough."

You've done enough. He'd taken them straight into a trap and nearly got them all killed. "I'm so sorry, Dad," he nearly sobbed. He couldn't catch his breath.

"He's delirious."

"His heart is seizing." Gen cursed viciously, a filthy one Jak was surprised she knew.

He opened his mouth to tease her about it but had no breath to speak. The black rolled up and over him, taking him under. Drowning him in the airless depths.

His father would never let him live it down.

GENTLE SUN SHONE on the sparkling aqua sea so distinctive to Annfwn. A young woman strolled on the white sands, long dark hair glinting with a hint of red, her movements shy and quiet. She wore a simple, light gown, short enough to show off her tanned legs, which Stella found surprisingly sexy. The young woman's body, too, looked so lovely—delicately curved, moving enticingly under the clinging material. The woman glanced back over her shoulder, and Stella realized she was seeing herself, as she'd been years ago.

Past Stella's expression was somber, eyes stormy gray, brow smooth, but also shadowed. Her lips curved into something not a smile, but lessening the sense of a frown.

Did she really look that way to other people?

"Jak," she said, reproach in her tone. "You have to stop following me."

"I wanted to give you something." Jak's voice coming out of her own mouth startled her. This must be a dream. But from Jak's perspective? He held out his hand, the Star shining on his palm. That's right—he had to give it back to Stella. She had to save them all.

"Why do you have the Star?" Past Stella asked, frowning in truth. "Jak, what's going on? I don't understand."

"My star, I need your help."

"Jak, I don't understand."

"Help me. I can't find my way."

"Nilly, it's all right. Go back to sleep."

She blinked up into Astar's beloved summer-blue eyes, his hand holding hers like being wrapped in comfort. *You touch Astar all the time—why is he different? Maybe because we shared a womb? Touching his hand is like holding my own. So, a matter of familiarity and trust, perhaps.* "Willy," she said, a world of love in it.

He smiled and brushed her hair from her forehead. "Go back to sleep. You need the rest. And you're safe now."

The dream floated back through her mind. Why had she thought she was Jak, talking to herself? *My star, I need your help.* Jak. She bolted upright, startling Astar into almost falling backward. "Where's Jak?"

"Don't worry about Jak. You need to rest and recover."

Astar was hiding his thoughts behind an opaque wall. "Is Jak all right?"

"He's fine."

He was lying.

"Take me to him. Right now." She pushed to her feet, staggering with the weakness in her limbs as Astar tried to both support her and stop her from going anywhere.

"Nilly," he said, a world of hopelessness in his voice.

"No." She shook her head, denying the possibility. "Oh no. You're wrong. Let me see him."

"Let her see him, Astar." Zeph came up and put her hand on shoulder. She looked pale and drawn. "You'd want the same."

"But she can't—" Astar stopped. Sighed. "Fine, but I'm carrying you. You're weak still." With that, he swept her into his arms like a bouquet of flowers. She looked around as he carried her out of the room and into a hallway. Zeph paced alongside, a line of worry between her brows.

"We're at the Midway Inn?" Stella asked. She remembered arriving, the tentacle monsters attacking, trying to summon the magic to send them back, Jak fighting like a whirlwind of blades. Then nothing.

"Yes," Astar replied tersely, passing a number of empty rooms, their doors standing open.

"We're the only ones here," Zeph added, sliding Astar a look, like she'd expected him to say as much.

Astar was tense, still burying his thoughts where he believed she couldn't read them, but his anxiety and sorrow leaked through the cracks. He never had been any good at lying. Astar was simply too sincere to carry it off. Even when they were kids and getting into trouble, Astar would blurt out a confession at the least bit of pressure. It had been up to Stella to cover for them. Funny to think about that now.

Bypassing all the rooms, Astar carried her down to the first floor, then carried her into the inn's gathering room, where most of the tables had been pushed to the sides, the chairs stacked.

Except for a table in front of the fire, where Jak was laid out, wearing the scarlet outfit he'd sported at the Feast of Moranu ball, his gleaming weapons arranged formally around him, his profile still as if carved from wax. His skin pale as death.

Lena, who'd been sitting beside him, leapt to her feet. Her mouth fell into an astonished O, her eyes red and swollen from weeping. Her shock burned fast into fury. "What is she doing here?" she demanded, putting herself between Stella and Jak, as if she might hide him behind her.

"She insisted," Astar replied shortly.

"Concealing the truth won't change it," Zeph said, the gríobhth remorselessness in her voice, though her gaze resting on Jak was full of grief. "Nilly has a right to know."

"Put me down," Stella told Astar as he carried her to the makeshift bier. As he complied, slowly and bracing her in case her legs gave again, Stella felt for Jak's presence inside the cold body. A flicker of life deep within. "He's not dead."

Lena made a sound of incoherent sorrow, pressing her knuckles to her mouth, and Astar tightened his arms around her. "I know it's difficult to face," he said, sounding unutterably weary. "We tried to save him, but he lost too much blood, got too cold. His heart stopped."

"You don't understand," Stella replied impatiently. "I'm telling you he's not dead." *My star, I need your help. I can't find my way.*

A sob escaped Lena's whitened knuckles. Astar hugged Stella close. "I'm so sorry," he said, tears in his voice. "I wish it wasn't true."

Stella shook him off. "He isn't dead. Let me go. Let me work."

"Let her do it," Zeph said.

"But, Zephyr, she—" Astar protested raggedly.

"She's a sorceress, an empath, and a healer—which makes her wiser in this arena than all of us put together," Zeph snapped. "Let her try. Wouldn't you do anything to save Jak?"

"Not at the risk of losing Stella, too," Astar ground out.

"I'm all right," Stella replied absently, hands on Jak's cold skin. His dark beard stood out starkly against his pallor, along with bloodless cuts and purpling bruises. Otherwise, he looked like he might be sleeping—and likely to open his eyes and make some joke about fooling them all and only pretending to be dead. She touched the pulse beneath his ear. Nothing.

"His heart isn't beating, and he's not breathing," Lena said quietly from the other side of the table. Stella refused to think of it as a bier. "I keep checking."

I can't find my way. He was holding the Star out to her.

"Where's the Star of Annfwn?" Stella asked, not looking up.

"Lost in the fight," Astar answered. "Gen is out looking for it, but…"

"But it's been nonstop snow and wind ever since," Zeph filled in. "If it's out there, it's buried."

Stella could go right to it, but there wasn't much time. Good thing Jak had wakened her when he did. She send a thought to the Star, funneling magic into it so it would glow. "We need to warm him up," she said. "He's too cold."

"Nilly, please!" Astar nearly shouted, and Zeph hushed him.

"We can always freeze his body again," she said very quietly, though not so quietly that Stella didn't hear. *His body.* No, she wouldn't let it happen.

"There are blankets," Lena began, turning.

"No," Stella said, stopping her. "Use your weather magic. Warm the air around him."

"I didn't think of that." Lena put her magic to work, the air in the immediate vicinity heating like sand baking under a desert sun.

"Not desert," Stella said, stretching her senses to find Jak within the tomb of his body, healing his lacerations as she encountered them. "Think tropical, like Nahanau. Thick, clinging humidity."

As if she'd created it herself, the weather thickened at her order, the sweet humidity as fragrant and comforting as home.

"I still don't feel a pulse or heartbeat," Lena said.

"It's there, just very slow." There. Like teasing a thread out of a tapestry, she found a line to Jak's life force. He received her mental touch with a rush of welcome, relieved she'd found him. It took all she had to hold him in place. "Not yet."

"I'm not doing anything more," Lena replied.

"Not you." Her native magic wouldn't be enough. Already she was flagging. "I need the Star."

"Nilly." Astar sounded at wit's end. "I told you. We can't—"

"Found it!" Gen sang out, the inn front doors slamming. "I found the Star! It was glowing in this snowbank. I don't know why I didn't—Stella! You're up..." She trailed off, making it almost a question.

Stella held out her hand, snapping her fingers. "Give me the Star."

"Your wish, my command," Gen replied, an odd note in her voice. The Star, warm and exploding with magic, settled in to Stella's outstretched palm.

Pulling open Jak's fancy dress shirt, she centered the Star over his heart, holding it in place with both hands and carefully focusing her healing magic through it.

"What is going on?" Gen whispered.

"She thinks she can save Jak," Zeph explained.

"Did you explain to her that—"

"We tried," Astar cut off Gen's question. "Nilly isn't listening to reason."

"Don't talk about me like I'm a stubborn child," Stella said mildly. "I know what I'm doing."

Astar snorted. "Because you've raised so many people from

the dead."

"I told you: He isn't dead."

"Maybe she's delirious, or out of her mind," Gen whispered.

"Stella can't possibly hurt him, and she just might save him," Zeph snapped out, her staunch defender. "So everyone shut up and let her work."

An awkward silence ensued. Stella was peripherally aware that that Zeph had led Astar away to a chair, where he now sat with his head in his hands. Zeph crouched beside him, talking soothingly. Lena remained a solid presence across the table, maintaining the air temperature. Gen reappeared, a carafe in one hand, a mug in the other.

"If I were trying to save him," she said quietly, "I'd have him drink this. To warm up from the inside."

"Good," Stella answered without taking her attention from the Star. "He'll need that in a moment."

Aware of Gen and Lena exchanging helpless looks, of Zeph comforting Astar in the corner, of Rhy here and not here, Stella held them all in her expanded perception—along with the growing thread of Jak's presence, his life force weaker than theirs but no less present.

"This will be a bit tricky," she told him, mentally taking his hand. "The timing must be exactly right."

"*Fortunately, I have excellent timing,*" he replied in her mind, a phantom grin flashing.

"That cocky arrogance will serve you well."

"Is she…?" Gen asked.

"Shh," from Lena.

"All right, Jakral Konyngrr," Stella murmured, "let's do this." With her mental hand, she pulled hard on the solidifying thread, simultaneously pouring magic into his heart, brain, and other internal organs.

He convulsed, arcing on the table as if hit by lightning, a tight scream scraping from his throat. A chair clattered in the background, and Gen nearly dropped her mug. Stella continued to infuse Jak's body with healing magic, weaving his spirit back into his body, warming his blood and repairing the damage from freezing and lying inert for so many hours.

Without the Star, she could never have done it.

With the Star—and sorcery she'd never realized herself capable of—she brought him back.

~ 12 ~

Pain hit him like a mailed fist to the head—except it didn't stay in his head. It radiated through his body, all of it—bones, ligaments, muscles, even his skin—cramping with convulsive force. He was simultaneously viciously cold and burning up with fever.

"Stay with me, Jak," Stella coaxed, her voice like a gentle sea on a warm afternoon. "I know it hurts, but it won't last long."

She was right—already the first bloom of agony was fading into a dull, roaring ache. Forcing his eyes open, he found her lovely, serene face hovering over him, her eyes silver as the full moon, brimming with magic. Her dark hair spilled around them both, like the shadows of Moranu, the gentle, shrouding night embracing them. The fine point of her widow's peak marked the apex of a triangle framed at the bottom by her winged brows, the center opening into a third eye that gazed at him invisibly.

"Welcome back," she said with a sweet smile.

Lifting a hand, he slid it behind her neck and pulled her down for a kiss. Her lips, unbelievably sweet and soft, moved over his in a benediction, like life itself. With her healing magic thrumming through every cell of his body, it seemed she breathed him in with the kiss, the life flowing back through her cupped hands over his heart, pumping into his lungs, and breathing out again in an endless circle.

He kept it brief, aware of paining her, though he couldn't imagine how he could be any more a part of her than in that moment. "I nearly died without kissing you. No way I'd risk letting that happen again."

She smiled, eyes radiantly silver, and she seemed about to say something. Then her eyes dimmed, rolling up, and she collapsed over him.

IT TOOK SOME time to reassure Astar that Stella had only fainted. Thank the three for Zeph and her stern wrangling of Astar's crazed concern, because she managed to calm him down before he became a rampaging grizzly and tore his arms out of his sockets. Jak might be cocky and arrogant enough to take on the shapeshifters, but no one really wanted to fight a grizzly with a few daggers and a sadly now-bent-beyond-repair sword.

By the time Jak drank down a third mug of Gen's warm brew—Danu, he was thirsty!—Lena had confirmed that Stella was simply sleeping off the intensive healing, and Astar had come to embrace Jak in a bear hug that was all human and no claws. They'd stretched Stella out to sleep on the table in his place, and Jak sat near her feet, where he could keep an eye on her.

Jak had also taken in his changed circumstances, and had wit enough to ask questions. "Why am I wearing my Feast of Moranu outfit?" A memory came to him of the tentacle monster shredding the leathers from his body with each stinging lash. He groaned and raked a hand through his hair. "I'm out of clothes, aren't I? This is all I have."

Lena and Gen exchanged uneasy glances, and Gen nodded a bit too enthusiastically, while Lena shook her head. He raised a brow at them.

"We thought you were dead, Jak," Zeph said, raising a hand when they all tried to shush her. "Why lie to him? He's alive and with us, thanks to Stella. But we thought we'd lost you. So we washed you up and put you in your best clothes."

Jak glanced around the table he now sat on the edge of, dangling his booted feet as he sipped a fourth mug of Gen's tea. They'd draped the table with a blue cloth and had arrayed his weapons around him—though he'd already sheathed them all on his person. He was sitting on his own bier, a decidedly odd feeling. "Not every day a man gets a glimpse of his own funeral," he remarked. They all groaned or scowled at him, and he grinned at their discomfort. "But thanks for at least burying me with my boots on."

"It's not funny, Jak!" Lena was one of the scowlers, fists on hips. "We were going to *burn* you. The ground is too frozen for digging. If not for Stella, we would've consigned you to death while you were still alive."

"It's not funny at all, Jak," Gen chimed in, folding her arms and giving him a matching frown.

Zeph met his gaze, her sharp blue eyes glinting, and he

knew she at least found it kind of funny. Astar looked too guilt-ridden to feel anything but that, and Stella slept peacefully.

"Where's Rhy?" he asked, glancing around the room again. Just the six of them. "Is he—" Memory hit him like a fist. "Danu—he never came back?"

The grim expressions of the group verified it, Lena turning her stricken gaze to the window.

"How long has it been?" he asked, aiming the question at Astar. He'd do best to be thinking about next steps.

"Just since last night," Astar replied, shaking himself as if shedding water. "It's midmorning now."

Hmm. How long had he been dead, or close to it? Most of the night, sounded like. Not worth dwelling on, though. "Were those your tentacle monsters, do you think?" he asked Zeph and Lena.

Zeph shrugged ruefully. "Now we know what they looked like under that leaf detritus."

"Interesting," Lena added, "but I didn't need to know this badly."

"So, the same thing happened again," Jak mused. "They opened a rift and pushed some beasties through to attack us. And took Rhy back through?"

"Or he fell through," Zeph suggested. "It's easy to do, especially if it was on the ground or something."

"It is," Lena confirmed. "And it's still there. I'm getting better at sensing them. There's another out in the direction where the thing was taking Stella. Likely planning to take her with it back to the alter-realm."

Remembering the tentacle monster's determined trajectory, Jak had to agree. "If Zeph's experience holds true, then Rhy is stuck in wolf form in the alter-realm. He's canny and capable. Can he have survived this long?"

Zeph and Lena exchanged wordless looks again. "Zeph would've been fine," Lena volunteered, "if she hadn't been trying to save me. So I'm going to say Rhy will be sticking it out and waiting to be rescued."

"Depending on what part of the alter-realm he entered," Zeph cautioned. "That realm and ours don't match up exactly. What if he emerged in their equivalent of Lake Sullivan?"

"Wolves can swim," Lena replied staunchly.

"But they can't fly," Zeph pointed out. "What if he—"

"What-ifs are pointless," Astar interrupted that depressing tack before Jak could. "We have to assume Rhy is surviving and waiting for rescue. We have to go after him."

"I didn't mean to imply otherwise," Zeph said, sounding chastened. "I'll go."

"You can't go alone," Astar countered, looking like he really wanted to forbid her from going at all.

"I'm the only one who *can* go," she argued evenly. "My gríobhth form is the only way we know of to consciously travel to the alter-realm."

"And it nearly killed you to return last time," Astar informed her tightly.

"Believe me, I remember." She grimaced. "But we can't abandon Rhy."

"I wasn't suggesting that." Astar scrubbed his hands over his scalp. "We also can't keep expecting Stella to keep yanking us back from the jaws of death."

"I didn't die on purpose," Jak pointed out, stung.

"No, I didn't mean it like that." Astar inclined his head ruefully. "I'm just doing a piss-poor job of leading you all. I feel like we're blundering from one disaster to another here."

"Not blundering," Jak corrected, his gaze on Stella's fluttering lids. "We're being hunted. And Stella is awake."

Indeed, she opened her eyes, once again a calm gray. She smiled up at Astar, who'd immediately gone to her side. Jak squeezed her ankle through the long sleeping gown she wore—she must've been asleep and recovering, too, before she revived him—and she levered up onto her elbows, giving him an assessing look. "How do you feel?" she asked.

"You're the one laid out on the impromptu bier," he pointed out, "while I'm hale, hearty, and upright. So who should be asking that question?"

She laughed. "Clearly Jak is just fine. And so am I." She brushed off Astar's supporting hands. "I'm all right, Willy. That was just a big healing drain, even with the focusing power of the Star."

Jak pulled the jewel from his pocket and handed it to her. "Speaking of which, you left this inside my shirt when you were feeling me up." He gave her a slow wink, and she blushed.

Astar growled, a deep rumble in his chest, and Stella swatted him. "Stop that. You promised." When he lifted his palms in surrender, she scooted closer to sit beside Jak, her arm brushing his lightly, dangling her feet over the edge of the table. "I agree with Jak. Except I don't think *we* are being hunted. I think *I* am."

EVERYONE BEGAN PROTESTING, except for Jak, who only regarded her gravely. "It makes sense, doesn't it?" she asked him, trusting that he'd give her the truth. "It explains the pattern."

"Yes," he agreed, his dark eyes sober. "I thought so before, but this last attempt made it crystal clear. This intelligence from the alter-realm recognizes you and knows how to target you. And it seems to want to acquire you." His words gave her a shiver, remembering how those tentacles had held her immobile, how the intelligence mobilizing them had batted her sorcery away like a bothersome gnat. Jak seemed to follow her thoughts, his jaw firming. "Which is why you can't go with Zeph."

The others had quieted down to listen by then. "Who said anything about Stella going with Zeph to the alter-realm?" Astar demanded.

"No one said it, but Stella was considering it," Jak said. "Weren't you?"

"I'm small and light enough for Zeph's gríobhth form to carry," she replied, wondering how he'd divined her thoughts. His kiss still tingled on her lips, a delightful aftertaste of him. Did he realize? She didn't think so. For the moment, she held the amazing revelation close to her heart. "And Lena can't go back." Her gaze went to Lena, who had her hands folded together, fingers interlaced, knuckles white with tension, terror wafting chill off of her.

"I can go back," Lena asserted, but her voice wobbled, and

it didn't take an empath to know Lena couldn't face the alter-realm and its denizens. Not yet. Maybe not ever.

Stella turned to Jak, raising a brow at him. "If Zeph's locked into gríobhth form again, she'll need someone with her with words and opposable thumbs, just in case."

"Not necessarily," Zeph countered with a proud tilt of her chin. "Who am I going to talk to—the monkey-lizards? And thumbs aren't everything."

"How will you carry a wolf back?" Stella asked.

"He can jump on." Zeph shrugged, elaborately. "Rhy and I have been practicing."

"And how is a wolf going to hold on?"

Zeph opened her mouth and closed it.

"Exactly," Stella replied. "I'm the logical choice."

"And I'm the Emperor of Dasnaria," Jak said, lightly enough, but with a bite beneath it. "*You* can't even defend yourself."

Stella felt her jaw sag at the unexpected insult, then drew herself up. "I have sorcerous skills you can't imagine."

"Pfft." His huff of disgust actually blew back the hairs around her face. "What if your skills don't work there, or work sideways like Lena's?"

She didn't want to contemplate that lowering possibility. Someone had to go with Zeph, and that was all that mattered.

"Tell me," Jak said, leaning in closer. "Why did you need the Star to fight the tentacle monsters here?"

Searching for an answer that would appease him, Stella found herself wilting at the knowing spark in his eyes.

"You sent me for the Star," he continued, "because you

didn't have enough power on your own."

"Is that true?" Astar demanded, and Stella had to acknowledge that with a short nod.

But it made her remember... She'd reached out and spoken into Jak's mind. And he'd heard her, despite having no sorcery of his own. He'd let her direct his body, too—something Aunt Andi could do, but that had taken her years of practice to master—and Stella had been able to use the Star through him. Jak, dark gaze fastened on hers, nodded as if he followed these thoughts too. *A matter of familiarity and trust.* Could it be?

Finally, Jak tore his eyes from hers and looked at Astar. "I'm going with Zeph. I'm no heavier than Lena."

Astar looked incredulous. "I feel I should point out that you were dead until just a little while ago."

"Not entirely," Stella corrected, though it hardly mattered now.

"And clearly it didn't take," Jak said with a cocky grin that he slanted at her. "Thanks to our personal star."

"Still, are you even up for this, Jak?" Astar asked, frowning—though whether from concern or from irritation with Jak's flirting, she wasn't sure. Her twin was going to have to get over that, however, as Stella had no intention of indulging his overprotectiveness.

"Let's find out." Nimbly, Jak sprang down from the table, testing whether his legs would hold him. Pulling two daggers simultaneously, he spun them, then threw both in quick succession. Eyeing the point on the wall he'd pinned, he strode over to retrieve them. He moved well, with his usual liquid grace. The striking scarlet leathers he'd worn to the ball that long night at Ordnung clung enticingly to his leanly muscled frame.

"He looks good to me," Gen murmured in Stella's ear, having sidled close—and Stella didn't disagree.

"Good enough," Jak declared. "Let's retrieve Rhy from the evil clutches of the alter-realm and get away from this creepy empty inn."

"I feel I should point out," Lena said, calmer now that she knew she didn't have to go back, "that it's entirely possible the denizens of this inn all went into the same rift that Rhyian did. They might all need rescuing."

They fell silent, contemplating that. Jak spun a blade thoughtfully, expression neutral, but eyes dark with some unnamed emotion as they rested on Stella. "If they do, they do," he decided. "Zeph and I will change tack accordingly, as necessary. We'll bring everyone back that we can."

Stella didn't have to read Jak's mind to know that he thought the odds of the people surviving weren't good—and she had to agree.

"If you *can* even get back yourselves," Gen said quietly, then lifted her chin when everyone turned to look at her. "It needs saying. Zeph and Lena said they circled for hours searching for a return rift, and it was so narrow Zeph almost didn't fit through."

"You're right, Gen." Astar tipped his head in acknowledgment. "And you're not saying anything I haven't been thinking, too." His summer-blue gaze rested on Zeph, pain in his eyes. "I've been weighing the math. We're risking two more people to rescue one. We stand to lose all three of you."

Lena spun on him, fiery with outrage. "We cannot just leave Rhyian there! Or the innocent people from this inn."

Astar held up placating hands. "I'm not arguing for that course of action, Lena. Just pointing out that the odds aren't on our side here." He looked to Stella. "Do you see anything at all that would be helpful? If you're not too tired to look," he added hastily.

She felt surprisingly good, in truth. Better than she should for the massive effort that healing Jak had required. Vigor and spring-green vitality circulated with abandon through her body, as if she herself had benefitted from healing. Recalling how it had seemed she inhaled her own magic back again from Jak's kiss, she considered him thoughtfully—then set it aside to contemplate later, and cast her internal gaze to the future. "I see this inn in the near future, bustling with people. I can't be sure they're the same ones, but they seem familiar with the place, not new stewards of it. And I see us, all of us, including Rhy, arriving at a snowy castle that could be Marcellum." Very carefully, she avoided looking past that moment in time. But the vision seized her anyway. Her alone in the tower in a field of lilies. Never leaving it.

Astar gave her a searching look. "Anything else?"

"No, that's all." She pasted on her most sincere expression, and Astar nodded solemnly in thanks, though Jak studied her with a too-knowing gaze.

Astar shrugged ruefully. "I think we have to try. I don't like it, but perhaps Zeph and Jak—especially better prepared this time—will be able to return more easily."

"I have an idea," Stella said, thinking it through as she

spoke. Though Astar would be the one to make the decision, she found herself positing the suggestion to Jak. "Lena and I will be staying behind. We can make ourselves useful. We've gotten better at closing, or at least narrowing the rifts," she said to Lena, who nodded cautiously. "What if we work in the other direction—holding the rift open?"

Lena widened her eyes. "That's a clever idea."

Jak shook his head vigorously. "No, that's a tremendously stupid idea."

"Why?" she demanded, a bit stung. Even Lena, easily the smartest among them, thought it was clever.

"What about what comes through the rift from the alter-realm to here while you're standing there holding the door open for it?" Jak demanded, stalking up to her, his anger—and fear for her—palpable. "You admitted you think the intelligence—and I still think we need a better name for it—is hunting *you* in particular. What are you going to do when, not if, it sends something even worse to grab you?"

She set her teeth against his scathing disdain for her skills. "I won't be alone and helpless. Lena will be helping me, and Astar and Gen will be there to defend us. Their grizzly and saber-cat forms are formidable."

"Let me remind you," he snarled, dark eyes flashing, "of our battle with those tentacle creatures *just last night*. You had Lena helping you, and Zeph and Gen at their most fearsome fighting the thing. Plus you had me, and I'm a better bladesman than Astar—no offense."

"None taken," Astar replied soberly. "You are."

"And that's when he's not doing double duty with claws,"

Jak continued remorselessly. "And still you were snatched by that *thing*." He gritted out the words as if each one pained him, which she knew they did, feeling with him that desperation and hopelessness as he chased after her. "Don't risk yourself," he said in a low voice. "I'm begging you."

Even though her heart throbbed in sympathy with his, she firmed her resolve. "I could ask you the same."

"I'm not risking myself foolishly," he retorted. "I know what I'm doing."

"Oh, and I *don't*?" she spat back. "Don't pull that Dasnarian manly-man-must-protect-the-fragile-females attitude, lest you begin to sound like my brother."

"Hey," Astar protested, but Zeph shushed him.

"It's not because you're female." Jak was fully incensed now, much too close, almost close enough for her hard nipples to brush his chest.

"Then what is it?" she spat back at him, the jaguar in her snarling, the woman wanting to claw and taste.

"Where the fuck were your daggers?" he demanded.

Her daggers? "Don't shout at me, Jak."

"I will shout at you when it's important," he countered, though he lowered his voice. "Answer my question. Your Silversteel daggers that I showed you how to use not two days ago. Where were they when the tentacle creature seized you?"

Oh. Hrm. She couldn't quite meet Jak's gaze and looked past him. "In my bags."

Nobody said anything, the expectant silence thick. She found herself flushing for no good reason at all. Jak didn't speak a word, but he audibly *fulminated* from a handsbreadth away.

"Why," he asked, very quietly, though no doubt their audience could overhear just fine, "are your weapons packed away where they won't do you any Danu-cursed good?" He finished on a near shout again, flinging the not-a-question at her.

Wetting her lips, she looked to Astar, who only regarded her with a neutral expression, making it clear that if she didn't want him to interfere in her relationship with Jak—such as it was—then he wouldn't interfere at all. Zeph's eyes glittered sapphire bright with fascination, Lena and Gen also watching with great interest. So lovely to know they were entertained.

"Answer my question, Stella," Jak said with fevered intensity. When she still couldn't quite meet his eyes, he took her chin in his hand, making her look at him. His touch sang through her skin. Not hurting her. Had he even noticed? He'd kissed her, too, when he'd first awakened. Firm, arousing, devastating—and too quickly over. Dropping her gaze to his mouth, she craved that taste again. Those enticing lips moved, curling with demand. "Answer me," he repeated.

"You don't get to order me around," she finally answered, though her voice trembled.

"In this, I'm going to," he replied, sounding calmer as he released her, but his eyes held a wildness. "If you'd had your daggers on you, where they should be at all times, you could've cut yourself loose from those tentacles like Lena did."

With a sinking sensation, Stella realized she had no argument there. She nodded slightly, conceding the point.

Jak relaxed, but barely. "If you don't want me out of my

mind worrying about you getting dragged off again while I'm possibly fighting for my life in the alter-realm, then you are going to get those daggers and satisfy me that you *will* use them."

She wanted to argue. She hated the idea of shoving those blades into another living creature. "There's no time for that," she ventured, glancing to the others again.

"There is, actually," Gen offered, her smile bright and helpful. "Jak hasn't eaten since midday yesterday, and that was road rations, and Zeph hasn't eaten much either, what with all that's happened. Both of you should eat a hearty meal before you go, to give you the best chance. I'll need at least an hour to cook. Two would be better for a substantial meal."

"I'll help," Lena offered.

Jak smiled thinly. "There you go. Let's get your bags. We'll do some knifework while Gen and Lena cook."

"I'll help with the blade practice," Astar offered, taking a step toward them.

"No, you won't," Zeph declared, hauling him back and fluttering her lashes. "You're going to give me a proper goodbye. Just think—we might never see each other again."

"Zephyr," Astar protested, stricken. "Don't say things like that."

Behind Astar's back, Zeph gave Stella a satisfied simper, perfectly aware that Stella would've been grateful for someone else to ease this humming tension between her and Jak. She'd never seen Jak like this. Where had the happy-go-lucky friend of her youth gone, and where had this simmeringly danger-ous—and sexually fierce—man come from? Worse, now that she'd been so thoroughly a part of him, they'd be able to physically touch without it hurting her.

The revelation came with a rush of joy underscored with stark fear.

She had no reason to hold him off.

She had no excuse to hold him off.

And her future still hadn't changed.

"Your daggers, Stella," Jak reminded her, as if there were some possible way for her to have forgotten already. "Your bags are where?"

"In my room," she huffed in resignation. "I'll go get them."

"I'll come with you."

"I can meet you back down here," she said. The idea of being alone with Jak in her room gave her stomach an unfamiliar flutter.

"We might as well practice in there," he replied. "As good a place as any."

"It's small," she pointed out dubiously.

"I'm sure, but what you need to learn is close infighting. How to deal with an attack that has made it through the rest of us. A confined space is actually better." He returned her gaze evenly, a glint of challenge in his dark eyes.

"Come on, then," she sighed. "If you insist."

~ 13 ~

H E DID INSIST. In fact, he'd been moments from falling to
his knees and begging her to become a bird and fly far,
far away from this wretched hellhole. That she'd agreed that
the intelligence from the alter-realm was seeking her specifically had rimed his heart with a fear he'd never felt for his own
hide. He needed to protect her with a primitive urgency that
defied logic.

He didn't care how much it pissed her off: She was going
to learn to wield those blades or... He didn't know what, but
something. He wasn't afraid of going to the alter-realm, but he
was gut-wateringly terrified of coming back to find her gone.
Or worse.

In a rare temper, Stella flung open the door of a room on
the second level. An unmade bed took up most of the small
space, her minimal baggage on a low table nearby. With her
back firmly to him, she rummaged in her bags, searching for
her blades. Jak leaned against the wall, arms folded, watching
her, keeping his body loose and relaxed—but fighting his own
mounting temper as she took forever to find the fucking
things.

At last—minutes later, during which a toddler could've

skinned and gutted her—she exclaimed in relief and turned to show him the daggers. Her triumphant smile faded at whatever she saw in his face. Probably good that his expression got the point across, as the next step would be throttling her.

"Put them on," he instructed softly, not trusting himself not to shout at her again.

She sighed in exasperation. "Is it really necessary to—"

"Yes," he bit out. "See how the pretty daggers sit in sheaths on that lovely belt? You buckle the belt around your gorgeous hips, and then you wear them. All. The. Time."

Her eyes darkened, thunderclouds gathering. "There is no need to be sarcastic with me."

"Isn't there? Then, pray tell, what *will* get through your thick skull?"

The sense of a pending storm thickened. "Don't you speak to me that way, Jakral Konyngrr."

He rolled his eyes, making his disdain clear. "I'll speak to you any way I like. Not as if you can do anything about it."

Lightning flashed in her eyes. "You forget that I have offensive magics. Powerful ones."

"Useless ones," he sneered, goading her further.

"How dare you!" Her streaming dark hair stirred as if in an unseen wind.

Though the hairs stood up on the back of his neck, he didn't move, considered yawning in her face, but even he didn't have the balls to push her that far. Instead he lifted a shoulder and let it fall. "I dare because I'm a better fighter than you are. Not because you're female, but because you're defenseless. That's why you need protecting. So, quit whining about everyone being overprotective and accept that you need a big strong man to—"

With an incoherent screech, she dropped the knife belt and hurled a ball of blue lightning at him. As it flew toward him, he pulled a dagger, threw it, and ducked. The lightning grazed his shoulder with a light tingle—he hadn't even needed to evade that tickle—and his blade shaved off a long lock of Stella's hair before thudding into the wall behind her.

Stella gaped at him. Without speaking, she dropped her gaze to the severed lock of hair lying like a snake at her feet. "I..." She lifted her eyes to his, shock clear in them. "You... you threw a knife at me."

"You threw lightning at me," he pointed out.

"Because you provoked me!"

"Yes, I did. Worked pretty well, except that was the most pitiful lightning I've ever seen. If that's the best you can do, then—"

"It isn't," she snapped.

"Why not?" When she didn't reply, he pushed away from the wall. "Because you pulled your punch."

Unhappily, she watched him pick up the lock of hair. Coiling it into a tight circle, he stuck it in his pocket. A nice keepsake. "All the magic in the world does you no good if you won't use it," he said.

"I can use it."

"I know you *can*. I also know you won't."

Pressing her lips together in something just shy of a mulish pout, she glared at him. "Are you saying you wish I *had* hurt you?"

He tugged the shortened lock of hair. "I can take it."

She didn't smile. "You're not immortal, Jak."

"And yet I survived a brush with death, thanks to you." He grinned jauntily at her, unbothered that she didn't return it. "Let's try that again, but this time, try harder."

"But I don't want to hurt you!"

He blew out an impatient breath. "If something is trying to kill you, then it's your enemy and deserves to be hurt."

"You aren't my enemy," she pointed out.

"I'm glad to hear that, but you still need to learn to strike true. You can always heal me again."

"True…" She gazed at him, uncertain.

"I'd rather you hurt me a little bit now than deal me a mortal wound by getting injured or killed. I couldn't survive that."

Her eyes widened, and he considered maybe he'd said too much. "Besides," he added with a grin, "at this rate, you'll have no hair left, and I'll be untouched. I'm really not worried." Drawing a new blade, he spun it through his fingers, picking out a new lock of hair to sever.

She growled low in her throat. "You wouldn't."

"I would, and I will," he said, letting his grim resolve show. "Or maybe I'll just aim for that sleeping gown. It won't last long against my blades and would be a fun striptease." He leered at her. "Finally I'll get to see you naked—a dream come true."

With a shocked gasp, she blushed hot. "You—" She bit down on repeating the challenge, possibly reading his utterly serious intent. Briefly, a jaguar stood where she'd been, then she reappeared in her fighting leathers, her hair tightly braided back, a smug look on her face.

"Do you think that will spare you?" he murmured, just to see her blush deepen. "I could still slice those leathers off you."

"But you won't," she replied with confidence, "because you'd risk cutting me, and you would never hurt me."

That was true. Too bad she knew it. "Moving on. What was your first mistake?"

"Pulling my punch."

"No, that was your second mistake." Scooping up the knife belt from the floor, he dangled it in her face. "Never, ever throw away your blades."

"You throw your knives all the time," she pointed out.

"Yes, but I know what I'm doing, and it's still a calculated risk. *You* will do best to keep your blades in your hands." Threading the belt through the loops on her pants, he settled it low on her hips, moving the sheaths to the optimum position. "How's that for drawing?"

He glanced up as he asked, finding her face very close to his. The storm in her gray eyes had subsided, leaving them the clear misty color of the sea just before sunrise. "I feel the same," she said, briefly confusing him. "When I thought they might be right, that you really were dead, I thought I might break apart into a million fragments."

For once, no clever remark leapt to his tongue. He smoothed her hair back from her face, careful not to brush her skin. It clung like silk to his fingers, and he knew she was right—he would never jeopardize her beautiful hair, he loved it too much. The thought of slowly cutting away her clothing, however... Well, it was a good thing he was getting practiced at exercising iron control over his lust around her. Her lips parted, her kitten tongue darting out to wet them. So tempting to kiss her just then.

But time was short, and this was more important.

"We'll just have to keep each other alive, then," he replied. "Now, try drawing your blades."

With a sigh—was she disappointed he hadn't kissed her? If so that might work to his advantage—she drew one blade. He shook his head. "No, both at once."

She tried again, far too slow and clumsy. Biting back his impatience, as she clearly hadn't practiced this at all, he moved behind her. "Like this."

Grasping her wrists over her leather cuffs, he aligned his arms to hers. Deliberately slow, he guided her hands to the sheathed daggers, though that didn't help to adjust her grip on the hilts. "Do you have your gloves?"

"You can touch my hands," she said, sounding like she was holding her breath.

He caught his own breath. "Are you sure?"

She huffed out a small laugh. "Jak, you kissed me before, on the table."

He appreciated that she didn't call it a bier. "You were healing me at the time, so I thought it might not be as painful." In truth, he hadn't been thinking at all, but he didn't want to admit that. It had been unforgivably selfish of him. But she'd looked so beautiful, and he wanted her so badly...

"It wasn't," she breathed, leaning her delicate body back against his, her deliciously round bottom nestling against his groin. "It felt... wonderful. I think—I'm pretty sure you can touch me now."

"I can?" His chest felt tight, holding in too much hope. "What changed?"

"A matter of familiarity and trust," she whispered. "When you let me inside your mind to use the Star through you, I think you became like a part of me."

He groaned, releasing her wrists to slide his arms around her, one embracing her slim waist, the other splayed over her flat belly, perilously close to slipping just a bit more to cup her sex. Sternly ordering his hands to stay put, he buried his face in her fragrant hair, holding her against him, indulging in the longing and the temporary sating of his craving for her. He wanted to take her, right then and there.

He wanted her to stay alive even more.

She tried to turn in his arms, but he stopped her. "No."

"Jak, if this is our only chance to be together, then—"

"Then we'll have to make sure it isn't our only chance. That means using this time wisely."

"I never realized how single-minded you are," she grumbled.

Delighted with her, about out of his mind with desire, he pressed a kiss to her temple, lingering there to taste her skin, to savor the scent, texture, and flavor of her. Savoring her answering tremble of need. "I'm surprised to hear you say that," he murmured, "as you have turned out to be the one person I'm single-mindedly fixed on."

Then he made himself let go of her and put his hands over hers—lightly at first, testing for any signs of discomfort from her—then lacing their fingers together when she didn't flinch. Hers felt fine as lace, soft and elegantly boned. "Is this all right?" he asked quietly.

"Yes," she replied on a feathery sigh. "It's lovely."

Guiding her hands to the hilts of her Silversteel daggers, he wrapped both their hands around them. "Like this. Feel that angle? Hold them like you might an egg—don't crush the shell, but hold on firmly enough not to drop them. Good. Now draw them like this, easing them from the sheaths. No—don't jerk them. Treat them like a cat you wish to pet, ease them along."

"Are they cats or eggs?" she asked, but on a laugh—and she was doing much better.

"Whatever metaphor works." With reluctance, he released her hands and came back in front of her. "Show me. Good. Much better."

"Will wonders never cease?" she griped, but she looked pleased with herself.

"I want you to practice that," he told her. "Every spare moment. Over and over until you don't think about it."

"Is that why you're always playing with your blades?" she asked curiously. "I've wondered."

He smiled, charmed beyond reason at the idea of her wondering about him. "Keep practicing. Don't stop just to talk. You can do both at once. Your resheathing should be as smooth as your draw. Don't fumble for the opening or scrape the sides of the sheaths. Better. And yes, Mom taught me this same way. Having a blade in your hand should feel natural, like a part of you. At this point, I have to remind myself *not* to draw my blades and play with them. Royalty and diplomats don't always respond well."

She smiled softly at his grin. "I think you could charm anyone into putting up with anything."

"A nice thought." Really, it shouldn't make him feel so giddy to hear such things from her. It was like being drunk on the smoothest, rarest whiskey in the world. "Ready for the next step?"

Her smile faded. "Maybe."

He backed up a few steps. "Sheathe your blades. I'm going to attack you. You will pull both daggers and use them to defend yourself *and* hit me with your magic at the same time."

She frowned, looking at her hands. "I'm not sure I can."

"Do you *need* your hands to shoot lightning or whatever at me?"

"Well, no, but it's—"

"There's no 'but' to it," he interrupted. "Your hands belong to your daggers."

"It's easier to use my hands to shape the magic," she insisted.

"This isn't about easy. This is about life and death. Learn to do it the hard way." He leapt at her.

She shrieked in surprise, fending him off with her bare hands.

"No!" he shouted in her face, seizing her wrists and backing her against the wall. "You just died."

She gaped at him, hurt in her expression that was like a dagger to his own heart. "You scared me."

"Good!" He wanted her to be scared, didn't know how else to get her to react to danger.

"That's harsh, Jak."

"Yes, it is." He leaned his forehead against hers, hating that he'd had to frighten her like that. "Time is slipping away. I don't have the luxury of easing you into this. Fight me."

"All right," she agreed shakily. "You just took me by surprise."

"I know. Enemies don't usually introduce themselves before they attack. This has to become reflex." Releasing her, he backed up a few steps.

This time, though shaky, she watched him warily. She held her hands poised near the sheaths. Too much of a tell, but they could refine that later. This time when he leapt at her, she drew the daggers and managed to hit him with a puff of something that burned a little. He still pinned her to the wall because she didn't actually point the daggers at him, but it was a big step.

"Better." He grinned at her. "Again, but stronger. Don't let me pin you. I pin you like this, you're dead."

She looked up through her lashes, eyes crystal through black lace, her body thrumming against his. "This isn't exactly a punishment."

"No," he agreed. "If we had time, I'd exact a toll from you each time I managed to pin you."

"Like what?" She moved against him, her hips pressing into him, though he doubted she was aware of it.

He shouldn't play this game, but it was far too tempting to tease her. "You'd forfeit a piece of clothing for each failure," he murmured, caressing her cheek with his lips. She trembled, but not in pain. "And once you were completely naked, I'd put you over my knee and spank you."

Her whole body moaned. "That... doesn't sound like a punishment either," she breathed.

"Danu, Stella, don't say that to me." Everything in him slavered to make that image come true. He made himself let her go. "Let's do it again."

She groaned in frustration, sheathing her blades. "You're a tyrant!"

"When it comes to saving your gorgeous ass, yes I am." He grinned at her consternation, then leapt.

IT WAS A full two hours before Gen and Lena announced the meal was ready. By then, both he and Stella were drenched in sweat—and he was sporting new bruises from hitting the wall when she blasted him with her magic, and bleeding profusely from a decent slice across his chest.

"Well, well, well," Zeph said from the doorway, arching her brows. "I've heard of blood play as kink before, but..."

Stella pointed a finger at her. "Don't start. Jak made me do it."

"I'm sure that's what all the girls say," Zeph drawled, then ducked with shapeshifter speed as a fireball winged at her head. She watched it splatter against the wall behind her, leaving a singed spot as sparks showered down. Whistling, Zeph eyed Stella with new respect. "I didn't know you could do that."

"I didn't either," Stella admitted. Going to Jak, she traced the cut on his chest, the tingle of her healing magic as profound as if she'd stroked his cock. Jak stared firmly at the wall so Zeph wouldn't detect his misery. "Jak's an excellent combat teacher."

"If that's what you kids are calling it these days," Zeph agreed cheerfully. She shone with happy satiety, practically preening her unseen feathers, leaving no doubt how she and Astar had spent the last two hours. Jak envied them, but he couldn't be bitter about it—Stella really had come a long way. "Anyway," Zeph continued, "the meal is almost ready. I've been sent to summon you."

"We'll be right down," Stella replied absently, infusing him with a general flood of well-being to catch the last of the bruises.

"As you say," Zeph replied and skipped off, humming a bawdy tune he recognized, about pirates deflowering maidens.

"Any pain?" Stella asked, looking *through* him with silvery eyes.

"None at all," he lied. Between the physical proximity to her and the repeated healing, he'd reached a state of almost transcendent need. Agonizing, but also giving him an edge that would serve him well on this mission to the alter-realm.

He leaned back against the wall, settling his hands on her hips and drawing her to lean against him. A side benefit of the last grueling hours was that—paradoxically, given how he'd repeatedly attacked and frightened her—she'd grown used to touching him. She wasn't skittish around him at all, immediately softening against him.

Splaying her hands over his chest, she fiddled with the slice in his fancy dress shirt. "I'm very sorry to have ruined these."

"I'm not. I might be in a bad way for clothes, but I'm glad to know you'll use those blades with a solid strike. That's worth any price. Remember: if you can see them, go for the eyes and ears."

She made a face. "Eyew."

"Lovely, squishy targets."

"That does *not* help, Jak."

He laughed, but she regarded him gravely. "Promise you'll come back?"

"What will you give me if I do?" he teased.

"You'll have to come back to find out," she replied, a hint of humor sparkling through her obvious worry for him.

"Then you have to promise to be here when I return."

She nodded somberly. "If anything comes at me, I'll be ready."

"I know you will be." She'd come so far, showing rare grit and determination. Once she got over the fear of hurting him, she'd demonstrated a delightful predatory side. He had to trust in that.

"We should head down to eat," he said, though he made no move to go.

"We should." Her gaze went to his mouth. "But first... Jak?"

"Yes?" His heart thudded, and it took everything in him not too hope for too much.

"Would you kiss me? For real this time."

"The first one was real." Though he understood her point.

She shook her head solemnly. "We were both... caught up. I want you to kiss me without the healing between us, without anyone watching. Just us." Her gaze went to his lips. "I want to feel you."

"Are you sure?" he asked, though his hands tightened on her hips of their own accord. "I don't want to hurt you."

She smiled, sensuous and all woman. "Surely that's my line."

"A point to the lovely lady," he agreed, then sobered. "Seriously, I can wait. I meant it when I said we can take this slow."

"I know, but..." Moving slowly, she slid her hands behind his neck, skin to skin, no healing sparkle to it. Tasting and absorbing him. "I'm finding I like the feeling of you being in my head."

"Probably a good thing, since you've been in every part of my body."

She cocked her head, her stroking fingers on his neck driving him wild. "I wasn't sure if you remembered that."

"I remember everything."

"Did you—do you—mind?" she asked hesitantly. "I know that had to be strange, having me take over your body."

"I don't mind." He smiled at her, his heart feeling as if it might overflow. "My body is yours."

She caught her breath. "I'm going to hold you to that."

"I hope you will." Pushing his luck, he slid his hands down over her perfectly rounded ass, enjoying the widening of her gorgeous eyes. Tipping his head slightly, he eased closer, giving her time to change her mind, but she held still, her eyes fluttering closed, until only breath whispered between them.

He brushed her lips with his, aware of the stuttering hiss of her response. Pulling back just enough to speak, he asked, "Too much?"

"No," she breathed. "More, please."

A smile curved his lips, and then he touched his mouth to hers again, light, butterfly-wing kisses to lure her in, to soothe and delight. She responded hesitantly, a trace of caution in it, but soon warmed, deepening the kiss of her own accord, opening to him like a fragrant flower under the moon, petals unfurling, her heated scent enveloping him and making his head swim. Making him want to drag her to the floor and strip her naked so he could kiss every fingertip of skin, to bury his mouth in her sex and taste her until she screamed his name.

Stella moaned, deep in her throat, and he knew she'd caught the fantasy in his mind. So tempting to make it real, right then and there. So not something that could happen. Yet.

So he lightened the kisses, gently pulling back, until he could gaze into her beloved face again. She gazed back, soft and dreamy—but this dreaminess was all for him, her lips rosy and full from his kisses, her eyes silvery with desire, full of the awareness of what they brewed between them.

"We should've done that a long time ago," she murmured.

"I tried to tell you." He gave her a cocky grin, certain it fell short in the face of the emotions storming his heart. "But maybe we needed to travel this path, and this is the exactly right moment."

"It feels right," she agreed, then searched his face with an edge of anxiety in her eyes. "You *will* come back?"

"Only death can stop me," he vowed.

She flinched. "I wish you hadn't put it that way."

"What is death?" he asked lightly, releasing her and setting her on her feet again, then taking her hand and lacing their fingers together. "My sorceress lover is more powerful than mere death."

"Am I your lover, then?" she asked shyly.

"Yes," he replied firmly. "If you'll have me?"

"I will." She nodded, as if confirming to herself. "Though obviously we're not lovers in truth. I must caution you again— even though this touching is fine, that might be all. It might be that we never can be lovers in truth."

"We already are," he told her. Lifting her hand, he kissed the back of it, delighted to feel her shiver, to see her eyes light with joy. "In every way that matters."

"Just remember," she said, sobering, "that if it's not enough for you, I'll let you go. No tears or recriminations. I'll understand."

She clearly did not understand, because he had no intention of letting her go. Ever.

~ 14 ~

"So," LENA SAID, sidling up and looping her arm through Stella's, "did I win the bet?"

Stella tore her gaze from anxiously watching Jak adjusting the riding harness on Zeph's gríobhth back. The storm had finally cleared, and Zeph shone like a second sun in the midday light, fur and feathers bright as hammered gold. Her eagle's head was turned backward, and she clacked her lethally curved beak at Jak in incomprehensible advice while he kept up a running monologue of good-natured retorts.

"What bet?" Stella asked, her mind a blank. Her mind had *been* a blank since that devastating kiss. And it hadn't been devastating in a painful way either—though it had been invasive. Bits of Jak's thoughts, his native exuberance and vitality, swirled inside her mind and blood. Her lips still tingled from the caress of his, and she lifted her fingertips to them, feeling as if the kiss must show.

Lena watched her knowingly, and Stella dropped her hand. "You have that *look*," she said, then sighed wistfully. "I remember feeling like you look right now. I miss it."

Gen came up and took Stella's other arm. "I've *never* felt like Stella looks right now, and *I* miss it."

"Don't be silly," Stella said, though her protest lacked force. "Nothing happened between me and Jak."

"*Nothing?*" Lena raised a brow. "Nothing at *all?*"

"A kiss," Stella admitted, her face heating with the blush. "A lovely, long kiss."

All three sighed dreamily.

"Still a virgin, then." Gen leaned around Stella to waggle her brows at Lena. "Two more nights and you'll have lost the pool, and we know nothing will happen tonight since—" She slammed her mouth closed, then groaned and rubbed her forehead. "I'm really sorry, Nilly. That was beyond thoughtless of me."

"We're all on edge," Stella soothed her, squeezing her arm. She eyed Jak, who was on Zeph's leonine back now, arguing with her about the placement of some strap. Astar stood nearby, offering his advice, and both appeared to be ignoring him. "And we'd be foolish to assume that Zeph and Jak will simply go and come back."

They all absorbed that in silence.

"I feel it should be me going," Lena said quietly. "Rhyian would come for me."

"Sometimes loving someone means standing back and sending the best people for the rescue," Stella said. "Jak can do this."

"Of course he can," Gen agreed staunchly. "They'll bring Rhy back with them, and all of the folk from the inn—and *they* can cook for us tonight."

Jak vaulted from Zeph's back, striding toward them. For the first time, she noticed that the sword that hung from his belt was Astar's Silversteel one—the match to the daggers Ash had gifted her with just before they left on this journey. Jak's own slim sword had been bent out of true during the tentacle-monster attack, and he'd declared his smaller blades sufficient. Stella breathed easier knowing Jak would have the indestructible Silversteel sword.

Jak gave them a cocky grin that didn't match his underlying feelings, but Stella could appreciate the bold face he put on things. Behind him, Zeph ducked her head against Astar's chest, her long tail sunk low, waving sadly as he stroked her feathers.

"Ladies," Jak swept them a bow. "We are ready if you are."

Stella detached herself from the support of her friends, glancing at them to confirm. "We're ready." She produced the Star of Annfwn, holding it in her palm.

Jak frowned at it. "Do you have to hold it in your hand?"

The man never gave up. "I suppose not," she conceded. Another habit to break. She already felt riddled with cracks and creaking strain from changing so much about herself in such a short amount of time. Casting about for a place to put the round jewel, she settled on tucking it into the silk underwear supporting her breasts under the fighting leathers.

Jak followed the stowing of it with his eyes, which danced with amusement and desire when he lifted them to hers. "There are so many things I could say."

"But you won't," she retorted, unable to keep from smiling.

"Good luck, Jak," Gen said, giving him a hug. "I'll guard Nilly's back with my life."

He kissed her cheek. "I know you will, valiant Gen."

Gen took a step back and became the white saber cat, pacing over to the area they'd marked off in the snow to show where the rift lingered.

"Thank you for doing this, Jak," Lena said with quiet intensity.

He lifted her hand and kissed it. "I'll bring him back to you."

"We'll hold the door open," she promised, then went to join Gen.

"He gave you his sword," Stella said to Jak, dipping her chin at the Silversteel.

"Yes." Jak touched the hilt, emotion moving through his eyes. The gift had touched him deeply. "Astar says he prefers the broadsword, and he wants me to keep this, but we'll see."

"You must keep it," she urged. "It fits you."

His lips quirked, doubt in his dark gaze. "I'm not convinced a prince's sword fits a simple sailor."

"That's not all you are, Jak," she replied gravely. "In fact"—she reached for her own Silversteel daggers—"we should trade."

"Absolutely not." He stepped back, holding up his hands. "You need the best possible weapons, and those will serve you well. *If* you remember to use them."

"I'll remember," she assured him, far from the first time.

"If anything starts coming through the rift," Jak added, "I want you to close it. Don't worry about us. We'll find our own way back."

"You think about your job. I'll think about mine," Stella

replied evenly.

He grimaced ruefully. "Good advice, but my thoughts will be with you anyway."

"And mine with you." Abruptly, emotion clogged her throat. It could be from the others, with everyone leaking anxiety, but much of it was her own.

"Do I get a goodbye kiss?" Jak asked, cocking his head uncertainly.

With an incoherent cry, she threw herself into his arms, holding tight as he kissed her. This was no gentle exploration as in her room, nor was it the kiss on his almost-bier, infused with healing magic. His mouth moved over hers with desperate intensity, the power of it rattling her to the core, her body leaping in response. When he broke the kiss, staring down into her face, she throbbed with unfulfilled desire. How had she lived all her life without this?

How could she let him go, never having drunk fully of this cup she'd barely tasted?

"We can finish this when I get back," Jak vowed shakily. "In whatever way we can."

"Good incentive," she agreed.

"As if I needed more." He pressed a kiss to her forehead, right below the point of her widow's peak. "Remember to use your blades. Go for the eyes and ears."

She laughed and pushed him away. "Enough! I will, Mother."

He grinned at her, and they went to Zeph and Astar. "Ready to save the day, stalwart steed?"

Zeph clacked her beak, managing to convey an eyeroll, and

he vaulted onto her back, fastening the straps of the harness around his leanly muscled thighs. "I'm not falling off like *some* people," he taunted Lena, who made a face at him.

Did he realize that Lena had deliberately fallen? Perhaps he'd guessed. It would be like Jak to give Lena reinforcement of that aspect of her story. Stella faced Lena from the other end of the rift, focusing her sorcerous gaze on that slice of oddness, that fold in space that marked the entrance to the alter-realm. It felt odd to draw on the focusing power of the Star from where it nestled near her heart, but it worked just as well. Lena's intent blue gaze met hers, a breeze lifting the caramel strands of her hair as the atmosphere around her shifted with her weather magic. Astar drew his broadsword, holding it two-handed and taking a position to guard Lena from anything that might emerge from the rift. Gen took a similar position at point near Stella, her saber cat's body poised to pounce, claws extended, and an anticipatory gleam in her eye.

With Lena's and her magic interweaving, Stella guided their mental hands to the narrow rift. She really wanted to use her physical hands to mimic the gesture, but Jak was right that the habit had become a crutch. Aware of his gaze on her, she kept her hands down, near the daggers at her hips, and levered open the rift with her mind.

It felt like opening a door into a tropical forest, the warm air riffling out, redolent of rich soil and decomposing vegetation. And there, within that alter-realm, the intelligence sensed her presence, turning to *look* at her with surprise and growing agitation.

She refused to flinch or distress Jak by revealing the discomfiting scrutiny. "It's open," she said calmly.

"Let's do this," Jak declared. Wings half mantled, Zeph leapt into a leonine gallop, plunging into the rift. Just as they went, something within the fold shifted, the air going cool and oddly odorless.

And they were gone.

JAK HAD BEEN braced for a lot of things—including tentacle monsters and a barrage of monkey-lizards—but he hadn't expected the polished stone of the perfectly flat expanse Zeph galloped onto. She immediately slowed her pace, turning in a wide circle so they could take in the landscape. If you could call it that.

Nothing showed in any direction except the black flat under a violet sky, the horizon as perfectly circular as if they were out at sea. Jak whistled, low and long. "So much for your forest."

Zeph clacked an unhappy reply.

"Yeah, no sign of Rhy or any people," he agreed. "And no good jumping-off point for you either." While Jak was lean enough, he still outweighed Lena—and it had been difficult enough on Zeph's wing power to lift off from ground on her own, much less with Lena's weight, let alone his.

She flexed her wings in suggestion, but he shook his head. "I don't want to tax you unnecessarily. We might need your wings if it comes to a fight or escape—and we don't know that we'd see anything more from the air than more of this anyway.

Can you keep circling?"

Obligingly she paced a slow circle while he focused his eyes, searching for any kind of detail. "Do you see anything besides this black flat and violet sky?"

She shook her eagle's head. Then cocked it, stilling as if listening to something.

"Yeah, I hear it too." Straining his ears—wishing his hearing was as keen as his vision or, even nicer, sharp as a shapeshifter's—he closed his eyes to concentrate on hearing and tried to identify the sound. A lonely rising note. A wolf's howl. "Rhyian."

Zeph dipped her beak in confirmation, taking a few steps in that direction.

"Wait," Jak said. "We need to mark this spot somehow, so we can find the rift again." But how? A screeching sound caught his attention, and he looked down to see Zeph scratching an arrow into the shining stone surface with her claws, pointed at the rift. "Smart," he agreed. "Let's go."

Zeph bounded into a run.

Riding a lion turned out to be nothing like riding a horse. Jak did his best to move with her instead of fighting the undulating series of leaps, lying as low over her outstretched neck and under her tightly folded wings as he could to cut wind resistance. Leaning to one side, he peered around the side of her neck, scanning the horizon. Still nothing.

Abruptly, the bottom fell out. Zeph screeched in surprise, matching his startled yelp, and her wings snapped out, pumping to change their plummeting fall to a glide. When Jak managed to swallow his gorge again—maybe that massive meal hadn't been such a great idea—he patted Zeph's shoulder, the powerful muscles bunching rhythmically as she found steady flight.

"My hero," he told her, beyond glad he'd been strapped to the harness or he'd have been a goner. "That was an amazing save."

She rumbled deep in her chest, something between a growl and a purr, a response he could absolutely sympathize with. Glancing up, he took in the parallel straight edges that defined the steep, vertical-sided canyon they'd fallen into, a stripe of empty violet sky beyond. Then, moving carefully, he peered down. The defile was deep and narrow, so much so that the walls appeared to meet at some infinite point of inky blackness that could be the bottom. "Well, this is charming. Do you hear Rhy anymore?"

She shook her head slightly.

"I vote we go back up, then, try to listen for him again. *If* that howl wasn't a lure to lead us into this trap," he added bleakly. Zeph began flying along the course of the defile, her wide wingspan very nearly brushing either side, gradually accelerating and using the lift to gain altitude. She'd been practicing her techniques while scouting and really had gotten impressively good at it. Jak palmed a dagger, just in case, as they reached the surface again. Yes, the riding harness was nice for keeping him from falling off, but mostly he'd wanted to have both hands free.

Nothing awaited them, however, and he sheathed the blade as Zeph landed on the featureless black plain, folding her wings with a relieved huff of air. "Need me to get off so you can rest?" he asked, but she shook her head, canting it in an attitude of listening.

Jak couldn't hear anything, but waited quietly for her. Finally she clacked her beak in annoyance. "Same," he replied. "I say we go back to the rift." She swiveled her head backward to stare at him in patent astonishment. "Working on the theory that the howling was a deliberate distraction," he told her, "to draw us away from that place." Glancing in that direction, though he knew it was right there, his eyes still couldn't pick out the sharp borders of the defile. The black on black blended seamlessly, and he couldn't fault Zeph for falling into it. He'd have done the same—and *he* would have plummeted to his death.

Or would be still falling, if the thing had no bottom. Horrifying thought.

Zeph pointed her beak at the sky, then clacked it at the defile, then up again. No, he didn't like that idea much at all. "You want to use that as a jumping-off point and go up to look around from on high?" he guessed, resigned when she nodded. "All right, if you're feeling up to it."

It was worse this time, knowing what was coming. Jak had never minded heights, having been climbing rigging pretty much as soon as he learned to walk. He'd loved hanging out in the crow's nest, the sense of being on top of the world, alone amidst the perfect circle of sea and sky.

Falling from heights turned out to be decidedly different. Wings spread, Zeph galloped for the edge, and Jak clenched his teeth so he wouldn't scream unmanfully again. They dropped—but not nearly so far, and she controlled the fall, quickly ascending again.

All the same, Jak did not look down at that infinite vanishing point.

Zeph circled as she pumped higher, and he set himself to scanning the landscape in a standard scouting pattern, essentially running transects with his gaze. From this height, he could pick out the line of the defile more easily. And, he noted grimly, the many more exactly like it. They ran in perfectly straight lines, parallel and perpendicular, forming a massive grid.

"This is so not natural," he mused, and Zeph clacked in unhappy agreement. Why would something create such a thing? The perfection of the pattern implied an intelligence at work—probably their old friend popping up again—but what could the purpose be? It reminded him of a board for playing a strategy game. Which made them the game pieces, pawns ignorant of the rules. Not a comforting insight.

Off to right, he saw something flutter. "There!" He pointed, and Zeph swiveled to follow the line of his arm. She saw it too, pivoting on wingtip to fly rapidly in that direction.

As they drew near, he could make out a banner of sorts, made of several shirts tied together, flapping as three people held onto one end, signaling them. They looked like regular folk from the Thirteen Kingdoms. "This isn't the square we landed on, right?"

Zeph shook her head and pointed a paw off to the front and side. Yeah, that was where he thought it was, too. Then, if these were the people from the inn, how did they get onto this square? Because no way could they have crossed those defiles.

Unless he was missing something. And he really hated feeling like he was missing something.

Several of them screamed at the sight of Zeph, dropping the banner and huddling together. Zeph landed well away from them as a woman pushed several children behind her and brandished a cast iron skillet. Jak hastily unbuckled himself from the harness.

"It's all right," he called in Common Tongue, belatedly wondering if these people were even from the same realm as him. They looked like it, but that didn't mean anything. He held up his palms in the universal sign of peaceful intentions— he hoped it was universal, anyway—and walked slowly toward them. "We're friends, here to help you."

A man stepped forward, meaty fists clenched. "Begone, foul monsters!" the man yelled, face contorted with belligerence and fear. At least he screamed at them in Common Tongue.

Jak could take him out easily with a thrown dagger to the throat, but he left his blades sheathed, palms upraised. "Friends," he repeated. "Sent by Her Majesty High Queen Ursula," he hastily improvised, "to rescue you."

Several of the people began murmuring among themselves, the tone turning to hopeful. "Then why are you with that monster?" the man demanded, pointing at Zeph—who flicked her tail and hissed in irritation. Jak gave her a warning look, and she subsided sullenly.

"She's Tala, from Annfwn," Jak replied, going with the truth. Ursula would rather the Tala keep their more mythical forms discreetly hidden, but here in this bizarre alter-realm, all bets were off.

"Oh yeah?" the man sneered. "Let's see it shapeshift, then."

Well, shit. "She can't. Not in this alter-realm. The laws of magic are different here."

"A convenient story." The man glared, unconvinced.

"Seriously?" Jak spat at him. "Because everything else here makes so much sense?"

That had them exchanging uneasy glances, so he pressed his advantage. "You're from the Midway Inn in Erie. You were lured or dragged into a rift behind the inn and ended up here—a land of square grids with uncrossable defiles between."

"The children," the woman spoke up, lowering her skillet. "The children found the hole and disappeared. We set out after them. We've been here without food or water, we don't know how long. Can you get us home?"

"Yes," Jak told her with a firm confidence he didn't feel. There had to be two dozen of them, children and adults. Zeph might be able to hop the kids across to the square that held the rift to home, but not most of the adults—and certainly not that big beefy guy. Except... There must be a rift on this square or they wouldn't be here. "Do you know where you came through?"

The woman pointed. "Over there. But we can't go near it because there's a wolf. We got as far away from it as we could without getting too near this edge. We lost young Ilano before any of us even saw these canyons."

"Biggest damn wolf I've ever seen," meaty guy agreed. He eyed Jak's sword. "Maybe you can kill it for us."

Jak grinned as relief washed through him. Rhy was wisely

sticking close to the rift, though something must be preventing him from crossing back on his own. But if the rift at the inn dumped Rhy and the people here, why had he and Zeph landed in a different spot? Also, it seemed possible that, if they crossed back through the rift on this grid, they might end up somewhere else entirely. At least they could hope it would be in their own world again. After that, getting back to the inn would be a matter of plain geography.

This place made his head hurt.

He glanced at Zeph, whose curved beak hung open in an unsettling smile at the news that Rhy was alive and nearby. "You want to go ahead, find Rhy, and we'll follow?"

She snarled happily and took off in an easy lope in the direction the woman had pointed. The group of people watched in stunned awe.

"Sir?" A kid had slipped their keeper and tugged at his sleeve. Jak crouched to meet the kid's brown eyes. "What kind of monster is that?"

"She's a gríobhth," he answered, using the Tala word. "A gryphon in the Common Tongue."

The beefy man snorted. "Gryphons are a myth."

Jak just shook his head and stood, addressing the group. "She's as real as you or me, and her name is Zephyr. I'm Jakral Konyngrr. You can call me Jak."

"Konyngrr. That's a Dasnarian name," the man said with suspicion.

"Gotten honestly from my Dasnarian father," Jak agreed cheerfully. "My mother was one of Her Majesty's Hawks. We're loyal to the high throne."

Even the big man was mollified by that.

"Hi, Jak. I'm Rika," the kid said.

"Ready to go home, Rika?" He held out a hand, and Rika took it trustingly.

"Will the greebtha kill the wolf?" Rika wondered.

The pronunciation was close enough. "No, because they're friends."

"Figures," the man muttered, and the woman shushed him.

They all began walking, some of the adults carrying the children. They all looked weary and worse for being stranded. "Did you ever see anything else here?" Jak asked the group in general. "Any signs of life besides the wolf?"

Mutterings and head-shaking answered him. "What is this place?" the woman with the skillet asked. "Nothing lives here."

"We don't really know," Jak hedged. Surely he was the worst choice for a diplomat. What would Astar have him say? "Her Majesty has sent us to find out." That was true enough. "And to help anyone who—"

He broke off at a strange hissing sound, a slithering of scales across a smooth marble surface. *Danu, what now?* Not really wanting to look, he casually glanced over his shoulder.

And saw a snake the size of a castle moat bearing down on them. "Run!" he shouted, shaking free of Rika's surprisingly fierce grip, drawing the Silversteel sword and palming a dagger. As the adults snatched up the children and began running, Jak took his own advice—but in the other direction, directly for the snake.

If he could hold it off, maybe Zeph could get everyone

back through the rift. Everyone but him.

"If I live through this, I'd better get a fucking medal." Of course, if he didn't survive, they'd probably give him a posthumous medal, and what use was that? But then, what kind of idiot ran straight into the fanged maw of a giant snake? "Strike that," he muttered to himself. "Hold the medal. I'll deserve a slap upside the head for sheer stupidity."

He picked a spot to make a stand—*don't think of it a last stand*—pretty much at random. It wasn't as if he had handy cover or high ground to choose from. Just that barren expanse of unnatural nothing. Which had birthed an enormous snake. Probably there were rifts popping in and out of existence all over this place. Would be nice to have Stella's skill at detecting the things.

Taking a defensive stance, he spent those last, rapidly vanishing moments to observe the snake. It looked like a regular Dasnarian copper viper, if they grew to three times his height instead of the diameter of his little finger. It was moving fast, but not with hot speed. Not surprising given the temperate-to-cool temperature of this place. A definite advantage there. The narrow head quested, flicking a forked tongue to taste the air for his presence, bead-black eyes set back on its head. He wouldn't spend any time wondering how a Dasnaria copper viper got to this place—and grew to gigantic size—but he would assume that it was equally venomous.

The snake drew up, neck ratcheting back into strike position. Feeling oddly like he was squaring off with a sparring opponent, Jak waited. "First move is yours," he murmured.

The snake struck. Jak threw the dagger into the snake's

mouth as it opened, leaping to the side and bringing the Silversteel sword around in a sweeping arc, laying open the head, but just missing the eye. The snake reared back and struck again just as fast, unbothered by the blade it had swallowed. The nearest fang came down, easily Jak's height, the breath of its passage hissing along his cheek. He flung a second dagger into the snake's soft palate, hoping to hit the brain from the closer distance.

Two daggers down. Three left.

The snake snapped back, striking again with blazing speed—so fast that he didn't have another dagger ready yet. Stella would laugh. Or not, it occurred to him as he tumbled out of the way.

And as burning venom lanced down his shoulder. *Fuck me.*

Already hit, he sifted through his options like shuffling a deck of marked cards. He couldn't win at this point. All he could do was his best to take out the snake so everyone else could make it home.

The snake struck again, and he rolled out of the way, pulling a dagger from his boot and throwing as he came around. It buried itself to the hilt in the soft scales over the mouth—right as the twinned fangs came down on either side of him. No hit, but he was down to two daggers and the sword. The latter wasn't much use if he couldn't stay within—ha!—striking distance of the snake.

Inspired, he leapt to his feet, briefly dizzy from the venom, and ran toward the snake again and to its side, slicing at the scaled body. The scales parted as the Silversteel carved deeply—Danu bless that sword—and the snake reacted, jerking away, pink flesh showing. But it seemed otherwise undaunted.

Repositioning, it coiled back to striking position, drawing a bead on Jak. "Double or nothing!" he shouted, sheathing the sword and drawing his last two daggers, one in each hand. The snake struck. Keeping steady focus, Jak hurled the twin blades at the serpent's eyes—lovely, squishy targets—and nailed them both. "Gotcha!"

He took off running as the snake reared back, shaking its head in confusion. Jak had no idea if he ran toward or away from the rift and the others—he'd totally lost track of direction during the fight, and the cursed place had nothing in the way of defining landmarks. But all that mattered was running. As long as the snake was stretched out pursuing him, it couldn't strike again.

Not that anything would save him now. Jak's eyes burned, and his breath came in short rasps, his steps growing clumsy. Paralysis setting in. Though his eyes watered, he kept them sharp, watching for the edge of the defile. Even so, he nearly ran off, barely throwing himself back in time. Changing course to run parallel, he risked a glance back to see the snake patiently tracking him, following its flicking tongue and his slowing progress. Soon he'd fall in heap, and the snake could dine on him at leisure, while he was still alive.

Hmm. Falling forever or being eaten alive?

Decisions, decisions.

Then, just as he'd about made up his mind to jump, with the hope that the snake might at least die with him, his legs fell out from beneath him, sending him smacking painfully into a faceplant on the hard stone. *Ow.*

The snake slithered closer, scales on marble, the quiet flicking of its tongue the only other sound. Pushing himself up to his knees through sheer force of will, he thumped the black stone with the meat of his fist so the snake would feel the vibrations. It did, pointing its snout straight at him and coiling back for the strike. Praying to Danu to give him the speed he needed, Jak held in place, the defile a palpable pit behind him. With nothing else to do with his hands—no way could he handle the sword in his condition—he fumbled for the coil of Stella's hair from his pocket and wove it through his fingers. For luck.

Whether he managed to dodge or not, the snake was going over. The only question was if they'd go together.

At least he wouldn't fall for eternity, because the venom would kill him soon. Small mercies.

The snake struck.

~ 15 ~

A T FIRST, NOTHING happened. Though Stella felt like a rabbit freezing under the sharp awareness of the predator's gaze, the intelligence did nothing overt. It simply stared at her, curiosity and consuming interest foremost, anger following behind as it recalled how she'd driven it away from Gieneke. There was also hurt at the way she'd repelled it, which had her feeling guilty even as she knew Jak would scoff at her tenderness. *If something is trying to kill you, then it's your enemy and deserves to be hurt.*

But *was* it trying to kill her? The tentacle monsters hadn't injured her—only dragged her away—and the injuries the others sustained battling them and the monkey-lizards hadn't been mortal wounds. She couldn't ignore that Jak had nearly died, of course, but that had been a combination of brutal weather and fighting to retrieve her. Did any of the creatures really want them dead, or was it something else?

The intelligence seemed to be listening to her thoughts, and the sense of its attention reminded her sharply of the lake monster's placid gaze—which had been unsettling, yes, but never felt threatening. But then, the stone giant at Gieneke had never emanated aggressive or hostile emotions either, even as it was pulling living beings apart and sticking them back together, so that was no good measure.

With a glint of mischief, almost a mental snicker, the intelligence withdrew its attention. It belatedly occurred to her to warn it—perhaps plead with it?—to leave Jak alone. But would that have been good strategy anyway? If the intelligence knew of her concern for Jak in particular, would it treat him better or worse?

It was too late anyway. The intelligence was gone, and something else hurtled toward the fold. "Incoming," she called tersely.

"Can you close the rift?" Astar asked, taking a defensive stance, both hands grasping the hilt of the heavy broadsword.

"Yes, but what if it's our people?"

"Can't you tell?"

Stella couldn't. She looked to Lena bracketing the other side of the gateway, her wide brow furrowed in concentration. Without speaking, Lena shook her head slowly. "We're keeping it open," Stella told Astar firmly.

"Goddesses preserve us," Astar muttered, staring hard at the nothing between Stella and Lena. Gen lowered her chin so it nearly grazed the frozen ground, rear end high and twitching in anticipation, tail waving in deceptive laziness.

They both reared back in shock when a dragon's snout poked through the gateway, Gen actually tumbling backward in her scramble. Astar recovered, charging with sword swinging.

"No, Willy!" Stella shouted, and he skidded to a halt.

"Dragon!" he yelled back, pointing with his sword as if

she'd somehow failed to notice it.

"Only part of one," she explained soothingly. "It can't fit through."

Indeed, it was only part of a dragon's muzzle, mostly one large black-scaled naris—the nostril as big in diameter as Astar was tall—angling to fit as much through as possible, its heated breath whuffling in curiosity. A few scales fell off, stripped away by the dragon's shoving at the restrictive portal. Stella felt the gateway shiver with the dragon's magical might, but she was able to hold the edges in place. It took concentration, and the focusing power of the Star helped immensely, but it also occurred to her that being in her own realm made a difference.

Clearly the dragon possessed some magic-nullifying power in the alter-realm, as the shapeshifter versions of dragons did in her own realm. But her own magic held strong against the alter-realm dragon in way she wouldn't care to test against Kiraka in dragon form, or even Zynda.

If Astar could find his way to dragon form again, it would be interesting to test herself against him. As it was, she relaxed slightly, not too worried about the dragon coming through. What was happening on the other side of the portal was another question, however. "We're holding the gateway size stable," she said, checking for Lena's confirming nod that she felt the same.

"Looks like it's trying to change that," Astar noted warily.

"It's mostly curious," Stella replied, assessing the dragon's mental state. "Magical creature, sensing the rift and all. But the dragon coming through is not the problem."

"No, the problem is none of our people can come through if there's a giant fucking dragon in the way," Astar grated out, his worry making him unusually harsh.

Gen slunk forward and slapped the naris with outstretched claws. The dragon snorted, fire spurting out to singe Gen's gray-striped fur. She yelped and rolled in the snow. The snout withdrew briefly, replaced by an enormous eye. Astar let out a war cry and flung himself at it, sword swinging in a broad arc. Before Stella could utter a warning, the eye disappeared, and Astar's momentum carried him right through the portal.

Stella spat out a curse that was also part plea to Moranu to preserve her foolishly heroic twin's hide. Hopefully he hadn't emerged midair and was now splatted on some forest floor, being devoured by tentacle monsters. Lena regarded her soberly. "That makes officially more of us in the alter-realm than in our home realm."

"Is that important?" Gen asked, briefly back in human form.

"I don't know," Lena replied. "Simply a data point. Balance can be important in my magic, anyway."

"Are you all right?" Stella asked Gen.

"I am, now that I shifted to heal. Should I go after Astar?"

"No," Stella and Lena said as one.

"Astar will be lucky if he's not neck-deep in leaf detritus battling tentacles right now," Lena said with a grimace, echoing Stella's thoughts.

"And we need you here to defend us," Stella added. "Just in case worse comes through or something strains our hold on the portal. So no matter what, please stay with us." Internally, she cursed Astar's bravery—and shortsightedness. The rift quivered. "Something else is coming."

It was their old friends the monkey-lizards. A pack of them came bounding through the portal, chittering angrily. Gen, back in saber-cat form, attacked in earnest, batting them with her head-sized paws, sending some back through the gateway in a surreal version of a child's game. Others she simply crunched in her fanged jaws and left limp.

One monkey-lizard leapt at Stella, and she barely remembered in time that she didn't need her hands to hold the gate open. She wouldn't call it reflex, but she did draw her daggers—just not before the vicious little thing latched onto her leg with four limbs and a prehensile tail. And sunk its sharp lizard teeth into her thigh.

"Ouch," she screeched, and Gen whirled to look. "I can handle it," Stella told her through gritted teeth. Jak would say it served her right for being slow and unprepared, and he'd be correct. Lena had no problems using her daggers to fend off the monkey-lizards, despite her greater need to concentrate on the unfamiliar sorcery. She was creating a nicely impenetrable perimeter with her blades—using techniques Stella recognized from what Jak had tried to teach her.

"Ow, Moranu take you!" she screeched as the monkey-lizard gnawed determinedly at her thigh, and she poked it with the tip of the blade. Ineffectively, as it only bit down harder. *Go for the eyes and ears.* It had big liquid eyes and upright ears. It would be cute, if it wasn't chewing on her. She pointed the dagger at its eye... And couldn't do it. In her head, Jak gave her a disgusted look and shook his head. If only she'd kept it off her in the first place. As it was, the small creature's fear and defensive fury—so immediate and overwhelming with its teeth sunk in her flesh—had her feeling sorry for it.

So tempting to shift to jaguar form, shed her attacker's grip, and give it a few swats. The jaguar didn't much scruple about hurting anything, so that made fighting in that form easier. But she'd lose her grip on the portal if she shifted, and Lena couldn't hold it open on her own.

Bracing herself, she tried a double poke with the dagger tips, like trying to pry off a biting burr—and with no effect. Then a white paw swatted the thing away, Gen's mighty jaws biting down with a crunch that finished it.

Gen took human form again, giving Stella a perplexed and disgusted look very like the one Stella had pictured on Jak's face. "I know you said you could handle it, but…"

"Thank you," Stella said, very sincerely. Glancing around, she saw that all the monkey-lizards were dead and no more were coming through the portal. Lena was cleaning her blades, also giving Stella the side eye. "Please don't tell Jak," Stella begged them both.

Gen and Lena exchanged glances. "We'll discuss a price for that," Gen informed Stella loftily.

"He's going to notice the bloody rip in your leathers regardless," Lena pointed out, "even after you heal yourself shifting."

Moranu take it, Lena was right. "Something's coming through," Stella warned them.

And Astar came careening through the portal, skidding as he hit the snow. He looked around wildly, as if unconvinced of his safe arrival, then blew out a huff of relief. A moment later, a huge black wolf followed him.

"Rhyian," Lena breathed, straightening as if a crushing weight had dropped from her shoulders.

The wolf shook his fur vigorously, then transformed into the man. Rhy shuddered and stretched, much as the wolf had done, his glossy black hair shivering into place, his deep-blue eyes going immediately to Lena. A moment of wordless communication hummed between them. Their longing for each other, the deep and turbulent emotions suffocating under layers of old anger and careless duplicity, throbbed so thick in the air that Stella thought she might choke on it.

Tearing his gaze away from Lena, Rhy took in their surroundings, noting the bloody carcasses of the monkey-lizards scattered across the snow, raising a brow at Gen's saber cat, who came purring to rub her cheek against his leg. He turned to Astar and held out a hand. "I am beyond grateful you came for me. You didn't have to, and—"

"Shut up, cousin," Astar growled. Ignoring Rhy's hand, he seized their cousin in a bear hug, and they thumped each other on the back with brusque enthusiasm, the emotions beneath considerably softer. When they parted, both men had to blink moisture from their eyes. "Besides," Astar said, "Stella and Lena are the ones doing the hard work of holding the gateway open. And Jak and Zephyr are the ones searching for you in the alter-realm. Didn't you see them?"

"No." Rhy looked around, as if the pair might suddenly materialize. "They came after me?"

"Before I did," Astar told him, then glanced at Stella. She

had no answer for him, and a pall settled over the group like the falling snow from the gathering clouds.

"I saw mossbacks, almost certainly from the inn," Rhy said, thinking it through. "But they were afraid of me and ran away. I stayed close to where that tentacle monster yanked me through the rift, just in case. In that empty expanse of nothing, I was afraid I'd never find the spot again."

Lena frowned. "Expanse of nothing—then you weren't in my forest?"

"I wish," Rhy replied fervently and with a wolfish grin. "At least then I could've eaten tentacles. I've had nothing to eat or drink since..." He glanced at the gray daylight sky. "Last night?"

"Last night," Astar confirmed, scooping up a packet of food and a flask of water Gen had insisted they have ready for anyone they managed to rescue. Rhy took the stuff gratefully, immediately tearing into it with rapacious ferocity.

Lena shot Stella a concerned look, and Stella smiled back reassuringly. But yes, Rhy had been in wolf form for a long time, longer than was advisable. She could maybe help him settle back into human skin, but not until she was done holding the portal open. It was becoming more of a strain, either because her native magic—and Lena's—was wearing thin or because it was trying to close. Possibly both.

And where were Jak and Zeph? She tried to set aside the plaguing fear, as it would only distract her, but like the bloody wound on her thigh, it continued to ache, quietly festering.

"This place was different," Astar was saying, watching Rhy devour the food with a concerned look of his own. "Flat, unnaturally so. Black, polished stone, with nothing in any direction."

"Except sheer defiles," Rhy put in, swallowing. "The inn people were discussing them. Very difficult to see until you're right on them. Several of their number nearly fell off to certain—" He broke off in horror. "I can go back in raven form and look for Zeph and Jak. On wing, I could—"

"No," Astar said, shaking his head grimly. "Not yet anyway. They might not even be in the same alter-realm you were. This place didn't look anything like what Zeph and Lena saw. Could the rifts be opening into different places?" he asked Stella.

Feeling ill, she nodded. "Different places, different times. We don't know anything about how these portals work or what they're connecting."

"I'll graph this out, using the data we have, so we can see the trends better," Lena said, "but so far we know that this gateway"—she gestured at the space flanked by Stella and her—"has taken Astar, Rhyian, and at least some of the inn folk to the same place at more or less the same time. We know this because they saw each other there."

"So Zeph and Jak might've gone to the other alter-realm," Astar said.

"Or one we haven't seen yet," Lena agreed glumly. "There could be many of them. But Zeph and Jak went through considerably after Rhyian and not long before Astar. Timing isn't a factor, then."

"So, it bounces around." Astar gripped the hilt of his sword, staring fiercely at the space between Lena and Stella.

"We can't count on these gateways taking us to the same places in either direction. Jak and Zeph may have gotten to a place, found no one, and already returned, just not to here."

A truly depressing thought. Though not as bad as imagining Jak falling to his doom down one of those defiles.

"If they are in our realm, they're flying back to us now," Lena said firmly. "If they're on the other side of this portal, they're depending on us to keep it open for their return. Our task is unchanged."

"Always so logical," Rhy said to her, though without rancor.

"You know me," she returned, her smile mirthless.

"Not as well as I used to," he replied wistfully, "if I ever did at all, being so bone-headed."

"Rhyian..." Lena looked determinedly away from him.

"Lena is right," Astar said firmly. "Our task is to keep this portal open and guard it. How are you holding up?"

Lena looked tired, but Stella was able to bolster her end with additional magic, taking on more of the burden. "Holding fine," she replied. "I wouldn't be able to do this much if I didn't have the Star, but—" She cut herself off, cursing her big mouth, Rhy's furious hurt swamping her.

Rhy stared at her, eyes like black pools. "Mother gave you the Star of Annfwn," he whispered, and Lena closed her eyes at the pain in his voice.

"I was going to find a way to tell you," Stella tried, wishing she could go to him. Her left little fingers twitched, and she desperately wanted to put them in her mouth. Instead, she pulled a blade and gripped it, understanding now why Jak found it comforting.

Rhy laughed without humor. "I don't blame you for keeping it from me. It was cowardly of you, but—"

"Enough," Astar cut in forcibly.

"It's only temporary," Stella told Rhy anyway, aching at the way she'd hurt him. "Just for this mission."

Shaking his head slowly, Rhy gazed past her. "We both know it's not."

"Discuss this later," Astar instructed. "Keep your attention on the here and now."

An uneasy silence settled as they obeyed, tensely waiting, emotions vibrating thick in the air.

"Something's coming," Stella said, almost relieved at the break from the discomfort.

The other three all whirled into defensive stances. And Zeph came prancing through in gríobhth form, wings spread just in case, with three kids perched on her back, gleefully squealing. Shifting fast so they wouldn't see the saber cat, Gen rushed forward in human form, Rhy right with her, plucking the kids from Zeph's back.

Astar also ran to Zeph, seizing her on either side of her beak and kissing her between the eyes. "Is this everyone?"

Relieved of her burden, Zeph shifted to human, giving Astar a real kiss. "No, the rest are right behind me."

"She really is a lady!" one of the kids squealed.

"A really pretty lady!" replied another.

"Rhy, you're here!" Zeph cried out, but Astar stopped her from running to him.

"Zephyr," he said forcefully. "Where's Jak?"

"Playing rear guard," she answered. "What has your tail all fluffed?"

"Long story," he said, "but the short explanation is that the portal bounces to different locations, maybe different times. I was just there and brought Rhy back through. He never saw you and Jak."

"Yeah, we came through on a different grid."

Stella was sure that made sense somehow. "And Jak?"

"Holding off a giant snake while we came through." Zeph scowled at the portal. "Where are the others? They were right behind me."

"Mommy..." one of the children wailed, and Gen shushed them soothingly.

"I'll go back for them," Zeph declared.

"No!" Astar practically shouted in her face. "You are not budging from this spot, Zephyr!" When she raised a brow at him, he released her and took a step back, raking a hand through his hair, fury and despair leaking off of him. "No one is going *anywhere.*"

"Willy," Stella called to him. Then she switched to subvocal, holding out a hand to him. *"Come over to me."*

Responding to that ingrained call between them, if nothing else, Astar came and took her hand. Zeph flashed her a grateful smile behind his back as she went to embrace Rhy. Stella fed some of her diminishing healing energy into Astar, calming him down.

"No one expects you to solve this," she reminded him.

He gripped her hand, desperation in it. *"I should send her back, I know, but I just... can't."* His roiling emotions buffeted her, as they seldom did coming from her twin, but he was barely holding on. They were all barely holding on—and comforting someone else gave Stella something to focus on besides her own misery. Detriment or not, that was how she managed.

"*Sometimes loving people is hard,*" she told him. "*It makes us vulnerable in new ways, and this love is very new for you. This situation is extreme and the strain is hard on all of us. Take a moment to breathe.*"

"*You never show the strain.*" He sounded both admiring and accusing.

She nearly told him that was because she always felt the strain of her surroundings, that she hadn't lived a day of her life without the pummeling stress of others' emotions. In many ways, more or less strain didn't make that much of an impact.

And, for the first time, she wondered what she'd be like without it. It seemed odd to contemplate, a perspective of herself that had never once occurred to her as possible. Until Jak suggested the possibility.

Her senses tied to the gateway twinged. "Something's coming through," she called in relief. Hopefully not premature relief. *Moranu, please let it be Jak and the other people.*

A big woman carrying an iron skillet stumbled through, blinking in surprise at the gathering and the inn. "We're home," she declared, as if someone might argue with her. One of the kids ran to hug her, and Gen eased them both out of the way.

More adults emerged, all exclaiming, all looking worn to the bone. Stella watched each one, waiting for Jak's familiar swagger, expecting his cocky grin and some teasing remark about her wound. She would take him scolding her about her lousy defensive skills, even put up with him upbraiding her and bullying her into practicing if he'd just come through.

Come on, Jak. You promised to come back.

The people from the inn were all gathered around, talking with loud excitement. Half of them seemed to have decided they'd only dreamed that Zeph had been a gríobhth—and possibly that the whole improbable experience had been a result of food poisoning. Astar waded in, bringing them to order with diplomatic reassurances. He didn't introduce himself, which Stella counted as wise, since that would only lead to more excitement.

"Is this everyone?" Astar asked.

"Except for young Ilano," a big man said, shaking his head sadly. "Wasn't watching his step and pitched right off the edge. That thing had no bottom we could see."

Astar nodded sympathetically, offering his sincere sympathies, evincing so much patience that Stella wanted to scream at him.

"Nilly," Lena called softly. She looked drawn, shadows under her eyes. "I'm running low," she said, and Stella nodded, understanding perfectly well.

"We'll have to let it close," Stella acknowledged. "Go ahead and let go of your end, I've got it."

"But what about Jak?" Lena protested.

Astar came back to her side. "They say that's everyone," he told her somberly.

"Everyone but Jak," she replied, having to say it out loud.

Playing rear guard against a giant snake. She unknitted her magic from Lena's, pulling the gate to be anchored on herself—and on the Star. Rhy still wouldn't meet her eye, and she ached for that.

Astar nodded, clenching his jaw, then shook his head. "Every time I send someone through after another of us, I risk losing you both." He switched to subvocal. *"I want to do the right thing, and I... don't know what that is,"* Astar confessed, searching her face for answers.

"Oh, Willy. I know you believe there is always a right way, the noble path, but sometimes there isn't. Most of the time there isn't. It's a balance. We weigh the risk against the result and decide what we're willing to gamble."

"Now you sound like Jak." Astar's expression didn't lighten, but a smile touched his voice.

"And, like Jak, I'm going to tell you that sometimes what we choose to risk isn't up to anyone but ourselves."

He frowned at her, suspicion growing. "Stella, what are you—"

Before he could finish, before anyone could stop her, she stepped through the gate that was herself, and closed it behind her.

THE FIRST THING she noticed was the utter lack of emotional noise. It came as a crashing relief, as if loud music that had been playing in both ears had suddenly stopped. Like the sudden cessation of chronic pain you'd endured for so long that you'd forgotten what it was like to live without it until it disappeared. Stella almost staggered with lightheadedness, giddy with the effervescent silence.

Was this how everyone else felt all the time? No wonder she seemed so dour to them.

Turning in a slow circle, she took in the featureless black plane that seemed to stretch in all directions, though she reminded herself of the defiles that tricked the eye and the unwary. No Jak, but at least she'd landed in the same alter-realm. He had to be here somewhere.

An alien violet sky arced above. Not even wind moved here. No signs of life, not even the dragon or monkey-lizards. No sense of the intelligence watching her either, though she didn't want to scan to intensively for it, leery of attracting its attention here, in this place, where it held all the power. For that much was unmistakable. The others had called this alter-realm unnatural, and it was. It had been deliberately created for some arcane purpose, and the intelligence was no doubt its architect.

Her empathic senses still worked—she'd wondered if that magic had been lost to her like the others had lost shapeshifting ability or as Lena had lost some of her weather magic—so she gradually expanded her awareness, seeking Jak.

Despite the tense circumstances, extending that mental sense felt amazingly good, too. As if some part of herself had been starved of blood, so tightly clenched, and unfurling it at last filled her with tingling warmth and excitement.

With heady relief, she sensed Jak. He was some distance off, so she began jogging in that direction—more of an uneven stagger than a run, as her wounded thigh throbbed—scanning the path ahead for sudden bottomless pits. As it was, she saw him, lying in a crumpled heap, heartstoppingly close to the edge of one of the infamous defiles. In fact, one hand dangled limply over the edge.

She crouched beside him, getting a grip on his jacket to drag him away from the edge. He sported a few new injuries— probably him choosing to fall in love with a healer was simple self-preservation, what with the scrapes the man managed to get into—but none were enough to have weakened him so. A few hand-sized iridescent copper discs were scattered about, and it took her a moment to identify them as scales, no doubt from the giant snake. If it had been venomous...

Turning him over, she sat cross-legged and pillowed Jak's head in her lap—and sent a prayer to Moranu that her healing skills would work here. Otherwise she'd have to drag Jak back through the portal somehow and heal him back in their own world. Hopefully Moranu could hear her in this place seemingly ruled by one being.

For whatever reason, her healing magic flowed normally. Even better, the snake venom paralyzing him was familiar to her, as if from a snake of their own realm. It hadn't stopped his heart or lungs yet, though it would have, given much more time to work. The slowing of his system had worked in his favor, reducing the spread of the venom. Flushing him clean of the venom first, she made sure none remained in his body before she coaxed his heart into a faster rhythm, setting it to match her own, then bringing his breathing into harmony with hers. Once his body had the new tempo, she gradually withdrew, keeping light tendrils of attention to make sure he wouldn't falter.

Opening her eyes, she found him staring up at her, dark gaze sparkling with wry amusement. "Bringing me back from the dead is becoming a full-time occupation for you," he commented.

~ 16 ~

"**F**UNNY," STELLA REPLIED with a quirk of a smile. "I was just thinking the same thing." Though her expression sat in her usual solemn lines, her gray eyes were dazzlingly clear, bright with happiness.

"See? We even think alike. Another sign we're destined for each other."

"Or simple logic: a reckless idiot who thinks he's immortal needs a healer on retainer."

He reached up to touch her smooth cheek, missing the rain of her dark hair around them. But she had it tightly braided back still, and she wore her black fighting leathers. Because she'd been prepared to battle creatures coming through the rift she and Lena had been holding open.

Memory—and with it, alarm—flooded him, and he sprang to his feet, momentarily confused that no blades leapt to his hands. That's right—he'd thrown his last daggers in a desperate attempt to kill the snake. He drew the sword instead. Looking around wildly, he saw nothing but the empty landscape, a few scales from the copper viper, and the perilous defile nearby.

"Did you happen to see a really big snake?" he asked Stella, who gazed up at him in bemusement. He offered her a hand, and she took it, rising gracefully to her feet.

"I think I would've noticed," she replied gently. "I've seen only you since I arrived here."

Then he hadn't dreamed it. He had dodged in time, and the snake had gone over the edge. "The others? Zeph and Rhy?"

"All safely back. *You* are the only one who didn't make it."

He studied her, her luminous presence so very odd in this sterile landscape. "And how is it that *you* are here?"

She raised a black-winged brow. "The same way you got here," she replied very seriously.

"And Astar just let you come after me?" He couldn't imagine that happening and began to have a bad feeling.

"No, Jak," she replied patiently. "I didn't ask for or need permission."

Wonderful. And he had no daggers left. Only the Silversteel sword. A chill of dread washed over him, and he scanned the landscape. "It isn't safe for you to be here."

"It isn't safe for anyone to be here. What are you doing?" she demanded as he grabbed her hand and pulled her into a jogging run.

"We have to get back to the rift," he informed her shortly, then skidded to a halt. She'd been limping as they ran. He looked more closely at her, observing her disarray—and the rent in her pants with bloody flesh showing through. "You're injured."

She grimaced, putting a hand over the wound as if to keep him from noticing. "A monkey-lizard bit me."

It hadn't just bit her—it had chewed on her for some time, by the look of it. "Where were your daggers?" he asked after taking a deep breath.

"In my hands!" She widened her eyes just a trifle too much for true innocence. "Belatedly," she admitted. "And then I couldn't get it off me."

He dropped her hand to wave his in the air. "You had daggers for that!"

"Can we discuss my poor fighting skills later?" She pulled her Silversteel daggers. "In fact, you take these for now, since you're better with them, and you seem to have misplaced yours."

"Yeah, well, a snake ate them." And didn't that sound ridiculous? "If you'd been there, you'd understand." He took her blades and sheathed them. "Why didn't you shift to heal yourself?"

"I didn't have time. I had to come rescue you."

He set his teeth. They'd argue about that later, too. "Go ahead and shift now. You can't run like that." And they might need to.

She shook her head slowly and somberly. "I don't think that's a good idea. I might not be able to in this realm. And even if I can, what if I can't shift back?"

Well, she had a point there. He sheathed the sword and turned his back. "Climb on, then, and I'll carry you. We have to get back to the rift before the intelligence notices you're here."

She cast a wary gaze to the sky, wise enough to look worried about that possibility. "I think it already has," she confided quietly.

He swore viciously. "Get on. We have to run."

"Jak—the portal is closed."

"It's... what?"

"Lena was exhausted, so I pulled it closed behind me so nothing else could get through to attack them."

Nothing *else*. He glared at her, unclear how he could both want to throttle her and cover her in kisses. To prevent either impetuous action, he punched his fists to his hips. "You closed it behind you," he echoed, hoping it would make more sense if he said it. Nope.

"There was a dragon trying to push through," she explained. "A real one. Without me to restrict the size of the portal, it might've been able to push through into our world. I *had* to close it."

All right, then. He took another deep breath. Let it out. It didn't help. "What in Danu *was* your plan?"

"I thought I might be able to open a portal from this side," she said. "I'm getting better at it. I was able to step through to the right time and place, so I was hoping I could simply take us back through again."

"But no?"

"But maybe. My empathy and healing are working, but the sorcery isn't. It would help to find an existing rift."

"There might not be any more on this section of grid," he explained through gritted teeth.

"That would be a problem, then," she replied evenly.

"We're going to die here," he mused aloud, then focused on her. "Explain to me again why you thought this was a good idea?"

"Because I needed to rescue you," she snapped, poking him hard in the chest. "Which I'm regretting now."

"You should be regretting it because that was an incredibly foolish decision. And you call *me* reckless!"

"You *are* reckless," she shouted back at him. "What kind of stupid man thinks he's such a heroic warrior that he stays behind to single-handedly battle a giant venomous snake?"

"What kind of person thinks she's such a powerful sorceress that she waltzes between worlds to rescue that stupid man?" he countered.

Abruptly, she smiled, one of her rare smiles like the sun breaking through storm clouds. "A sorceress in love with that stupid man," she said, her voice quiet and shy.

That stopped him cold. Floored, all frustrated indignation draining out of him, he stared and her, mouth working to speak words his numbed brain had yet to supply. "You have an incredibly bad sense of timing," he finally said.

Her smile took a rueful twist. "You're no doubt correct there. But I also thought you should know. In case we die here."

"Yeah." He studied the toes of his boots, keeping his hands on his hips. Then he looked up at her again. So breathtakingly beautiful, so incredibly tempting. She was everything he'd ever wanted. The only woman he'd ever truly wanted. And she was in love with him. The moment should be celebrated, and they couldn't because they might be swatted like bugs at any moment. "I'm in love with you, too," he offered.

"I know." She smiled impishly at his consternation. "Astar

told me."

"I'm gonna kill him," Jak said to the sky. Had something up there shifted? Like a cloud in a cloudless sky. That was a weird shade of violet. He narrowed his eyes, searching for whatever had moved up there. "If we live through this, I'm going to make him pay."

"Hmm." Stella was looking up, too. "Something is coming."

Jak lowered his gaze to hers. "Whatever happens, stay behind me."

"I don't think your blades will help with this," she said, looking past him.

He spun, keeping her squarely behind him, and tried to make sense of what he was seeing. The air itself seemed to be condensing, visibly thickening into the shape of a man built like himself, but several times taller. "Why do they all have to be giant?" he muttered, drawing his sword and palming one of Stella's daggers.

In nonchalant defiance of his instructions, Stella stepped up on his dagger side. "That's a question worth considering," she murmured. "Though perhaps when we have more leisure to do so."

The being continued to take form, the black stone they stood upon now rising up in a fountain, like liquid pouring from below to fill a vessel in defiance of the laws of gravity. As the man became more solid, he took on different coloration— ending up looking a lot like Jak himself, down to the sword and dagger.

"I'm much better looking than that," he noted with considerable disgust.

"You are," Stella agreed—not complimenting him, but with almost academic interest. "Remember how the stone giant became a gryphon like Zeph after it saw her, but kind of blurred?"

"Yeah." She was right. This thing looked like a squidgy copy of himself. How Jak might look in fifty more years if he spent that whole time on a whiskey bender. *Note to self: maybe I should start drinking less.* He looked like shit with a drunkard's bulbous nose. "What does it want—can you tell?"

"It's... curious. Not aggressive. And..." She closed her mouth on whatever she'd been about to add, chewing her full bottom lip uneasily.

"The stone giant was curious if you could tear people in half, stick the odd pieces together, and still have them work. That was pretty aggressive," he felt he had to point out.

"I'm not arguing that its interest in us hasn't been destructive," she murmured. "Just answering your question."

The stone man smiled at Stella, a sick parody of Jak's jaunty grin. "Eeyem wuv wittoo," it said.

Stella sighed. "Oh dear."

"You understood that?" Jak demanded. The stone man mimicked him as he raised his sword. The thing's stone version of the sword didn't look sharp, but it would work just fine as a club to bash their brains out. "What did it say?"

Stella slid her gaze to his, trepidation in her expression. "It said it's in love with me." Grimacing at whatever she saw in Jak's face, she added, "I'd say it's just mimicking you from before, but it means it. At least, those are the emotions I'm sensing."

"Fuck me," Jak swore, stepping in front of her. "You can't have her," he flung out. Gauging the distance, he considered nailing the thing in the eye with his dagger. Hitting the target wasn't the problem. Doing it damage would be. Battling that stone giant at Gieneke had been like chipping at marble, and he doubted this would be any different.

"Eyem gonnah killem," the man said, advancing on them, waving its sword-club.

"No need to translate that one," Jak bit out as they backed up. The man took several more steps, gaze clearly fixed on Stella.

"Wuv wittooo!!!" it roared.

The defile was behind them somewhere. Jak felt its gaping maw like a chill wind on the back of his neck. He angled them away from the stone man, but it flanked them, backing them toward that edge. This wouldn't end prettily. "You'll kill her, man," he shouted at the thing. "She goes over that edge, she dies, and you'll never have her."

The stone man slowed, cocking his head as if thinking.

"Jak, I have an idea," Stella said, putting a hand on his back.

"Absolutely open to suggestions right now."

"I think we should jump."

He couldn't risk glancing over his shoulder, but he'd give a great deal for a look at her face right then. "Are you going for the tragic ending to our love story, jumping to our deaths because at least we'll die together?" Come to think of it, that would be preferable to being bludgeoned to death knowing he'd be leaving Stella to the brutal attentions of this monster.

"Dasnarians," she muttered in disgust. "Always looking to be tragic heroes."

"Yeah, well, it comes naturally to us." He feinted to the side, and the stone man took one step to neatly cut him off.

"Apparently. But no, I think I sense a rift down there. If we jump, maybe we can fall through it and get back home."

A laugh escaped him. "I'm *pretty* sure you're not crazy."

"I'm not. I have my reasons to think it'll work."

"Wuv wittoo!" the stone monster howled, sucking up more stone to grow even larger.

"Also," Stella said in a fainter voice, "its feelings are quite... sexual. I think I'd rather risk jumping."

Better and better. As much as he hated facing that endless drop, dying together was better than the alternative. His father would be thrilled to know Jak had that much fatalistic Dasnarian in him. He sheathed his sword and dagger and took her hand. Giving her one swift kiss, he grinned. "The only bad part is no one will see this to compose the ballad."

She laughed, sounding wild, her eyes fierce. "Then we'll have to live."

"Your mouth to Danu's ears."

"Moranu's ears."

"Double the blessing."

They turned as one. And leapt into the void.

~ 17 ~

S TELLA HAD FLOWN many times but had never fallen, certainly not in a human body. Jak gripped her hand, a howl ripping from him, and she surprised herself by screaming too. The atavistic terror made it difficult to concentrate, but she found the rift she'd sensed, wrenching it wider. It was too much off to the side and needed to be bigger. Bigger. Without the Star, she couldn't have done it. Straining her mental muscles, she forced it wider.

And felt the brief disorientation as they passed through the rift.

"Oof!" Both their screams cut off as they hit ground. Fortunately they seemed to have landed in a giant snowdrift, but still, the hard landing had a stunning effect.

"Are you all right?" Jak asked after a while, his voice rough.

She prodded herself to think of a reply. "You know that joke about how falling feels like flying until you hit the ground?"

"Never heard that one," he wheezed.

"Well, it doesn't. Falling feels nothing like flying, even *before* hitting ground. I never want to do that again."

"At least we hit snow-covered ground and lived through

it," he replied reasonably. "Or did we? I'm getting so used to dying that I might not be able to tell the difference anymore."

"I hurt too much to be dead."

"Good point. And I'm too fucking cold. Should it burn like this?"

"Cold might be good," she ventured. They should probably get up. Eventually. "It could mean we're back in Erie."

"Next time find us a portal to Annfwn. Or Nahanau," he suggested. He pushed himself up, groaning as he did, and brushed snow off his face and hair before scanning the landscape. "This looks like Erie, unless our chameleon shapeshifter has created an alter-realm to mimic ours."

"I can't think about that." What if it started doing that, though? They'd lose all sense of what was real and what was manufactured to... to do whatever it was the intelligence wanted from them. Jak leaned over her, smoothing her hair back from her forehead. "Shift, my star. Heal yourself."

She didn't think she was seriously injured from the fall, but there was the monkey-lizard bite that ached all up and down her leg now. Still, she sighed, laying a hand on his cheek. He flowed into her, but she was becoming familiar with him, feeling him inside and out. It was beginning to feel more right to have his presence inside her skin than not. "It doesn't seem fair that I can and you can't."

He grinned and kissed her nose. "Except you can work your healing magic on me. And you can shift into a horse and carry us out of here."

"Oh! Really good idea." She shifted into her jaguar First Form, so comfortable in its long familiarity, and took a moment to sniff the air before returning to human form, showing Jak her relief. "We're not far from the inn."

"Thank the three," he replied fervently. He'd been running some forms to warm and limber up. "Let's go."

"Don't you need healing first?"

He shook his head. "The venom-purging stuck. I'm feeling good—if cold. Honestly, all I want is to get by a fire as quickly as possible, so I'll take a ride. If you're willing." He cocked his head, searching her face. "I shouldn't assume."

Absurdly, she found herself blushing. Though the shapeshifters in their crew had become accustomed to giving the others rides of various kinds, it *was* a kind of intimacy. And though Jak had ridden her before, it felt… *different* now. She blushed harder, imagining Zeph's risqué remarks on the subject.

"Hey," Jak said, touching her cheek lightly. "We can walk."

"It's not that," she assured him.

He smiled, not his cocky grin, but knowingly, a sensual mischief behind it. "Not how you imagined getting between my legs?"

"Jak!" Her face went near to bursting with the flaming heat. "You've ridden me before."

"I know." He trailed his finger down her cheek, caressing the underside of her jaw so she shivered, and not from the cold. "I understand how you feel. Things are different between us now. You said you love me."

She took a deep breath. "I do, but Jak, I—"

"Let's save the 'but Jaks,'" he suggested wryly. "I have a feeling I'll want plenty of whiskey to have that conversation."

She hated to put off the conversation, or lead him on to believe they could have more than would ever be. Being in love when you were about to die was one thing. Trying to work that into a life with no place for being in love was something else entirely.

But she closed her mouth and shifted into horse form. Jak wasted no time vaulting onto her back, his agile weight barely a burden, he balanced himself so well, aligning to her movements as she galloped over the snow. She tried not to think about the way his strong thighs gripped her sides, but by the way he stroked a hand over her neck as he lay low against the wind of their passage, she knew without reading his emotions that he was savoring the contact too.

And, like her, he was craving more. Her skin against his. She wanted that, too, more than anything. But he'd have to understand it could only be for a short while. The vision of that lonely tower pressed on her, ever closer in her immediate future. If she stood at a crossroads, then the other roads, if they'd ever even been possibilities, were shrinking away. A single future squeezed out all the others. Jak wasn't in it.

Well, they would discuss it. And perhaps she'd have some whiskey, too.

They reached the inn just after full dark, their friends plus locals all pouring out into the once-empty torchlit circle with cheers and exclamations of relief. Jak tensed as they approached, and she heartily agreed. She hated the sight of the snow-packed circular drive too. And if she'd been thinking, she would've shifted back to human before they were spotted. She hadn't been thinking, though. She was so very tired. Shifting put flesh back together as she intended it to be, but it didn't restore vitality. Jak's exhaustion permeated her consciousness, too. After all they'd been through, it was a wonder they were on their feet at all.

"We'll tell them to save the interrogation for morning," Jak told her. "I'll tell them we're refusing to open our mouths except to stuff food in them and ask where our beds are."

She bobbed her head in weary agreement. And even after Jak sprang down and she shifted back to human—drawing gasps from the local crowd—she was more than happy to let him take the lead. Astar wasn't at all happy with her, but he embraced them both, informing them that they would be having a long conversation the following day, particularly about following orders. That last was delivered with a significant glare for his twin, though Stella was too tired to care.

THEY LEFT THE inn so early the next morning that the northern winter darkness had yet to pale. That wasn't saying much, and Stella found herself agreeing with Jak's suggestion that they take a portal somewhere warm and sunny, if only for a few hours. Too bad they didn't seem to work that way.

Though they'd all gone to bed early—stuffed to the gills by the inn's grateful and enthusiastic cook—everyone was still tired, in mind and heart, if not in body. Rhy had continued to avoid her, which was just as well, as Stella had no more idea of what to say to him now than ever.

True to his promise, Astar rode in the carriage with Stella and Jak, lecturing them on their reckless behavior until she irritably told him to stuff it. Astar looked frankly shocked, hurt wafting off of him, though Lena, riding inside also, had to smother a giggle. Beside Stella, Jak kept a solemn expression on his face, but his amusement crackled lightly off the air, his affection for her like a caress.

"Willy," Stella said on a sigh, then reaching across the space between them to take his hand. "We're all being pushed to our limits here. Including you. I'm trying to remember that you're doing the best you can. I'll ask the same consideration from you."

Astar set his jaw, the muscle there twitching, then he ran his free hand over his face and squeezed hers where they were joined. "Fair enough. I know I've been making a hash of leading this quest."

"You haven't," Jak said firmly, Lena nodding in solidarity. "This is unknown territory. Stella is right that we're all just doing the best we can."

"Well, we need to start doing better," Astar replied bitterly, "or we'll all end up dead."

"Some of us several times," Jak noted, sliding Stella a grin.

She snorted at his black humor. "Don't get comfortable thinking I'll drag you back from Glorianna's arms every time you end up there."

"I'm not sure Glorianna would have me," he mused. "At any rate, Your Highness, consider me properly castigated and apologetic. I should get up top and relieve Zeph of the reins before she drives us off the road."

Astar waved a hand at him. "Give it a little time. Zephyr is determined to prove she can do this, and she's feeling guilty about abandoning you in the alter-realm."

"She shouldn't feel—" Jak started.

"But she does," Astar interrupted. "So let her do this for you. Take today to rest. Try to stay warm."

"You can snuggle with me," Stella said when Jak opened his mouth to argue. Tugging the fur blanket more fully over both of them, she scooted up against him, making a show of shivering. "Brr."

Jak raised a dubious brow at her, not really fooled, but he put his arm over her shoulder and drew her close. The chill bothered him more than he'd admit to, and Gen had explained that it was common for people who'd nearly frozen to death to be susceptible to the cold, and to find it painful. Even with the healing, it would take time for his body to equilibrate again.

"You can keep an eye on me this way," she added, and he relaxed, happy with that much. Jak worried more than he'd said that the intelligence had taken such an interest in her, and he kept replaying that scene in his mind, fretting over it. Both of them had, by unspoken agreement, glossed over that aspect in their report to Astar.

They spent the day cuddled together in the carriage, discussing their various adventures and debating the implications. Zeph, Gen, and Astar took turns driving the carriage, scouting in hardy winter forms and coming inside to warm up. Rhy never came in, assiduously avoiding her. It was a very long day, but at least nothing attacked them, though Jak maintained vigilance, refusing to doze as she'd hoped.

By the time they reached the next inn, situated on the banks of the frozen River Eva, they all barely managed to eat before they crashed, exhausted, into their individual beds.

THEY REACHED CASTLE Marcellum the following afternoon, delighted to find the lovely, comparatively small castle amid picturesque snow-covered rolling hills. Frozen lakes in crystal blue nestled in the valleys, surrounded by forests frosted in ice.

"It's like a winter fairyland," Gen commented, her eyes wide and wistful.

Rhy, who'd finally conceded to pressure to rest in the carriage—though he still brooded and wouldn't look Stella in the eye—made a disparaging sound. "Looks like boring mossback farms to me."

Gen poked him in the arm hard enough that he scowled at her and rubbed the spot. "Farmers are good people," Gen informed him. "Without agriculture, there's no foundation for a stable civilization."

"Stability is overrated," Rhy replied.

"Not everyone is a predator, Rhyian," Lena said. She'd been talking to him more the last couple of days, perhaps in the vacuum of his determination to ignore Stella. Or maybe just trying to find something of a friendly common ground between them. Almost losing Rhy to the alter-realm had frightened Lena enough that she wanted her ex-lover to be a friend again, but she also couldn't forget how he'd betrayed her all those years ago. Stella didn't know what she'd do in

Lena's place.

Hopefully she'd never have to find out.

"There's a great deal to be said for a stable community," Lena continued when Rhy didn't immediately retort. She gazed out the open carriage window, a wistful smile on her face. They'd drawn back the heavy curtains so they could see, the climate around Marcellum gentler, free of the biting winds of the high plains. "Peace and prosperity, along with a stable food supply, allows for other endeavors to flourish. Scientific study, the proliferation of the arts, refinement of crafts and tools."

"Is that the kind of life you want?" Rhy asked, sincere curiosity in his voice.

Gen and Stella exchanged covert glances, doing their best to be unobtrusive. Rhy and Lena having a civil conversation—and one where he seemed to be genuinely listening to her? Near-death experiences were terrible to deal with, but they certainly resulted in interesting changes of character.

"Is it?" Lena mused, still staring out the window. Then she met Rhy's gaze, her mouth in a curve that was both bitter and rueful. "I don't know. I thought for a very long time that I only wanted to be left alone to my studies in Aerron, but now that feels long ago and far away. I've been so clear on what I didn't want that I think I haven't given much thought to what kind of life I *would* like to have."

"One blissfully free of my presence, no doubt," Rhy said without rancor.

Stella held her breath for Lena's explosion, but her friend only laughed, softly and without music. "Rhyian," she said, "after you—after we broke up, it never once occurred to me to imagine you would ever be a part of my life again." She returned her gaze to the frozen landscape. "It simply wasn't a possibility."

Pressing his lips closed, Rhy nodded, gaze lifting to Stella, where she sat across from him. The pain there caught her like a cramp, and she sent him a wave of compassion. He closed his eyes briefly, then inclined his chin in silent gratitude. A start, anyway.

They rode the rest of the way to Castle Marcellum in silence.

"It was so thoughtful of Queen Nix to spare us the formal audience," Lena commented on a groan, flopping back onto the bed in the suite of rooms she, Gen, and Stella would be sharing. Castle Marcellum wasn't big enough for them each to have their own room, but Astar and Zeph had gotten a room of their own, with Rhy and Jak sharing another. They were all looking forward to spending the rest of the afternoon thawing themselves out in hot baths.

"And having a ball in our honor!" Gen exclaimed from the hot bath she'd lucked into the first turn at. "I can't believe they can put one together on such short notice."

"I suspect we're a welcome excuse," Stella commented, well familiar with Ordnung's social occasions and what kind of planning was involved. "Midwinters here are no doubt dull. It's a long stretch between the Feast of Moranu and Glorianna's spring festival. Tonight won't be especially fancy, but it's not as if the people around here have much that they're suddenly dropping to make this happen."

The door burst open, and Zeph practically flew in, carrying a bundle of glittering silver fabric.

"Why are you here?" Gen demanded. "I thought you had plans to debauch Astar into unconsciousness."

Lena giggled, as those had been Zeph's exact words.

"Done and done," Zeph declared, swanning toward Stella, looking far too pleased with herself. "The poor bear is worn out, so it didn't take much. And look what I found!" She unfurled the fabric and held it up against Stella. "It's tiny, like it's made for a doll, so I'm thinking it's perfect for our Nilly here."

"Wow, um, thank you?" Stella said, taking hold of the dress that Zeph thrust against her.

Zeph smiled radiantly. "I mean that in the nicest way."

"Yes," Gen added. "We'd all love to be as delicately built as you are."

"I wouldn't," Lena protested, levering to sit on the edge of the bed. "I'm very happy with my body."

"Because you're built like a warrior queen," Gen grumbled. "I'd kill for your figure."

Zeph rolled her eyes dramatically and adjusted Stella's hold on the gown. "Anyway, Astar passed the word that some of us have wardrobe emergencies, like darling Jak, and Queen Nix had a whole pile of clothes delivered to our rooms. I'll have the rest brought here once Astar wakes up, but I spotted this one for Stella to wear tonight and had to bring it here immediately."

"I have a formal gown I can shift into," Stella said. One considerably less showy than this one.

"And Jak has seen you in it as many times as I have." Zeph glared at her fiercely. "Tonight is special."

"Tonight is not special," Stella protested weakly. "You know me—I probably won't even stay at the party very long."

"You only have to stay long enough for Jak's eyes to pop out of his head," Zeph promised. "Because the special part happens *after* that."

"Are you just aiming to win the bet?" Lena demanded. "I can't help but notice that tonight is night five."

"You're just bitter that you lost," Zeph replied airily. "But for the record, no. It's just that tonight is an opportunity. Who knows when we'll have another?"

"Zeph is right," Lena said, sliding to the floor and coming over to examine the gown.

"My favorite words," Zeph replied, blowing her a kiss. She returned her predatory gaze to Stella. "You, darling Nilly, are getting a makeover."

"Yes!" Gen pumped a fist in the air, excited enough to abandon the tub.

Lena clapped her hands together. "Hooray!"

Stella eyed them all with jaundiced bemusement. "I understand Gen and Zeph getting excited about girly primping, but you, Lena? This is hardly logical and scientific."

"I can be girly." She took the dress from Stella and hung it up, smoothing the glittering folds. It had been intricately sewn with crystal beads, swirling in patterns like the eddies of water, onto a sheer fabric transparent as air. It went over a satin sheath of a platinum shade so light, it looked almost white. "This is a beautiful gown. It will look truly amazing on you, Nilly."

"It will look truly revealing," Stella said dubiously, noting how deeply the neckline plunged—the back almost nonexistent—along with a very high slit in the skirt in front.

"Exactly," Zeph crowed. "Now into the tub with you."

STELLA HADN'T BEEN the subject of such attentive primping since she'd gotten old enough to refuse to be her mother's dress-up doll. Which, to be fair, had been by about the time she was five. Sometimes being a shapeshifter came in very handy, especially when your parents couldn't shift into a form fast enough to chase you.

Whether it was because she knew she'd never escape her friends because of their well-meaning enthusiasm for the task, or because she was actually enjoying herself on some level, Stella submitted to the makeover with grace. She even allowed Gen to put up her hair, as all three of her friends insisted she had to do, as the back of the gown dipped so low and must be shown off. Lena applied cosmetics from her own supply, meticulously applying the shadings with deft artistry. And Zeph made a trip back to the room she shared with Astar to root through the remainder of the delivered wardrobe, selecting gowns for the rest of them, along with shoes and other accessories, before sending off the "boy things."

With considerable trepidation, Stella slipped on the high heels that looked more like jewelry than shoes. "I don't know if I can even stand in these things, much less walk or dance."

Zeph swatted her shoulder. "Your First Form is a cat. You have natural balance and feline elegance."

"The tail helps with that a lot," Stella pointed out, but she stood tentatively, trying to think feline.

"Maybe you should selectively grow a tail, then," Gen said with a giggle. "That will get Jak's attention."

"I already have Jak's attention," Stella replied.

"I wish I had your confidence." Gen sighed wistfully.

Stella didn't think confidence had anything to do with it—or she wouldn't feel so awkward in the revealing gown—but she also didn't want to try to explain that having Jak's attention weighed heavily on her conscience.

"Yes, you do have his attention," Zeph agreed seriously. "That's not the point. Tonight is to show him how very much you deserve and appreciate his unswerving attention. Jak already thinks you're the most beautiful woman in the world. It's time that you felt the truth of it for yourself. Take a look," Zeph instructed as Stella opened up her mouth to argue. Zeph nodded to Lena to uncover the full-length mirror they'd thrown a rejected gown over in order to get Stella to stop fretting about what they were doing to her appearance.

"Absolutely gorgeous," Gen gushed.

"You know," Lena murmured, gazing at her, "I never thought you looked all that much like Queen Amelia, but looking at you now, I wonder how I missed your resemblance to your mother."

"I'm not sure that's a good thing," Stella replied cautiously. She almost didn't recognize herself in the lovely woman reflected in the mirror. The sheath of the gown fit her body like a second skin—where it wasn't revealing her actual skin— the glittering gauzy overlay clinging lovingly, softening and emphasizing curves she'd have said she didn't have. The bodice dipped daringly low, revealing the inner curves of her smallish breasts, which, for once, looked almost voluptuous. The high slit in front parted to nearly mid-thigh, the jeweled heels giving her legs elegant lines they'd never possessed before.

Turning and looking over her shoulder, she took in the naked expanse of her spine, the way the gown barely clung to her rear end, very nearly revealing the cleft of her buttocks. And yes, she was blushing, the color high on her cheeks—her mother's bone structure, yes—when she faced herself again, her eyes looking larger and sparkling with excited embarrassment. Her lips, which had always been simply there, now looked lush and full, as if begging for kisses.

For Jak's kisses. She flushed even more, the color pinkening her breast, her nipples peaking visibly under the clinging silver silk. "I cannot go out in public like this," she announced firmly.

"Oh, but you have to," Gen cried out, wringing her hands together.

"Not only *can* you," Zeph said, taking her by the waist and turning her away from the mirror, then marching her toward the door, "you're going to, right this moment."

Stella tried digging in her heels, which only unbalanced

her. Clearly she'd have to practice such moves in the teetering things. "I'll shift," she warned Zeph.

"Go ahead. I'll shift, too, and I'll win."

"And I'll help," Gen chimed in, hastily opening the door to the hallway.

Gritting her teeth, Stella had to acknowledge the truth of that. Especially if they teamed up on her. She could use sorcery against them, but... who was she kidding? She wouldn't do that to her friends.

"Astar is going to have an apoplectic fit when he sees me dressed like this."

"I'll handle Astar," Zeph replied almost grimly. "The man means well, but he needs to get out of your way."

The three of them—who'd bathed and dressed while they took turns on Stella's transformation—flanked her through the halls. Everyone they passed stared at Stella. "I feel naked," she muttered.

"You don't *look* naked," Gen reassured her.

"You just don't like being the center of attention," Zeph noted. "No playing the shy, retiring wallflower tonight. You, my darling Nilly, will be the belle of the ball."

"It's honestly past time you were," Lena added with a warm smile. "Also, if and when you decide the crowd is too much for you, I imagine Jak will be happy to keep you company."

"Obviously nothing will happen between us tonight," Stella said, hearing the nerves in her voice, not sure if she was relieved or disappointed.

"Oh, I doubt it will be *nothing*," Zeph crooned, batting her long lashes salaciously and still managing to look like the gríobhth as she did.

"But go at your own pace," Gen advised. "I know Jak will respect that, but... take my advice and don't rush things."

"Oh, Gen. I'm so sorry." Stella slowed, feeling Gen's residual pain and shame over what had happened with Henk.

"No." Gen held up her hands as if to fend Stella off. "Tonight is *not* about me. I'm sorry I said anything."

The sounds of music and talking crashed out of the open arches leading to the ballroom gallery, and Stella thought longingly of the black alter-realm, with its utter absence of psychic energy.

"You don't have to stay long," Lena murmured in her ear. "Just try to have fun."

Fun. Of all the things Stella thought about at social events like this—supporting Astar, keeping a finger on the emotional pulse of the various personalities, wondering when she could politely withdraw to the relative quiet of her rooms—trying to have fun had never been one of them. She nearly said she wasn't sure how to do that, but decided it would sound pitiful.

Then she saw Jak, and all else faded away.

~ 18 ~

H E'D CLEARLY FOUND new clothes in the largesse provided by Queen Nix, as he wore a close-fitting suit of black velvet that showcased his dark eyes and lean build. A froth of white lace failed to soften his jawline, his beard neat and glossy. Spotting their arrival, he spun, showing off the flowing tails of his jacket, then struck a pose—abruptly spoiled when Zeph and Lena stepped aside to leave Stella with no one to hide behind.

Jak froze, goggling at her, his mouth actually falling open.

Behind him, Astar also stared—though with a decidedly different expression on his face—and started toward her, halted when Rhy seized his arm in a firm grip. Giving Stella a smug smile, Zeph swooped over to take Astar's other arm, the pair of them forcibly escorting her brother away. Lena and Gen followed, giving her little waves of encouragement.

Stella hovered where she was, feeling quite lightheaded and definitely naked, especially with the way Jak stared at her, his gaze raking her from head to foot and traveling up again. Recovering his poise, he glided up to her and bowed, dark eyes full of the emotions he held tightly controlled. "May I?"

He offered a hand, and she placed hers in his, bracing herself for the flood of his thoughts and feelings. But he was restrained, only the warmth of his admiration reaching her. Brushing a kiss over the back of her hand, he straightened. "You are always beautiful, my star, but tonight..." He took a deep and shaky breath, then smiled ruefully. "You are both breathtaking and so stunning that I have no breath to speak the words that wouldn't do you justice anyway."

"Those were pretty good words," she replied, hearing the hitch in her own voice.

"Is this for me?" he asked, letting his gaze run over her again, his gaze like a caress on bare skin.

"Yes," she acknowledged. "Courtesy of Zeph, as I'd never have been so bold on my own."

"I knew I loved that naughty shapeshifter," he mused. "And look at us, you in white and me in black. We're a matched pair."

"More like polar opposites."

"That explains the magnetic attraction." He raised a hand to a passing servant and snagged them two flutes of sparkling wine. Passing one to her, he lifted his in a toast. "To the most beautiful woman in the world."

She blushed, of course. "We both know that's my mother, not me."

"You are to me," Jak replied with frank honesty, still with his flute poised, waiting for her to seal the toast. "You're everything to me. The sun, the moon, and the brightest star in the sky."

She had to laugh and clinked her glass to his. "I notice you've found some smooth words again."

"You inspire me." He smiled broadly, sipping his wine as she did.

The golden effervescence spilled over her tongue, bright and delicious. To her surprise, she realized she *was* having fun, and she hadn't even had to think about how to do so.

"Would you dance with me?" Jak asked. "Or would you prefer to stay out of the crush?"

How well he understood her. She gazed ruefully at the crowded dance floor, just the sight of it warning her of the headache she'd get if she plunged herself amid all those people. A headache was the last thing she want to have that night. Maybe she could stand it, for the opportunity to dance with Jak. But first things first. "I should present myself to King Cavan and Queen Nix," she said. "Her Majesty would expect me to do so."

"Of course." Jak presented her with his arm, and she slipped her hand through the crook of his elbow. "Astar has already presented himself, so I should've realized that would be the first thing you'd want to do also." He deftly maneuvered them through the outskirts of the crowd, neatly deflecting anyone who came too close to touching her. She never even sloshed her wine, he moved so smoothly. "I'll remember that for the future," he added, dimples showing as he smiled at her. The gold hoop in his ear glinted, incongruous with the somber attire—and oddly perfect, too.

"You don't have to do this, Jak."

He slid her a curious look. "Don't have to what?"

"Don't have to… make a study of me," she replied with a helpless shrug. "Don't have to accommodate all of my obligations and odd ways."

"You're *not* odd."

"Oh, come on, Jak," she said, laughing, feeling so utterly self-conscious. "I know how strange I am. Another woman would've jumped at the chance to dance with you."

"Good thing I don't want another woman, then," he replied easily. "And you're not strange."

"I'm as strange as they come. That's why I've never—" She broke off, unwilling to expose herself even more.

Halting their progress, he drew her into an unpopulated corner. A pretty palm tree had been planted in a large pot, seeming to flourish there. Jak took her empty flute—when had she drained it?—and set it aside with his. Taking both her hands in his, he studied her face intently. "Why you've held off your admirers," he finished for her. "Why you've never let any of them get close enough to be noticed by you, let alone admitted to the intimacy of your friendship."

She opened her mouth and closed it. "That's not what I was going to say."

"No," he agreed. "I imagine you were about to say something like that's why you've never been open to romance, because you think you're destined to live your life alone, like some sort of sorcerous hermit."

That came uncomfortably close to the truth. "I *am* able to see my own future," she told him, pulling at her hands.

He let her go and set his hands on his narrow hips, sweeping back his jacket to do so, smiling knowingly as she couldn't help remembering the body beneath the clothes. "Have you looked lately?"

"Ah, I—" she stammered, blushing hotly. Truly, she should resign herself to a permanent blush. Belatedly she realized he didn't mean looking at *him*.

His dark eyes sparkled with amusement, seeing through her predicament. "At your future," he clarified helpfully. "Have you looked at your future lately?"

She frowned. "I don't have to." And she didn't want to. The lonely tower in the field of lilies frightened her. For the first time, she considered how unnatural that landscape was, with a chill of foreboding, it occurred to her that it might be an alter-realm.

No wonder it felt like that future loomed ever closer.

"Stella, my love." Jak kept his hands off of her but edged her deeper beneath the cover of the potted palm. Her back hit the wall—the cool stone reminding her how bare it was—and she shivered at the look in Jak's eyes. Much better than the chill of that lonely future. "I may not be a sorcerer, or a very good student, but I paid attention to any of the lessons that helped me understand you better. I know very well that the future can change, that our actions and decisions change it."

"What are you saying?" she breathed, wondering if he'd kiss her right there in the ballroom. And if she'd let him.

Or if she'd give in to the heat between them and kiss him.

His lashes lowered as his gaze swept down, no doubt noticing her tightly peaked nipples. "Maybe you should look," he murmured.

She did—and saw that the gown left nothing to the imagination. Her breasts stood out taut, nipples straining, as if begging for Jak to notice them. With a groan of mortification, she clasped her hands to cover her breasts.

He laughed, gently tugging her hands away. "I *meant* look at your future," he teased. "Please don't cover yourself. You look gorgeous. I only have one problem with this gown."

"That it leaves nothing to the imagination?"

"Oh, it leaves plenty to the imagination," he assured her, "in the best possible way. But then, I have an excellent imagination. I do not, however, see your daggers on you."

She groaned in exasperation. "Seriously?"

He regarded her with absolute seriousness. "Yes. You should be armed at all times."

"At a ball."

"Perfect time to take you by surprise."

"*Where* would I put daggers in this dress?" she demanded.

He leaned in close, his voice an intimate whisper. "I'm happy to help you find hiding places."

"I'll just bet you are," she muttered, and he laughed. "I suppose you're wearing blades?"

"A few," he replied with a grin.

"Well, I have my *other* weapons," she informed him archly. "Invisible sorcerous ones."

"Have you been practicing those, then?" he asked with a suspicious glint in his eye.

"Some," she admitted, then grimaced. "Not enough."

Nodding, he didn't chastise her. "We can work on that tomorrow, since we'll be cooling our heels here another day or two. I can come up with some dummies for you to practice on, so you won't be worrying about hurting anyone."

"That could work." She smiled, grateful for his thoughtfulness.

"Ready to face the royal lions?"

"I suppose I'd better," she said on a sigh as he tucked her hand in the crook of his arm again, escorting her out from the shelter of the potted palm.

"You'll dazzle them," he promised. "And while I know you don't wear anything this revealing as a rule, it's truly tamer than what most court ladies wear."

"That's my point: I am not most court ladies."

"No, you're a princess destined to be a queen," Jak agreed easily. "Which means, to continue our earlier conversation, that I'm perfectly happy to make a study of you, as you put it. If I'm going to have a place in your life, then I plan to be good at it."

They were approaching the dais where King Cavan and Queen Nix sat on their thrones, heads bent together in some intimate exchange. With her hair white as snow and his silver-threaded black, they looked like an echo of what Jak had said about the two of them, a black and white matched pair. "Jak…" She took a deep breath. "I love you, but I don't know if there's a place for you in my life."

There, she'd gotten it out. She'd been honest with him, even if she had equivocated more than she meant to.

Unperturbed, Jak patted her hand. "I know that's what you think. That's why I intend to carve one out." He slid her a cocky grin. "I'm an excellent bladesman."

"I know that," she gritted out, "but Jak—"

"Ah-ah-ah." He wagged a finger at her. "We agreed to no 'but Jaks' unless there's whiskey involved."

"I never agreed to that."

"You did, tacitly."

"Choosing not to argue with you isn't the same as tacit agreement."

"It's a lot like not drawing your blades to defend yourself when something attacks you," he replied, sliding her a pointed look. "If you want a different outcome, you'll have to take a stand."

"You're impossible," she hissed as the royal couple's seneschal waved them forward.

"Not at all. I'm possible. Very possible. Even probable." He set a hand on the small of her back and slipped behind her. "I'll be right here, waiting for you."

Composing herself, Stella moved forward and inclined her head to the king and queen of Erie. The etiquette involved was a bit hazy. They were subject to the high throne, but Astar was crown prince still, not high king—and regardless, Stella was his sister and though generally expected to be queen of Annfwn someday, she didn't have much in the way of her own rank. Even if she did, presumptive someday queen of an equivalent kingdom to theirs didn't match their current rank.

And yet, the perception of her position, particularly as widely known apprentice to Queen Andromeda occasionally amplified reactions to her. At Elderhorst, it hadn't been an issue, as King Groningen had been as apt to chuck her under the chin and remind her what a troublesome toddler she'd been. With the reclusive monarchs of a distant subsidiary kingdom, she was on less solid footing. A flicker of movement caught her eye, and for a moment, a white horse seemed to prance past and was gone. Magic, of a kind she'd never before encountered, shimmered in the air.

"Princess Stella," Queen Nix said warmly, startling her from her reverie. "It's a delight to receive you here in our court."

"Indeed," King Cavan said with a charming smile. "You are the spitting image of your mother."

"Oh, Cavan," the queen chided, rolling her eyes. "Her Highness looks like Queen Andromeda if anyone, with all that dark hair. Prince Astar has their mother's coloring."

"Astar looks very much like our father, Your Highnesses," Stella said with a smile. She could swear she could see a horse. There and gone again. "Neither of us can hold a candle to our mother's goddess-gifted beauty, though I'm flattered by the comparison."

"Well, my old dress looks lovely on you." Nix smiled and patted her flat belly. "After seven children, my waistline no longer allows me to wear it. You'll take it with you, I hope."

Startled, Stella realized she and Nix were very much of a size, though Nix had a fuller, mature woman's figure. "Thank you so much, Your Highness. I will treasure the gift."

Nix's gaze went past her. "And who is your handsome escort?"

Stella glanced back to find Jak waiting at relaxed attention where she'd left him, hands folded behind his back, dark eyes alert. Gesturing him forward, she noted a flicker of surprise in him—perhaps unease?—before he strode up, sweeping a deep bow to the royal couple. "Jakral Konyngrr," Stella told them. "A longtime friend."

"Konyngrr." Cavan tapped his chin thoughtfully. "Related to Prince Harlan, Her Majesty's consort?"

"My uncle, Your Highnesses," Jak agreed, a hint of reserve in his voice. Wondering at it, Stella opened her senses to him, finding him surprisingly tense.

"Aha!" Cavan nodded. "I've placed you now. You're General Kral's son, the man who sought to be emperor of all Dasnaria and became a sailor instead."

Jack settled into his apparently relaxed stance again, arms folded behind his back. So as not to be tempted to draw a blade, Stella realized. "The very one, Your Highness."

"Is it true," Cavan asked in a conspiratorial tone, as if everyone present couldn't hear, "that your father's ship, the…"

"The *Hákyrling*," Jak supplied easily, his tension increasing.

"Yes, the *Hákyrling*—has it truly engaged Kooncelund frigates south of the Sentinels?"

Long habit allowed Stella to keep her expression cool and remote, but this was news to her. Jak made a show of frowning, though Stella read the lie in him clearly when he answered. "I've no knowledge of such encounters."

"Hmm." Cavan narrowed gray eyes gone sharp. "I wonder if—"

"Cavan," Nix said, interrupting him with a hand on his arm. "This is a party. Tomorrow is time enough for political conversations. Our young visitors have come on a quest, after all."

"Fine, fine," Cavan replied genially, stroking his silver-threaded, dark beard. "Your brother mentioned you hoped to travel to the Isles of Remus to meet with our son, Isyn."

Something in his forbidding demeanor warned her the answer wasn't promising. "Yes. Her Majesty specifically requested we pay a visit to King Isyn, to make diplomatic overtures. Will we be able to accomplish her request?"

Cavan and Nix exchanged glances. "That's something of a complicated answer," Nix replied. "We'll explain in full tomorrow. For now, please enjoy the party."

Dismissed, Stella inclined her head, and Jak bowed again. As he escorted her away, guiding them to the fringes of the crowd, she bent her head closer to his. "What's this about the *Hákyrling* encountering Kooncelund ships?"

He rolled his eyes. "How can rumor fly so fast when we can't get clear messages from Ordnung?"

"Jak."

"Stella."

"You're ducking the question."

"I have an idea," he said, quickening his pace toward a set of glass-paned doors leading onto a terrace. Opening one, he stuck his head out. "Not too chilly. And there are fire pits." He tugged her out with him, leaving the door ajar so music swept out behind them.

The terrace was empty of people, the firepits scattered around circled by chairs in conversational groups. Out in the open air, the psychic pressure of the crowd lightened, and Stella breathed a sigh of release. "I want you to tell me about the Kooncelund ships," she said, determined not to be distracted.

"And I want to dance with you," Jak replied, sweeping her a bow. Straightening, he grimaced at whatever he saw in her face. "I'll tell you all about it tomorrow. Danu knows Cavan seems intent on grilling me. For tonight, I just want to savor being with you, in this beautiful dress you wore just for me." His gaze caressed over her bosom, and she had no doubt the chill had her breasts standing at more attention than ever. To think she'd forgotten about her dress for a while.

Jak held out his hands, inviting her to step into them, so she did. His upper hand closed gently over hers, his other arm going about her waist. She set her hand on his velvet-clad shoulder, meeting his dark, intent gaze. Feeling suddenly shy, she searched his face. *Tonight is to show him how very much you deserve and appreciate his unswerving attention.* Having Jak's full attention was a heady experience, and she felt stripped bare by it.

"Are you cold?" he asked softly.

"No." In fact, she felt overwarm, flushed and needy.

"Good." His voice was an intimate murmur amidst the firelit shadows. Catching the upsweep of the music, he moved her into the dance, leading with the deft agility that characterized everything he did. His eyes never left her face as he moved them in ever-widening circles, whirling them faster and faster over the stone terrace, their only audience the crackling fires. A laugh welled up inside her, ebullient and effervescent as the sparkling wine, and she threw back her head to release it. The stars shimmered overhead, brighter and denser than she'd ever seen them.

Jak laughed with her, releasing her to twirl at the tip of his fingers like a spinning dagger, then reeling her back into his arms. The music hit a crescendo, the notes swelling and throbbing like a heartbeat, then drifted away. In the ensuing quiet, only the flames snapped. Jak splayed his hand on her bare back, caressing her lightly there. "Is this touch all right?"

"Yes." Her voice came out on a whisper. "I'm growing accustomed to feeling you in my head."

His lips quirked. "That doesn't sound like a positive, but I'll take it. I have to say, I really love this dress." His fingers glided up the line of her spine to the exposed nape of her neck and down again. "And I love hearing you laugh."

"I laugh," she countered.

"Not often." He caressed the length of her spine, making her shiver with heat. "You're always so very serious."

"I warned you that I have no sense of humor."

"I don't think that's true. You just have a different way of seeing the world."

"Strange," she agreed. "Odd."

"Delightfully enigmatic." Pressing his hand into the small of her back, he drew her closer against him. "I'm always wondering what you're thinking behind those summer-thunderstorm eyes."

"Probably nothing very interesting." She couldn't quite catch her breath, overwhelmed by this closeness to him. Jak's presence overpowered her thoughts, like a mighty ocean filling every sense. Because she could, she slid her hand behind his neck, stroking the soft skin in the hollow there, as he had with her. His eyelids lowered, a hum of pleasure coming from him.

"What are you thinking now?" he asked.

"I can't think about anything but you," she confessed.

"Good. Because I'm the same." His gaze wandered over

her lips. "Can I kiss you?"

She thought she might die if he didn't. "Yes."

Though she was ready for it this time, the brush of his lips over hers undid her. The taste, the sensation of him, the heat of his desire all flooded her, and she clung to him like her only salvation in a storm-tossed sea. He kissed her like a drowning man, drinking her in like his last gasp of air, his hands fierce on her kiss. When she dragged her mouth from his, needing breath of her own, he kissed the underside of her jaw, nipping the tender skin lightly. The sensation drilled into her, her bones going liquid, and he dragged his teeth down her throat, holding her in a firm grip as she bowed backward over his arm.

His hot mouth trailed lower, following the skin bared by the daring gown. Reaching the hollow between her breasts, he slowly licked the inside curve of one, then the other. A sound of raw, shuddering need escaped her...

And she was on her feet again, Jak decorously stepping back and putting his hands on his hips. They were both out of breath, and he laughed raggedly.

"Is something wrong?" she asked.

"Too right," he replied ruefully. "I thought I'd better stop before I went too far."

"I didn't want you to stop," she said before she knew she'd speak the words.

Jak cocked his head, listening very carefully. "Anyone could come upon us out here."

True. And that wouldn't be good.

"We can dance some more, if you prefer," he suggested.

"I think I've had enough of the party," she told him hesitantly. "I'm sorry."

"You don't have to be sorry." He took her hands and en-folded them in his. "That's who you are. Shall I escort you to your room?"

She didn't want to be alone in her room either. Perhaps for the first time in her entire life, being alone didn't sound desirable. "I don't think I want that either," she ventured.

Jak studied her face. "Would you come to my room with me?" he asked very carefully. A breath of insecurity leaked from him, part of him braced for disappointment. "It's all right to say no. I said we'd take things slow, and I meant it. We have all the time in the world."

But what if they didn't? They might not have any more than tonight. That tower loomed ever closer. "What about Rhyian?"

Jak grinned in sheer happiness, excitement leaping in him and fueling hers. "He owes me. I told him if the door was bolted to find somewhere else to sleep, and he agreed."

"You planned this?" She wasn't sure how to feel about that, though the girls had all seemed to assume something like this might happen.

"A good warrior prepares for all eventualities," he replied, a bit smug. He adjusted her dress, then offered his arm. "Shall we?"

Feeling as if she were taking an enormous step—like leap-ing into a deep and bottomless defile—she slipped her hand through the now-familiar crook of his elbow. Inside, the close heat of the ballroom hit her like a wall, the gamut of emotions loosened by wine and exertion pummeling her. "Steady," Jak murmured. "Close your eyes if it helps."

"What if someone notices?"

"What do you care? You're strange and odd."

"Jak!"

He laughed. "It will only add to your air of mystery, sorceress. Close your eyes. I'll have us out of here in a moment."

She did as he suggested, surprised to find it did help. As he had in the dance, Jak led her through the crowd with deft agility, so that she never questioned her footing, or so much as brushed against someone else. Feeling the cooler, fresher air of the hallway on her face, she opened her eyes, finding him grinning at her. "That *did* work," she exclaimed. "How did you know it would?"

"A guess," he admitted. "A trick Mom taught me. When I'm trying to see a long ways or pick out detail, I cover my ears. It helps me to focus. I figure your sensing emotions is like an extra sense. A crush like that can be overwhelming even to those of us with the usual ones, so it makes sense that eliminating at least the sight of all those people lets you concentrate on keeping them out of your head."

"Very clever," she conceded.

"As I keep telling you I am," he replied, turning down another hall and stopping before a closed door. "Still on board with this voyage?"

And here she thought she'd already taken the step. Unable to meet his intent gaze, she stared hard at the door, as if it might hold answers. "I want to, yes, but I don't know how much I can... That is, I—"

"Stella." He waited for her to lift her eyes to his. "We can stop anytime. Only as much as you're enjoying. I mean it."

Mutely, she nodded. Moving slowly, he opened the door and gestured her in. Stepping inside, she paused in wonder. Candles were lit around the bedchamber, with hothouse roses spilling from vases in florid splendor. The bed was turned down, rose petals scattered over the sheets. She raised a brow at Jak as he finished bolting the door and turned. "Is this part of the eventualities?"

He took in the sensually appointed room, slowly shaking his head. "I'd like to take credit, but I didn't do this."

"Zeph," she said on a sigh, exasperated and moved at the same time.

"Ah. Of course it was."

"I should tell you…" she started, then hesitated, wondering if she really should.

Jak raised a brow and waited.

"The girls," Stella continued, figuring herself stuck now, "they made a betting pool, on when I'd lose my virginity to you."

Jak's brows rose higher, dark eyes sparkling, though he didn't crack a smile. "Are we in Zeph's window tonight?"

"How did you guess?" she asked wryly, and now he laughed.

"Zeph has a nose for these things," he conceded, "though it might not yet happen. Who has after this?"

"Gen. She picked eight to ten days, Zeph had five to seven, and Lena bet on one to four."

Jak stroked his hands down her arms, looking terribly pleased and interested. Of course, the man loved a good bet.

"I'll have to thank Lena for the vote of confidence in my seductive skills. What was the starting date?"

"The night you, Astar, and Rhy went to the tavern," she admitted, face heating.

A wide smile cracked his face. "That was before I discussed anything with Astar."

"Yes, but *after* the incident in the carriage," she pointed out, almost primly.

"The *incident*," he purred, drawing her closer. "You mean when I showed you what could be yours."

She looked up at him uncertainly. "Mine?"

"Remember what I told you before. My body is yours." He plucked a pin from her hair, discarding it and coaxing the long strand to uncoil. "All right if I take your hair down?"

"Yes." Feeling the shiver of his gaze on her sensitive skin, she turned. Instead of plucking more pins, however, he feathered a caress down her spine, then pressed a hot kiss to the naked small of her back. She gasped at the sensation, melting with it.

"Have I mentioned how much I love this dress?" he asked against her skin. "Gotta admire Zeph for working hard to win the bet. Serious competitive spirit here."

Stella giggled, a sound she was sure had never escaped her before. "She set the lure for you, yes, but I have a mind of my own."

"No one could be unclear on that." Jak's lips traveled up her spine, leaving a blazing trail behind, his skillful hands anchoring her by the hips as she sagged. His mouth brushed over the nape of her neck, shivering need through her. Sliding his arms around her waist, he snugged her back against him, his velvet-clad erection hard against her bottom, his lips finding another spot beneath her ear that made her weaken further. "How is the touching feeling?"

"Amazing," she breathed.

"You'll tell me if it hurts?"

"I would, yes." She turned in his arms and looped her hands behind his neck. "Remember when the tentacle monster was dragging me away and I sent you to retrieve the Star?"

His eyes hardened, expression going remote. "Till my dying day."

"And I had you do Danu's Dance so you'd enter a trance state, allowing me to enter your mind."

His expression thawed with curiosity. "I didn't realize that's what happened."

She nodded, hoping he wouldn't mind what she was about to tell him. "You let me into you so completely that it's as if the barriers between us softened. Your thoughts and emotions are no more painful to me than my own. Even if they are sometimes... brasher than mine."

"That's one word for it." Lowering his head, he kissed her softly, with devastating thoroughness, tracing his tongue along her lower lip before he pulled back, studying her face. "So... that's good?"

"It is if you aren't bothered."

A line formed between his brows. "Why would I be bothered?"

"You are pretty much an open book to me now. I can read your thoughts and feelings from any distance."

"Is that how you knew I wasn't dead? And how you found me in the black-stone alter-realm?"

She nodded. Of course it wouldn't take Jak's canny mind any time to put it all together. He pursed his lips, considering, then smiled. "You could just rummage around in my head and extract the information about what happened with the Kooncelund ships."

Her mouth fell open. "I *wouldn't*," she said on a gasp. "That would be—"

He stopped her words with a swift kiss, his tongue slipping within to plunder her mouth, sending her mind swimming until her thoughts were pinprick stars in a midnight sea. "That would be fine," he said against her lips. "All yours, remember?"

~ 19 ~

STELLA GAZED UP at him, her eyes dreamy and softly gray—and for once he didn't have to wonder what deep thoughts preoccupied her, because she was focused entirely on him, pliant and warm in his arms.

And she loved him. It still seemed so tentative and fragile, that new reality, and yet he'd begun to believe in it. Here she was, alone in his bedchamber, wearing that dress that made her shine like a star, and that had been driving him out of his mind with the need to strip it off her gorgeous body from the moment he'd laid eyes on her.

Because she hadn't said anything more, he resumed plucking the pins from her hair, savoring the satin spill of her dark locks as they unfurled against her creamy skin. The candlelight gleamed on them, bringing out the red that lay banked beneath, like the glimmer of crimson fire in otherwise black coals. That was Stella through and through—quiet, unobtrusive, until the breath of flame awakened and she billowed like an inferno.

She trembled under his hands, so sensitive and receptive to the least caress. He'd reined himself in with fierce determination, keeping his raging need tightly leashed. He'd do nothing that might frighten her, or even give her a moment's discomfort. For her, he would be all gentleness and patience.

Of course, he reflected grimly, he might have to step away for a moment and relieve the unrelenting erection that had become truly painful in the hours since he first saw her in that dress. The upside was that it wouldn't take long. He was opening his mouth to offer some excuse when she looked over her shoulder at him, her eyes glowing with sensual understanding.

"Don't step away to do it," she murmured, gaze traveling down his body as she laid her delicate hands on his chest. "Let me do this for you."

He breathed a laugh, not exactly embarrassed, but… "I thought you wouldn't invade my thoughts," he teased.

"Some things I can't help hearing," she replied in a wry tone. "Particularly if you're thinking about saying something, the thoughts form loudly and clearly in your head in the moment before." Her lips curved in a smile. "So you have to stop telling me so many pretty lies, because I'll know."

He feigned shock. "You made a joke!"

"I didn't." She seemed astonished at the suggestion. "I wasn't joking at all. That's perfectly true."

"Uh-huh." He put his hands over hers, lightly curling his fingers around her wrists, vividly imagining what might come next. "What am I thinking now?"

She blushed furiously, but didn't tense up. "That's what you want from me?"

Oh, Danu, I so owe you for giving me this. And Moranu, and Glorianna. I owe all of you generous sister goddesses. "If you'd like to." He tried to keep his feelings open about it, to not pressure her by showing how very desperately he needed her touch.

"This is all mine, isn't it that what you said? So I can do as I like with you." She was definitely teasing him now, this gamine side of her a delightful discovery. Her nimble fingers worked the buttons of his waistcoat, pushing it off over his shoulders along with the jacket. Working intently, she undid the laces of his shirt, gaze caressing him as she undressed him. She pressed her lips to his bared chest, then glanced up when he jerked under the kiss. "Is this all right?"

"Can't you feel that it is?"

"Yes, but your feelings and mine, they're tangling—and this is all very intense."

"I understand that." He took a breath, instructing himself to calm down. "It's intense for me, too, and all very good."

"I'm glad." With a wicked sparkle in her eyes, she undid the fastening of his pants, easing them over his hips. Jak held very, very still, closing his eyes, certain that the smallest wrong move would have him spending with ignominious speed. "Should I do this like you did?" Stella asked, peeling the fabric away so his turgid cock sprang free. "In the carriage."

He groaned, the memory only spurring him to greater extremity. "I think it's not going to matter," he gritted out, then risked looking at her. Her dark head was bent as she studied him, and he nearly came right then simply from having her look at him. "My star," he nearly panted, sliding his hands through her hair. She looked up, eyes wide and dark with desire. "Please."

She smiled, softly and sweetly. "A kind of healing." Setting her hands on his abdomen, she slid them down, following with her gaze, her native green magic sparking through his skin— and she wrapped her hands around his shaft.

His eyes rolled back in his head, his whole body going rigid, and an inarticulate, strangled gargle of sound erupted as he fisted his hands in her hair. Probably much too hard, but he couldn't help himself, and she didn't seem to notice. Gripping his cock firmly at the base with one hand, she stroked up with the other. She *had* been paying attention in the carriage, her technique perfection, her healer's hands striking the exact balance between firm and gentle. His knees went to water, and he sank to the floor, Stella following him down.

Kneeling before him, she watched him gravely. "This is good, yes?"

"Danu, yes." He tried to relax his grip on her hair, but she stroked him again, and his hips rode up in helpless need. "Stella..." he ground out.

One more stroke of her exquisite hands and he lost himself, body arcing, spending his seed in convulsive bursts that left him sagging, breathing ragged, face buried in the silken mass of her hair. She stroked him soothingly, attuned to his sensations, following along with meticulous attention.

"You are a miraculous lover," he whispered.

"Am I?" She rubbed her cheek against his, finding his mouth with a searching kiss, then studying his face with grave attention. "I want to be for you. It's lovely to give pleasure this way, like healing, only there's no pain to overcome, so it rises to another, even better level."

As her words penetrated his pleasure-fogged brain, he got a

grip on himself, unwound his hands from her hair, and gently moved her hands from him. She gave him a questioning look. "Is something wrong?"

"No." Rising to his feet again, he brought her with him, then kissed her and stepped back. "But let me clean up. We're going to start over."

"Start over?" Looking at her hands covered with his fluids, she licked one finger curiously. The sight had him hardening again. "Tastes like the sea," she said, crystal-gray eyes alight with innocent wonder. The artlessness she brought to their lovemaking stirred him more than all the practiced techniques of his more-experienced lovers.

"Starting over," he replied firmly, going to the attached bathing chamber and wetting two towels, bringing her one to clean her hands and using the other on himself. "And turning the attention on you," he added, lowering his voice to a sensual burr, just to see her blush.

"There's no need to start over." She sounded shy, lashes lowering as she diligently wiped her hands clean. "I don't need attention on me. I liked doing this for you. I want to make you happy, Jak."

She was babbling. Shy and nervous. He tossed the towel aside and firmly fastened his pants again. They were going to stay that way for a while. "Finished with this?" He plucked at the towel in her hands, then tossed it aside also when she nodded. Moving slowly, he threaded his hands through the silk of her hair, pushing the mass of it back over her shoulders, coaxing her to lift her face to his. "Did you find it exciting, doing that for me?"

Mutely, she nodded, the blush high on her cheekbones.

"That's how I'll feel, giving you pleasure," he explained. "Enough of you tending to me. I want to touch you. That would make me happy."

Doubt filled her eyes, a sense of that feeling curling into him, too. He would have to practice discerning her emotions from his. Especially with Stella being such a giving person and him—well, who was he kidding?—him being accustomed to taking whatever he could get, it would be a challenge to make sure he gave to *her*.

"I see..." she said slowly. "What do I do?"

"Nothing at all," he replied as seriously as he could, given that he wanted to laugh with sheer delight in her. "I'll do all the work. You stop me if I do something you don't like."

"Go ahead." She visibly braced herself, closing her eyes and even curling her fingers into loose fists at her sides.

He studied her. "Maybe we need that whiskey after all."

Her eyes flew open. "I did not 'but Jak' you!"

"Not verbally." With a mental sigh for his obtuseness, he took her hand and led her to the chairs by the fireplace. Seating her in one, he poured them both a finger of the excellent and rare Branlian whiskey he'd purchased with his winnings from the tavern contest, which felt like an age ago. Stella held hers tentatively, as if it might sprout wings and flap away. He took a fortifying sip of his whiskey, savoring the smooth burn. "I think there are maybe things you want to tell me that I need to listen to."

"Oh." She reflected on that, turning the cup in her hands. "I just... It's that..." She blew out a breath. "I do love you."

It still gave him a thrill to hear it, even mitigated as it was in that moment by the clear hesitation in her voice and manner. He could wish that she was an open book to *him*. "But Jak…" he prompted, lifting a brow.

She laughed a little, then actually sipped her whiskey, eyes going wide. "How do you drink as much of this as you do?" she gasped, waving a hand as if cooling flames.

"Practice," he informed her seriously, then grinned. "The second sip is smoother."

Judiciously she sipped again, then nodded. "True."

"So," he said, crossing one leg over his knee. Realizing that might come across as defensive, he unwound and leaned his forearms on his knees, dangling the glass between them. "You love me, but…"

"But I really don't think that there's a future for us." She grimaced. "I know there isn't."

He bit back the automatic argument and forced himself to slow down and consider her words. "Because you looked?"

She nodded unhappily, then shook her head. "We have to face that you and I are very different people. Once we're no longer on this quest, what would we have in common? Where would we live? You can't be forever guarding my back and escorting me about."

"Why not?" he asked, very reasonably, he thought, given the frustration boiling up inside him.

"Because that would be no life for you!"

He stared into the whiskey, knowing full well it didn't contain any more answers than it ever did. "Is it that I'm not good enough for you?" he asked evenly, unwilling to see the truth in her face.

"What? No. Why would you think that?" Real distress sounded in her voice, so he made himself meet her earnest gaze.

"I'm not a prince," he reminded her. "Not magical. Not a shapeshifter. I'm just a sailor—and sometime pirate, it's true—who happens to be good with a blade."

"Jak," she said, clearly stricken, "that doesn't come close to encompassing all that you are."

"But all that I am doesn't fit anywhere into your future." He sounded as dead as he felt inside.

"It's not because of you," she whispered. "It's me."

He nodded, mostly because he didn't trust his voice. It was an old insecurity, one he thought he'd left behind long ago, but apparently not. When you're friends with the children of kings and queens, of sorcerers and dragonkin, you couldn't get too caught up in comparisons. He'd always known he wasn't good enough for Stella, but that hadn't stopped him from wanting her. That was the pirate in him, he supposed, always reaching for unearned treasure.

"Jak, please talk to me," Stella said quietly, her tone beseeching, her voice strained.

With a hoarse laugh, he looked at her, so incredibly beautiful in the candlelight, her skin glowing against that remarkable dress that teased with what it nearly revealed. Her dark hair cascaded around her like a cloak of night, and her eyes were silver as the moon. Quaffing the rest of the whiskey, he considered drinking the entire bottle. Maybe that would kill the pain. "I thought you knew everything I'm thinking already."

"Not at the moment, I don't. The emotions are too strong. All I know is how upset you are."

"I'm thinking this is not how I envisioned this night going," he said, trying to keep it light and failing miserably.

"Jak..." She sounded miserable and broken. The little fingers of her left hand twitched, and he more than half expected her to chew on them. But she curled them into a fist instead. "I'm so sorry. See? I'm no good at this. I'll only bring you misery." Standing, she smoothed her dress. "I'd better go."

"Yeah, you do that." He didn't care that he sounded bitter. "Actually, wait. Tell me this: if this is how you felt all along, why did you agree to letting me court you? Why are you even here with me right now?"

She twined a long lock of hair around her fingers, twisting it in her agitation. She hated hurting him, and she'd done it anyway. "I wanted to test the waters. To try to see if I could make it work with you."

"But you *didn't* try," he hurled at her, a well-aimed throw because she flinched and paled. "You're so far from testing the waters that you're standing on shore, perfectly dry, and do you know why?"

"It sounds like *you* know," she said with a testy edge. At least he could get under her skin this way. "Why don't you explain myself to me, Jak?"

Standing, he poured himself more whiskey, because why not? "You're afraid, Stella. That's why you're always extending yourself to help everyone else, because you can't bear for anyone to see inside you, to truly touch *you* emotionally."

"You don't know what it's like for me." A quaver laced her voice, and she looked away from him. "I've told you: letting people inside is painful."

He barked out a humorless laugh. "I have news for you, sweetheart. It's painful for all of us. But you've developed a dodge, always being the one giving because you're terrified of needing anyone or anything."

"That's not fair," she replied, but her mouth wobbled.

"Isn't it? You're the one who's figured out a way to avoid being close to anyone."

"I'm close to Astar."

"Not anymore," he persisted ruthlessly. "You're letting him go, too. Remember how you worked so hard to make sure Astar didn't know you felt abandoned by his falling in love with Zeph?"

"I didn't want to impinge on his happiness. To behave otherwise would be selfish."

"Oh, right." He gestured with the mug. "You and Astar, both so fucking noble all the time. Has it ever occurred to you that clinging to this honorable ideal is the most selfish thing of all?"

"No, Jak, it hasn't. And you getting drunk isn't going to solve anything."

"Also wrong," he snarled. "Getting drunk is how us lowly mossbacks deal with emotional pain. Something else you wouldn't understand."

"Which thing wouldn't I understand?" she snapped, finally losing her cool reserve. "Emotional pain or using liquor as a crutch to escape it?"

"Besides which, I'm far from drunk. Something I intend to remedy, so unless you want to keep me company—or commit to a real effort to make this work between us—you might as well leave."

"Fine, I will." She strode to the door.

"You do it so well, after all," he called after her. "Enjoy your life alone. Just remember that you're the one who made it be that way."

She slammed the door behind her. He poured himself more whiskey.

It was going to take a lot.

STELLA DASHED THE tears from her eyes, glad she'd at least managed to keep them from spilling over until she made it out the door. Once in the empty corridor, she paused, glancing back at the firmly shut door, more than half expecting Jak to come storming through it, demanding that she come back and resolve the argument.

But he didn't.

He really was, finally, letting her go. She should be happy. Relieved.

What had she done?

Feeling too shattered to walk to her room, unable to face running into anyone, friend or stranger, she leaned for a moment against the wall. Pressing her forehead against the smooth, plastered surface, she let the tears fall. Giving in to the need, she tucked her left little fingers between her lips, the taste odd from the crystals Gen had glued to her nails. Sucking on them just a little, she splayed her other palm against the wall, the stone structure beneath old and rooted in the ground. Steady and solid in a way she wasn't. Especially in that moment, she was as fragile and ephemeral, no substance to her at all. She hated that about herself. Back when she'd told Astar she wanted to test the waters with Jak, it had felt possible to be someone else, someone strong.

But she honestly wasn't that person, and never would be.

"I take it this means I get to sleep in my own borrowed bed?"

Stella jumped, tucking her hand guiltily behind her back and jerking her head away from the wall—how foolish had she looked, standing there like that?—and faced Rhyian. He lounged against the same wall, shoulder against it, arms folded, one ankle crossed languidly over the other. Clearly he'd been there a while, and she'd been so fogged in by her own turmoil that she hadn't even noticed.

"Ah, um, yes," she stammered. "If you hurry, Jak might not have drunk the entire bottle of whiskey yet." She tried a smile, but it came out wobbly, along with a fresh spate of tears. She never had been any good at humor.

"That bad, huh?" Rhy cocked his head at her, and she braced herself for a cutting remark. "Want me to go tell the girls you need some hand holding?"

"No!" That came out way too forcefully, and her nose was dripping. With nothing else to use but the beautiful dress, she wiped her nose with the back of her hand, certain that her mother, no matter how far away, knew and was cringing. Rhy handed her a folded cloth from his pocket, and she took it, bemused both that he had it and that he'd thought to offer. "I don't really want to talk to anyone right now," she amended.

Rhy nodded but didn't move. "I'm like that, too. Prefer to lick my wounds in solitude. Has the added benefit of allowing me to feel sorry for myself."

She should offer to listen, to give him comfort, but she didn't have it in her. "Rhyian, I…"

"I was really angry at you," he continued. "I'm sure you know that. Beyond furious that Mother gave you the Star of Annfwn."

Groaning internally, absolutely unable to deal with this conversation at that moment, she nodded. "I know. For what it's worth, I am sorry. Neither of us wanted you to be hurt."

He shrugged, the gesture rippling through him though he stayed in the same pose, blue eyes keen on her. "I was especially pissed that you felt you had to keep it secret from me."

"I shouldn't have. I—"

"Of course you should have," he interrupted. "And my being hurt, being pissed, is *my* problem, Nilly. Anyone can see that you should have the Star. You are the logical heir to both Annfwn and the sorcerous legacy of Salena's line."

"Oh." She didn't know what to say to that. "Thank you."

Shaking his head, he made a face at her. "Don't thank me. You're the right choice because of who you are. You're a powerful sorceress, and you'll be a good queen. Though you'll need to work on your alpha presence. If you're going to be queen, you'll have to get a lot more commanding."

She had no idea how to do that. "Maybe you should be king of Annfwn, and I'll handle the sorcery."

Grimacing ruefully, he unfolded his arms to wag a finger at her. "It doesn't work that way. Father was king without being a sorcerer, and that went badly for Annfwn. Nope, you'll just have to buck up."

Wonderful. Maybe she could think about that when she didn't feel so wrung out.

"Want some advice?" Rhy asked. "I realize I am not the guy people come to for sage advice, but I think I have something useful for you, since you and I are a lot alike."

She blinked at him. "We are?"

"Yes, cousin." He gave her a wolfish grin. "Old Willy the golden boy, he's so different from me, you wouldn't even know we're related, but you and I—we're the same inside. Haunted by the shadows of Moranu's hand, ever changeable, never fixed. If we had less-charming personalities, they'd call us capricious. Fickle, even."

"I am not—"

"Why are you out in the hall weeping when everybody knows that both you and Jak wish you were inside that room?" He jerked his head down the hall.

"We argued," she answered weakly.

"So? People argue. The more they care, the more painful it is. What you do is go back in there and sort it out."

"Like you did with Lena?" she asked, stung enough to say what she normally wouldn't.

"Exactly," he replied softly. "Like I *didn't* do with Lena. Because I chose to lick my wounds and suffer in solitude rather than dealing with her and the consequences of my actions. All because I was afraid. Lena got to me. I loved her, and I couldn't stand to be that vulnerable to her."

You're afraid... you can't bear for anyone to see inside you, to truly touch you emotionally.

Rhyian eyed her knowingly. "A lot alike, you and I. The big difference is that you cope by diverting attention from yourself by tending to everyone else, while I deflect by being a sarcastic asshole." He grinned, though it quickly faded. "Take my advice, cousin of mine: Don't fuck this up. Go back in there and fix it. Because if you don't do it now, you might not get another opportunity. Learn from my great cautionary tale. Someone should."

Pushing himself off the wall, he gave her a jaunty, if slightly sarcastic, salute. "I'm off to find somewhere else to sleep." He shoved his hands in his pockets and started walking back down the corridor. "Tell Jak the debt is paid," he tossed over his shoulder.

"When did you gain so much self-knowledge?" she called after him, still more than a little annoyed. Galling, for Rhy to be giving her advice.

He glanced back, eyes smoky with remorse. "The thing about licking your wounds in solitude? Gives you a lot of time to think."

~ 20 ~

I T TOOK MORE courage than she believed she possessed, but Stella made herself walk back down the quiet corridor and open that door. It would've been polite to knock—and she nearly did, knuckles poised near the carved wood—but if Jak came to answer the door, they might end up continuing the fight in the hallway, and she didn't think she could bear that.

So she turned the handle, holding her breath lest Jak had bolted the door behind her. It opened easily, and she stepped inside. The candles all still glowed, the petal-strewn bed untouched, her hairpins and Jak's clothes piled on the floor where they'd left them before she ruined everything.

"Rhy, man," Jak called from the fireplace where he stood, shirtless, trousers hanging low on his narrow hips. He still wore his glossy black boots, and he had his forearm braced against the mantel, head bowed as he stared at the fire, whiskey bottle dangling loosely from his other hand. "I know I said if the door's unbolted to come on in, but if you love me at all, you'll leave. I'm in a foul mood."

Stella closed the door and bolted it.

"Stay at your peril, then." Jak snorted, setting the bottle on the mantel, then starting to turn. "Or maybe we can brawl.

You couldn't beat me up any more than—Stella."

"Me."

"Came back to claim your hairpins? I think they're on the floor there with the pieces of my heart. Hey, gives you another opportunity to grind the still-bleeding shreds of it into the rug with your delicate, pointy heels."

She rolled her eyes, advancing on him. "Oh, that's not dramatic."

"Dasnarians excel at that kind of thing," he informed her, tucking his thumbs into the belt that held his blades. "Really, it's good that you broke my heart. Now I have a tragic tale of love unrequited to tell at the taverns."

"You'll need better alliteration to earn your way as a poet," she retorted, "since you won't be earning coin throwing knives when you're a drunkard."

He bared his teeth and reached for the whiskey bottle. "It takes a lot more than one bottle to dull my wits, sweetheart. Why are you here?"

Screwing up her courage, she went to him, neatly plucking the bottle from his hand. On impulse, she hurled it into the fireplace, satisfied by the shattering glass and the whoomph of billowing flames as they consumed the volatile liquid.

Jak eyed the flames, too, then her, a glint of wariness in his dark gaze. "That was really expensive whiskey."

"I'll buy you another."

"My royal patron." He waved a hand foppishly in the air, making a grand and courtly bow. "So kind, so generous." He straightened, eyes hard and black. "So cruel. I still don't know why you're here. Destroying my stuff and all."

"I wanted to finish our argument, but you're clearly too drunk. Forget it." She spun on her heel, heading for the door, cursing herself for listening to *Rhyian*, of all people.

"Uh-uh. I'm not that drunk." Jak caught her around the waist, easily lifting her and carrying her back to the fire. Depositing her in a chair, he leaned on the arms of it, effectively caging her there. "I let you run once. More than once, come to think of it. You came to finish this—though, funny, I thought you *did* finish it between us, before we even got started—but go ahead. Tell me what you have to say. I'm *listening*." He hissed the last word with an edge as lethal as any of his blades, his face set, his thoughts dark as his eyes.

She gazed at him, her mind suddenly blank. She had no idea what she wanted to say. In truth, she only wanted to run her hands over the corded muscles of his arms, to taste his skin again, to trace the lines of his lean chest and abs. Maybe she thought he'd tease out her words, as he usually did, that he'd take the reins and guide her through this treacherous conversation. But he only stared at her, fierce and expectant, waiting her out.

Don't fuck this up. Go back in there and fix it.

She didn't know how to fix it. If she could, she'd walk back time to before she ruined everything by being afraid. Start over. Instead, she'd have to tell him what she'd never told anyone.

"I apologize," she said softly, but making herself meet his demanding gaze. "You are right and I am wrong. I was—*am*—afraid, and it was easier for me to push you away, to try to convince you that there's no place for you in my life, than to face the truth."

He blew out a breath, then lowered himself to a crouch, hands still braced on the arms of the chair. No longer looming over her, he gazed up at her no less demandingly. "And what is that truth?"

THE TRUTH? "FALLING doesn't feel like flying at all," she told him, knowing it made no sense.

But he nodded, as if it did. "Do you feel like you're falling?"

"All the time," she confessed. "Bracing to hit the ground."

He searched her face. "I'm trying to understand."

"I'm not explaining it well." She dug her nails into the velvet covering the arms of the chair. "I don't know what kind of life I should have. Some people think I'll be queen of Annfwn, but I don't see it. Jak—I can't see anything about my own future past a certain point."

He cocked his head in question. "You said you had seen it. Pieces, ever shifting, but there."

"I lied," she confessed. "I'm not that good at seeing the future, not like Aunt Andi, and when I do—I don't see myself. I'm forever hurtling toward a single place and time and after that is nothing. Jak... I think maybe I don't live very long."

With an encouraging nod, he firmed his jaw. What she'd said clearly pained him, but he was listening. "Have you... seen your death?" he asked with careful neutrality. A vivid image came from him, of the intelligence of the alter-realm, swinging its blunt sword like a club.

Had she? "Not exactly, but what I see is... awful in its own way."

"All right. What is that?"

"I've never told anyone."

Folding down to his knees, he took her hands in his. "You can tell me."

Maybe she could. "I'm in a tower, with no way out, surrounded by an endless field of lilies." He waited patiently, and she blew out a breath. "And that's it. It sounds silly when I describe it, but..."

"It doesn't sound silly," he corrected. "You're alone in the tower, maybe in the whole world."

"Yes," she breathed, beyond grateful that he understood the quiet horror of it. "And there's no future for me after that. It just stops, there in that tower."

Nodding absently, he studied her hands, stroking his thumbs over the backs of them. "It sounds like an alter-realm, though one we haven't seen yet."

"That only recently occurred to me, too."

"How soon?"

"I don't know. Sooner than it used to be."

"You haven't told even Astar?"

"I'm too noble," she replied wryly, throwing his accusation back at him. "I don't want to worry him."

Jak lifted his gaze to hers. "I apologize for that. I shouldn't have said it. You are the least-selfish person I've ever known."

Extracting one hand, she laid it over his cheek, stroking the silky beard. His gaze on hers, he turned his head and kissed her palm, lingering there, sending renewed shivers through her body. "It was a well-aimed strike," she admitted. "It is easier for me to wall everyone out, rather than to risk..."

"Risk what?" he asked, searching her face, rubbing his cheek against her palm.

"I know you laugh at me, but I don't want anyone to be hurt when I'm gone and don't come back."

"Oh, my star." He gazed at her, emotions welling through him like the swells of the ocean. "So many people would grieve your loss. And that's how it should be. It's not wrong to be loved."

"I know that in my head."

"Well, know this in your heart: I'm not letting you go. Where you travel, I'll be with you."

"In my vision, you're not there."

"Because you didn't let me be with you until now. But this," he said, squeezing her hands, "this is forever. I'll always be right here, guarding your back."

Her heart squeezed as if he'd taken that in his hand too. Perhaps he had. "All right," she said. "I want you to be with me, no matter what."

"I want to promise that I won't hurt you," he said solemnly, "but I know that I did. You've been crying." He lifted a hand to stroke a gentle finger over her cheek. "I'm sorry for that."

People argue. The more they care, the more painful it is. "Well," she said, a smile breaking through to crack her lips, "it's *your* heart in pieces ground into the rug over there."

With a groan, he dropped his head into her lap. "Danu, that *was* overly dramatic, wasn't it? I blame the whiskey, and misguided Dasnarian poet hopefuls in my ancestry."

Cupping his jaw, she lifted his head. "Jak, they say three

time's a charm."

His dark eyes gleamed. "What are you saying?"

"I'm asking for one more start-over. Can we try this again?"

"Ah, my star," he breathed, "as many times as you like. Again and again and again." Levering up to his knees, he stroked her hair back from her face, touching her with devastating tenderness. "Though I feel I have to say, we can still go slowly. I don't want this pending destiny of yours to create pressure."

She threaded her fingers through his dark hair, feeling finally and completely sure. "Jak, when I walked out the door, the only thing I felt was regret. I wanted to be in here with you. I won't let being afraid stop me."

"All right, then," he breathed, placing a kiss light as a butterfly on her temple. Then to her other temple, then on each eyelid as they fluttered closed. She held still for it, resting her hands folded in her lap as he rained gentle kisses over her skin. Letting the sensations soak in, allowing Jak in all his masculine exuberance to permeate her. So much passion in him, so much need, his edges sharp.

But his desire was tempered by love. And that felt sweet as water in the desert, softening the parched soil of her heart. Perhaps she'd grown so accustomed to walling out emotions that she'd gone too far, repelling the good along with the uncomfortable. Still, it took more effort than she liked to stay with him. Part of her waited, tense with anxiety, expecting pain.

"How are you doing in there?" Jak murmured against the

corner of her mouth.

She opened her eyes, finding him regarding her intently. "This is nice."

He cracked a dubious half smile. "Hmm. Nice isn't what I was going for."

"It's good," she assured him. "Is this all right with you?"

Narrowing his gaze, he feathered light fingers down her throat and over her collarbones. "I'm not the one we're focusing on here. I want this to feel good to you."

"It does feel good," she insisted.

"But Jak?" he teased.

And she sighed. "It's a lot. I feel... vulnerable."

Sitting back on his heels, he took her hands—having to gently pry them apart, she realized, so she made herself relax—and set them on his naked shoulders, moving them so her hands glided over his skin. "Isn't that part of lovemaking—to be vulnerable to each other?" he asked.

Catching her breath at the delight of touching him, she nevertheless cocked her head in curiosity at that. "Is it? Nobody talks about it that way."

He smiled ruefully. "I suppose that's true. People tend to talk about the clash and storm of it. But it's more than that. It's this." Now that she'd taken over touching him, he stroked gentle fingers over her throat again, tracing the sensitive skin between her breasts, watching her face as she stilled at being touched there. "We can stop," he reminded her, "if it's too much."

"I'm not afraid."

He cocked his head at the nails she was digging into his

chest.

"Oh!" Abashed, she released her grip on him and healed the marks she'd left. "I'm so sorry."

"Don't be. That's part of it, too. As long as that's coming from a place of desire, not fear."

"It's some of both," she admitted. "But I don't want to let fear hold me back anymore."

"I can understand that." Moving slowly, he eased in, pressing his lips to the tender skin between her breasts, stroking with long, hot licks of his tongue, sending waves of heat through her. Letting out a long breath, she sighed in pleasure, arching her spine to offer more. Her breasts swelled, nipples peaking again, and Jak made an answering sound, sweeping his hands up her bare back under her hair, encouraging the yielding, his mouth feasting on the skin revealed by her gown.

She clung to his shoulders, enveloped in their twining desire, wanting to be overwhelmed now, needing him to sweep away her thoughts. Anchoring her with one corded arm, he set a hand on her hip, caressing upward until it rested just below her breast. He trailed his teeth lightly over the exposed inner curve of her breast, humming when she moaned. Dipping his tongue beneath the confining satin of the bodice, he sought untouched skin—and cupped her breast.

She stiffened in surprise at how his hand relieved the empty ache. When he paused, she pushed her breast into his hand. "Don't stop," she pleaded.

With a low chuckle, he squeezed, lightly massaging the fabric-covered side, kissing and licking the bare skin of the other. And, trapped between the two, her nipple stung with a sweet, tingling ache. When his thumb brushed over the turgid nub, she cried out at the intensity of it.

Still holding her, brushing her nipple, Jak lifted his head to kiss her softly and lingeringly. "Is that a good scream or a bad one?"

"I didn't scream," she gasped, wriggling against his touch.

"Good scream, then," he decided, a smug note in his voice. "By the way, screaming is most welcome. Especially my name."

"I don't—*Jak!*" His name ripped out of her as he firmly pinched her nipple.

"Exactly like that." Backing off, he helped her to her feet. "As you know, I love this dress, but how do I get you out of it—do I have to cut it off?"

"They did sew me into it, but I don't want it ruined. I'll shift, so I can keep it."

"As much as I'd enjoy the process of stripping you naked, that's probably a good plan," he conceded, stepping back to give her room.

Deciding that this bandage would sting less if quickly removed, when Stella shifted back to human form, she came back naked.

And immediately regretted the choice, covering herself with her hands, knowing she was blushing furiously. Jak made no move toward her but smiled warmly, dimples deepening as he took her in. "So beautiful," he murmured. "But why hide yourself from me?"

"I don't know," she answered in a pained whisper.

"The vulnerability thing?" he asked, easing closer, stroking his hands down her arms, the way she'd seen him soothing the horses.

"Maybe," she allowed. He moved her hair behind her shoulder and kissed the side of her neck, renewing the heat that seemed to rise at his command. "It's funny," she continued, tipping her head to the side, allowing him in to kiss and taste more, "I used to love being naked as a little girl."

"I've heard the stories," he murmured, laughter in his voice. "Queen Amelia despairing of keeping you clothed, and you running naked through fancy balls."

She groaned, a small part from embarrassment and a great deal from his teeth closing with gentle insistence at the juncture of her neck and shoulder. *"Princesses don't run around naked,"* she said, mimicking her mother's exasperation. "It took her so long to drill that into my head that now I…"

"Don't want to run around naked anymore?" Jak asked with a teasing smile.

"I suppose so," she conceded.

"Maybe that means you should."

"What?" Scandalized, her cheeks flaming, she clutched her hands over herself even tighter.

"Run," Jak repeated, letting go of her and taking several steps back. "Naked. I'll give you a head start."

"But Jak, I—"

"Better run," he interrupted, "because when I catch you, I'm going to do obscene things to that gorgeous body."

Crouching, he flexed his hands, his grin full of wickedness, thoughts giving her glimpses of—*Oh my.* With a squeal, she turned and ran.

It wasn't a big room, but he also didn't try very hard to catch her. She ran, dodging furniture, darting past his reaching hands, shrieking with laughter. Heedless of her nudity—freed by it—she scrambled across the bed when he trapped her in the corner, squealing when he caught her by the ankle, which became a triumphant hoot as she managed to extract herself and bounce to the other side.

Accessing her shapeshifter speed, as she so rarely did, she eluded the laughing Jak several more times, until he feinted convincingly in one direction, catching her by the waist when she fell into his trap. With a shout of victory, he tossed her on the bed and pounced, caging her there with her wrists pinned, his body straddling hers as she panted to catch her breath.

"I claim a forfeit, Your Highness," he said, also breathing hard.

"What will you have of me, pirate?" she inquired haughtily, aware that her body strained toward his.

"I believe I shall divest you of your maidenhead." Lowering his head, he kissed her, starting out gentle, the kiss turning greedy as she opened her mouth to him. "If my lady agrees that the prize is mine."

"Take what you will, you rogue," she breathed, her heart pounding, sex slick with need.

"First, I will slake my thirst." Instead of getting up as she expected, he dipped his head, kissing her lingeringly, then trailed kisses down her body. Following the trail of the territory he'd previously explored, he soon moved to kiss her nipples, driving her mad with the sweet kisses and occasional nips.

She squirmed beneath him, fingers tangled in his hair, thoughts blissfully scattered to the winds by the desire he stoked in her. Holding her breath as he moved lower, she steadied herself for what he clearly intended to do. When he eased her thighs apart, sliding his tongue along the hollows of her hip bones, she allowed it willingly enough. Needed him there, his warm breath a tease, the ache in her sex desperate to be eased. But she also froze, morbidly embarrassed for him to see her there.

Of course, he sensed it, pausing in his caresses, laying a firm, warm hand on her belly just above her curls. "But Jak?" he asked softly.

"Do you have to?" she asked, feeling foolishly virginal.

"No, but it will help if we're going to do the full deed. Make it hurt less."

"But it will hurt regardless."

"Probably," he said with a rueful smile, placing a kiss on her thigh, making her quiver. "I understand it can, and I'm on the big side."

"So I've been informed," she replied a bit tartly.

"Ah, gossip." He shook his head, then kissed her other thigh. "Remember that it's all for you. You can have me any way you like, or not at all. We can stop here."

The tense need in her body clamored with a resounding no. "I don't want to stop."

"Then shall I..." He dropped another kiss on her inner thigh, closer to her sex, and she shuddered at the intensity of it.

"Are you sure you want to?" she asked, still hesitant.

"Read my mind."

She did, and nearly came apart at what she found there. Winding her fingers into the bedsheets, feeling the fresh crush of rose petals against her palms, their fragrance rising to intertwine with the scent of hot candlewax and Jak's skin, she offered herself to him. "Slake your thirst, pirate."

"Tastes like the sea," he murmured, and she relaxed, oddly comforted to hear that, having liked the taste of him. Then his tongue swept through her folds, and her mind shattered in a thousand directions. Crying out at the intensity of the sensation, she bucked beneath his mouth, aware of his gently restraining hands. He held her there and drank from her indeed, his hunger rising sharply, feeding her own.

She rose like a wave, towering ever higher, until she crashed into his arms, crying out his name. And he answered wordlessly, driving her up again, slipping a finger inside her where she felt so very empty, stroking her there with impossible intimacy. Patiently, meticulously, he built her to even greater heights, his deft fingers and agile tongue finding the exact rhythm, driving her wild. And holding her there, teetering at the edge.

She was begging him—just he'd promised she would, back in the carriage when it all started—thrashing in her need, when he abandoned her. Though only long enough to shuck his boots and trousers. Finally, he slid up her body, nestling between her welcoming thighs. Bracing himself on his elbows, he lowered his forehead to hers, breathing hard as if he'd been running. She lifted her hips, wanting, needing him inside. "Please, Jak."

"Let me take it slowly," he gritted. The need boiled in him, to thrust, to take, to savage—all tightly leashed with his disciplined control. So tempting to unravel him, to cut those bonds he used to restrain himself, to unleash the mighty storm within him. But he would never forgive himself if he wasn't gentle with her, so she nodded.

He reached between them, stroking her lightly, reverence in the caress as she thrummed beneath his touch, then he positioned his cock at her entrance, slowly pressing in. Feeling the stretch, she stilled, torn between the twin pulls of wanting to retreat and also draw him deeper in. Firmly nestled in her entrance, Jak moved his hand beneath her hips, tilting her to a better angle, then met her gaze.

His dark eyes, black as the ocean in a storm, bored into hers. "Ready?" he whispered, his nerves strumming at a pitch as high as hers.

She wound her hands behind his neck. "Yes. I love you, Jak."

"I love you, my star," he replied, kissing her with sweet yearning. Lifting his head again, he held her gaze as he pressed into her.

It did hurt, a quiet stretching tear, but her driving need for him overrode it. "More," she murmured.

He breathed a laugh. "Oh, there will be."

Setting his jaw, he flexed his hips, withdrawing slightly, then pressing harder, so she gasped. He brushed her cheek with the thumb of his hand positioned next to her head, and she turned to brush it with a kiss, the blooming emotions making her eyes fill with tears.

"Too much?" he asked.

"Not enough," she replied with a weepy smile. "Give me everything, Jak."

With a released breath, he kissed her again, feeding on her lips, then surged into her, both of them crying out together. So impossibly full, she squirmed beneath him, discovering the unexpected delight of his skin all along hers, their bodies slicked together, joined as one, her movements rattling them both. He flexed into her more, groaning as if unable to help himself, and she expanded, receiving him. His skin against her most intimate skin, and she wanted more.

Lifting her hips, she wrapped her legs around his narrow hips, embracing him in every way possible, and sighing out his name as he sank into her to the hilt. "Jak," she sighed into his ear, kissing him and then dropping her mouth to bite his neck. "More."

He laughed raggedly. "I'm doing my best here, my only love." But he began to move, gently at first, then with more vigor as she met him stroke for stroke. Pushing himself up, he reared over her, working his hips to find the point of deepest pleasure, teeth bared in a fierce grin as he gazed down at her, dark eyes glittering, his heart open.

When she convulsed, arching as she screamed his name, he threw his head back too, loosing a hoarse cry, emptying himself into her, his mouth descending to drink in her cries in return. As she fell, spiraling, and loosed of her own tethers, he followed, holding her firmly in the circle of his arms and his abiding love.

For the first time in perhaps her entire life, she felt utterly safe and at ease.

~ 21 ~

PROBABLY HIS BRAINS had leaked out of his ears.

That would explain the emptiness of his skull, which seemed to contain only dreamy wooziness. Stella enfolded him, her exquisite legs wrapped around his waist, her tight sheath gripping him with her sweet, wet heat, her arms holding him against her delicate body as her hands drifted caresses up and down his back, her mouth pressed into the hollow beneath his ear. Taking his earring gently in her teeth, she nibbled, toying with it—and sending delicious thrills straight to his groin.

"I've been wanting to do that for a long time," she purred in his ear.

"Do it as often and as long as you like." He should move. He was probably crushing her.

"Don't move," she murmured. "I like your weight. We should stay like this forever."

With a laugh, he snuggled against her, savoring her deliciously soft skin touching him everywhere. This was the place he'd so longed to be, and he never wanted to part from her. "I know what you mean, but would it be practical?"

"I *am* a princess," she mused. "I could command the servants to feed us."

"*Another* joke?" He feigned utter shock. "Who are you and how did you get in my bed?" Palming her small, perfectly round bottom, he added, "Not that I'm complaining, mind you."

She giggled, a particularly sweet sound since he'd never heard that uninhibited, girlish laugh from her before. "It wasn't a joke," she replied gravely. "I'm perfectly serious."

"All right, then," he said agreeably, turning his head just enough to nuzzle the sweet hollows of her throat. "At least this plan positions me to service my lady as often as she requires." As if hearing the suggestion, his cock swelled within her, alert to the call of action.

"Jak," Stella breathed, squirming beneath him in that delightful, artlessly sensual way of hers. "Again?"

"Unless you're too sore?"

"Not right now, I'm not." She lifted her hips. "Though I can't tell if I need you or if you need me."

"Mirrors of one another," he murmured, lifting his head to kiss her deeply, drowning in her. "We each need the other. Try this." Holding her against him, he rolled, turning so he lay on his back. Still joined to him, she sat up, pushing back her wild mane of hair. Tousled, catching the light of the last flickering candles, it fell around her like a cape of black fire, framing the pale, delicate curves of her body. He cupped her small breasts, delighting in their sweet, soft fullness that just filled his palms, her nipples drawing the globes of them to taut and perfect peaks.

She arched into his touch, leaning into his hands and drawing her fingers in a titillating caress over his chest, flexing her hips experimentally—and drawing an answering arch from his spine. "My star," he breathed, then lost himself in the delirious sight of her riding him, slowly and sensuously. Flickers of green fire sizzled from her fingertips, sparking through him to heat his blood even hotter. Feeling completely at the mercy of this dark sorceress, he succumbed to her rhythm, following her lead and giving her whatever she asked of him.

A knowing smile curved her lips, her eyes silver as the moon, and he half believed Moranu possessed his body now, milking his cock for her pleasure, and with a cry of ultimate surrender, he gave himself over to her, spending his seed, yielding everything to the woman he loved more than his own life.

HE WOKE WITH the sunrise, the ship's bells that lived forever inside his head tolling the advent of dawn, though the room remained dark as night, the heavy curtains drawn against the winter's cold, the candles merely frozen pools of wax, the fire a sullen pile of coals.

Stella lay snuggled against him, a slight weight draped over his body, her head pillowed in the fold of his shoulder and hair streaming over the pillow she wasn't using. With a smile of pure happiness, he drew the goose down comforter higher over her bare shoulder, cuddling her closer against him. *We should stay like this forever.*

He fervently wished they could. But the world would

reach out to them. Jak couldn't set aside that the intelligence seemed to be hunting Stella. That, along with her vision of being trapped in a tower in what surely must be an alter-realm, had him worrying. He'd do his utmost to protect her, to keep her safe—but how?

"You're thinking awfully loudly for someone who should be asleep." Stella lifted her head, pushing her hair out of her face, and blinked at him owlishly in the dimness.

He stroked a hand down her back, the graceful line of it as exquisite as the rest of her. "Sorry," he murmured. "Go back to sleep."

She settled back against him, snuggling like a kitten in her sweet softness. "You always wake up so early."

"Sailor's habit," he replied wryly. "Plus I really need to piss."

She giggled. "Me too."

"Summon the servants with the chamber pots," he suggested, "so we don't have to leave this bed."

"I'd rather summon them to bring a hot bath," she reflected, trailing her fingers down his chest. "I feel sticky in every crevice."

"You could just shapeshift clean."

"It's really not the same. I come back to human form clean, yes, but I don't feel like I've washed, if that makes sense. I really want to wash."

"Regrets?" He rolled his head on the pillow, trying to see her face.

She lifted her mouth to kiss him. "Only that I let being afraid hold me back from this for so long. I love you."

"I love you," he replied simply, returning the kiss, thanking all the goddesses for this moment. He'd made them a promise, so he'd find a way to protect Stella, no matter what happened.

Stella smiled impishly. "I also regret that we aren't at Castle Elderhorst. I really loved having hot running water right in my room."

"We'll steal the design and replicate it at every place we live," he promised.

"Groningen would no doubt share it freely if I asked."

"Where's the fun in that?" he complained. "But fine—whatever gets us hot running water, because I agree. That was the best." Loathe as he was to leave the warm bed and warmer woman in it, he got out, shivering against the cold, and went to the bell pull that would summon servants. Finding his pants from the night before, he pulled them on. Stella was sitting up in the bed, bare-breasted, hair falling around her, watching him with an intent and solemn expression. "Everything all right?" he asked her.

"I like looking at you," she admitted, somewhat shyly.

Crawling onto the bed, he kissed her with enough enthusiasm that she began giggling. He could spend his whole life making her laugh like that. "Look as much as you want," he said. "I like looking at you, too."

A knock at the door heralded the servants. He went to arrange for baths, received the tray of hot beverages the girl brought with her—a prescience he greatly appreciated—along with a message that they were expected for an intimate breakfast with the king and queen at a remarkably early hour for royalty. Stella had wrapped herself in a blanket to visit the attached bathing chamber and returned, taking the cup of sweetened black coffee he handed her. Her eyebrows went up at the first sip. "Annfwn coffee?"

"They apparently are digging out all the good stuff for their royal guests." He winked at her. "Did I get the balance right?"

"Of course. Though I don't know when you learned how I like my coffee."

"I'm a clever guy. And you are my favorite subject of study. Does an intimate breakfast with the king and queen of Erie mean fancy dress?"

"Oh, are we summoned? They're getting an early start."

"That's what I thought, too."

"So, yes, not as fancy as what you wore last night, but definitely more formal than the phrase 'intimate breakfast' suggests."

"Hmm. That might be a problem." He went to answer the knock, allowing in a parade of servants with buckets of hot water to fill the tub in the bathing chamber.

"You really have nothing left?" Stella asked with a frown.

"Last night's stellar outfit and my scarlet suit from the Feast of Moranu ball, which is considerably worse for wear," he admitted. He'd hoped to buy more clothes on the journey to Castle Marcellum, but the overland route across the wintry steppes wasn't exactly a shopping extravaganza. "If I didn't know better, I'd think there was a conspiracy to keep me naked." He lifted a brow at her.

Shaking her head, Stella stopped a servant and asked that a tailor be sent to them with at least one suit of clothes that could be quickly adapted in time for breakfast, and more for later. The girl curtsied and agreed with alacrity, as if the request weren't odd for daybreak, and skipped off to roust the poor tailor from their bed.

"You didn't have to do that," he said, once the last of the servants had gone, wrestling the unfamiliar sense of irritation at the feeling of being managed.

Stella gave him a considering look. "Why did that annoy you? You need clothes."

"I'm used to providing for myself." He could just imagine what his Dasnarian friends—and his father—would say about him being a kept man.

"Did you mean it," Stella asked, wrapping the blanket tighter around herself, "when you said that about arranging for hot running water in every place we lived?"

He frowned, confused. "Yes. Why?"

"Because if I do have a future, you want to live with me," she clarified, "wherever that may be."

"Yes. And stop questioning whether you have a future. We're going to make sure of it. I love you and I want to be with you." When would she get that through her head? "You better not be thinking up ways to cut me out of your life."

"Don't get snarly." She came over and worked a hand out of the blanket wrapping to lay it on his chest, soothing energy coming from her. "I want to be with you, too, but this is what being part of my life would mean. If you're going to be my official consort, you'll have to look the part. Sometimes that will mean letting me provide for you."

He tamped down the thrill of being named her official consort. For whatever reason, he hadn't thought that far ahead—but of course Stella wouldn't give herself unless she meant forever. Laying his hand over hers, he grimaced. "Yeah… All right. I'll swallow my manly manly pride and take the clothes. But I don't relish being the pauper to your princess."

She regarded him seriously, no doubt sorting through his conflicting emotions better than he could. "It would be part of the deal—and I wouldn't blame you for wanting no part of it. Being independent, to the point of disregarding manners and rules, is part of who you are. I don't want you to change that for me."

Lifting her hand, he kissed her fingers, then gave her a cocky grin. "I don't think I can change that, even for you. As long as you're willing to put up with me, I'm in."

She smiled, the happiness lighting her face. "It won't always be easy."

"But we'll figure it out," he promised her. "As long as we agree that loving each other and being together is worth the difficulty."

"I believe it is."

"I do, too." He leaned in to give her a real kiss, drawing her up against him, tempted to drag her back to bed. Instead, he patted her adorable rear. "Take your bath while it's hot. I'm going to run some forms while I await the sleep-deprived royal tailor."

"Are you sure you don't want to go first?" she asked with a concerned frown.

"Tough and manly," he reminded her. "I don't mind tepid bathwater. It's warmer than the cold arctic seas I bathed in as a child."

"I've been on the *Hákyrling*," she retorted primly, "and I recall having hot water for baths."

"You ruin all my stories," he complained as she laughingly skipped away and shut the bathing chamber door.

With her safely out of temptation's reach, he settled into Danu's Dance, the movements warming his muscles and the grace of the goddess clearing his mind.

Nothing, however, could quite remove his dread of what they might yet face. *A tower surrounded by an endless field of lilies...*

FEELING MORE SELF-CONSCIOUS than she liked, Stella entered the cozy dining hall on Jak's arm. At his insistence, she wore her daggers on a jeweled girdle he'd improvised to go over her morning gown of deep-blue velvet. For his part, Jak looked unusually subdued—and especially lethal—in another black suit, this one of Chiyajuan silk with a jacket of gold brocade. He'd complained about looking like a court dandy until she pointed out that he'd worn scarlet to the Feast of Moranu ball at Ordnung and that it didn't get dandier than that.

He grumbled something about there being a difference between swashbuckling rogue and court dandy, but he subsided with good grace—at least until he'd started badgering her about being armed. She was surprised at herself, at how much she enjoyed bantering with him, and how *different* she felt, sated in a way that had her feeling deliciously fulfilled. It was as if she'd been starving for some nutrient without realizing it. As if some sort of essential loneliness had finally eased. She just wished she didn't have to face people again so soon.

"Courage," Jak whispered, kissing her cheek, and she smiled at him.

The king and queen hadn't arrived yet, but all their friends had, observing with expectant and delighted—or, in the single exception of Astar, carefully stoic—expressions. Zeph even did a little shimmying dance, subsiding only when Astar raised his brows at her. Even Rhy, slouching against a decoratively carved pillar, smiled and tossed her a little salute.

Fortunately King Cavan and Queen Nix entered just then, with no fanfare, but with two young royals with them. The young woman, who looked to be about Stella's age, with hair as dark as Cavan's and his slate-gray eyes, must be Princess Marjolein. The slightly younger prince had his mother's ivory hair and lake-blue eyes. He was introduced to her as Prince Wilhelm, who gallantly bowed and kissed her hand with an appraising look in his eye.

Jak stood back, appearing nonchalant, but tapping his fingers on his lean thigh very near one of his sheathed daggers, eyeing the young prince like a target. Stella flicked him an inquiring glance, and he grinned. Without taking his eyes off her, he said something in reply to Rhy, who was eyeing Wilhelm as the young prince kissed Lena's hand, clearly renewing an acquaintance of the night before. Princess Marjolein greeted Astar with a wistful smile, an unhappy look on her face as she took in Zeph on his arm, flashing Salena's ruby ring and looking carelessly glamorous as usual.

Apparently Stella had missed a round of royal matchmaking at the ball the evening before. Thank Moranu that Jak had spirited her away.

The ensuing bustle of everyone being seated and beverages served took up everyone's attention. Stella found herself at the queen's right hand at the large round table, Prince Wilhelm beside her. Astar flanked Cavan on the other side of the king, with Zeph beside him—Stella breathed an internal sigh of relief that Cavan and Nix recognized Astar's engagement—and Princess Marjolein sat on Zeph's left. Rhy sat beside Marjolein, looking bemused by her opening flirtations. Lena had been seated on the other side of Prince Wilhelm, likely in an effort to allow him to charm both apparently eligible princesses.

Jak had been placed next to Lena, and Gen sat on the other side of Rhy. Gen looked decidedly glum at how they'd been distributed according to rank and marriageability. Stella would have to talk with Gen after breakfast. Hopefully Jak didn't mind his exile to the far end of the circle, though he seemed cheerful enough. He caught her looking, dimpled at her, and held up the whiskey a servant had brought to go in his coffee, pouring some into Gen's tea before she could stop him.

Stella laughed softly. Zeph had a flute of sparkling wine and was happily sipping it. That was good. Everyone might as well enjoy staying at least the two nights at Marcellum. They all could certainly use a day of rest and indulgence. Perhaps she and Jak could retire to his room again, and... The horse caught her eye.

It was absolutely real and present, despite prancing

through an intimate dining hall, shimmering with ethereal magic and transparent as a ghost. The servants set plates before them—an unusual dish of fluffy bread that had been dipped in some sort of crunchy batter and fried, served with berries and a dark, sweet syrup—and Stella sampled hers, finding it delicious and herself ravenous. She began eating, while keeping an eye on the ghost horse.

"You see her, don't you?" Queen Nix smiled when Stella jumped. "My horse, Falada," she clarified. "You see her as well as I do. I should have guessed you would, being of Salena's line."

"Are you a sorceress?" Stella asked, not quite willing to acknowledge Nix's canny guesses.

The queen gave her a knowing look for the diplomatic dodge. "Nothing like my mother was. Isyn is named for her and holds her throne now. The magic in the Isles of Remus is different from here. Falada is fae. Though her mortal body was sadly murdered long ago, she remains with me in ethereal form. Such is her loyalty to me."

Falada had come over to them, silently whuffling Nix's ivory hair and canting her head to give Stella an assessing look.

"Ah," Nix breathed, nodding. "I agree, and I'm glad to hear it. She likes you," Nix said to Stella, "and she's agreed to accompany you to find our son."

~ 22 ~

"**I**S KING ISYN missing?" Jak heard Stella ask of Queen Nix. She spoke quietly enough that Jak might not have heard her over the general hubbub of the meal, if he hadn't had most of his attention trained on Stella. At least that too-pretty Prince Wilhelm wasn't trying to charm her at the moment. Jak had been distracting himself with jollying Gen out of her dour mood, telling her that the presence of available whiskey proved they weren't actually sitting at the table intended for little kids.

He wasn't the only one to hear the question, everyone falling silent, King Cavan giving his queen a resigned look. "I believe 'missing' would be putting it too strongly," he said.

"I never said Isyn was missing," Nix returned evenly, holding her ground despite her ethereal appearance. "I said he needed to be found. Falada has agreed to go with them."

The king's brows rose nearly to the bottom of his crown, Wilhelm and Marjolein becoming exceptionally attentive. "She has?" King Cavan tendered, as if not quite believing what he'd heard.

"She has," Queen Nix confirmed, no doubt in her voice or expression. "It's time, Cavan," she said more softly. "He's never been out of contact for this long. Ever since that magical eclipse, there's been nothing from the Isles. If anyone can find him, Falada can."

Cavan cast an uncomfortable glance at their attentive audience. "Their Highnesses Prince Astar and Princess Stella have come to us on a pleasure journey, and Prince Astar already explained to us that the eclipse was nothing unusual."

"I'm sure that diplomatic explanation worked in most of the places our guests have visited," Queen Nix observed tartly, "and I don't blame Her Majesty for wishing to spread a soothing tale to calm fears. I know better, however. I'm sure it's no coincidence that magic rifts have opened between worlds at the same time an unprecedented eclipse occurred, and that the crown prince arrives on our doorstep wishing to visit the epicenter of the problem." She leveled a gimlet stare on Astar. "Is it?"

Astar cleared his throat. "Ah, no." He inclined his head to Queen Nix—and seemed to receive some message from Stella that decided him. "It's no coincidence. The seven of us have been specifically selected by Her Majesty, on the advice of Queen Andromeda, to travel to the Isles of Remus and discover the source of the problem. And hopefully remedy it."

King Cavan considered that with some consternation, though Queen Nix only nodded. "Sailing to the Isles will be no easy task, as I'm sure Andromeda foresaw, especially at this time of year, but if anyone can guide you there, Falada can."

Stella met Jak's inquiring gaze across the table, her eyes crystalline with intrigue. Whatever was going on, it had caught Stella's interest.

"I beg your indulgence, Your Highnesses," Astar said, his gaze going around the table as if he'd missed an introduction, "but who is Falada?"

Stella knew. Jak could see that much in her face. Everyone else, however, looked equally mystified.

"A friend," Queen Nix replied. "Her Highness Princess Stella is able to see her, though I believe only she and I can." She sighed, an old sorrow in it, and Cavan put his hand over hers, squeezing it.

"Princess Stella can see Falada?" Marjolein demanded, sounding most put out. Not that she'd been chipper all through breakfast, casting longing glances at Astar and resentful ones at the oblivious Zeph. Jak would put good money down that Princess Marjolein was on the infamous list Her Majesty had pressed on Astar, of approved princesses to wear the engagement ring Zeph now flashed at Marjolein.

Perhaps Zeph wasn't so oblivious after all. Jak could hardly blame her for wanting to make her claim on Astar's affections perfectly clear. Jak would be happy to take pretty-boy Wilhelm down a few notches himself. Stella, however, true to form— Danu, he loved that woman—seemed to barely notice Wilhelm's existence, much less pay attention to the youth's extravagant compliments.

With a start, Jak realized Wilhelm was likely no younger than he was, though Jak felt positively ancient compared to the pampered princeling. Good thing he and Stella had skipped most of the ball the night before. Watching Stella dance with Wilhelm might've been more than he could take. As it was, he'd like to hurl a dagger or two at him. Not to kill or maim.

Maybe just knock the fork out of his hand that he was waving so extravagantly through the air as the princeling expounded on fae magic, Marjolein's question having opened a flood of excited conversation. It would be easy to do. Likely he could be fast enough the princeling wouldn't know what hit him.

Zeph caught his eye across the table, lifting her flute of sparkling wine to him. In grim acknowledgment, he quaffed the remnants of his own whiskey without diluting it with coffee. Odd bedfellows, he and Zeph, both in love with the royal twins and destined to deal with a future of this kind of thing. He'd have to discuss with her. Perhaps he and Zeph could partner together, run interference for one another, all to reduce potential injuries to incautious competitors, naturally.

Astar cleared his throat. "If I may…" he said, loudly enough to carry over the general hubbub, silencing the group and gaining everyone's attention. "Thank you," he continued with a half smile, then turned to the king and queen. "We're grateful for your offer of assistance and naturally accept the company of your envoy to guide us. Stella, you are willing to be liaison to Falada?"

"I'm happy to," Stella replied with equal decorum. "And allow me to echo my brother's sentiments. We are so grateful for the trust you and Falada place in us, and we will do our utmost to find King Isyn and restore contact between you."

The king and queen heard Stella's "but" as clearly as Jak did, both waiting intently for her to continue.

"But can you explain," Astar said, picking up smoothly, "what makes this journey such a challenge, why we need a guide, and how an entire island chain can fall out of contact?"

Speaking of partnerships, Astar and Stella worked as well together as any fighting team, only wielding diplomacy instead of blades. Observing them closely, Jak recalled how Stella had alluded to a communication system that required them to be close. Knowing what to look for, he picked out the subtle flexing of their throats as they spoke silently. Subvocalizing to each other. Clever.

"I can address the last two questions first," Queen Nix replied. "Though I'm afraid I have an incomplete answer. I grew up in the Isles of Remus, and even I don't completely understand the phenomenon, but the islands sometimes... shift from one plane of existence to another. I know it sounds impossible, but there's no other way to explain it. Sometimes the Isles are in this world, and we can travel back and forth freely. Other times... not."

Across from him, Stella was in profile to him as she watched the queen with keen attention. "It sounds entirely possible to us," she assured the queen, and their group all nodded, some grimacing.

"Your Highness," Lena spoke up, "can you clarify—I take it that this phenomenon is not new, that it occurred long before the eclipse?"

Queen Nix nodded. "As far back as our history goes, which is a very long time."

Lena looked thoughtful. "My mother indicated as much, but there's not a lot of information on the magic of the Isles, not even in our library."

"Even the famed library at Nahanau has its limitations," Queen Nix replied with gentle understanding. "And our Isles are far more ancient than yours."

Rather than looking daunted, Lena brightened with interest, very much her mother's daughter.

"Thank you for explaining, Your Highness," Astar said, inclining his head to her. "I take it Falada can penetrate this shifting reality to guide us to the Isles?"

"If anyone can, Falada can," Queen Nix replied.

Jak didn't love that she promised nothing there, but he supposed that was as good as they'd get. Better than sailing blind.

"*If* you can even make it there," King Cavan said to Astar with a thoughtful frown. "That speaks to your first question. Though the Strait of K'van is narrow this far north, and the distance to the nearest of the Isles not great, the seas are quite treacherous this time of year. The wise traveler would set sail from the Grace River estuary and approach the Isles from the south."

"But it would be a shame for them to backtrack when they've already journeyed so far north," Queen Nix put in. "I've made that purportedly 'easier' journey overland from the estuary, and I don't recommend it. It is long and arduous in other ways." Her lips pinched with old pain, and Jak watched Stella's silvery gaze following their invisible companion, tracking it as if she saw it behave in agitation.

"I won't ask my sailors to undertake such a perilous voyage from the coast here," King Cavan said decisively, placing a hand on his queen's shoulder when she would've protested. "Isyn would say the same and you know it, Nix."

"Perhaps, but as a mother, I—"

"If I may, Your Highnesses," Astar broke in. "I apologize for the interruption, but there's no need for concern on this aspect, at least." He nodded at Jak. "We only need to borrow a vessel. Jak can sail it for us."

Everyone looked at him, the four royals of Castle Marcellum regarding him with so much surprise a lesser man would take insult. Instead, he toasted Astar with his heavily whiskey-laced coffee. "My prince's confidence warms my heart." *Or maybe that's the whiskey.* He discreetly suppressed the quip, but Stella clearly heard it, eyes dancing with laughter.

"*You* can sail a ship, all by yourself?" Wilhelm inquired archly.

"Provided it's of a size appropriate to the seven us and no larger," Jak answered without rancor. "I'm assuming Falada doesn't take up much space. And I don't have to work all the rigging on my own, as my companions all have opposable thumbs most of the time, and they take direction well."

Zeph muffled a snicker with a cough that fooled no one. Stella's gaze still held amusement, but she narrowed her eyes in warning.

"You can't mean..." Marjolein began, then paused with lifted brows. "I'm sorry, Jim, is it? I can't imagine that you plan to ask Crown Prince Astar, Princess Stella, Princess Salena Nakoa KauPo, and Prince Rhyian to perform manual labor."

"Not really a prince," Rhy said to her, as if confiding a secret, and she frowned.

"You're the son of King Rayfe and Queen Andromeda of Annfwn," she reminded him.

"Nevertheless," he countered with false cheer, "the Tala do

things differently, and there's no actual rank like 'prince' in Annfwn. The good news there is that means I can join Zeph and Gen in sullying my hands with manual labor."

"Even if it means following *Jak's* orders?" Gen emphasized his name with a hard look at Marjolein.

"There's an old saying that the captain of the ship outranks everyone on it," Jak informed them cheerfully. "You'll follow my orders and you'll like it."

Marjolein actually choked on her shock, her mother sliding her a reproving look. "Honestly, Marjie," Queen Nix scolded, "I don't know when you became such a snob. I once spent my days as a goose girl and—"

"We know," Marjolein and Wilhelm chorused, exchanging weary looks.

The queen of Erie had been a goose girl? How interesting. Certainly a story there.

"I, for one, have never heard Jak's supposedly old saying," Lena put in, giving him the hairy eyeball.

"It's Dasnarian," he supplied helpfully.

"Or you made it up on the spot," she countered.

"And you without a library handy." He grinned at her consternation. "Guess you'll have to wait to look it up."

"Actually, we have an excellent library," Wilhelm said, jumping on the opportunity with admirable alacrity. "I'd be delighted to escort you after breakfast, Princess Salena Nakoa KauPo."

"I'll go with you," Rhy drawled, lounging back in his chair, gaze resting on Wilhelm with lethal intent. "You know how I love a good library."

"Me too," Gen piped up, looking between Rhy and Lena. Good. Someone needed to play referee there. Wilhelm didn't look happy, but everyone else relaxed.

"And we have a great deal to discuss," King Cavan said to Astar. "I've assembled my advisers, and Nix and I are prepared to discuss what you've brought from Her Majesty. We'll meet you in an hour in the council chambers?"

"Yes, indeed," Astar said as they all rose. The king and queen proceeded from the room, and Astar offered a hand to Zeph, helping her rise. Bringing her hand to his lips, he kissed the ruby engagement ring. "What are your plans, lovely Zephyr?"

"You'll be in these meetings all day," she said on a sigh.

"Most likely," he conceded. "But you don't need to attend."

"You can join us," Jak said, coming around the table to assist Stella from her chair, putting himself firmly between her and Wilhelm. She had cleaned her plate, he noted with satisfaction. "Nilly and I plan to work on her offensive sorcery. She could use a living target with feathers she wouldn't mind singeing," he added with a wink.

"Jak, that's not true," Stella protested, though she giggled. Everyone but Wilhelm and Marjolein paused at the sound, looking at her in astonishment, then at him. He couldn't help grinning. Yes, that was *his* giggle.

Zeph threw a significant glance at his groin. "Apparently rumor didn't exaggerate, and it's exactly as magical as the stories make out."

Stella blushed furiously as Astar ran a hand over his face,

groaning. "*Zephyr.*"

Zeph patted him on the cheek. "You'll get used to it over time, darling. Come on, let's go for a walk or something, get some fresh air before we have to sit in meetings for the rest of the day."

He cocked his head at her. "You know you don't have to—"

"Yes, I do," she said firmly. "Queen Nix seems like an excellent role model, so I'm going to watch and learn how to be a good queen."

"You'll be amazing," he replied, and they left the room, heads bent together.

Marjolein watched them go with an odd look on her face. "He's really in love with her," she murmured.

"He is," Stella replied in a firm but gentle tone. "And that's our grandmother Salena's ruby ring Zeph is wearing."

"I know she's your friend," Wilhelm said, "and certainly an incredibly beautiful woman, but she doesn't seem to have what it takes to be high queen."

"Oh?" Stella asked, still mildly, but magic thickened around her, making the hairs on the back of Jak's neck stand on end. "What *does* it take?"

Wilhelm was clearly taken aback by the question. "Well, I... ah. Hmm."

"Isyn trained all his life with Mother and Father," Marjolein put in, "learning what he needed to know to take the throne in the Isles of Remus. Wilhelm and I have done the same, though neither of us knows yet which of us will be heir."

Wilhelm smiled at his sister, looking far more genial than he had so far that morning. "I still say we hold the throne as siblings."

"Given the scarcity of potential spouses in this forsaken corner of the north, that's looking likely," Marjolein agreed with a wry twist of her mouth.

"While your point is a fair one," Stella said to them both, "Astar has also studied his entire life. Her Majesty has spared no effort to ensure my brother will be an excellent high king, when his turn comes. One of the many skills he's learned from the high queen is how to judge character. Astar isn't blinded by love; he fell in love with Zephyr because she is of sterling character. Loyal, brave, loving, fiercely intelligent. As you've observed, she's committed to learning how to be the best high queen she can be. What she doesn't know, Astar can teach her. The Thirteen Kingdoms will flourish under their rule, far more so than if my brother married out of duty, rather than love of someone who makes him whole."

A small silence pooled among them in the wake of Stella's speech. Even Marjolein and Wilhelm seemed to understand that Stella rarely spoke so much.

"Forgive me, Your Highness," Marjolein said, curtseying to Stella. "I made hasty conclusions in my surprise—and disappointment." She smiled ruefully. "News of the crown prince's engagement had not made it to us yet."

Stella inclined her head regally. "I'm happy to have had the opportunity to allay your concerns." None of them clarified that the high queen herself had only recently learned of the news—if the missive Astar sent from the manse on Lake Sullivan had even made it to Ordnung—and no one could predict what Ursula's reaction would be. Jak was privately betting that Her Majesty would turn out to be a softie in the face of true love. He'd been around her and Uncle Harlan enough to know. Still, monarchs could be unpredictable creatures.

Glancing at Stella, he wondered how it would go when her family learned of their relationship. His own parents would be likely pleased enough—even if his mother didn't have a high opinion of monogamy. Reading at least some of that thought, Stella squeezed his arm. *"I have far fewer obligations than Willy does. Ash and Mother already love you. It will be fine."*

He raised a brow at her, surprised to hear her voice in his head as he had that night the tentacle monsters almost abducted her.

"Do you mind?" She searched his face, relaxing when he subtly shook his head and smiled at her.

"Well," Wilhelm said, "now that we've extracted our feet from our mouths, shall we venture to the library?" He offered an arm to Lena. *"You* are not engaged, are you, Your Highness?"

Lena didn't so much as glance at Rhy. Taking Wilhelm's arm, she smiled. "Why, no, I am not. And please, call me Lena."

Rhy retained enough manners to offer Gen his arm, but his expression held murder as he stalked behind them, gaze focused on Wilhelm's unguarded back. Jak caught his eye. *Don't kill him*, he mouthed, and Rhy curled his lip in a snarl as they all left the room.

"Oh well," Jak said aloud, guiding Stella to the other door so they could return to his room. "If Rhy does kill Wilhelm, I can help him hide the body."

"But what excuse will we make to Cavan and Nix?" Stella mused, tapping a finger on her lip.

"One joke after another," he said, grinning down at her.

"I was being perfectly serious," she replied with a grave expression. "It's not a simple matter to dispose of a prince, even a young and silly one, and pretend you've simply misplaced him."

"Have you dealt with that problem often?"

"You have *no* idea." She sighed heavily, then hugged his arm, her eyes sparkling as she looked up at him. "You make me happy, Jak."

"See?" He bent close, nuzzling her ear. "My cock does have magic properties."

She smothered a scandalized giggle. "Poor Astar. I should say something to Zeph."

"I think she knows what she's doing. I say let her practice managing him."

Stella gave him a considering look through her lashes. "Is that what you intend to do with me?"

"Absolutely," he agreed cheerfully. "I plan to keep you sexually sated and deliriously happy."

"Is that why we're going back to the room?"

"That can be on the agenda for later," he conceded. "After you practice your offensive magic."

She groaned. "You're a tyrant."

"With a magic cock," he amended. Setting his hand over hers on his arm, he snugged her in close enough to surreptitiously caress the side of her breast through her gown, making her shiver. "If you're a very good girl, I'll teach you some tricks for managing *me.*"

"I suspect I already know a few," she replied loftily.

"I look forward to being managed, then," he told her warmly. "*After* you practice."

"Yes, master." She rolled her eyes.

Because he really needed to take his mind off the arousing conversation, he said as they turned down the hall to the room, "You were kinder to those two than you needed to be."

"Was I?" She glanced at him, following the change in topic without difficulty. No doubt it helped that she could sense his thoughts for context. "I don't think so. Either Marjolein or Wilhelm—or both of them—will rule Erie someday, which means Zeph will be their high queen. And neither of them had malicious intentions; they were sincerely puzzled. Whatever I can do to assist the peaceful transition of the high throne, I will do."

"I hadn't thought of it that way," Jak admitted, opening the door for her. "Apparently I have study ahead of me, too."

"Well, we can—" She broke off on a gasp, and disappeared.

~ 23 ~

J AK FLUNG HIMSELF into the void faster than he could draw a blade. Hopefully whatever portal she'd fallen through would remain open long enough for him to make it through also.

As fast as he moved, he was almost too late, the closing edges of the gateway scraping his arms painfully. Wrenching himself sideways, he pushed through, hanging onto the sense of Stella in his mind with every fiber of his being.

He popped out into a vast meadow of lilies. Soft sunshine beamed down, the heady scent of the lush blossoms filling the warm air, bees buzzing as they moved lazily from blossom to blossom. It should have been beautiful, but his blood ran cold at the sight.

No sign of Stella.

Or a tower.

Jak spun in a circle, a blade in each hand, scanning the deceptively lovely landscape. If Stella had gone to a different alter-realm, he was out of luck. Even if the others came after them—which they'd undoubtedly attempt, though it might be a long time before anyone knew they were gone—this looked like an entirely different alter-realm than any of them had been transported to before.

And it matched Stella's vision too closely to be anything but that. She'd been deliberately abducted. Jak felt it in every bone in his body. Danu only knew what the intelligence planned for his captive sorceress, but it wouldn't be good. And Jak had no intention of letting it happen.

"Stella!" he yelled at the top of his lungs.

"*Jak!*" Her mental voice came so loud in his head that he spun to look over his shoulder before he realized she wasn't physically present. "*Are you really here?*" her mental voice shouted with anguished hope.

"Of course I am." He grinned so she'd feel his confidence. "I told you: I'm not letting you go. Where you travel, I'll be with you. I'm right here." As he spoke, he spun, searching for her, for a tower. Nothing but lilies and bees.

"*Oh Jak…*" She pulled back the tumult of her emotions, but she still sounded frightened when she added, "*Please help me.*"

"I'm coming to get you. Just tell me where you are."

"*I… don't know how to. I'm in a tower, and all I see out the windows is lilies. Just like my vision, Jak.*"

"I know. But I'm here, so the future has changed. We'll change it together. Shapeshift and fly out of there."

"*I can't. I tried.*"

"I'm coming. I'm in the field of lilies, and I came through right behind you, so I must be close, but I don't see a tower." Covering his ears to eliminate the distracting eternal buzzing of the bees, he focused his far vision, scanning for anything like a tower. Nothing. He tried jumping up and down, waving his arms. "Can you see me?"

"*I can't look out the windows right now.*"

Something about her mental voice gave him pause. "Is something in there with you?"

"...Yes." Stella had hesitated too long to reply. And fear that she'd been trying to hide from him broke through, crashing like a wave on the beach.

"Guide me to you. Right now. Get in my head and walk me there. I know you can."

"I can try. Run your forms to induce trance state."

"Is there time for that?" He still turned in slow circles, seeing only the endless field of lilies, colorful, graceful, sweetly redolent—and utterly loathsome.

"Maybe not."

Fuck. He viciously leashed his rising panic. Stella always soft-pedaled threats to her well-being. This was serious. "Take over my body, immediately. Do it, Stella," he ordered, as firmly as he knew how.

"You have to trust me enough."

"I do. Remember? My body belongs to you." Imagining himself in bed with her, lying back as she rode him, surrendering to the tidal wave of love and desire, he opened his will to her. It was easier than the first time, to let her take over his limbs, though definitely odd to feel his head turn of its own volition. *I trust you.* He said it mostly to remind himself as his instincts bristled, wanting to thrust her out. His body started walking through the lilies, the direction no different to his eyes than any other.

"I trust you. And, Jak, I want you to know that I love you. No matter what happens, you've made me happier in these last days than I've been in all my life."

Blending his intention with hers, he pushed into a jog, then a run, more alarmed by her words and the sense of goodbye in them than he could bear. "I look forward to hearing you tell me that every day for the rest of our lives," he gritted out.

She didn't reply, the sense of her in his head fading. Pouring on more speed, he kept running in the same direction. Toward nothing. Toward everything.

"*Stella?*" he asked mentally, so as to save his breath. The thick, sweet scent of the lilies made it difficult to breathe. "*Stella, answer me!*"

He ran smack into a wall.

He hit it so hard that the pain and impact stunned him, dropping him in a crumpled heap. "Fuck me," he groaned, forcing himself to his feet, swallowing back the nausea. His head spun, and moisture poured down his face, stinging his eyes. Wiping it away, he found his hand covered in bright blood. Fucking head wounds that bled so freely. "Get tough," he instructed himself.

Pulling off the fancy cravat that went with the new outfit, he bound it over his forehead. Couldn't afford to have blood in his eyes. At least the trend was holding of him destroying yet another set of clothes. That had to be good luck, right?

Hands outstretched, he edged forward, finding the invisible thing he'd run into at full tilt. A wall, slightly rounded. The stone felt smooth under his hands, though his brain had a hard time dealing with the fact that he still saw lilies beyond. Closing his eyes helped, though that made him think of Stella closing her eyes at his suggestion in the ballroom, implicitly trusting him to guide her through the crush. He would not break that trust.

He followed along the wall, tracing a circle about the size of a cottage. Could be a tower. Unfortunately, he made it around to his own trampled track through the odiferous flowers without encountering a door. *A tower, with no way out,* she'd said. "Stella?" he called.

No reply.

He cranked his head back, seeing only empty air. Hopefully this was the right place. Though, for all he knew, the landscape was studded with invisible towers. But Stella had brought him here, so he'd trust in that. Nothing for it but to climb.

He yanked off his boots and tossed them aside. Pulling a blade, he clenched it in his teeth so he'd be prepared. Closing his eyes, he felt for a seam between stones, digging his fingers into the crack, then skimmed his hand up the stone for the next. It at least felt like a standardly constructed stone edifice, with blocks at regular intervals. Settling his fingers into the next crack, he felt with his toes for a seam above the ground.

And began to climb.

It was far from ideal, the seams yielding very little grip. He tried to tell himself that he only climbed the rigging of the *Hákyrling*—and at least this mast didn't sway and dip with the sea. But the precariousness of his hold had his heart hammering.

That and the utter silence where Stella should be in his head.

Even though he'd been climbing steadily, it was painstakingly slow and tedious. He had no sense of his own progress—

and he didn't dare look. He had zero doubt that if he so much as glanced at the nothingness he clung to high over the ground, that he'd lose his head and likely his grip. So he kept going, his world reduced to feeling for the next hold.

And listening to the least whisper of Stella.

Nothing. Nothing. Nothing.

At one point, he had to pause, hanging on with one hand, body pressed tightly to the invisible wall, toes trembling with strain, as he plucked the dagger from his teeth and used it to dig out a better grip. Really a bitch to do with his eyes closed.

Putting the dagger back between his teeth, he tasted the grit of stone. It was real—and it helped to remind himself of that. Not being able to see the tower he climbed didn't make it any less solid. Forcing his exhausted body to continue, he climbed ever upwards.

Maybe it was a good thing he hadn't been able to see how tall the fucking thing really was, or he wouldn't have attempted the climb.

Though, who was he kidding? Nothing would keep from Stella.

Hear that? he thought viciously. *You can play all the games you want to, but we won't give up. I won't give up. Stella is mine, and you will never, ever have her!*

"Jak?" Stella's mental voice came, thready and weak, but there.

"I'm here! I'm climbing the tower. I'm almost to you."

"No, go back. Save yourself."

"Fuck that, Stella! Just hold on." Good advice for himself as one shredded and bleeding set of toes gave way, losing their

grip and nearly pulling his arms out of the sockets as he strained not to fall.

"Jak, please…" The tears and despair in her mental voice, whether for him or herself—or them both—galvanized him. With a snarl, he reached for a new hold and nearly lost his balance when his hand met empty air. In a desperate shove, he grabbed down—and clamped his hand over what felt like a window ledge. It could be he'd fling himself over only to fall through empty air, but there was no going back.

Taking the leap of faith—and a literal leap of body—he levered up and hurled himself through the opening.

"AWAKE NOW?" THE grating voice asked her.

Stella fought through the swirling depths of disorienting unconsciousness and opened her eyes to find herself lying on the bed she'd seen when she landed in the tower room. She'd been in a panic, battling the sheer terror of seeing her vision come true, the black despair threatening to drag her under. When she found she couldn't shift, that her sorcery was a mere trickle, she considered jumping out the high window and ending it all right there.

Then she'd heard Jak's voice, and her world righted. She wasn't alone. He was here somewhere. She'd been guiding him to her when she grew suddenly dizzy and…

And the man standing over her was *not* Jak.

The intelligence had gotten better at its mimicry, coming closer to looking like Jak, though it still made itself bigger. It preened internally at her observation, as if it believed larger was automatically better.

"I *am* better," it said. Its words had gotten clearer, too, though its voice retained an odd cadence. "I can please you better than he can. I love you."

She shuddered, carefully sitting up and scooting back on the bed as it approached her. "Did you knock me unconscious?"

"Yes." It grinned, an unearthly parody of Jak's cocky smile. "You were bringing *him* here. We can't have that. I am the only man you need."

"You are a handsome man," she agreed, feeling her way through the thing's emotions. The lust and possessiveness was so distasteful she nearly gagged, but she kept at it. She had no sorcery, but her ability to sense—and manipulate—emotions worked just fine. And she had her daggers, which she surreptitiously palmed. "I don't need him," she added.

"Yes. He climbs to you now. I will kill him, and then we can be alone. I love you."

"*Jak?*" she called, feeling the unsteadiness in her mental voice. Whatever the creature had done to her to knock her out had also left her mentally drained.

"*I'm here!*" Though his relief flooded her, so did his exhaustion. He was hurt and near the end of his strength. "*I'm climbing the tower. I'm almost to you.*"

"*No,*" she begged him, not daring to tell him why. Telling him the intelligence was with her and planned to kill him would only strengthen Jak's resolve to get to her. "*Go back. Save yourself.*"

"Fuck that, Stella!" His voice snarled through her head, determined to hurl himself to his death to save her. *"Just hold on."*

"Jak, please…"

"No!" the creature yelled at her. "You don't talk to him! Only me." It grabbed her by the arm, yanking her close and embracing her in a bruising, clumsy grip. No longer made of stone, its flesh still didn't feel quite living. With a queasy burst of revulsion, she wondered where it had gotten the flesh to assemble this body.

Then she didn't have to wonder, because the physical connection opened its thoughts and emotions to her. Much as she wanted to wrest free, she forced herself to allow them to flood her. In the back of her mind, Jak's solid confidence bolstered her, his unwavering love giving her the foundation she needed.

And Jak himself came hurtling through the window.

She caught a glimpse of him: scarf tied around his head like a feral pirate, face smeared with blood that spattered the white lace trimming his shirt, dagger clenched between his teeth. As he tucked, rolled, and sprang to his feet, he drew the Silversteel sword and pulled the dagger from his teeth in the same motion, roaring, "Unhand her, foul beast!"

The creature thrust her away, spinning and running at Jak.

But she held on to its emotions, twisting them tight in her mental grip. Even as it dove at Jak, it staggered, clapping its hands to its head.

And Jak ran it through with the Silversteel sword.

It screamed, the sound like a jungle chorus of animal

howls, the death shrieks of countless prey and the snarls of predators as they killed. Recovering, it fastened its big hands around Jak's throat, lifting him off his feet and throttling him.

"Stay back!" Jak yelled in her head, even as he brought his dagger around to slice open the thing's fleshy throat. No blood spilled out, and its thoughts barely registered the wound. The Silversteel sword, however, that burned, the borrowed flesh around the metal shriveling away, necrotic, returning to the death it had been stolen from.

And Stella knew what to do.

Still twisting the creature's emotions around themselves, she ran up behind it and plunged both daggers into its ears with all her strength. An unholy wail went up as it stiffened, dropping Jak. Stella staggered back—realizing belatedly that she shouldn't have let go of her daggers, and the creature turned on her.

Its face was distorted, as if made of candle wax that rapidly melted under an unseen flame. "I love you," it said, bewildered, betrayed, and furious in its hurt. "I love you!" it roared, gobbets of flesh falling away. The Silversteel sword clattered to the floor. Jak, already on his feet again, snatched it up. The thing's body continued to collapse, the head teetering to the floor atop a mound of decaying flesh, her daggers sticking out of its mushy skull like absurd silver ears.

It stared at her, beseeching. "I love you," it pleaded, the words dribbling away as its mouth melted into nothing.

She and Jak stared at each other across the mound of still-dissolving flesh. "Are you all right?" he asked.

Laughing breathlessly, she gestured at his battered and

bloody self. "I should be asking you that. As usual, you've undone all my good healing work."

He glanced down at himself ruefully. "And ruined yet another set of clothes."

She laughed again, but it turned into a sob. "Oh, Jak."

Then he was there, enfolding her in his arms, encircling her in all his strength and love. "Hush now, my star. You're safe. I promised I'd come for you."

"You did." Letting the tears fall, she wrapped her arms around his lean waist. "I knew you would."

The tower trembled beneath them, shuddering and teetering. "The tower may be melting like our friend here," Jak muttered. "How high up are we, anyway?" Letting her go but taking her hand, he pulled her to the window and peered out. "Fuck me."

"You didn't know how tall it was?" she asked, perplexed, then braced herself against the wall as the tower tipped and swayed.

"It was invisible," he answered absently, then glanced at her. "We're too high up to jump out."

"I landed in this room, so there must be a portal here. I'll find it and open it."

"You sound sure."

"It's gotten clever about hiding the rifts, but I learned some things from being in its mind." She shuddered, and Jak squeezed her hand.

"Steady on," he instructed gravely. "You came this far. Find that rift. I'll get your daggers."

She spared a glance for her blades, mired in the muck that

was the creature. "Ugh. Leave them."

"No way. They're Silversteel, and that might be the best weapon against this thing." Jak looked up from plucking the daggers from the fleshy soup. "Unless you think you killed it."

"I wish, but no. We only destroyed this particular incarnation." She felt the shimmer of the rift, staggering as the tower shifted again. Stones rained down outside. A hole in the ceiling opened. "I found it. Hurry."

Jak dashed to her, wrapping his arm around her waist and giving her a sound kiss. "Take us home."

As the floor dropped out from beneath them, wrapped in the arms of her beloved, she left the tower that had haunted her visions all her life. Suddenly, her future opened up, a bright and shining road ahead of her.

With Jak, always by her side.

The story continues in
The Dragon's Daughter and the Winter Mage
Coming September 10, 2021

TITLES BY JEFFE KENNEDY

FANTASY ROMANCES

HEIRS OF MAGIC
The Long Night of the Crystalline Moon
(in *Under a Winter Sky*)
The Golden Gryphon and the Bear Prince
The Sorceress Queen and the Pirate Rogue
The Dragon's Daughter and the Winter Mage (September 2021)
The Storm Princess and the Raven King (January 2022)

BONDS OF MAGIC
Dark Wizard
Bright Familiar (July 2021)
Bonds of Magic #3 (October 2021)

THE FORGOTTEN EMPIRES
The Orchid Throne
The Fiery Crown
The Promised Queen (May 2021)

THE TWELVE KINGDOMS
Negotiation
The Mark of the Tala

The Tears of the Rose
The Talon of the Hawk
Heart's Blood
The Crown of the Queen

THE UNCHARTED REALMS
The Pages of the Mind
The Edge of the Blade
The Snows of Windroven
The Shift of the Tide
The Arrows of the Heart
The Dragons of Summer
The Fate of the Tala
The Lost Princess Returns

THE CHRONICLES OF DASNARIA
Prisoner of the Crown
Exile of the Seas
Warrior of the World

SORCEROUS MOONS
Lonen's War
Oria's Gambit
The Tides of Bára
The Forests of Dru
Oria's Enchantment
Lonen's Reign

A COVENANT OF THORNS
Rogue's Pawn
Rogue's Possession
Rogue's Paradise

CONTEMPORARY ROMANCES

Shooting Star

MISSED CONNECTIONS
Last Dance
With a Prince
Since Last Christmas

CONTEMPORARY EROTIC ROMANCES

Exact Warm Unholy
The Devil's Doorbell

FACETS OF PASSION
Sapphire
Platinum
Ruby
Five Golden Rings

FALLING UNDER
Going Under
Under His Touch
Under Contract

EROTIC PARANORMAL

MASTER OF THE OPERA E-SERIAL
Master of the Opera, Act 1: Passionate Overture
Master of the Opera, Act 2: Ghost Aria
Master of the Opera, Act 3: Phantom Serenade
Master of the Opera, Act 4: Dark Interlude

Master of the Opera, Act 5: A Haunting Duet
Master of the Opera, Act 6: Crescendo
Master of the Opera

BLOOD CURRENCY
Blood Currency

BDSM FAIRYTALE ROMANCE

Petals and Thorns

Thank you for reading!

ABOUT JEFFE KENNEDY

Jeffe Kennedy is an award-winning, best-selling author who writes fantasy with romantic elements and fantasy romance. She is an RWA member and serves on the Board of Directors.

She is a hybrid author, and also self-publishes the romantic fantasy series Sorcerous Moons. Books in her popular, long-running series, The Twelve Kingdoms and The Uncharted Realms, have won the RT Reviewers' Choice Best Fantasy Romance, been named Best Book of June 2014, and won RWA's prestigious RITA® Award, while more have been finalists for those awards. She's the author of the romantic fantasy trilogy, The Forgotten Empires, which includes *The Orchid Throne*, *The Fiery Crown*, and *The Promised Queen*.

Jeffe lives in Santa Fe, New Mexico, with two Maine coon cats, plentiful free-range lizards, and a very handsome Doctor of Oriental Medicine.

Jeffe can be found online at her website: JeffeKennedy.com, every Sunday at the popular SFF Seven blog, on Facebook, on Goodreads, on BookBub, and pretty much constantly on Twitter @jeffekennedy. She is represented by Sarah Younger of Nancy Yost Literary Agency.

jeffekennedy.com

facebook.com/Author.Jeffe.Kennedy

twitter.com/jeffekennedy

goodreads.com/author/show/1014374.Jeffe_Kennedy

bookbub.com/profile/jeffe-kennedy

Sign up for her newsletter here.

jeffekennedy.com/sign-up-for-my-newsletter

Made in the USA
Las Vegas, NV
18 April 2021